M000007165

REFLECTIONS

of the Journey to Streets of Gold

LUCY BYERS

-A Novel-

Copyright @ 2017 by Lucy Byers

Library in Congress Cataloging in Publication has been applied for.

All rights reserved. Except for use in any review, the reproduction or utilization of this work in whole or in part in any form by any electronic, mechanical or other means, now known or hereafter invented, including xerography, photocopying and recording, or in any information storage or retrieval system is forbidden without written permission.

Reflections of the Journey to Streets of Gold is a work of fiction. Any references to historical events, real people, or real places are used fictitiously. Other names, characters, places, events, and incidents are either the product of the author's imagination or are used fictitiously, and any resemblance to actual events, places or persons, living or dead, business establishments, or locales is entirely coincidental.

Print ISBN: 978-1-54391-808-3

eBook ISBN: 978-1-54391-809-0

LucyByers@Facebook or LucyByersBooks.com on the Website.

TABLE OF CONTENTS

DEDICATION

To my wonderful husband and best friend Joe,
Thanks for your endurance
of the long hours spent to complete
one of my long-time dreams.

To my belated mother
whose inspiration and
love this book is
dedicated.

Dedication to my grandfather and grandmother
for their decision, courage, and determination of coming to
America to find a better life.

PREFACE

As the amber sunlight fades across the autumn sky and the leaves fall to the ground in death, life is renewed for Francesco stepping into America on November 7, 1913 to find the place that promises *streets paved with gold*. On this cool crisp autumn day, the headlines of the New York Times announced that the *Stampalia* sailed into the New York harbor called Ellis Island after a 25-day journey from Napoli, Italy. Three million Italians had immigrated to America from 1900 to 1915, but in 1913 is the year that a record high of Italians immigrated. Francesco and his two brothers, Vito and Alberto, are on the ship included in the record count. They had dreamed of coming to America for many years. The dream now became a reality. For Francesco, his arrival is an early birthday celebration because he will turn 19-years-old on December 11.

Francesco is the middle-aged brother of the first three sons born to Maria and Giovanni with Vito being the oldest and Alberto the youngest with a two-year age difference between each of them.

To make this dream happen, many sacrifices were made. There was a small, copper-colored tin can put on a shelf where excess lira amounting to pennies, nickels, and dimes in American money is dropped preparing for their departure. The one-way fare for steerage passage in 1913 is approximately $15 a person.

They put the many miles of Italy behind crossing the ocean to begin their life anew in America. Frightened, alone, and tired with minimal cash to sustain them with food and shelter, the brothers bind together through many difficult hardships of coming to this unfamiliar land. There are many lonely nights without family and friends, language barriers, and economic difficulties.

Meeting Lucia after arriving in America sends Francesco in a different direction than he originally planned. He claims his love that happens suddenly and is overcome with happiness that seems to be unending fulfilling his deep desires. Leaving New York to begin their life together in the countryside holds magic for their love to blossom.

Then, the Great Depression sweeps across America turning the tide across the land. A fire ignites turning into a tragedy. Now the moments of their magical love found on the streets of New York turns into setting Francesco's world upside down causing much pain and heartache.

The fond memories that life held turns once again into a challenge. Deep dark secrets must be thrown in a closet for no one to see. Francesco wants to hold on to the high expectations of life before coming to America, but now his world seems to be falling apart. Will he ever find the place that promises *streets paved with gold*?

Francesco's journey is a passionate love story when difficulty and great sorrow is thrown in his way dampening his expectation of a better future with the happiness he desires for a brighter tomorrow. It is a life-changing quest for the promised *streets paved with gold*. *Reflections of the Journey to Streets of Gold* reflects on the magnificent power of hope when life doesn't turn out the way we plan.

CHAPTER 1

BARI, ITALY

The ocean pours forth shells all along the shores perfecting each shell before coming to the surface. While the shells are deep under the ocean, the shells are carved into beautiful images by the waters rushing over them day by day. It's the same with man molding him into the image of who he is because of the waters he has passed through in life.

Once again, Francesco stood on the banks overlooking the Statue of Liberty. The reflections in the waves sparked his memories of his life back in Bari, Italy when suddenly the face of a woman appeared. The woman was walking through the waves with an incredible smile on her face lifting her hands to Francesco. Something deep within him was awakened when the familiar voice in the distance called out his name. She was moving toward him when breathlessly he staggered to avoid toppling to the ground as she then disappeared.

As he stood unsteady on his feet looking out once again to the ocean, the voices of children were echoing in his ears reminding him of the day's gone bye. "Come play hide and seek with me," he heard a small audible voice saying. Was this only a fragment of his imagination? Were the tiny voices he once heard each day silent after all these years?

Were the hands of time being turned back? He longed for the days when life was simpler and carefree. There was nothing compared to the desire that flared within him from her touch.

He stood looking across the ocean visualizing the fishing village clinging to the limestone hillside with its picturesque view echoing reminders of his childhood days. He vaguely saw in the corner of his mind the "Castle of the Mountain" (*Castel del Monte*) built by Emperor Frederick II with its symbolic significance and the Trulli (the *Trulli of Alberobello*)—limestone dwellings that resemble the pyramidal dwellings in the prehistoric time. He remembered the journey that brought him to America and his extraordinary love story of Lucia entering his life.

The story begins in Bari, Italy in the early 1900's. Bari is the second largest city of Southern Italy and is the capital of the Apulia or Puglia region. This province and its ports face the Adriatic Sea, which is described as the arm of the Mediterranean. The old city with its medieval streets and monuments is best known for its agricultural and fishing industry. Corso Vittorio Emanuele is one of the main long roads dividing the city between two different periods in history. It is lit with traditional street lamps winding into the ancient part of the city while the Via Capruzzi is the other main road that winds through the most modern part of the city where many large shops and local markets are located. Bari connects with Naples (Napoli) by roadway.

The old limestone house with its rough dry-stone floors sits upon the slopes of the countryside amid a carpet of Olive trees, which Giovanni and Maria called home with their six children Vito, Francesco, Alberto, Leonardo, Theresa and Angelina.

They have only the bare necessities to sustain them. Their dwelling designed with a conical roof has a sizable dining and living room combination plus a bedroom, and another large room is divided by curtains creating two bedrooms for the children. The dining area with its oblong wooden table and benches has unpainted rough timber open shelving against the wall where they store their dishes and food supplies. Black cast iron skillets and tin pans hang on hooks situated above the fireplace for cooking foods. The fireplace is located on one side of the back wall of the dining area, which serves for cooking and heating the few rooms once the weather has a chill in the air. A large tin bucket filled with coal and pieces of wood sits by the fireplace. In the dead of winter, Maria and Giovanni rise throughout the night to throw a few shovels of coal in the fireplace producing heat for the family's warmth. The bedrooms are furnished with a bed, chest of drawers with mirror, and a hand-made oval braided rug to shield their feet from the cold. The coldest months are usually January and February with temperatures generally in the 40s when the house is difficult to heat.

Today the sunlight glistened across the morning sky sending warm rays through the window pane indicating that spring once again is here. Now, there is more daily sunshine.

The smell of coffee brewing sounds the alarm that morning has arrived. The scent signals the eldest sons that it is time to arise out of sleep to start the day to accomplish all the tasks needing completed before the day ends. After the brother's finish eating breakfast, Vito pours the boiling coffee into his cup from the silver metal kettle. Out the door he darts with his younger siblings not far behind him.

Francesco shouts, "Let's get a move on it today to begin our barnyard chores."

Alberto answers, "The shovels are over there by the barn leaning against the inside wall."

Vito, the oldest of six, stands leaning one shoulder against the side of the old rustic wooden structure used as a barn with his coffee in hand. He stands for a little while watching the brothers amid their farm chores while sipping his coffee. Standing in thought for a short moment Vito yells out, "Francesco! Alberto! Come over here. I need to talk to the both of you about farm chores that need to be worked on today. We need to get started early this morning while the day is bright before the sun sets."

"Vito, what does it look like that I am doing?" replied Francesco from a distance.

"Yeh….do you think we are playing around?" Alberto let out a yelp as he chimed in.

Dropping their shovels from picking up manure, Francesco walked a little closer gazing into Vito's eyes and looking back and forth over his shoulders to let him know that he was fully alert listening to his directive. There sure was a scent in the air reminding him of the job he was doing.

Vito, being the oldest, always looked out that the work at the farm was accomplished. For the last few years, most mornings began the same way once spring arrived.

A frown wrinkled Francesco's forehead as he started speaking. "Vito, I have a list of small chores that I need to complete today. Does this chore really need started right now?" questioned Francesco. "I already had my plan in place for today."

Alberto was now walking closer whistling softly to contain his temper. So far it was a peaceful protest, but if he and Francesco thought too long and hard, it could develop into a brotherly quarrel. Vito was good at giving orders, and sometimes it went a little too far for them to adhere.

Vito's throat tightened before speaking from the expressions displayed on Francesco and Alberto's faces. "I thought uh…. uh…. we would repair the fence posts today. We've talked about repairing the fence for quite some time, but we haven't started the job yet. We need to get this job finished before long, for we don't want the few cows and horses running away. Now that the weather is warming, the cattle will be grazing outdoors more often."

Alberto hesitated as he then nodded briefly placing his hands in his pockets to let Vito know that he would cooperate. "Well, I guess we can't stand around thinking about the job, let's get busy while the day is fresh. The best part of a day is morning when we have a lot of energy after a good night's sleep. We may as well get started by digging the holes. Then, we can set the posts in the ground."

Francesco looked at Vito, then back at Alberto, who was standing straightening his hat. Francesco shrugged as he took a deep breath to take air into his lungs to keep his composure. "Before long, hopefully, we will be going to America. Then, we won't have to struggle with all these jobs here at home."

Vito replied, "Yes, but we must finish these jobs before we leave to make it easier for Mama. I wonder if we will find these *streets paved with gold* in America."

Their annoyance faded with the sounding of the house door swinging open. Bursting through the door was Leonardo dressed in blue jeans with a red checkered shirt and navy jacket with tousled black curly hair. He is the fourth child in line and is ten-years-old. He is like any other ten-year-old wanting to play more than work most of the time, but his parents require him to do some chores on the farm. He stood clapping his hands as he was jumping up and down on his feet.

"I'll help! I'll help!" The echoing voice from Leonardo rang out. "I'll fetch my shovel to help dig the ditch or clean up the manure. I'm dressed for a workday today."

Vito paused a moment ignoring Leonardo. "Uh…. uh…. where are Theresa and Angelina? Do you need to watch them play while Mama is doing some housework?" questioned Vito.

Disappointment seemed to flood his facial expression as he replied. "Theresa and Angelina are still in bed. They will be helping Mama with the dishes from breakfast once they awaken. Last night, I asked Mama if I could help you with the chores today. She said that I could," explained Leonardo.

"Let the sleepy heads sleep while we get an early start," exclaimed Vito.

Theresa was seven and has a little independence, but Angelina is like any other four-year- old requiring more care with eating, bathing, and dressing being the younger sibling.

"Come along. We'll put you to work," snickered Vito. Vito loved his baby brother always looking out to keep him happy. "Look across the pasture, Leonardo. The calves are running around the fencing in playfulness to get our attention. It is delightful to watch their fun and games."

Leonardo giggled, "Vito, look at Blackie. He's rubbing his head against the fence. His head must be itchy."

"Their heads get itchy like ours. They have to have a way to scratch too." Vito laughed. "Maybe we need to give them a bath. We could get out the shampoo and brush to wash their heads and backs. After you shampoo and scrub them good, I'll get a bucket of water for you to rinse the soap off."

"You're being silly," chuckled Leonardo.

Vito said, "Seriously, since you are a big boy now and want to help, I'll give you some direction. I'm glad to teach you the ropes in hope that one day you will be able to take over the chores once we older boys leave home. Go take Blackie farther out to the pasture to eat."

Each boy had their orders of work to get the fencing repaired. The orders filtered down from Giovanni to Vito to the younger siblings. The day would be done in a blink of an eye for the hours would pass by quickly due to the busyness as each one helped in accomplishing the job. The hard work of all the family members proves to help in the provision of food and income for the family's survival in these hard, poverty-stricken times.

Back at the house, Giovanni had to arise for his daily adventure. His sons were presently starting the farm work outside. Usually, he was off to the seaport for his day of fishing; but today was a little different. He was running late.

Giovanni was a farmer and fisherman by trade, which he was quite proud to be a part of that profession. Neither job paid any money, making life hard. Typically, he would dress in his knee-high boots, knickers, and a buttoned-down, opened-neck, long-sleeve shirt with a flat, front brimmed hat set upon his head. Off he would go with net in hand in the early morning hours ready to board the boats to make his catch for the day. He had to do this to provide for his family and make the dream possible for his sons to discover the land of promise.

Returning to bed after starting the coffee at the crack of dawn, Maria was slumbering in bed as Giovanni bends down to kiss her before leaving for his daily trade.

"Maria, I must go now to meet up with the other fishermen to make the dream happen."

Opening her eyes, Maria smiles reaching her arms up around his neck kissing him in return. "Don't work too hard, my love. I will be waiting upon your return." As Maria released her hold, Giovanni whimpered softly knowing how much Maria means to him.

Maria laid there observing how fortunate she was to have such a handsome man. Giovanni is of a bronze tone complexion having dark, curly hair with graying at the temples. Little in stature with strong arms and back, but he sure has a kind, gentle spirit with a great big heart—never complaining of the hard-manual labor he had to endure. Hard-manual labor for Giovanni is working through the day as a fisherman pulling up the heavy nets over the boats with the other fishermen. Some days, he would return home working the farm alongside his sons until darkness settles in across the land to complete the unfinished chores of the day. Strong muscles and bones are being built constantly from all this physical exertion encountered allowing Giovanni not to tire easily.

Giovanni was happy to have a few idle moments in the morning of quality time alone with the woman he adored. Most days, the children and the farm work take up most of Maria's time.

"Maria," he said in a teasing voice hesitating to leave, "will you go fishing with me?"

"I'd love to come, but you know that I can't—not today anyway," said Maria. "Uh…. Giovanni, who would take care of the children and work here on the farm if I went with you?"

He was silent for a little while. "You'll have to think about it sometime. Maybe we can arrange something in the future. Not that I would make it down to the seaport for work, but we could spend the day away from here for a few hours just you and me. There is too much to do anymore. It seems that we never have any quality time together to call our own. Life is passing us by these days."

"Giovanni, if we haven't had any quality time we could never have borne our six children," Maria smiled as she spoke softly. "I know you like to have some playful time with me. It would be pleasant to take a walk together to hold hands and talk. Some days, it would be nice not to have a care in the world like in our younger days. It does seem that each day we are striving to make ends meet at our home. I guess that's how things change when people get married and have children."

"Maria," Giovanni replied, "it would be enjoyable to have some time alone with you now and again. It could be sort of a date day to spend together like the old days. The older boys could watch the younger children while we go down to the seaport to look across the sea watching the ships come in to shore or attend a dance in Bari some night. The seaport with its turquoise waters is beautiful. It would be nice to walk along the shore to have some relaxing time together."

"I promise I'll think about it," she snickered as she rolled over in bed and watched him leave the room. An alarm went off in her head when he left for work, it was time for her to rise and shine for today's grind had to begin. Most days, she would be in the kitchen preparing breakfast before Giovanni's departure for the seaport. Today, she thought for a moment what Giovanni had said as she lay there in bed. Maria whispered out loud to herself. "Maybe you are right Giovanni. Life is passing us by quickly, and we may not have tomorrow together. It sure would be a pleasure to dress in my best apparel and style my hair to attend the local dance down at Bari. I will think about this tomorrow; but for now, I must get out of bed and start my daily chores."

Giovanni returned to the bedroom once again before his departure for the seaport. Maria was standing at the corner of the room with her back to him trying to straighten out the bed. Looking at her huddled in the corner made him have second thoughts about leaving for the seaport.

He murmured, "Maria, you are never more than a thought away from my mind for I love you with all my heart. I guess you are right that we have had a little quality time in life for as you said earlier we would never have had the six children without it. Maybe today, I am having a melancholy feeling or longing for the younger days when life wasn't so complicated. There is a great responsibility running a household and raising a family. Some days, I wonder if working like we do is worth it. I feel life is short, and I want to spend as much time with you as I possibly can before we are no more. I will dread that day."

Maria turned around as she responded, "I love you too. Hopefully, that day is a long way off. Now, you must get going for the vessels will leave without you. If you don't soon go, we will be going back to bed for some real lovemaking." Maria laughed, moving over to where Giovanni was standing, and placed a kiss on Giovanni's cheek to bid him farewell. She then placed her pink, terry-cloth robe on, tying the belt around her waist, before heading to the dining area.

Giovanni grabbed a couple of breakfast rolls and a cup of coffee and out the door he ran waving to his sons doing their morning chores. He was late leaving today. He needed to hurry to the path. He saw no one in sight, but he knew he would catch up with several other fishermen on the paths through the woods heading in the same direction. Giovanni walked several miles every day from the village on the hillside down to the seaport. Stories, singing, and laughter would often begin the day as the group of fishermen walk along the pathway. Upon arrival, nets and fishing reels were waiting inside the boats that were moored in the harbor.

CHAPTER 2

DAY AT SEA

There are storms of life that can be raging tossing us to and fro like the tempest of the sea, but if we follow the light through the darkness that is shining from the lighthouse standing in the distance, we will land safely to the shore.

Upon arrival at the seaport, Giovanni noticed that the coastline lined with seaside towns is beautiful. It stretches out as far as the eye can see unfolding the pastel colored fisherman homes with verandas that twist down a maze of lanes lining the sea.

As usual, at sunrise the Adriatic seaport is extremely calm and serene as the fishermen arrive to begin their day. Seagulls are sitting along the shores making loud noises welcoming the visitor to their home. The fishy smell of the sea fills their nostrils as the sounds of the waves penetrate their ears making known that they are situated close to the sea area. Many cliffs rest in place at the aqua sea.

As the men are approaching the sea at this early hour, the dim lighting reflected from the sky reveals the land surrounding the body of water with its large structured warehouse buildings, gray colored rocks, and green flooring with hundreds of trade boats tied to the big rocks along the banks.

Giovanni yells to a few of the fishermen standing nearby. "I find it soothing to breathe in the fresh salty smelling sea air while standing here on the docks." He was aware that once the sun rises, radiance will fill this place with its turquoise waters and clear blue skies with a few white puffy clouds floating overhead and over the whitish structured buildings. "No one could ask anything more for this is like heaven right here on the earth. There are days that I wish I could stand here for hours in my own thoughts and enjoy it without reporting to work."

Dominick replied, "You are right Giovanni, but if we don't move faster, we are not going to get to board the vessels. Look out there to the sea. The fishermen are boarding vessels all along the shores where they are tied in a huge circular position. We are running a little late this morning. We really must move faster to get closer to where the boats are docked."

In the distance, a few of the fishermen wave and yell to let Giovanni and his companions know that they saw them. The unclear echoing sound confirming, "We will wait for you!"

Giovanni with a few other fishermen make it to the dock. They all begin boarding the vessels breathless from that fast pace from their lateness. The lead fisherman makes sure that ice and bait is in the boat for their daily catches.

Giovanni shouts, "Let's head out to sea. Everybody, grab the large paddles on both sides of the vessel. With all of us rowing, we can make our way to the section of the sea quickly to make our catch for the day. We can then drop our anchor where we want to spend our time today to wait on the fish to bait."

Dominick shouted above the noise, "Doesn't it feel wonderful all the saltiness that lingers in the air this morning filling our nostrils and making our souls feel alive? It is the best part of the morning closing ourselves into a meditation like state while we wait for a catch. We all know that the better the catch for the day, the better it will be for us to provide our families with food on the table."

Dominick lived on a small farm a mile down the road from Giovanni. Giovanni and Maria would visit Dominick's place when time allowed. Dominick and Philomena had three boys and two girls. Dominick loved to dance and sing when he had leisure time to spend with his family. When summer arrived, Dominick would bring his guitar in hand out of his villa to the rustic stone front porch as his children would gather around to sing to the tune.

After rowing for quite a while, Giovanni called to the fishermen, "Let's drop the anchor to begin our day's work. This looks like as good as place as any for catching fish."

Another fisherman hollered, "The fish like to hide in this seaweed that's showing through the water's surface. There is a lot of seaweed here at this place. Let's go for it and hope to catch a lot of fish."

The fishermen baited their hooks with mackerel, sardines, or squib from the container inside the boat before dropping their lines in hope of catching tuna.

Giovanni replied, "There is other factors as well that can play a part in catching fish. The weather, water temperature, and current must be right for us to have bites. Hopefully, we'll get a lot of bites today."

Giovanni continued reiterating, "Today, it looks as though in this area, the fishing may be plentiful. We might be lucky enough to see other sea creatures. Let's drop our lines and nets to sweep the sea of fish. The sooner we make our catch—the sooner we get to end our day and go home."

One of the fishermen roared, "Let's put our empty nets down and hope to pull the heavy nets up with fish all day long. This type of work sure is tiring on the arms and back, but we will remain positive anticipating that we will catch some fish quickly."

"This type of exercise of putting nets down and pulling them up sure has a way of building the arm and back muscles," said another fisherman.

Suddenly, a burst of *a cappella* music echoed across the sea with the sound of a man's choir piercing the ear with harmonizing tunes in the distance. It appeared that one boat would start the singing as the others chimed in until most of the vessels passengers were singing.

"Sometimes, I swear this noise-making scares the fish away. We probably would do better if we were silent," spouted Giovanni.

Dominick proclaimed, "I guess that the music has a way of lightening the atmosphere of the heaviness felt by many of the men in this hard way of life. The life span sure isn't too long for most people in this part of the world with the hardships endured. If only there was an easier way for us to make a living, but there is none. The area is quite depressed these days with only a few paying jobs. At least, everyone is happy while they are working with little time to think."

Giovanni shouted, "It feels that our nets are getting heavy with fish. Let's bring them up. Hopefully, it isn't a bunch of jellyfish."

As the group of fishermen raised one of the nets, a fisherman yelled, "It looks as if we have caught several fish in our net. They are mostly sardines today. This salty sea sure is rich in these fish. If we don't like the look of the catch, we can drop some of it back into the sea hoping for better. We will need to keep some of the live sardines and place them in our chest container for tomorrow's bait."

Dominick espoused viewing a creature, "I think we caught an octopus too. Octopus in these parts is a real delicacy for the meat goes a long way when feeding a large family if prepared into a Sicilian octopus stew. Octopus brings in more money than most fish to the hotel, restaurants, and markets along this coastal area."

Giovanni said, "Octopus is an eye-catching advertisement at most of the places. This fish brings satisfaction to the human taste buds. I can't believe we caught it in our nets for octopus usually hides in dens and under rocks through the daylight hours. They appear usually at night when they become prey hunters. I must say that this is a rare occasion."

Dominick hollered, "I think I caught something. Help me reel it in. It's heavy whatever it is!"

Giovanni cried, "It's probably a tuna. They are quite heavy. Wow, we are going to have a fight on our hands reeling this fish in because of its size and weight! This may take us a few hours to get this monster into our boat."

"If I caught a tuna, there is probably a lot more from where it came from for they like to live in flocks," said Dominick. "Let's begin the fish fight!"

Giovanni grabbed the reel from Dominick. "Oh, whatever this fish is, it is quite strong." Then, he lost his balance and was thrown down on his buttocks.

Dominick laughed and yelled, "It's a tuna fish! Everybody come over and help lift this creature into the boat." For several hours, the fishermen wrestle with getting this approximately 100-pound tuna catch into the boat. Once in the boat, Giovanni pulled out his knife and slit both sides of the fish to drain the blood before the men would place it on ice to take back to the docks.

Giovanni said, "This made for a great day today! We are all weary and tired. Let's head back to the harbor."

Dominick replied, "It did make for a great day, and we will get paid more than usual for this big catch. This is our lucky day!"

Giovanni roared, "Let's call it a day! We have caught a fair amount of fish. Let's head to the port to make our exchange from the catch, which will amount to an attractive sum of money for all of us to top off the day. Then, we can return to our little village that sits on the hillside overlooking the seaport until tomorrow to begin our day once again."

Dominick confided in Giovanni as they traveled on foot daily to and from the seaport. "Sometimes, I wonder if this job of fishing is worth the effort for the money that is paid to us. It is not enough money for the work that we do."

Giovanni chimed in, "The work that we do is out of necessity because opportunity is limited in this part of the country. How else could we get any money for our families to live? I do a little farming, but there isn't any money in that trade either. Let's not think about it."

Dominick said, "I'll see you in the morning." Dominick waving his hand in the air stopped a moment then proceeded to walk the path to his house.

CHAPTER 3

NIGHT TIME AT THE FARM

———◇———

*Tapestry on the underside is ugly with all the threads
hanging out, but on the top, it's beautiful; the same as our
life shapes into beauty with the trials making us over.*

Suppertime was now upon them when Maria called the boys in from the fields. Since returning from the seaport, Giovanni was resting in his chair from the hard day down at the docks. He opened his eyes when he heard the boys enter the house. Theresa and Angelina were carrying utensils to place on the table by the place settings. In the dining area, a home-made square rough oak table sat in the front left corner at the entrance with two wooden benches, one on each side, for each family member to sit while eating. Everyone took their place at the table for a little family conversation and food to appease their hunger from the day's work.

Lighting is provided by a kerosene lantern sitting on the ledge of the fireplace. The fireplace provides some lighting throughout the room and takes the chill from the air on these spring cold nights. Coldness seemed to settle in once the sun goes down, but it wouldn't be long until the blazing heat of summer would be here to stay for a season.

Getting up from the table after finishing his meal, Francesco began speaking, "Let's go over by the fireplace to keep warm and get a few games out to play."

"Yeah…. yeah," cheered Angelina and Theresa together.

Leonardo ran over to fetch the checkerboard and checkers, "Here I'll set the checkers up and Theresa and I can play this game."

"Ok," said Francesco. "Vito, Alberto, Angelina, and I will play a game of Chinese checkers. I'll get the different color marbles out for each player to choose what color they want to use to play."

Vito chuckled, "Maybe I'll let Angelina win, if she's good. The time is passing quickly, and we will have to retire for the night as soon as we finish playing these games."

Giovanni and Maria were at the corner of the fireplace sharing stories from the day's events as the children were enjoying their game playing. Giovanni loved to share many stories about his happenings at sea.

"You're cheating," cried Theresa.

"I am not cheating," replied Leonardo. "You forgot to jump my checker; therefore, I win the game."

"I quit! I quit! I quit!" screamed Theresa.

Leonardo was about to reply when Maria jumped up and chimed in, "Both of you should go to bed if you continue to spat. Children, you need to finish your games quickly and get to bed. It's getting late!"

Vito got up and started toward the bedroom. He said, "Let's get under the covers to keep warm."

Francesco replied, "Yes, it sure feels good to snuggle up with other body heat under the heavy quilts in bed to keep warm."

Maria made the quilts from materials that she would purchase down at the marketplace at a sale price. Sometimes, she would use the fabric from the children's clothes that they would outgrow piecing each square together. Usually, Maria's hand-made quilts could tell a story about one of the family members from the fabric square sewed on to the quilt. Quilting was done in the dead of winter when no other work could be done.

Giovanni and Maria were still sitting by the fireplace by an end table in the flickering dim lighted room even though the children retired for the night.

Giovanni spoke softly while Maria was listening intensely. "We both know that times are hard, and wages are quite low and modern conveniences aren't available while economic opportunity and famine are prevalent stretching across the land. The workers at most jobs are laboring from morning until evening to provide a few necessary commodities such as food, clothing, and shelter for their families."

Maria said, "I know, but we must not complain. We must do what we must do each day to meet our budget and to avoid starvation for our family. You know that happiness isn't measured by material things Giovanni, but happiness prevails for the love each one of us feels for one another in the little things in life."

Maria noticed that Giovanni appeared to be troubled as he started speaking once again to her. "We have talked many times that we would work by the sweat of our brows to acquire enough money to fulfill our dream. We have had this precious dream that we hold dear to our hearts for several years. I tell you Maria that we must make this dream happen one way or another."

Agreeing Maria said, "Yes, we must make it happen."

Giovanni struggled speaking, "I don't want our sons working the family farm for the rest of their life. We want to send a few of our older children to America where life would be much better. It will take team effort with all our family working hard to make this dream happen. We will place our own desires aside for a little while to make life better for our children. We do not want our sons having the hardships we have had in our life experiences. We will make the necessary sacrifices to achieve this dream coming true. We must be determined to make it happen. We must! We must!" Giovanni banged his fists down on the end table.

Maria joined into the conversation by stating, "Giovanni, you must contain yourself. The children will hear the noise and come running to see if everything is alright. I know you are troubled about not having enough money to send our sons to America, but we must be patient to make this dream come true."

Giovanni replied, "I'm tired of being patient."

Maria continued speaking, "I know that there is talk all over Europe of how America is where one's dreams come true. We have never traveled to America to know what's there, but we choose to believe all the chatter of the good life in America. If only a few of our sons could get to America, life may be easier for everyone. It would be worth everything for us to see this happen. There would not be as many mouths for us to feed. A sum of their money that they earn in America could be returned to us here in Italy to help our family."

Giovanni replied, "Once in America, our sons could send for the rest of our family to make the journey if we so choose."

Giovanni resumed speaking, "We know that leaving one's country is never an easy task; for even though the heart gets homesick and longs to return, it is usually impossible for lack of funds. Also, making the journey on the ships to America is an extremely hard experience. Getting one glimpse of the land of promise, they will never turn back." Giovanni thought for a moment then he said, "I will make sure that this vision of a better tomorrow comes to pass. I have made a vow that I feel will not be broken before my Creator regardless whether the other members of the family remain in Italy forever. It still would be worth sending a few of our sons across the ocean to a new world for a better life. Of course, we would miss them very much."

Maria spoke softly almost at tears. "The older we become the harder it will be for us to leave our country with our roots in place. It will be worthwhile, though, to remain in Italy to hear the stories of America from our sons and to dream for a little while what our own life could have been granted the opportunity in our younger day. I guess you could say that self-denial has a way of making one's heart joyful."

As Giovanni was sitting next to Maria, he placed his arm around her and lightly placed a kiss on her cheek. "Maria, my dear, you have such a good way of looking at the bright side of things. We will need to take this subject up another night, but for tonight, we must go to bed for morning will arrive quickly." Giovanni reached his hand into Maria's pulling her close as he led her into the bedroom to go to sleep.

CHAPTER 4

SUMMERTIME ON THE FARM

———◆———

*Some memories are realities and are better than anything
that can ever happen to one again. (Willa Cather)*

At the crack of dawn, Giovanni arose to return to the seaport to fish, while most of his family were slumbering. Summer was now upon the land. The farm was well attended by his family that he always felt assured that everything was alright with his Maria over-seeing the farm chores. Giovanni only worked as a fisherman from spring through fall and was at the farm the rest of the year when the weather was cold. Of course, in the winter there were minimal duties that had to be done on the farm including attending to the livestock.

Maria was up early today serving Giovanni his breakfast of cornmeal and toast. If the hens laid enough eggs, breakfast would consist of scrambled eggs; and other days, porridge was served. When possible, he liked a good hearty breakfast before leaving for the seaport. Some days, that's all he ate until his return home at eve-ning for the dinner meal. Maria sat down with her coffee for a short time after Giovanni left for the seaport before arousing the children from their sleep. It was good to have some quiet time to reminisce about things of life.

Maria drifted back into reality. She walked over to the old ket-tle to check if enough hot cornmeal remained while toasting the bread for the children. She would throw a few berries or bananas over top the cornmeal to sweeten the taste. She yelled back through the two bedrooms, "Wake up sleepy heads! It's time to arise to begin our day's work! Your father is off to the seaport, which means that it is now time for you to awaken out of your sleep."

Francesco laid their yawning and stretching before placing his feet on the floor. "Come on Vito and Alberto. Mama has called us to start our day. We better get up. We can work in the early part of this day while we still have a lot of energy for the chores needing done."

Vito would lie in bed making noises of the wild before he arose. "I know I need to get up, but Francesco there is some days that I would like to sleep until noon instead of working in the fields and feeding the animals."

"Nice dreaming of sleeping until that hour," chimed Alberto, "but it will never happen as long as Papa has this farm. He's at the seaport trying to make a living to feed his family while we must take responsibility to do the chores. Vito, you sound like a big grizzly bear with all the noises you make upon awakening."

Leonardo was rolling around in bed laughing at the statement Alberto made. He was trying to get a little attention from the older brothers. "Do I have to get up too?" Leonardo propped his head up with his hand resting on his elbow.

"You know the answer to that question before you even ask it," replied Vito. "You must help your younger sisters today inside the house with chores."

Alberta yelled out, "Mama, we are all awake. We will be coming to breakfast in a few minutes as soon as we straighten our room and get dressed."

Alberta continued speaking to his brothers. "Let's get dressed, make our bed, and then we can eat as I told Mama."

Maria left the eating area to go inside the other bedroom to help the younger girls dress. Angelina was giggling while Theresa was chattering to Maria. Upon dressing, Theresa left out a yelp, "Let's hurry to breakfast. We'll pretend that we are in a race, and we can get to the table before they do to win the prize."

The girls yelled, "We beat you to the table. We are going to have our bowls of cornmeal before you do."

Vito teased, "You better save me a little bit of cornmeal for I will be quite hungry if I don't get to eat."

Leonardo laughing chimed in, "It's best you put some honey on your cornmeal for bears like things sweet. We don't want to hear your grizzly noises."

Maria laughed, "We must all eat a hearty breakfast with all the hard labor we will be doing today. Don't eat too fast for the cornmeal is quite hot, and I sure don't want anyone burning their tongue."

After breakfast, Maria went to the bedroom to dress for the day's work. She dressed in her long blue tattered dress with a yellow colored apron wrapped around her thin waist with a big brim red hat on top of her head and high-top shoes on her feet. Speaking to the children upon her return from dressing she commented, "I love to weed and hoe the garden at the crack of dawn while it is still cool outside. Everyone seems to have more ambition the first thing in the cool mornings."

Francesco replied, "I agree. Early rising to avoid the heat of the day is the trick to getting things done faster."

Maria responded, "I am going to pull up my hair under my hat to keep my neck cool from the severe heat today."

Maria is of a well-proportioned size woman with her long flowing black tresses arousing pleasure to a man's eye. Her soft-spoken voice reflects her inner loveliness that shines as the brilliance of a star.

"Sometimes, Francesco, I do get weary from all the work I do. I feel that when it comes to work, though, I have the strength of a horse never stopping to rest. Plowing, planting, and harvesting are a few of the usual jobs I know must be done. With your father going off each day for his catch to provide for us, chores are many; and I know that my body can't afford to be weak." Maria continued, "I have the responsibility of taking care of this farm while your father works the seaport. My dainty little hands are unlike most other women's hands for they have hard calluses because they are accustomed to the grip of the hoe. Hoeing is an essential part of gardening keeping the weeds under control making for healthy plants. I am very grateful to all of you for I know that it would be impossible to keep this little farm going without you. There are times, though, that conflicts arise over the work, but you are all very obedient when it comes to your father and my demands." Maria reflected for a moment not knowing why she was giving this lecture. "You younger children can stay in the house and do your chores while we're outside working the fields."

Vito said, "Let's get moving outside for we have work to do before our father returns."

Today, Maria stood admiring the three oldest sons working in the field. They were attired with little red and navy trimmed flat-brimmed caps to shield their heads from the sun along with their navy knickers, red plaid button-down cotton shirts with sleeves rolled up, and high-top black button-up shoes. The colors were eye catching to any spectator looking across the field with their bronze complexion.

Vito, Francesco, and Alberto are standing alongside their mother helping to cultivate the garden. They had planted sugar beets, beans, lettuce, artichokes, tomatoes, and potatoes and other varieties. The garden was huge stretching out across the countryside. The artichokes are a perennial plant taking six months to harvest when first planted. Not only were there the vegetables to care for, but the apple, cherry, fig and olive trees not to name the many vine-yards of grapes flourishing along the hillside. Also, there were the few livestock consisting of horses, cows, pigs, chickens, and goats. Each family member had his job to help lighten the workload. It was a fact that "*many hands make work light.*"

Back at the little dry-stone farmhouse the three younger sib-lings Leonardo, Theresa, and Angelina remain doing some inside chores. Dishes, dusting, and pushing a broom save Mama a little time for there are more important jobs this time of year that needs done. These days, as soon as you are old enough to walk, the children are delegated a job.

Angelina yelled, "I am going to do the sweeping today. Give me that broom, Theresa."

Theresa smirked, "No, you do the dishes. We can go out and get some water in a bucket at the water pump. I will get you the step stool for you to stand at the basin to wash the dishes. There is still some hot water in the kettle from breakfast that we can mix with the outside pump water that we can pour into your basin to begin your task."

Angelina squealed, "You always get your way. I wanted to do the sweeping, but now that Mama isn't here I will have to listen to you and do the dishes. I'm going to tell Mama on you when she comes back to the house."

"Go ahead you tattletale," screamed Theresa. Angelina and Theresa would argue many times about the housework—who would do the sweeping. Angelina was a little too young at age four to do a good job at any task even though she thought she could.

Today, Leonardo was on the other side of the room using a dust cloth to pick up dust.

Maria returned to the house and spoke to the children as she came through the door. "I am finished gardening for today. I picked a few beans that will need snapped. It's starting to get too warm out there for me to keep working outside. I am going to do some inside work of the chores that you younger children were unable to accomplish here in the house once I see what still needs finished."

"Mama, tell us what you want us to do to help you, and we will be glad to do whatever it is to get the chores done," Angelina replied.

Angelina was at the age that she wanted to help with everything, but sometimes her help wasn't proven to be the best help. Sometimes, Angelina would wet a rag to use as a dust cloth to run over the furniture or get a broom from the closet to sweep the floor to help in the weekly cleaning process. Her cleaning was best described as a lick and a wipe.

"There are several jobs that still need done outside. You will all have to go up to the garden and look how the vegetables are growing from the seeds you planted. Maybe, tomorrow in the cool of the day, I will have you do a little weeding to make the crops flourish. Children, why don't you go out and feed the chickens?" Maria questioned. "Go and see the boys at the barn for some corn to throw to the chickens while I stay inside to finish the household chores."

Angelina ran out the door faster than the eye could capture for she loved helping with any outside chore. She loved the animals and considered them as playful pets.

Leonardo following behind called, "Angelina, you are going to fall and get hurt running so fast. We'll get to the barn by walking if you wait for me and Theresa."

"I know, but I thought I would race you to make it there first." Suddenly, Angelina burst through the door where the older boys were now taking care of the other animals in the old barn. The animal's body heat served as a heater in the colder season, but today the place was hot with the doors and windows propped open.

"Vito, give me some corn in a bag to feed the chickens," shouted Angelina.

"I'll get it for you, but you will need some mash too for the younger chicks."

Vito stood up from the stool as he swung Angelina around. Their laughter rang out as the two held on to each other by their hands twisting around through the air. Leonardo and Theresa stood waiting until the playfulness stopped. They were waiting for their brother to hand them a bag of feed to help in the chores.

Francesco and Alberto came over to where the children were standing to talk to the youngsters.

There next to the limestone abode was an old wood frame building they called a Spring House used to store food from one year to the next. Inside there were wooden steps leading down below the earth where the temperature was cool even in the hottest months making it ideal for storage of food. There was a pipe coming out of the ground on the lower level where a trickling stream of water ran from the hills that was fetched for drinking or watering the animals. There was an opening at the far corner of the Spring House for the excess water to run down over the hill to the cistern.

Alberto said, "I'll fetch the spring water in a bucket for you from the Spring House to water the chickens after you get the feed." He turned around to leave and Leonardo followed behind to help him with the bucket. Vito and Francesco handed the girls their bags of feed for the chickens. Watching his sisters' exit the barn, Vito returned to his duties once again.

The rough wood on the outside of the barn looked rustic with metal screening serving as windows where square openings appeared. Vito sat on the little stool milking the three goats while Francesco and Alberto feed the other livestock. Feeding the livestock and milking the cows and goats was a small part of the day's chores. Goat's milk helped supply the family with milk to drink and cheese to eat. Each goat had its special name and a reason for why the name was picked. There was Ivory named because of the whiteness of her coat, and Bones named for his thinness. The two other goats were Elvira and Sabrina. They were named for their feminine traits. Many times, Elvira liked to come over and bump you while Sabrina waited for popcorn to devour it right out of your hand. Each one had its personality.

"Francesco, come quickly. I need help with Sabrina." Francesco ran to where Vito was sitting with Sabrina the goat. His face was instantly hit by warm milk flying up in the air running down his cheeks. Wiping his face with his hands, the warm milk kept pouring onto his face flooding his eyes causing them not to focus. Vito sat there laughing. Francesco realized that his brother was playing one of his pranks on him for Alberto came from behind howling with laughter. Now they were all laughing. Some boyish play was good for lifting the spirit where hardships plagued the land.

Once again, nightfall fell across the land when all the family was united in the little dwelling to talk, eat, and retire from another day's work.

Tomorrow, another day would begin taking on with the same routine as the day that passed bringing one season into the next season.

After many days of labor, the day arrives to start reaping the harvest that is sowed.

As Maria spoke, she was organizing the schedule for what fruits and vegetables had to be picked. "Vito, you and your brothers will need to gather several baskets for the potatoes and beets that need to be dug from the ground. Potato and beet planting is more work than the other vegetables because of the digging. Once all the potatoes and beets are dug, I will decide the amount to sell and the amount to retain to sustain our own family's need until next season."

Vito affirmed, "You decide what amount of potatoes and beets that we need to keep, and we will bring them to the Spring House to store for the winter."

Francesco said, "Alberto and I will go and get the shovels and hoes to begin."

Alberto chimed in, "We will let the potatoes and beets lay on top the ground that is dug for a little while before taking them to the market. It will make it easier for the earth surrounding them to fall off before they are placed in bushel baskets. Patrons look for nice new big clean potatoes and hearty beets. Hopefully, they sell fast."

Maria stood taking in what the boys were saying. She nodded, "Once the potatoes and beets are dug and the vegetables are picked, you can all go off to the market to make a sale, which will put a little extra money in the old tin can for the dream."

Vito speaking, "We will pick olives next week too. The trees are still flowering. We will pick some olives that have ripened once the flowering is done. We will then have to get our nets to drop the olives in to save on time having to pick them up off the ground."

Francesco mumbled, "While the potatoes and beets are drying out, we will pick the other vegetables, Mama. The big red slicing tomatoes will be very appetizing if they are ripened and ready to be picked. The beautiful redness makes you feel like reaching out and grabbing one to sink your teeth in to suck the juice right out of it. There is nothing better tasting than a fresh garden red, ripened tomato."

Alberto said, "Maybe another week we can pick the grapes. This year the grapes seem to have flourished along the hillsides cascading down from the vines waiting to be picked to lessen the weight. Patrons at the market look for firm, ripe grapes to make the best quality wine for drinking."

Now that all their chores were finished, Vito, Francesco, and Alberto filled baskets with tomatoes, lettuce, potatoes, sugar beets, and various fruits and vegetables that were ripened and fully grown.

The baskets with a wide variety of fruits and vegetables would be loaded onto the wagon to take to the marketplace in the morning to sell to feed the little ones and save enough money for the dream. There were several other necessities carted along such as the wagon's canvas covering, money bag, a light lunch, and water in preparation for the all day stay.

Presently, the wagon sat desolate waiting to be loaded with all the fruits and vegetables for the sale at the marketplace. Punctually was the key at the marketplace to obtain a place for the wagon and selling their items. Only a few days a week were devoted to selling at the marketplace in the summer with all the chores that need finished at the farm.

Another day has begun, and the plan today was to go off to the marketplace with the loaded vegetable and fruit baskets. Before leaving for the market, the older boys had breakfast. Breakfast today consisted of porridge with brown maple syrup, toast, and coffee. Mama would whip up the porridge in the black iron kettle on top the grid of the old fireplace with a flame underneath. They had to eat heartily for dinner was a long way off in the day. With all the hard work that was done in a day, appetites were sparked with hunger.

Upon finishing off his porridge Francesco said, "Mama, it won't be long until we are ready to go to the marketplace. We will complete a few of our necessary daily chores first before we leave. Vito can milk the couple of cows and goats while I throw some food and fresh water out for the other animals. I'll let the feeding and watering of the chicks to the youngsters when they arise. We will be back as soon as our fruits and vegetables are sold."

Maria stepped over to Francesco patting his arm saying, "Thanks, I never need to worry when you boys are around for you all help to make the farm run." She started over to the fireplace to mix some more porridge with water to have ready when the younger children arose.

Vito's mouth was full. His cheeks were shaped as balls from the last few bites of toast stuffed into his mouth. He continued to chew upon rising from the table before making his exit saying, "We'll be back as soon as we can. Tell the sleepy heads that we'll see them tonight since they are still in bed."

Maria smiled. "Actually, I will. Your father has left for the seaport earlier this morning."

Alberto lifted his cup to down the few sips of coffee left in his cup before heading out the door. Francesco rose from the table and waved to Mama following Alberto through the door to complete the farm chores before leaving for the marketplace.

Maria nodded as she returned his wave.

Coming toward the old barn, they gazed at the old wood planked wagon with four wood end posts that made the wagon sturdy. It was structured with a long handle on each side and the creaky metal wheels made the wagon quite heavy without any vegetables loaded.

Francesco motioned lifting his hands in the air as he was speaking to Alberto. "While Vito and I do the few farm chores, why don't you load the baskets onto the wagon making it ready for us to leave for the marketplace?"

Alberto replied, "I'll be glad to load the wagon. You two go about the chores for it will save on time if I take care of the wagon." Alberto went over to where the baskets were placed the night before and lifted the baskets one by one onto the wagon.

Vito and Francesco exited the barn looking at all the produce that sat upon the old wooden wagon. "The vegetables really look appetizing with all the bright colors. We sure had a nice crop this year," said Vito. "It was a lot of hours of labor, but I guess it's worth the effort when we see how lovely the crop turns out here."

Francesco said, "Let's get started. Here's the plan. Let's pull the wagon through the narrow pathways to make our way to the market. It sure is easier when the path takes us on a downhill walk than carting it on an uphill pulling, but we have no control of the downhill or uphill path."

Alberto replied, "You're right, but sometimes it seems there are more uphill paths than going downhill especially when we have a load of fruits and vegetables on it."

Vito stood shaking his head in agreement to Alberto's statement. "Stop complaining Alberto. We all know it isn't easy taking the wagon to the market, but if we want to make some money and sell our vegetables, we must push the wagon to get there. Let's begin our journey. It looks like everything is loaded. The sooner we get there the sooner we can begin our selling."

Francesco yelled out from behind the wagon, "It sure is good we aren't weaklings for it makes us able to maneuver the wagon without much trouble through the pathways on our way into Bari. At least coming home is somewhat easier without the load on the wagon. We must admit that it's a pleasant journey meeting people along the way to the market talking as we walk to our destination."

Passing by the back-narrow alleys upon arrival into the Old Town, men and women stood in open doorways in their baggy rag clothing by big wooden barrels.

"Good morning," yelled an old man as they carted the wagon past the door.

Francesco nodded his reply speaking, "Maybe next week we will bring our crop of grapes to the market to sell. We will stop by and see if you are interested in purchasing any of our grapes. We didn't bring any today for our wagon is full, but we are thinking the grapes will be better ripened by next week when we come to the marketplace."

This was the place where the grapes were brought to be crushed from their skins to begin the process of old-fashioned wine making. Sugar and yeast were added to start the fermentation process. This was a steady process for the best wine is bottled and placed on a rack refraining from drinking for one full year. To keep a supply of wine on the Italian table, grapes had to continuously be crushed and placed in fermenters for bottling to begin. This was a vicious cycle.

The man responded, "Do stop by next week, and I will look at your crop to decide if I want to buy the grapes."

Continuing through the maze of alleyways and courtyards, they came upon Cathedrals and monuments before reaching the market. Bari housed a lot of magnificent architecture if one opened their eyes to gaze upon it. Beauty was everywhere inside the city as well as beyond. One could stand looking out as far as the eye could see across the seaport imagining the memory of the medieval sailors.

In the distance, echoes of music could be heard from a few villagers with their music boxes in hand trying to make a few cents in their tins. People came from all over the village seeking fresh food for a cheap price. The market was always lively with a vibrant atmosphere in the summer with the sellers and buyers filling the streets. On both sides of the street, the farmer's market spread out with various homegrown fruits and vegetables. Several varieties of grapes, lettuce, tomatoes and mushrooms, juicy peaches and oranges, and succulent berries filled the market. Some farmers would sell an array of bright colored flowers. Beauty as usual is always an eye catcher. Some of the wealthy class enjoyed having cut flowers at their places to enjoy the sweet-smelling fragrance and lively colors beaming for all to see. On each side of the street, there were little village store's where home-baked bread, fresh-caught fish, red wines, and a variety of cheese produced by locals were sold. Mouths watered from the aroma permeating the air from the fresh-baked bread and odors of onion, garlic, and tomatoes simmering. Most villagers had large families to feed; and because of the lack of space to grow fruits and vegetables, they always welcomed the crop grower.

The markets were busy with hundreds of Italians rustling through the streets looking over the produce for sale. In their minds, they were thinking how to get the best buy of the day for they only had so much to spend and needed their little bit of money to go a long way to feed the little mouths in their households.

Vito, Francesco, and Alberto rolled the wagon into the marketplace looking for an open space to set up with the rest of the farmers. Today, they set up on the north side of the street. They unrolled the canvas cover they had thrown onto the wagon to serve as protection against the heat and rain. Then, it was placed upon the four end posts of the wagon.

Francesco said, "I don't think we need to worry about rain. It looks like the sky is clear today."

Vito agreed, "Yes, but we will need the canvas to avoid the heat today." Just then, Vito took a drink from the canteen. Looking over the wagon, Vito noticed that the sugar beets with their green tops lay to the side with potatoes piled high up in various baskets. They had only a small basket of beet tops for the heat would cause the tops to wilt making for loss of money. Good quality beet tops were young, fresh, tender, and clean without heavy-veined leaves that usually made the tops tough. Picking the beets while young was the key.

Artichokes were good growers in Bari. The freshness of the vegetable was indicated by its green color. After it has aged it becomes brownish. Artichokes were a chore to get ready to bring to the market. They had to be cleaned by cutting the stems and tough outside leaves with a thistle-like center removed. A rare number of patrons would soak them in salt water, then boil them, and add vinaigrette dressing to devour.

They stood organizing their wagon. The same type of vegetables and fruits were together. An Italian lady walked over to the wagon asking, "Are you ready to begin selling?"

"Yes," replied Vito. "What are you looking to buy?"

"I'm looking for some beet tops. I wash and boil them until tender for approximately a half hour. Then, I chop them coarsely and add butter and salt to eat. My husband loves them prepared that way."

Vito thought it was good that her husband loved them because it would be nothing that he would eat. Even though he didn't like them, they would harvest them for patrons that would purchase the item.

He pointed to the basket, "Pick out as many beet tops as you desire to buy." The woman seemed to represent the middle-class for her appearance didn't exactly denote poverty. Her attire was plain.

"Thank you," she replied. She looked down picking out several vegetables she desired placing them in a basket to carry to her house. "Here are the vegetables that I will buy today. Besides the beet tops, I am buying tomatoes, lettuce, and a few potatoes." She paid Vito for the purchase; then, slid the basket over her arm as she walked away.

Good beets had to be smooth and free from blemish. Beets that were rough or ridged with cracks would usually prove to be tough or woody. Sugar beets were always good to eat, but it sure was a messy job preparing them to eat. Cleaning the little bit of dirt away from the beet was difficult, but placing them into a pot to boil was the worst of the preparation. Beets had a way of bleeding into the water and staining everything that touched it including the hands.

Long ears of yellow sweet corn that was not fully husked sat behind the sugar beets and potatoes. A fresh green husk with well filled kernels made for a good ear of corn.

On the other side of the wagon was where the tomatoes sat. A good quality tomato was firm, smooth, and of a good color, but it was not overripe. Stacked beside the tomatoes were Romaine, Iceberg, and Oak Leaf varieties of crispy lettuces. Depending on what vegetable or fruit was in season was the item brought to sell for the day. Usually, the fastest product to market was the deep dark purple grapes that were used all over Italy. The boys planned on bringing the grapes to market next week. The small grape vineyard was surrounded by a circle of Olive and Cypress trees. Some of the ancient Olive trees with knotted robust trunks were 100-years-old regardless of their size. When the grapes are mature, they are plump and firmly attached to the stems. Red wine is drunk in most house-holds at meals for the water is a lot to be desired. One could not stop without tasting a grape or two. The sweetness saturates the mouth causing the taste buds to come alive from the natural sugar that is bursting with sweet flavor.

"Vito," shouted Francesco, "hopefully we can sell our items fast. Then, we can get out of this extreme heat." Sweat was pouring off their foreheads and their shirts were damp with perspiration from all the travel on foot to the place. Most local sellers hoped that the onlookers would stop at their place first. The day would be an early one once they made their sales, but many days that was not the case. Some days, it didn't take long for the crop growers to sell their items; while others, the day never seemed to end. Because of the short sup-ply of money, there were days that the average villager would only eat one meal where other days they ate nothing. Obesity was not a problem across the country.

Chatting among the locals made the day go fast. Vito was of an outgoing personality and could make conversation with about anyone. He would leave the wagon with Francesco and Alberto to do the job of selling returning a little later to check on what had been sold.

Vito returned saying, "I wish I had something cold to drink. I have been talking to several around the market, and it has dried my mouth from the extreme heat."

Alberto pulled out the canteen handing it to Vito saying, "This should help quench your thirst."

"Would it be safe to drink after your mouth has been drinking out of it?" questioned Vito.

"It's okay if you wipe around the opening before placing your lips on it. Anyway, beggars can't be choosers." Alberto answered.

Vito started talking to his brothers about his visiting in the market today. "When I went over to the wagon across the street, there was standing a gentleman. Do you see that man dressed in a blue shirt with suspenders holding his knickers up with a blue hat on his head?"

"Yes, I see him," Francesco nodded.

"I like his hat." Alberto chuckled.

"Well, forget the hat, but he was talking to different locals saying that he sells tickets for a Steamship Company that could buy their way to a better life in America. He said that he has been traveling from village to village selling tickets for a cheap price. Once we would acquire a ticket, it would secure our passage to America." said Vito.

"Do you think he really is selling tickets or is it a scam that he's trying to get some of our money?" asked Francesco.

Vito laughed, "No, he is selling tickets. In matter of fact, he sold a few today to some of the villagers for he said that the ship will be leaving from the port in about two months."

"Two months is a long way off." Alberto said in a questioning voice.

Vito continued, "Mama and Papa have talked our entire life about this dream coming true. Maybe, it's time to seriously act upon it. Maybe, it would make life easier that way we wouldn't have to work as hard. Supposedly, there is lots of money and beautiful women attired in long flowing dresses with wide brim hats waiting for us to arrive."

"Vito," said Francesco, "you are always thinking about beautiful women waiting for us. You're a dreamer. You should try to think of making money for a better life first; then, you can get any beautiful woman you want. Women usually cost a lot and like to have a good time. How can you give a woman a good time if you don't have any money? Do you really think she'll want you for your looks?"

Alberto chimed in, "Yes, I agree with Francesco, women fancy money to spend. You can buy her a comb for her hair or take her to a dance in the village if you have some money on you. I wish you would get women out of your brain for now."

Vito answered, "Well, I think it's worth checking out for if we can leave here for a better life; the two months wait is worth it all. We could begin living our dream."

Meanwhile, life back at the homestead, Maria had to take care of duties that are required in caring for the children and running a household. Leonardo, Theresa, and Angelina were now past infancy and into the early childhood years. It required less work now. From all the crops harvested, there was always something to prepare for the family from churning butter to pressing grapes for wine to drying fruits. Then, there was also laundering clothes on the wash-boards, baking bread, tidying up, and planting flowers—the work never ceased.

Sometimes, Leonardo and Angelina would play together while chores were being done. Little voices chattering filled the abode with laughter ringing out from their playfulness.

Now, the distinct sound of pounding was heard in the distance as the wagon made its way up the pathway for the return home after the day at the marketplace.

Francesco shouted, "Mama! Mama! Come quickly for we have many things to tell you! The day was splendid! We bumped into a man from a nearby village who makes vast amounts of wine to sell to merchants. After the encounter, he asked us to bring the beautiful grapes we grow to the marketplace next week. He assured us that he would buy the entire crop for his wine-making business. Other locals looked for us too for they know how perfect our crops are. Little by little the produce we had with us was sold. We have returned with nothing on the wagon. Mama, here is the money we made for the little tin to help provide the family with food and to help prepare for the future dream."

Vito smiled as he put his hand on Mama's shoulder, "Also, there was a gentleman selling tickets to the villagers to go to America. This well-dressed gentleman alluded to the fact that he has been all over Europe selling many tickets to help our villagers have a better life. Do you think he's for real?"

Mama replied, "All of us have often talked about the dream. The dream, which your father and I would never deny you boys, is of letting you three boys go to America. We have been saving money right along to fulfill this dream. When the day approaches that we have enough money saved, we will then let you go and have that better life. Maybe the time is closer than any of us think. It will be hard, though, for me to let you go; but I know I must when the time is right. When your father returns, I will tell him of your experience today."

Alberto sighed, "Vito was running around the market talking while Francesco and I sat at the wagon and sold the fruits and vegetables."

Vito responded, "I might have went around talking, but I'm the one that found out information about the ticket sales to America. If I would have stayed at the wagon, I would have not heard any of that information."

After a moment, Francesco said, "Vito, you're probably right. Let's go put the wagon away and get cleaned up for supper."

As he was speaking, out of the house ran the babes to greet the boys.

Angelina yelled as she ran toward the boys, "Did you bring us any chocolate bars?"

Francesco retrieved a candy bar from his pocket. "Here you go. You'll have to share it with Theresa and Leonardo for I only have one bar."

She started peeling off the paper from the bar to take a small bite. She looked up at Francesco, "I'll share. It will be a bite for each of us." Angelina was glad for a small bite. As Angelina stood smiling with her big brown eyes gazing at Francesco, she blurted out, "I have something very important to tell you, Francesco. It happened when you were at the market."

"Did something bad happen while we were away?" replied Francesco.

Angelina shook her head back and forth as she opened her mouth pointing her finger at the front of her bottom lip.

"You lost your tooth." said Francesco.

"Yes, that is what I wanted to tell you," said Angelina giggling. "I waited for you so that we can bury it in the garden outside. Then, a new tooth will grow in its place."

"Well, I hope you get a brand-new tooth for you sure are a special little girl," replied Francesco. "Tonight, I will make a wish for you to get a bigger and better tooth than you had."

"That sure will be swell," said Angelina. "I will check in the morning to see if a new tooth begins to come up in my mouth."

In the distance, a man was walking slowly toward the house. As usual at the setting of the sun, Giovanni returned weary and tired. Some days, he would bring a few fish home in place of money. This sure was putting a damper on fulfilling the dream.

He brought mostly sardines, bass, and tuna. Tuna was the fish that went farther feeding the hungry mouths of his family. Poverty plagued the land. He was told down at the docks that eventually when times get better he would be paid more for the fish. Many times, he wondered if that day would ever arrive. He was holding on to the dream despite circumstances.

As usual in the evening, each family member shared their daily stories with the other members of the family sitting around the dinner table in the dimly lit room.

Tonight, though, Papa's usual sea venture stories took a different twist. All ears were tuned into hear what Papa had to say when Leonardo asked a question, "Papa, why do you always wear long-sleeved shirts? Did sharks bite your arms?"

Papa replied as he rolled his sleeves up. "Do you see these scars on my arms?"

The children all nodded while they waited in anticipation for the details.

"I do not want to offend anyone, but the scars are very ugly for eyes to view."

Angelina spoke up smiling, "They aren't that ugly, Papa."

"Let me tell you a little story about how I acquired these scars. It was late at night with only the light of the moon shining down upon the earth. Your mother and I were awoken to hear the chickens cackling loudly like something was bothering them. I arose out of bed and ran out to the chicken coop with my lantern in hand to find a pack of wild dogs inside trying to attack the chickens. As I approached without warning, the dogs were growling, then, they turned toward me with their mouths wide open. They started biting my arms and legs with their teeth that felt like shark teeth. I was screaming and hitting them trying to get loose. As I dropped the lantern, fire broke out chasing the dogs away, but it was too late for the dogs left me with my skin ripped apart from their teeth. We left the doors open for the chickens to get out of the burning building and ran to the pond for water to get the fire dashed out before the entire building was lost. I was in excruciating pain from the bites, but I didn't realize how badly the dogs had hurt me until after dashing the fire out. My adrenalin was activated from the situation at hand. Then, I collapsed. Mama noticed the blood flowing out of my arms and helped me. She dragged me back to the house where I laid in bed with pain for days. She had to contact the doctor for I needed medicine given to guard me against getting rabies and infection.

Immediately Mama spoke, "I don't know how I had the strength to drag your father back to the house, but in an emergency, your body has immeasurable strength and is able to do impossible things you never dream it can do."

"The doctor from the nearby village visited daily caring for the wounds. My wounds were very sore with oozing pus and blood because of what the dogs' teeth had inflicted on my body. I was lucky. If I had not worn long pants and a long-sleeve shirt to bed that night, the damage to my skin would have been twice as bad. Also, dropping the lantern, which caused the fire, made the dogs run away. It saved me from more severe damage to my skin. Now, you all know the reason for my long-sleeve shirts and why I am terrified of dogs."

Angelina responded, "Papa, we hardly notice the scars on your arms. If you wouldn't have called our attention to them, we wouldn't even know that they are there. We love you despite the markings. It makes you special to all of us now."

Once dinner ended, the children left the table and went about playing games together in the usual way for a short time.

Francesco stood up yawning, "I'm tired! We've worked hard today with going to the market selling our crops. Tomorrow, we will have another busy day. I don't know about all of you, but I'm going to bed." Tonight, each one decided to retire early that they may be able to start an early workday tomorrow.

Many days tired and low in spirit, Giovanni would wonder whether he would ever have enough money to fulfill the dream for his sons. Many times, the dream seemed very far off. Though, the family had been saving the Italian *lira* for quite a while, he hoped that the dream was closer to being fulfilled than he believed. When waiting for a dream—sometimes the time seems to pass by slowly. One day would go into another as the years passed by with each family member fulfilling their obligation to make the dream happen.

CHAPTER 5

TRAVEL TALK

Watching the tide of the ocean washing into shore fills one's being with complete serenity. The sound of the waters and the seagulls calling out soothes the spirit of man.

Maria began speaking as she sank onto the bed in their bedroom. "Giovanni, today Vito came back from the marketplace all excited stating that there were men there selling tickets for passage to America."

"Maria, that doesn't surprise me for there have been men at the seaport docks when I arrive each morning for work," he replied. "The sellers are going across the land in an effort of routing thousands of steerage passengers to America. They will acquire some money by having a large group of passengers."

"Giovanni," she blurted, "you never said anything about the sellers! I am very surprised!"

Giovanni shrugged, "I didn't want to get your hopes up that now is the time to fulfill the dream that we have been planning for many years. I'm not sure we have enough money to pursue this adventure yet."

The pain in his heart was a little unbearable. He didn't make eye contact for he knew that he was not being honest with Maria.

He stuttered, "Maria, may…. maybe it's not that at all, but uh…... Maybe it's that I'm still not ready for the idea of letting the boys go now. I can't face the reality of the dream coming to pass. The boys are young, and I will miss them terribly when they leave us."

He looked at her for a long silent moment before beginning to speak. "One night, not long ago, I went to the old tin and counted the money while you and the family slept. I knew then that the dream had multiplied to become a bigger dream than what we ever imagined."

"What do you mean?" she questioned.

"Earlier, it appears the days passed with little vision of coming true, but now I know that all three sons can fulfill the dream for there is enough money to send each one of them," he confessed. "Like I said earlier, uh…. uh…. I'm not sure that I'm ready to let them go to an unknown land even though the boys are really men now. I thought maybe we could send the oldest first." Giovanni walked over to the bed and wrapped his arms around Maria.

She spoke as she gazed into his eyes, "I have my doubts that I want Vito going alone. He probably wouldn't want to go by himself anyway." Maria was trembling. "It's better that all of them go together for they can help each other in starting a new life again. It would be too hard going alone. They have worked hard during their upbringing and deserve the best. We have taught them well. It is time now that they make a life of their own by spreading their wings as the eagle. Vito is 20, Francesco; 18, and Alberto; 16. I feel that they are old enough to be on their own now and make their own decisions. Look at us, Giovanni." Maria chuckled.

"I know, Maria, I robbed you from the cradle, and we had our first child before you were 16," Giovanni laughed as he pressed a kiss on her cheek.

Then, he glanced worriedly at her for he knew she was upset. Giovanni noticed how gorgeous she still was as she sat relaxing on the bed. "I want to tell you that you are as beautiful tonight as you were when I met you!"

She lowered her eyes saying, "Thank you, Giovanni, but we are talking about the boys, not me."

He dimmed the lantern. "We can take this conversation up another time," he chided. He then took her lips under his and the cares of life vanished from his touch. As he lay down beside her tightening his arms around her whispering love expressions as their bodies melted together into an exquisite slumber from their lovemaking encountered.

Meanwhile, not a word was spoken about the dream since the night when Giovanni and Maria entered sweet bliss when the world seemed to stand still for a moment. Many days while work-ing, Giovanni kept thinking most of the time about America and the gossip from many of the Italians. The time was at hand that he had to share his thoughts with the boys soon. Before speaking to the boys, though, he hoped for Maria's approval. Maybe, tonight was the night he hoped to open that forbidden conversation?

Giovanni and Maria usually talked before retiring for the night about the day's events. Tonight, it was not different than any other night other than Giovanni felt prompted to share his heart with Maria about the dream. Giovanni and Maria were standing in the dining area. Giovanni moved closer to Maria. Not knowing how to begin the conversation, he pushed a few strands of black curls to the side of Maria's head smiling a stiff smile while placing his hand on her shoulder. Then, he began to speak, "Maria, we must tell the older boys that now the time has come to depart on their voyage to America for a better life. I feel that we must act now while the agents are available; otherwise, it will always be a dream and never happen. We talked about this a little while back, but we have not said a word since. We cannot keep avoiding this matter."

"Giovanni, the more that I think about it the more afraid I become. How can we let our sons go to a foreign land? They speak very little English. Besides, they know no one and will be homesick in such a far land. We'll never see them again."

Giovanni walked over to where the tin sat. He took the tin from off the shelf to count the money that was saved by his family as he had done many times in the past. "There is more than enough money for our sons' passage," Giovanni beamed. "From what I've been told, the cost of a ticket is approximately $15; and there are "free-lance" ticket agents traveling all over the seaports advertising these tickets. These tickets are sold without space reservations. They will also need a passport. The boys will have to answer many questions from the inspectors for the ship's manifest before embarkation, which I will review with our sons before they leave. I have collected the details over the years to have the passage organized. Though, I must teach them not to trust anyone in America, and I must tell them that there are many robbers in Napoli."

"Maria, we have talked for many years that we want to give our sons a better life than we will ever have here in Bari. The boys cultivated plans throughout their lifetime for this new experience. We introduced the idea to them years ago, and I believe that they have accepted it as something they want to pursue."

"I don't know if I can let them go, Giovanni," Maria responded emphatically.

"I do not want to hear those negative sayings out of your mouth again," he grumbled. "Was it only vain talk? You must stop being selfish!" Giovanni was becoming very annoyed. "We must give them something we never had or never will have! Let them go, Maria! Take your hands off them and let them be the men they need to be by letting them have the freedom to make a better life! Life here is too hard! All they'll ever know here is poverty!"

Maria froze taking in every word that Giovanni was saying. She couldn't ever remember Giovanni displaying heartlessness like he was displaying. Then she spoke softly, holding on to each word, trying not to anger Giovanni or to break down and weep. "Giovanni, I remember not long ago how Vito came through the birthing canal screaming at the top of his lungs, and I cradled him in my arms to stop the crying. He was the firstborn that was made in love. I was happy to bring a new life into this world that we made together with the hand of God! Francesco and Alberto came next with open arms of greeting. We fed them and sheltered them from the cold in hopes that they would have a good life here with us. We have many memories of their childhood that we will always hold dear to our hearts. They have had a good life regardless of all the poverty."

Tears of anguish welled up in Maria's eyes and her faint small voice quivered as she continued speaking, "Back then, we never thought of sending our sons to a foreign land to never see them again. We protected them..." her voice was fading "from whatever it was that came our way. Once things got hard here...the thought left my mind. A little later uh.... uh.... I know we talked of sending them away for a better life, but I guess I never thought that we would have enough money to make it possible. Please forgive me Giovanni for acting very childish! I can't help holding on to them for a while longer! They are my flesh and blood! I know in my heart I must let them go! I... still think of them as my baby boys! Giovanni, give me some time to get adjusted to the idea, and I will try and let them go!"

"Maria, time is what we don't have!" Giovanni snorted.

Tears started flowing down Maria's cheeks like a summer shower. Giovanni looked at Maria silently. He had upset her. Bending his head over Maria's, Giovanni took Maria in his arms to comfort her from the sadness she was feeling. Maria was very precious to Giovanni.

Giovanni didn't disturb her weeping as he started speaking softly. "Maria, I will give you some time, but don't spend too much time thinking about it or they'll miss their opportunity! When opportunity knocks, we must respond before it passes us by! When the time is right, Maria, we will tell the boys of our decision when we make one if we ever do! We must let them know that they will be sent with our blessings for a better future! Of course, if they decide that they really don't want to go to America, I am not forcing them to go. They will live with that decision. They have a home here with us for as long as they want to live in Bari. Now, let's get to bed for morning will be upon us soon, and we have a full day ahead of us tomorrow. Let's get some rest."

For a time, words were not spoken between Giovanni and Maria about the boys going to America since that night when Maria broke down weeping. Days passed with Giovanni sailing out to sea while Maria along with the boys worked the land. The younger siblings followed their daily protocol too. Maria must make her decision quickly for time wasted would fade out the dream. Finally, one morning she decided that she had to let the boys go to America. Giovanni was right. It was the time for the adventure. The decision was made. Preparation for the journey would soon need to begin.

One fine day, Giovanni returned from the seaport a little earlier than the usual time. He regretted the words that he had to communicate to his sons, but the words had to be said. He began the conversation slowly, "Vito, Francesco, and Alberto, let's go down to the seaport where the turquoise waters are sparkling like mirrors! I just arrived home from there, but I am filled with so much energy from the beauty bursting all around! Today, it seemed that the walk was shorter than the regular walk!" Giovanni knew that the right words would come out as he eased into the conversation.

"Papa, we finished our chores here at home earlier than usual. We can all walk down to the seaport with you. It will be nice to have some time alone to talk men talk," said Francesco.

Giovanni understood that this conversation was more than the normal men talk. He smiled as he ushered the boys through the door to get to the path that led down to the seaport.

"Vito, Francesco, and Alberto!" called Giovanni. He began to speak softly upon their arrival to the seaport. "It's a beautiful day here at the seaport! Really, it's a perfect day today with the sky of blue and the white puffy clouds floating as the sun rays are shining brightly through the clouds! Look at the water how it's very clear and sparkling! Do you see the reflection of us in the waters?"

The boys nodded as they stared at each other with a look of confusion on each of their faces. Their minds were racing with anticipation of what their father was trying to tell them. Suddenly Francesco spoke up, "Yes, we see our reflection Papa! What are you trying to say to all of us?"

Giovanni sighed as he tried to stand tall straightening his clothes showing little emotion. "It's…it's like a glass mirror waiting to shatter! This is the way my heart is right now, breaking up inside of me for what I must say to you! I must say it even though it's not easy!"

Alberto replied, "Is there something wrong? Are you sick?"

He continued, "No, it's nothing like that boys. It's about the dream that we have talked about in the past. We have been putting a little leftover money in a tin for many years with hopes of sending you to America for a better life if need be."

Vito spoke, "It's alright Papa if we can never get to America for lack of funds! We understand! Don't fret about it!"

Giovanni gasped, "No, no, that isn't it at all! Let me begin. I would like you to understand want I want to say to you. When we started, we never thought we would accumulate much money. The other night I decided to count the money to estimate how much more money we will need. I was excited to find that we have finally accumulated enough money that the dream we've been dreaming for such a long time can now become a reality. When we started talking, we only had plans to send one or two children, but after thinking about it, we decided that three children would be better to go for that way no one would feel alone in a strange land. You boys are very close knit because of growing up together and your closeness in age. You played together, worked together, and slept together. You really haven't been apart at all while growing up. There is some preparation to make before you leave, but we must hurry to get things ready before the ship sails. I will purchase the tickets and secure passports. There are other matters to attend to as well. I will see that this is accomplished before you leave. Since all steerage tickets are sold without space reservations, obtaining a ticket should be easy for now."

Francesco spoke up, "I don't want to go! I'm satisfied with my life here with you and Mama! I don't want a better life! We work hard, but that's all we know is work! We hear different ones talking at the marketplace how America is a better place, but when it comes down to it, who wants a better life? Not me! I'll settle for what I have! I wouldn't know how to deal with it! None of us know the English language or are we familiar with any of the places in America! We would be aliens in a foreign land!"

Giovanni answered, "Francesco, common sense tells you that everyone wants a better life if they can obtain it! Once you find that better life, there's not a person in the world who would return to the lesser when they can have more! Go with my blessing, and please don't look back!"

Francesco sighed dropping his head, "I heard that making the journey is very difficult. I'll have to think about it for a little while, Papa!"

Alberto spoke up in a questioning voice. "You don't think you want a better life, Francesco? What's there to think about in having a better life?" He continued speaking. "If you would get a glimpse of finer things, you would change your mind in a hurry like Papa said! What are you afraid of anyway? It would be fun taking a journey to an unknown land to explore it like Columbus did to find a new land. Maybe, we may go down in history!" Alberto chuckled. "You sure wouldn't be going alone. All of us will travel and stay together. We would be able to talk amongst ourselves. We would learn the language in time. It is fun learning new things! It keeps the mind going strong!"

Francesco stood by the sea gazing up into the sky with tears flowing down his cheeks. He was thinking in his mind that no one really understood how he was feeling.

He whispered, "You're right, we would all be together, but maybe that isn't enough for me! I know I can get use to this idea, but for now—I need some time to think. If I decide not to go, the two of you can go without me. I'm not stopping the two of you from going. Anyway, like Vito said before—there are beautiful women just waiting for our arrival!"

Vito interrupted, "Well, at least in America, we would have some money to show a woman a good time. First thing we would do is look for a job. Supposedly, there are a lot of jobs in the coal mines and steel mills. We could make a good living to provide for all our needs. If possible, we could send money back home to help Mama and Papa when we have a little extra."

Giovanni stood by the sea staring as if in a trance. For a long while, his body felt numb and lifeless as he was taking the conversation in but trying to make sense of it while holding his heart together. As he stretched out his arms, Vito, Francesco, and Alberto ran toward him as they all stood together in a circle embracing one another with tears flowing down their cheeks speaking words of consolation to each other. Each one expressed softly of how they will miss him, Mama, and the other siblings while Giovanni returned to them the same sentiment. They were assured that being far across the world, memories would help to sustain them when feelings of loneliness came upon them.

Finally, Giovanni spoke up, "Sons, darkness will soon be upon us. Let's go back home and tell your Mama how you are all looking forward to taking this adventure. We can then begin getting things ready for you to go. There is not much time until the next ship leaves, and we must get ready for your departure. Francesco, if you decide to stay here that is alright."

As they traveled up the hillsides by foot, each one was silent in their own thoughts. There were good thoughts of how life could be much better, but also feelings of homesickness flooded their minds for America was a long way from home. Once leaving, it was very unlikely that they would ever return to their homeland.

Upon arrival home, Maria felt that Giovanni had the conversation about the voyage to America with their sons. Maria and the other children were standing in front of the house. Despite her anxiety, Maria knew in her heart that now was the time. She held her head high smiling to hide her true innermost feelings. The younger siblings would help ease the pain in her heart for there still would not be an empty nest. The family would expand as the years pass by with grandchildren being born, but there would always be emptiness without the presence of the boys. She would try and keep a positive attitude that maybe one day the boys would return with their children. Even though, they didn't, she could write to them to help ease the pain of emptiness. Maybe, she and Giovanni would make a trip to America. One never knows what's down the road in life. Now that the blessing was given by Maria and Giovanni, preparation had to begin for this voyage.

After several days had passed, Francesco hesitantly spoke to the family one night after supper. "I have finally made my decision to start a new life by going to America. I am going along with my two brothers. I am certainly uneasy over this new experience with fear flooding my thoughts at times, but I will be going!"

"Don't be afraid, Francesco. We'll all be in this undertaking together," spouted out Alberto. "I am accepting it for an adventure that might prove to be a new discovery."

Vito said, "I am the dreamer! I am always dreaming of what might be. Clothes and food have to be packed, tickets and passports have to be obtained, English has to be learned, and emotions have to be brought under control for this long journey awaiting us."

Alberto continued, "It will be a major adventure getting to the port in Napoli from Bari."

Giovanni swallowed hard. "I will provide the wagon; and you can use one of my horse's, which upon arrival to the port both can be sold for a sum of money to help provide all of you with some extras if needed while waiting for the ship to come to transport you across the ocean to America. My understanding is that the Steamship Company required by our government will be responsible to house you in the boarding houses at the port until your ship comes in."

Vito espoused, "We know that there will be a waiting time for the ship to appear. Hopefully, they will house us travelers in private boarding houses that are located all along the port city coast boasting of their own "emigrant hotels.""

Francesco picked up on the conversation. "America has been an inborn hope for us to have a better life where our dream to own land and get a better job can be fulfilled. Common practice is that one member of a family goes to America first, then, saving enough to bring others over; but the plan for our family is different."

Vito continued, "Supposedly, the journey is long and hard with few conveniences that life offers while coming from Italy into the

New York harbor. There has been talk that some of the ones coming on the ships never make it for the ocean being rough and food is scarce with illness striking some of its passengers."

After listening a while, Maria spoke up to the conversation. Her voice was quite shaken from the heartache she was feeling. She began, "That's the risk that must be taken to capture the dream. There's usually a price to pay to obtain better things in life. Your father and I have instilled this thought in your minds for a better life. Life can be better elsewhere with more opportunities. We must not think negatively of the journey. Now is the time to take the chance. Here in Bari with all its poverty, there are days that some families eat one meal only. We understand that there is a great chance that you will never return to your homeland with money being very scarce and the voyage being too long and hard. We realize that this chance of a better life will separate you from our family forever. In America, you can work in the coal mines and steel factories that provide a better income. This is an opportunity of once in a lifetime. We will be fine back here in Italy! Maybe someday, we may join you."

Giovanni spoke softly looking at Maria, "In these kinds of matters, sacrifices have to be made! We must make the best of what little time we have left together before we must part. We will all hold on to our memories! I think it's time to retire for the night. Tomorrow will be another day."

CHAPTER 6

THE JOURNEY BEGINS

Men must have a vision as they pass through life.

As the weeks passed by with all the preparation being made for the voyage, finally the day arrived to say their goodbyes. The boys would be heading for Napoli their port of departure. There was no turning back. The morning was a beautiful day. The sun was shining across the hillside as the sky was of a brilliant clear blue radiating the beauty of the universe. Francesco stood and observed all that he could see to have the memory in his mind. Then, the eight of them stood hugging and holding on to one another. They formed a circle taking each other by the hand knowing that the circle could never be broken regardless of their absence. Their father led in a family prayer for protection, guidance, blessing, and wisdom as they were about to depart. There was not an eye that was dry as Giovanni closed the prayer.

Their spirits would always remain alive no matter wherever they traveled for each one was left with a memory that would be stored deep within the heart forever. It's impossible to take memories from the heart. Memories would always be embedded in its chambers.

One of the horses that Giovanni had as part of his small farm was hitched up to the small flat wagon as the luggage and food supplies were tied down with rope. From Bari, it was approximately 165 miles to reach Napoli, which would take them at least 5 to 6 days to reach the port. Napoli sits on the west coast. Some of the rough terrain may cause unforeseen problems, but they weren't dwelling on the unforeseen. Now that the wagon was loaded with a few personal goods; it was time to go. Giovanni and Maria were standing with arms wrapped around each other while the little ones were chattering about the beauty of the horse. The children had never noticed such beauty; they wanted to touch its mane. Maybe this was a plot of distraction to take their minds from facing the reality of the situation at hand.

Francesco pulled Angelina up by the arms to hold her one last time before boarding the wagon and kissed her cheek. "Probably the next time I see you, you'll have grown like a wild weed!"

Francesco made eye contact with Leonardo as his voice started quivering. "Leonardo, uh...uh...take care of Angelina and Theresa for now you'll be the man of the house while Papa is working! You will all need to help Mama with all the chores for there is a lot of work here to do. The harvest is over for now, but next year it will return once again. Of course, you all will be a year older. We will write as soon as we get an address to keep in touch with each other. We will miss all of you!"

Vito, Francesco, and Alberto climbed up onto the wagon with ticket and passport. Vito held the reins in his hand as each one waved their goodbye. "We'll let you know which journey is worse, the one to the port or the one to America. We love you! Take care until we meet again!"

Maria stood frozen trying to hold back the tears vaguely comprehending the conversation. God only knows.... she wanted to be strong for the family. She didn't want to speak a word for the boys to detect how upset she really was. She put a fake smile on her face lifting her hand waving as the wagon was about to leave.

Vito chuckled as he spoke, "Papa, I'll let you know if there are beautiful women in America!"

Alberto shook his head while smiling in disbelief of how in the world Vito could think about beautiful women now. Slowly, the horse started moving as each one waved their goodbyes and threw kisses to each other.

Angelina and Theresa broke loose from their hold running behind the wagon screaming, "Don't go unless we can go with you!" Tears were streaming down their faces.

The wagon came to a stop. Francesco jumped down with tears in his eyes. "You girls must dry those tears from your eyes! We will be alright! You must act like big girls now, and if you miss us too much, try and think of a good memory that will bring us into your heart! We will never be far from you or leave you for memories remain!"

Francesco turned the girls around to run back to Giovanni and Maria. He gave another wave as he jumped back up onto the wagon.

Giovanni yelled out, "Remember, watch out for robbers in Napoli and trust no one!"

Maria grabbed the girls and Leonardo as she felt sickened walking to the house. She softly spoke out loud, "Things will never be the same here at the homestead without all of you!"

Giovanni was deeply saddened to see his sons leave tearing his home apart. He stood there in a trance as he watched the wagon disappear wiping his eyes with a handkerchief as the tears continued to fall. Then, he clenched his fists raising his arms in the air walking toward the barn.

Speaking softly to himself, "Why does life have to be hard here in Italy that I have to make the sacrifice of sending my sons away to an unknown land? I know that I will never see my flesh and blood again! Why, tell me why things can't be easier?" Sadness beyond words was gripping his heart. He stopped dead in his tracks as he turned around to find his way home with his family. Life would continue as always, but there would always be empty chairs at the dinner table serving as a reminder of what was.

The boys begin the downhill journey to get on the narrow pathway that would lead them to the Napoli seaport. Francesco reiterated, "We have acquired the directions several times from Papa to memorize in our minds. We know that we will pass through several villages before getting to the port. If we become lost, we can always stop and ask directions."

Alberto replied, "I'm quite adventurous and not worried too much about our journey. I know that we will make it one way or another. We know that we must keep traveling west. We will definitely get to our destination."

Vito began, "It is fortunate that the season is now mid Fall when the weather is still mild that we can sleep under the stars without getting too cold. However, it is wonderful that Mama has given each of us a quilt that she made to keep us warm from the chill of the night. There is truly nothing like the treasures from home that can be carried along for memory sake!"

Alberto chimed in, "In the day, we can travel as far as we can—only stopping to feed and rest the horse while we eat our own food. When the terrain gets rough in places, we will get down from the wagon to make the wagon light. We can walk the horse with the wagon attempting not to topple it until we can reach the next village."

Francesco started speaking softly, "Night will soon be upon us. Let's build a campfire lighting up the darkness of the night. We'll keep the campfire burning through the night. It will help to warm our bodies while huddling together taking the chill off from the cool breeze. Once the sun goes down, there sure is a chill in the air! I'm told fire protects from danger like Papa told us the story of the wild dogs. We can share our stories tonight while practicing some of our English anticipating for our great adventure that is right around the corner."

Vito said, "We must be careful avoiding the wild attacks of animals while sleeping under the stars. There may be wild boars, brown bears, and wolves roaming out here. Let's place stones under the wheels to keep the wagon from moving. Later, we can bed down under the wagon for protection to sleep."

"I'll unhitch the horse," announced Alberto.

Excitement was in the air as they continued their journey, which is a downhill and uphill journey to reach Napoli. After several days travel, Francesco yelled out. "Look over there! Do you see the body of water with ships and several buildings in the distance? Smoke is hovering in the air from the ships and various buildings with the sound of honking to the ear!"

Vito snapped, "This must be Napoli where we will set sail to reach America! It seems to be a very busy place!"

There were masses of people milling about as they looked out into the distance over the harbor. Their hearts were pounding at the first sight of the seaport for there was no returning home once boarding the ship.

Francesco commented, "I believe we have arrived at Napoli! We will have to wait for our ship to show up. I'm not sure how we will recognize the ship. I am hesitant to make our way any farther for my emotions are exploding within my inner being! Right now, I feel like turning around and going back home!"

Vito snorted, "We must compel ourselves to go on regardless to how we are feeling!"

Arriving at the seaport, Francesco approached the building on the left while the two brothers remained with the wagon. There was a ticket booth where a little round man with a bald head sat. Francesco ran over to the window and began speaking in Italian asking, "Is this Napoli, the seaport where the ships take passengers to America?"

The man shook his head up and down in reply indicating they were at the right place. He asked, "Do you want to purchase a ticket, or do you already have a ticket?"

Francesco continued speaking, "We have our one-way tickets. My two brothers and I are waiting for a ship called the Stampalia. We are told that the Stampalia ship would be coming in to take passengers to America. I hope the ship hasn't already sailed on its journey."

Once again, the man smiled and shook his head up and down indicating this was the place of arrival. He talked back to Francesco in Italian, "No one ever knows the exact time when their ship will arrive for no schedule is generally given. You may have to wait days, weeks or even a few months. All I can tell you is that I know that it is coming soon. If you like, you can all be housed in a private boarding house located here at the port. If you have your ticket, you can stay until the arrival of your ship. The Steamship Company is required by the government to provide for its passengers their night's stay until the ship sails in. Otherwise, you can sleep under the stars."

Francesco didn't want to sleep under the stars. They had saved some extra money to pay for the various expenses aside from ship travel. He pulled out a small sum of money and laid it on the counter.

The man in the ticket booth cleared his throat and spoke once again. "Like I told you, there is no charge for anything. The Steamship Company is responsible for providing for you until you board the ship. If you have your passport, ticket, and paperwork, provisions are all set for you until you set sail. Before boarding, you will be asked approximately 29 questions recorded on the manifest. Some of the questions you will be expected to answer will include your name, sex, marital status, occupation, last residence, nationality, if you have at least $25, if you have ever been in prison or an institution, ability to read or write, race, physical and mental health."

Vito spoke up glancing at his brothers, "Uh…. Uh…. hopefully, we will be able to answer all the questions."

The ticket agent continued speaking, "Once you have answered the questions, medical exams will be completed, vaccination will be given, and most likely you will be disinfected with disinfectants that will give off a stinky odor. Then, you will be led on to your accommodations on the ship."

The man stood up as he exited the booth. Then, he instructed Francesco where he and his brothers could stay by motioning in the direction Francesco had to follow. "Go to the end of the dock to the last boarding house for there are several rooms available there for you to stay as long as is necessary. The doors are not locked. Take whatever room you feel like staying in. Make yourselves comfortable now for it's a long, wearisome journey once you are boarded on the ship," the ticket salesman said. "You will be led to the lower deck, which will be like a prison until you reach shore. Each day ships arrive to transport passengers to America. There may be 1,500 to 2,000 steerage passengers. We will hope that the ship you are waiting for will arrive soon," he replied. "Talk is that it should be arriving in a few more days, but it could be another week or two or possibly up to a month. I will know once I see it is coming into harbor."

Francesco turned around to leave as he started to inform his brothers by saying, "Our ship is to come in within a few days, but there's a possibility that the ship could take a month to get here. I'm in no hurry to leave here. Maybe by then, I will get use of the idea of leaving Italy or turn around and go home. Until its arrival, we have some business matters that need attended too before boarding the ship to America. One important thing is that we must try and sell the horse and wagon before leaving."

Vito replied, "I don't feel it will be hard to accomplish this task for passengers will be unloading the various ships with baggage coming to Italy. Passengers will need a way to transport their belongings across the hills."

Alberto chimed in, "This will give us a little extra money for our voyage. Papa has a few wagons. He wanted to help us in whatever way he could to make our voyage to America as pleasant as possible. He knows that we will send some money back to the family once we are settled."

Walking down the plank decking with the horse and wagon toward the front of the boarding house, Francesco grinning said, "Vito and Alberto, let's get some rest. We've had several tiring day's journey getting here. We will take care of everything we need to do tomorrow when we have clear heads. Let's hitch the horse to the post with the wagon."

Alberto shook his head. "We will need to take our baggage off the wagon and place it in the room. We don't have much baggage; therefore, it shouldn't take us much time."

Vito held open the door for his brothers. There was something cozy about slipping into the small room with only two small straw-filled beds. The room appeared clean. Alberto occupied himself for a moment by gazing out the window with his thoughts only his own.

Suddenly, it began raining. They were glad that they were indoors warm and sheltered from the storm once more with only the few necessities of life.

Vito stated, "Tomorrow, we will find a place to bathe for once we board ship we won't be able to bathe until we reach land again."

Alberto spoke up, "I don't want to wait until morning to bathe. I would like to bathe now before we retire for the night. The rain appears to be slowing down and will probably stop in a few minutes."

Francesco shook his head in consent saying, "I agree. Once the rain stops, let's go find a place to bathe."

As the rain stopped pelting down, Francesco and Alberto made their way to the door with Vito following behind. Once again, they went over to the counter where a little bald man was sitting in the booth and asked, "Where can we find a place to bathe?"

The man motioned them saying, "Right across the street to the little building is where you will be able to take a bath. There are wash basins and a few tubs. If you need a cake of soap, I have some in a cabinet."

Grabbing the soap, Francesco shouted, "Let get going! We'll return to our room to pick up some clean clothes!" They scurried off to the little building that promised them some refreshing from the days travel before retiring for the night.

Early the next morning, the trio dressed before making their way to a little coffee shop. As they entered the shop, the aroma of the brewing coffee embraced their smelling senses. Vito leaned over the counter.

The man behind the counter asked as they approached. "What will you have today?"

Vito replied, "We'll all have a cup of black coffee this morning with toast and scrambled eggs."

The man slid the coffee cups across the counter in front of each one. "Sit down over at the little round table, and I will bring your order in a few minutes for you to eat."

The brothers dropped down around the table removing their hats. Sipping their coffee, they began conversing about their plan for the day. The waiter brought over the eggs and toast placing it in front of each one. It felt good to have a hot breakfast like their Mama made when they were at home. Francesco laid down the money on the table as the waiter picked it up.

"Once we finish breakfast, we'll have to find someone that can help us with the sale of our horse and wagon," said Alberto.

"It will feel good to relax for a few days since we have traveled far to the seaport," said Vito.

Once they boarded the ship, bathing and food would be slim pickings on their journey across the ocean. They had packed dried salami, bread, and cheese and some other items that would not spoil, but they didn't know how much they would be eating with the roughness of the ocean would most likely curb their appetites.

It didn't take long to sell the horse and wagon for many ships sailed into port with passengers unloading luggage to prepare for their journey into the heart of Italy.

Time dragged as they waited anxiously for their ship to arrive for there was little to do while waiting—only to eat and sleep. A day felt like a week in time. Time seems to drag when anticipating an important event that will change the rest of your life. This event would paint the rosy future that they had dreamed.

After several weeks of waiting, the morning finally arrived as they were told it would. Francesco awoke from the loud shrill sound of honking. He arose out of bed as he looked out the window to see the ship pulling into the harbor. "Alberto! Vito! Get up! I believe the Stampalia is coming to take us to a better land where the *streets are paved with gold*! Hurry, we sure don't want to miss our passage to America!"

Vito replied, "How do you know this is the Stampalia ship? It could be another ship!"

Francesco scratched his head as he looked at Vito. "From the description I was given by several passengers waiting to board, it appears to be the closest image of the detail that I was given that matches."

Alberto said, "This Stampalia is the ship that is going to make our dreams come true!"

It was a ship that carried approximately 2,500 passengers from Italy to New York during one trip. The ship was built in 1909; therefore, it was fairly a new vessel. The trip usually would take at least 14 days up to a month to reach the shores of America.

Besides answering questions to board the ship, Francesco and his brothers were a little nervous regarding the anticipation of the questions upon arrival at Ellis Island. The boys only attended a minimal amount of school because in Italy it cost money to attend, and they lacked the funds. Francesco and his brothers finished eighth grade. They could read and write Italian very well. English was another story. They were very weary from all the days of waiting for their ship to arrive. Each day they remained at the boarding house was stressful with the anticipation of sailing but not knowing the exact time.

They were warned what the process was before boarding. At Ellis Island, they were required to go through a similar process. A wrong answer to a question could deport you. They were told that the United States Immigration Officer at the time of arrival was given the manifest lists of the alien passengers. The intent of the questions was to identify illegal entering aliens and criminals and people unable to support themselves upon arrival.

Hustling to get dressed while collecting their bags, the brothers ran out the door to make it to line up to board the ship. The brothers arrived where the ship now was docked. They had meager luggage that was going with them to their new home.

There were many people waiting to embark. The noise and confusion were beyond belief with at least 1,000 passengers boarding. They were met by the ships security. "Step over here to the right for processing. You will be led to that little building before boarding. Once you answer the questions, have the medical exam completed, and are given the vaccination, you will be able to board the ship."

Francesco whispered to his brothers, "Let's try and stay together so that we can board together. Also, let's go follow the crowd to the exam building."

Vito spoke up, "Yes, if we all pass their expectations, then we can be on our way. Do both of you have your ticket, passport, and paperwork?"

Francesco and Alberto shouted together, "Yes!"

After an hour of processing, they made their way back to the ship for boarding.

Alberto yelled, "All aboard! We answered the dreaded questions and had the medical exam."

Francesco shouted, "Hooray! Hooray! We have our paperwork and passport and vaccination for it is stinging. We sure are now ready to board the ship."

Vito spoke, "It was well worth us practicing our English to answer the questions correctly. I am happy that we all made it through the process to be able to board the ship."

With ticket and passport and paperwork in hand, the Stampalia was waiting as they were led down the deep stairways to the lower decks to their steerage accommodations. Upon arrival to America, the ships manifest would be turned over to the Ellis Island inspectors to confirm accuracy.

"It looks like we are going through that hatch on the deck," said Alberto.

Francesco was staring down at the floor. "Yes, there are two ladders leading down to the unknown. The area is dimly lit. I'll go first. Hold on to avoid falling or breaking your neck!"

The brothers arrived down to steerage. Vito explained, "If you notice, the floor is covered with sawdust. There are berths along the wall that are numbered on the rough wood boards stacked three to four high. Let's bunk together."

Francesco chimed in, "I wonder if we're assigned to a certain bunk number. We'll have to remember our number to stay in the same bunk the entire trip. We'll bunk over here. They'll tell us to move if they have assigned bunks. Let's put our belongings over here."

Vito said, "I'll take the top bunk. Alberto, you take the middle one and Francesco; the lower. It sure appears that there is no room to sit up. The buckets must be for people that need to throw up. It looks like in the corner is a toilet surrounded by a flimsy curtain."

Alberto started speaking, "No wonder that there sure is a smell down here, and it's a little warm from no windows for ventilation. Hopefully, it won't become too intolerable!"

Francesco frightened replied, "There are a few old wood rough benches in the center of the floor to sit on with some old barrels. It sure isn't too passenger friendly!"

Vito spoke with fear in his voice, "Well, I guess our prison now begins for the rest of our ocean journey to freedom! At least prison will be short lived. Freedom will be reached once we reach our new home if we survive. Let's get settled in to our new temporary home away from home."

CHAPTER 7

LIFE ON BOARD

A caterpillar in a cocoon struggles to get out then changes into a beautiful butterfly as he comes forth. The struggle creates the beauty. Life is full of many struggles, but if we endure the struggles, we come forth in rare beauty.

Francesco spoke loudly to Vito and Alberto trying to be heard over the sound of the engines and the other passengers talking. "There is barely any room to move down here now. If more passengers keep coming down here to steerage, the conditions will be overly crowded."

Vito hollered, "Maybe we should have waited for a different ship to come into port."

Alberto roared above the noise, "Francesco, the crowded conditions can be dealt with each day. How do we know that the next ship isn't crowded? This foul odor is going to be what's intolerable to me if it doesn't get any better!"

Francesco cried, "It's going to be a difficult trip with the odor and the dismal darkness that I notice here in this compartment! I have a weak stomach, and I hate to think that we must put up with this smell every day until we reach our destination! The time will sure drag! We treat our animals at home better than these conditions!"

Vito tried to shed some humor on the subject. "We should have brought clothespins for our nose! Maybe that's why this area is kept dark. Once we get settled in this compartment, it will really turn darker to avoid us seeing what is causing the odor. Perhaps after a while, we won't notice the smell. Hopefully, we'll adjust for the short time we have to reach our new home."

Alberto chimed in, "Short time? Huh, it could take us a month! That sure is not a short time with having to contend with this smell! One thing I must say about you Vito is that you always try to brighten up things. Vito, you could be standing in horse manure, and you still would find humor in doing it! The odor is overbearing! It's something more to contend with for the many days of our travel!"

Francesco laughing, "Hopefully, the odor isn't coming from horse manure! I hope they aren't transporting horses too!"

Francesco at this moment was shaking his head as he spoke, "I feel like turning around and running right out of this ship all the way home! We are very poor here, but maybe poverty isn't bad after all. I felt that the trip wasn't going to be pleasant, but I sure had no idea it would be crowded with neck to neck people. Besides the crowd, we also must put up with an odor. It's sure is going to be an unpleasant trip!"

Once again, Francesco stood observing their accommodations. He looked around noticing the iron pipes with little berths allowing only sufficient aisle space for several hundred passengers to navigate in this lower part of the ship.

Francesco stood speaking to his brothers. "Our new home away from home leaves a lot to be desired! I hope we will survive this long journey!"

Vito replied with a slight chuckle. "We are survivors! Try and think on pleasant thoughts! Despite these miserable conditions, we must keep faith alive in our future. Keep that thought in your mind! Too bad I didn't bring some clothespins and blinders for our eyes! We could all put a clothespin on our nose that way we wouldn't smell anything, and things would be alright. The blinders for our eyes would block out seeing the small accommodations."

Alberto commented, "The steerage passengers keep flooding down here to these quarters. Hopefully, the end of the line comes soon!"

Francesco heard the engines being fired up and the honking of the horns. Francesco yelled, "Do you feel the movement of the ship?" Once the ship left the Port, there was no turning back. Fear gripped his heart. "I wonder whether leaving our homeland and family behind to pursue a dream is the right decision to make! At this moment, I feel like we are cattle being placed for slaughter!"

A vision of having faith in unseen things from the creator was the factor that kept hope alive in his heart. All he and his brothers carried were clothes on their back, a few packed clothes, food, and approximately $45 in their pockets. Upon arriving in America, they could purchase their train ticket, food, and find shelter from the cold.

Francesco questioned privately in his own mind what the new world would be like and if the promise of a better life would come true. It sure was hard to imagine a better life with all the chaos that was going on in this ship. The brothers only spoke the Italian language fluently, which was fine for now. They were learning the English language, but at the present, they did not have it down pat. Because there were many Italians on the ship, language was no barrier; but once they migrated to America, it would be difficult because they were not fluent in the English language.

The various passengers were becoming acquainted with one another. After several days on the ocean, the travelers were becoming weary with one day leading into another.

After having turbulent waters throughout most of the nights, they walked up to the open deck where the morning was once again being captured. Alberto said, "We are all becoming exhausted from the length of travel and the hard conditions with such a small berth available. It is hard to get a good night's rest! The smell of vomit from the sick passengers is another problem!"

Vito replied, "I have had many sleepless nights due to the noise from the iron pipes and motion of the ship! Many noises echo through the night with crying infants and languages swirling through the air. The darkness of the night and a feeling of loneliness makes the mind to wonder. I hope there is a new beginning like we were told!"

Francesco stated, "Most of the passengers appear to be in a state of shock physically, mentally, and emotionally. The ocean is quite rough, winds are howling, and the weather is cold. Ventilation is poor! Dining rooms are not found on the ship on the bottom decks. We steerage passengers must eat on the benches in passageways near the sleeping compartments where odors from vomit and toilets are almost unbearable! The smell is getting worse as the days pass from the unattended vomit of the seasick and the odor of human flesh from the inability to bathe!"

Francesco stood still leaning against the berth in the dim light thinking to himself that who in their right mind could even have a desire for food with all the obstacles that one had to contend with during this voyage.

Francesco continued speaking to his brothers. "Most days I feel like vomiting too! I know I should drink coffee or water to stay hydrated, but I've noticed that most passengers eat only enough to survive because odors curb the appetite. Many times, fear grips my heart too! Constantly, I am thinking of survival! Hope keeps coming back to my mind, though, that life will be better once we reach our new home! It is good that we brothers have each other for support and hope to hold on to in this crisis. When one is discouraged, the other brother tries to say encouraging words to help all of us through the low point. At least, I feel secure knowing my brothers are with me. These difficulties will be behind us once we reach the new world."

Right next to them was a family of a mother, father, and a two-year-old boy. After several days out to sea, Francesco thought he would go out of his way to be friendly and try to hold a conversation with them. Francesco felt it would be wise to introduce himself and his brothers to this family. Maybe they were headed in the same direction once they left the ship.

"My name is Francesco. This is my brothers Alberto and Vito." Francesco stretched forth his hand to the couple waiting for a handshake. "We all have come from Bari, Italy."

Francesco continued speaking, "We are coming to America to start a new life where we were told that opportunity calls, and the *streets are supposedly paved with gold*. We are going to try to get a job in the coal mines once we get to America. We have heard that the coal mines and steel mills are hiring immigrants."

The young woman began speaking. "There are three in my individual family also. My name is Antoinette, my husband is Alexander and the baby is called Micah." Antoinette continued speaking, "Alexander is trying to provide a better future for our family. He decided to bring us to America. Presently, we aren't sure where we will be staying, but we were told that jobs are plenteous. I'm sure Alexander will find something to do."

Alexander was of a small stature with dark greenish eyes and curly black hair. He was approximately 20-years-old. Antoinette had a slim build with dark complexion wearing her long nearly black hair pulled tightly twisted in a bun. She would sing lullaby songs to the youngster each night trying to calm the boy from the sound of the howling winds and tossing ocean. Many nights she was vomiting from the rough waters but continued for the sake of the child to remain calm. Many nights the child spent crying wanting to get off the ship because of the loud noises and the dismal darkness. Micah was one of many children crying of the fear felt from their environment. Alexander would remain in his berth in a stupor caused by the foul air unable to help in quieting the child.

"I'm glad you came over and introduced yourself for I know that many nights Francesco you would come over and take our child in your arms and rock him to sleep to help me and the boy's father get a little rest since we have been very seasick. We are very grateful Francesco that you take Micah under your wing the way you do even though we didn't know your name!"

"The little boy reminds me of my own siblings back home that I already miss! Micah's little dark head of hair is soft and nice to touch!" Francesco sat down on the bench in front of her holding out his arm to grasp Micah. It felt good to cradle the child in his arms.

"Micah, I'm your friend. Did you ever see a cow?"

Micah shook his head up and down.

"What noise does the cow make?" asked Francesco.

Micah sat and stared not willing to answer.

"Doesn't the cow say moo, moo?"

This time Micah curbed his lips trying to imitate Francesco saying, "Moo! Moo!" in a giggling voice.

"I have a horse at home and the horse sound is, Neigh! Neigh!" It felt good to focus one's thoughts on other things until reaching shoreline.

As the days were passing by to make their way to America, Antoinette thought that truly Francesco was a great storyteller for children. He positively had a special way about him to get a child's attention. He certainly would make a good father one day.

Night after night Francesco would tell the little boy stories about the farm animals on his family's farm. He would continue making sounds like the cat meowing or chickens cackling. The little boy listened attentively and laughed until many times falling asleep in his arms. It felt good having a warm body pressed against his chest in the dark cool confinement of the compartment.

Alana and Nicholas, an elderly couple from southern Italy was on the other side of them. Alana began speaking in broken English, "We have relatives in America whom have invited us to start life again where opportunity for a better living can be attained. Our health is not too good anymore. If we can go to a place where life is easier, we feel this may help us live a longer happier life. We like to share our stories of the good old days in Italy with others. It's always nice to hear people laugh. It makes the atmosphere lighter."

Many of their stories were amusing and would go on for hours, but it was good for passing the time reminding all the listeners of the good times back home. Sometimes, their stories were repeated with adding more details to the story, but no one worried about it for there was plenty of time to waste. Older people have a lot of wisdom if only a person stops to listen.

To really stimulate the atmosphere as the days passed, the old man now and again would take out his music box and start playing and singing. Nicholas loved watching the sleeping come alive. Some would sing; others would dance. Dancing would take place right in the little confine that allowed them enough space to move around for the moment. The seasick seemed to recover for a little while. It's amazing how music has a way of reviving one's soul. Music made the time pass by quickly. Sometimes, the music and singing went on until the wee hours of the morning.

Another older gentleman called Domenico had a violin with him. He would take his old violin from the case and begin to play. The violin didn't seem to be worth much by its appearance, but when Domenico placed the bow on the violin, it was as though heavenly music began radiating the premises. A dance floor was made in the center for the children and adults to dance. A good time was had by all participants. The music seemed to lighten the atmosphere from the hardships that most of the passengers were feeling. Domenico seemed to be traveling quite light, but his most valued possession was his violin. He never left the violin out of his sight.

Over in the far corner, there were several men playing cards using the old wooden barrels as a table.

To pass the time because of the length of the journey, passengers had to stay occupied by playing cards, singing, dancing, storytelling, and talking, talking, talking. Much time was spent rehearsing immigration inspectors' questions, and hour upon hour was spent learning the strange new language.

Horns honking, engines roaring, and laughter filled the air after 25 days of traveling when the crowds on the ship came to the top deck screaming and hollering in amazement as the ship approached the New York harbor. Some were clapping, others crying, and many were singing songs of joy as they approached their new home. A fear gripped most hearts though, wondering whether their new home would accept or reject them. This land held a different view than did the Old Country.

The brothers went up to the top deck. At the tip of Manhattan, the first thing coming into view was an object. They were all standing looking across the ocean. Tears of relief came streaming down Francesco's face. "Alberto, Vito, look there is a huge object coming into view for us all to see!" In the distance, stood a lady with a torch held high to the sky.

"It's the Statue of Liberty!" yelled Alberto. "All who sees her knows there is freedom and liberty for those entering this land!" Amazement gripped their hearts of the bigness of the statue that represented the big new world. Alberto sighed, "Finally home!"

Vito, Alberto, and Francesco circled around each other with tears streaming from their eyes. They didn't know whether the tears were tears of joy or sadness from what they were feeling of reaching their new land safely.

A feeling of sadness swept over Francesco of leaving behind the acquaintances and friendships he had made on the ship on his way over to America. It was very unlikely that he would meet again with the many people he had bonded with on the journey here to America.

However, Francesco knew that if ever he would see a violin that it would bring back the memory of Domenico playing his beautiful melodious songs to soothe the passengers on their way to America. When he would see a curly, dark-headed little boy, his mind would re-capture his moments with Micah.

Upon docking at Manhattan, the medical inspectors boarded the ship for medical exams for the first and second-class passengers before they were released to their freedom in New York.

A security officer yelled, "Steerage passengers, please step over here to the pier where there is a waiting area! Stay in groups of 30. Be sure to wear your name tag with your manifest number for us to see clearly. Barges will then take you to Ellis Island, which is only a half mile more to your destination to freedom in America."

Vito nervously spoke, "Let's stay together! We sure don't want to lose each other! Come on, let's get on the barge taking us to Ellis Island! We want to get processed; then, we can be on our way. It's sure is great to see the light of day again!"

The passengers were packed on the top deck of the barges with their luggage on the bottom level deck as the barge started moving toward the Island. At the entrance of the building, upon arrival at Ellis Island, were many United States flags flying high welcoming them to America. Interpreters met them at the main doorway directing them up the stairs to the Registry Room.

Francesco said, "I don't know about all of you, but I am extremely exhausted and weary from these several weeks of travel.

The ground is swaying beneath my feet and with these loud shouts in different languages echoing the air is giving me a headache."

Alberto said, "Let's move over here with the other steerage passengers to the processing area. There is so much noise from the crying infants and the different languages echoing up and around the high ceiling of the huge hall here at Ellis Island that it would give anyone a headache."

Vito began speaking as they reached the top of the stairs, "It looks as if a doctor and interpreter are here waiting for us. If we don't get a white chalk X put on us, we are free to start our life here in America."

The doctor began, "It usually takes about three to five hours for the processing. Once I do the exam, move over to the right to bathe with disinfectant solutions. The final step will be questioning to verify information on the manifest by the inspectors."

Francesco said, "There sure is an odor from steerage passengers unable to bathe for days!"

Body odors mingling with the scent of disinfectant greeted the nostrils upon entrance to this building because of frequent cleaning of floors, benches, walls, and showers to avoid contamination by germs.

Vito snapped, "I hope we pass the dreaded questions and medical examination! What are the doctors looking for any way?"

The immigrants are assembled in groups of 30 according to the manifest, examined by a doctor proving they're fit to stay in America, and questioned with approximately the "29 dreaded questions."

Alberto answered, "We were told that the doctors are looking for tuberculosis, heart disease, mental illness, and trachoma. If any of these diseases are found, the immigrants must return to their own country. They are not permitted in the United States. The immigrants have to speak some understandable English."

Francesco espoused, "I am very nervous that something will go wrong, and we will all have to return to Italy. Either that or maybe one of us will have to return. I know that we don't have enough money to turn around to return home, but we were told that the Steamship Company was responsible for our return. If one of us must return, we made the pack among us that we would all return home."

Alberto started speaking, "You worry too much! Everything will be alright!"

Vito said, "I don't know which is worse, the smell of not bathing for days or bathing in disinfectant solutions before being cleared. I know that Ellis Island will always be memorable to us for it is the point where we immigrants started our process of becoming an American. Let's move into the bathing area."

Coming out of the bathing room the Inspector nodded his head as Francesco shouted, "Vito, Alberto—we passed the test! We're free! Free at last! Not that we smell very good from the disinfectant soap we were required to use, but at least, we're free to start our new life. My eyes are sore from the doctors using the probe to invert my eyes to look for trachoma, but the pain I'm sure will pass in a day or two. It reminds me of a woman in travail with a child. After holding that newborn baby, the pain is all forgotten. Hopefully, it will get better for us as time goes by. I feel the worst is over!"

Alberto stooping down to collect his baggage said, "Let go over there to the Money Exchange to exchange our lira for American dollars. Then, we can purchase our railroad ticket at the railroad ticket office and leave Ellis Island to head into New York City to catch the train."

CHAPTER 8

ARRIVAL IN THE NEW LAND

---

*What is a final destination that a human being longs for
in life? Each one focuses his attention differently.*

Before leaving Ellis Island, Francesco stopped to view one last time his entrance to America. In his heart, there was an invisible sign saying, "Welcome to America." The calm crystal waters reaching toward the clear blue sky with the big white puffy clouds brought assurance to his soul that all will be well once he reaches his destination. He pauses for a moment of silence thinking how serene and beautiful life can be in comparison to the ocean on such a calm sunny day. The ocean calm waters can change in a matter of seconds if a storm comes in to make the waters rough and raging. He knew the same is true of life situations for a time. He hoped that life would be beautiful here.

Francesco shouted, "Over there is our next stop! It looks like the railroad ticket office in the distance where we can purchase tickets to come to the end of our journey."

"Let's go to the ticket booth. Then, we can be on our way," said Alberto. "We can wait in the ferry terminal marked for Manhattan passengers. A ferry will shuttle us into the city to catch the train. Look! The New York City railroad ferry boarding area can be seen! It is only a short distance from the ticket office."

Traveling all these days made a bond of friendship with the various travelers and now it was time to say goodbye once again. Passengers were going in different directions to reach their ultimate destination. Different languages assaulted their ears.

For Francesco and his brothers, their destination was a place that each would feel solitude in his innermost being and would be able to earn a living. Francesco still had to find that place for he hadn't come to terms with it emotionally since leaving Italy.

Upon approaching the ticket office, there were mass lines of people waiting to purchase tickets for their destination. Vito alluded, "We will be waiting hours to get to the window for a railroad ticket.

Let's use our ferry pass to be ferried to the city and purchase our tickets another day."

Upon arrival in the city by ferry, Vito stated, "While we are here in this city, let's see a few sights for a short time and then be on our way."

Alberto agreed by saying, "Yes, we could explore the territory for we probably won't get back. Why don't we enjoy it while we're here? Vito, don't' you have some extra money for us to stay in a hotel or boarding room until we can leave?"

Francesco chuckled, "Alberto, you are always one to explore. There isn't any hurry to get to the place we're going. There surely isn't anyone waiting there for us. Maybe it would be a good idea to stay here a few months to find a job and earn some extra money that we may continue our journey. I'm sure the city is full of job opportunities that we can do. Besides, winter will be setting in, and it will be better to travel once spring arrives."

"Good idea!" replied Vito. "We don't know what will be waiting for us once we arrive at our planned destination anyway. We may not be able to start a job in the coal mines, railroad, or steel factory right away. It might be to our advantage if we make a little extra money here in the city. It is hard to search for a place to stay in the cold weather. After we're here a while, we might decide to stay here and not venture any farther. At least, we can become a little accustomed to this strange land before moving on."

They made their way through the streets looking toward the sky. Alberto yelled, "These are some of the tallest buildings that my eyes have ever beheld. There certainly are many sights to see."

As they looked across the street, Francesco cried, "Look! Over there is a park surrounded with large shade trees with benches located underneath. Sometime, we will have to sit and enjoy viewing the buildings and parks that grace this area."

Vito agreed. "There certainly is a lot of pedestrians here walking on the paved streets as Model T cars seem to be touring the roads while making their way through the city. There's a lot of similarities in the architecture of these marble buildings to the ones of our Old Country."

Alberto commented, "Skyscrapers line the sky with dome-shaped and steeple types of roofs that are stretching high above with a little smoke rising up through some of the chimneys."

A policeman was standing on the opposite side of the street shouting directions to the visitors especially for all Italians to make their way to a neighborhood located a few blocks farther down the street in Lower Manhattan that was known as *Little Italy*. It was a place that welcomed the Italian home for many Italians settling here after leaving Italy was his proclamation.

"Let's go to *Little Italy* and maybe we can find some lodging for the night," said Alberto.

"I agree." responded Francesco. "We must find a place to stay before night sets in. Anyway, I would like to drop off my baggage instead of carrying it while we explore. It's too heavy to tote through the streets. This would be as good as anywhere else—especially if it's a place where other Italians live. They will understand our language, and we can maybe find some information out about the city and where to look for jobs to investigate."

Vito knew that they would feel at home in this place far from home especially if it reminded them of their culture as proclaimed. They were all weary from traveling. It sounded good that they didn't have too far to go to find their heritage neighborhood.

As they approached the neighborhood, the architecture of stone buildings gracing the sky five to six stories high with some black iron work served as a reminder of their homeland. There were plenty of shops that sold fine Italian foods with the smell bursting through the air. There were many tenement houses and boarding houses standing as you glanced towards the sky. Apparently, it was a place for those coming through Ellis Island in search of a better life for a place to call home. Soon Thanksgiving would be arriving followed by Christmas. It seemed that Christmas trees with all their old-fashioned, fanciful decorations stood along the streets waiting for visitors to stop and notice the multi-colored bulbs.

Glass storefronts with plentiful amounts of rooms behind were waiting for the visitor to bed for the night. They stopped halfway through the street where a vacancy sign hung.

The trio went in and Francesco started speaking to a short, chubby, bald man that was sweeping the floor.

"We noticed a vacancy sign outside. We have arrived from Italy, and we need a place to stay. Do you know who we would talk to about this matter?"

"I am the landlord. You came to the right place. I have a room located on the first floor that would sleep three to four people. I require payment a week in advance before I would allow you to retire for the night. Uh…. uh…. I can show you the room if you like."

Vito said, "We will comply with your wishes on payment, but it is not necessary for you to show us the room. We are quite tired, or could I say exhausted from our journey and will trust your judgment in this matter!" Vito reached into his pouch handing the landlord the payment saying, "The rates seem reasonable; therefore, we will board here."

The landlord continued speaking as he took the money in his hand. "Perfect! It will be an ideal place to start your new life! You can stay for as long as you like. In the morning, we can talk more about the city and its opportunities."

The owner exchanged the key for their money as they now headed toward their room. Unlocking the door, they noticed that the room was plain but cozy. It would be a comfortable place to stay. The room contained only two double bunk beds, a chest of drawers, and a nightstand with a kerosene lamp. The beds were made up of a deep red and white chenille bedspread with a large multi-colored red burgundy braided rug thrown on the floor by the bedside. There was a bathroom off to the right with a small white toilet, and a pedestal bath sink with a large silver spout and facet handles, and a high cast iron porcelain tub with four claw type feet that would seat an individual comfortably. Clean white towels were draped across the side of the tub. The walls had no pictures but were painted a pale pink. A window faced the front street with a red cushioned window seat and a white painted wooden chair sat to the side of the window. The window had several panes of glass with no curtains where a lopsided roll-down window shade hung for privacy. There was a lot more space in this room compared to the place they slept as they sailed here to America. Anything now seemed acceptable.

Vito said, "Let's retire for the night, and tomorrow we can seek out some food and jobs once we regain some strength. At least on top of the night stand, there is a pitcher of water with glasses that we can drink some water throughout the night if we are thirsty. If we get hungry, we do have our box lunches they handed us at Ellis Island that we can eat."

Each one was tired from travel that it didn't matter where they stayed only that they had shelter from the cold was their main concern.

Alberto said, "Let's take a hot bath to get the smell of the disinfectant from Ellis Island off our bodies before retiring for the night. It will feel good to feel warm fresh water and the scent of sweet smelling soap over our bodies. The stench of not being able to bathe for days still is lingering in my nostrils from our clothing, but tomorrow we can find a place to do our laundry."

"Let's throw our laundry in a pile inside the bathroom and close the door to avoid the smell coming into the bedroom. We'll take care of the clothes in the morning," said Francesco.

Francesco was anxious in his spirit that he couldn't get to sleep right now. He ventured toward the seat at the window to watch his surroundings. Pulling the chair to the window, he sat down. With pen in hand and paper, he decided to write home and tell Mama and Papa that they all arrived safely here in America. He started the letter by telling them back home of their journey and their new acquaintances. He told them that they have not found the *streets that are paved with gold* yet, but they were happy to step their feet on ground here in America. Tomorrow, he would find a mailbox to mail the letter.

As he looked out the window, he noticed that people were walking up and down the streets. It was a city that was alive at night. The city was lit up as the day. It was a city where people seemed to never sleep. As he looked up directly across the street, he noticed a young woman in the window swirling around and then stopping to look at him. Could he only be imagining that this beautiful young lady with long black hair was gazing at him? Was it a fragment of his imagination? Was it a shadow dancing in the night? No, he was certain that it was a real woman swirling then stopping to watch him. What was she doing? Was she dancing? Was she a ballerina? Suddenly, the motion stopped once more; and once again, she was looking through the window at him. Did she have music to swirl to or was she making her own music? Francesco was tired, but it was ridiculous that he was now hallucinating. Maybe, he should go to bed.

Then, she stood still looking his way. He smiled and waved. She returned his wave. What would she be doing? Maybe, she was in the same predicament as he was—unable to sleep. Maybe, she thought that if she swirled around the room she would get tired and sleep. Who was in the room with her? Was she alone? Was she with family? Was she married? All kinds of questions were flooding his mind.

It was such a beautiful night. Stars were twinkling down upon the city as street lights were lighting up the street. With the Christmas season approaching, he remembered the story of how the star shone brightly in the sky as the Wise Men followed. Maybe, the true story was comparable to his life following and being led by the Divine star to what his purpose is in this life to fulfill on this earth. He sensed in his spirit that those that follow are truly the wise here on the earth. Silence sure had a way of communicating thoughts in one's mind, but he realized he had to be wise wherever this venture in his mind took him. As he sat in silence, he wondered whether he would ever have the pleasure of meeting this young lady. She resembled a porcelain doll if she was alive and not a fragment of his imagination. What would he say to her anyway? He never had the opportunity to share the company of a woman in his lifetime. He was at a loss to how a man should act. He never had the pleasure of kissing a woman. Why was he thinking about kissing? He whispered to himself, "I know I must be tired when I start thinking about kissing."

As he stood up, reality hit him. What would she want with him anyway? He had nothing to offer her but himself. Then, he moved away from the window, sealing the letter by licking the corners, and addressed it to mail in the morning. He retired as his brothers had for the night, but his mind kept seeing this porcelain doll. She was dainty and beautiful with her long black hair flowing around her shoulders. What would it be like to run his finger through her hair? As he laid there in his bed, he was imagining what it would be like sharing company with her as he slowly drifted off to sleep.

Morning approached too soon. Vito was up and ready to start the day.

"Let's go find a little café here on the street to eat our breakfast. It will feel good to have something hot to eat. We're all hungry from all the days of travel, and we do have a little cash for expenses," said Vito. "Later, we will find a place to do our laundry."

"I feel that after breakfast we need to do a few chores. Then, each one of us should look for a job to provide us with an income that we can all remain in New York for a little while to make some money for our future traveling. We could put our money together to have some extra cash for whatever we need to do," said Alberto.

"It sounds like a good plan to me," replied Francesco. "I wrote Mama and Papa a letter. I would like to post it this morning if I can find a mailbox. I'm sure they are wondering about our trip to America. I feel like I'm on the other side of the world with the distance we have come. This will ease their minds to know that we arrived safely."

Ready for the day's adventure, they headed down the street to the little café that sat on the corner. A glance toward the sky, Francesco said, "I see why the suggestion was made that we head to *Little Italy* for this place reveals similar sights of the Old Country with iron work detailing the buildings. An immigrant could surely feel at home here while searching for a better life."

Breakfast was being served as they entered the café. Each one ordered some bacon and eggs to satisfy their appetites. As they sat eating, they decided to split company for the day to pursue some type of job that would help with money. At least one of them should be able to acquire a job.

"Francesco, don't go too far from where we are staying to get lost. Go only a few blocks one way or another to remain close to our boarding room. We will all meet again this evening after looking for a job," said Vito.

They agreed not to venture too far from this neighborhood during their short stay. They didn't know the city, which had each of them feeling a little helpless in this foreign land. At least in this part of the city, there were many Italians that spoke the same dialect as they did to communicate effectively if they chose.

Many of the patrons in the café were speaking Italian, which was music to the ear. It was like being at home. The café was decorated with all the décor from Italy. There were little wrought iron tables with red tablecloths and black wrought iron chairs. Scents from various food aromas filled the air. In the corner stood a small live Christmas tree reminding all patrons of the season approaching. The smell of pine penetrated the area close around the tree, which was a welcomed scent compared to the smells that lingered in their memory of their past days. They were lucky that winter was around the corner. The weather was not too cold. Winter officially begins December 21, but it wouldn't be long, though, until the calendar turns. For now, it still felt like autumn. After finishing breakfast, Vito and Alberto headed for the street each in their own direction leaving Francesco behind for he was a slow eater.

After polishing off his coffee, Francesco headed through the door when suddenly, he collided with an object. He could not catch his balance however hard he tried. He was whirling and twirling as if to be dancing when suddenly down he went onto the street face first. He was feeling embarrassed and stunned all at the same time. What caused this catastrophe? For a moment, he was quite dazed. He finally got his wit about himself as he lay. He then turned over, lying on the street, looking upward toward the sky. Could it be that he was hearing unfamiliar laughter springing out? He shut his eyes and then opened them wide knowing he wasn't hearing things. Who was laughing anyway? Usually, it was Vito playing a prank, but he knew this time he wasn't around. As he glanced up, he saw a pretty lady with a petite voice calling out to him, "Why uh…. uh…. are you lying on the street?"

"Why am I lying on the street?" growled Francesco. "I'm lying here because apparently you knocked me down."

"I didn't knock you down," whispered the voice. "You fell on your own accord. You should be watching where you are going."

"Watching where I'm going. I think it is you that needs to watch where you're going. I can't see behind doors, you know," said Francesco angrily.

For a little while, he sat there staring at the unknown pretty face wondering if he recognized her from somewhere. Suddenly, it struck Francesco that this was the porcelain doll he saw last night and that the unknown face was familiar to his eye. This was the lady that he watched swirling about through his window last night. He could never forget that long flowing hair with the most beautiful face he had ever seen. Could this be magic? As he tried to get up, she held out her hand to assist him. He sat up annoyed—thinking it would be the last thing he would do was having a woman helping him to get up in his fallen state. Unable to get up himself, he took her hand in his and noticed how soft and dainty her hand was clutched to his hand. Her hand sent electricity through his body. He had such a wonderful feeling throughout his whole body upon placing his hand in hers. What was happening anyway?

"Thanks for the assistance," Francesco replied a little angrily.

"You're very welcome," the lady replied as she stood with her brown eyes fixed to him with a grin on her face.

"Do I know you?" asked Francesco.

"Not that I am aware," replied the lady.

"Are you from around here?"

"Yes, I live up the street from here. My family arrived here about a month ago from Italy to begin a new life. My father felt the only way he could support a family would be coming to America. It's been a little hard for us to get a start here in America, but my father is trying as well as possible to provide for us. My father is working in the butcher shop down the street. Both my brother and I have jobs to help out as much as we can."

It hit Francesco this face was certainly familiar to him. Stuttering, he spoke softly in almost a whisper. "Uh…. uh…. I think…. you are the lady that I saw in the window last night. If you recall, I waved to you as you were swirling around late last night." He was reassuring himself once again that he would remember that face with the long flowing hair cascading around it anywhere. She was the most beautiful woman he ever laid his eyes on. She was quite petite with light porcelain skin and dark brown eyes. He couldn't believe that at this moment he was talking to her.

"What do you mean I was swirling about last night?" She laughed. "The only thing that I know I was doing was that I was practicing my dance routine to get ready for my work later today. Were you being a peeping Tom?"

As she spoke, it was as though a magical spell came over him. "No, I was not being a peeping Tom. Truly, I arrived in the city, and I was invigorated with an abundance of energy that I couldn't sleep. I went over to the window to check out what was happening when I saw your face." Francesco asked, "Where are you going?"

"I'm going to have breakfast. Then, I must go to work."

"Would you mind much if I have breakfast with you?" Francesco continued speaking in a confused manner. "On second thought, I won't have breakfast for I already ate, but I will have another cup of coffee. Maybe, it will give us a little time that we can talk."

"Well, I guess it would be alright for you to have a cup of coffee with me," she replied softly.

"In matter of fact, I will buy you your breakfast or whatever you would like," Francesco said. He had put back a little extra money for this trip. This would not be a problem. With the lack of funds, he shouldn't have offered breakfast to a stranger, but she didn't appear to be a stranger. He must be going mad. It was like he had known this woman his entire life.

"You wouldn't be able to buy me whatever I would like," as she snickered continuing to speak. She paused a moment then said, "On second thought, maybe I should pass for I don't really know you— why should I have breakfast with you?"

"Well, that's the point of having breakfast with me that we could get to know each other because I don't know anyone here in America. I could always remember that you were the first person that I got to know in New York. You were the first to knock me off my feet. Besides, it will be a little incentive payment saying thanks for pulling me up off the pavement to obtain my balance."

She started laughing once again as Francesco glanced at her. Francesco wondered what she was laughing about anyway. What was funny? She must think of him as such an idiot being very clumsy especially when he viewed her from a distance last night swirling through the room in such a graceful manner.

She began speaking once again saying, "I'm sorry I'm laughing, but it was funny watching you trying to gain your balance and not being able to do it when you took your tumble. Well, I guess you could join me for breakfast, but I don't have a lot of time today for I must be at work in about one hour. If you insist, we could talk for a little while."

Francesco held the door as they both made their way into the café. In his mind, he was thinking that she was the most beautiful sight he had ever seen. He ached to touch her. "It doesn't take long to eat breakfast. Really, fifteen minutes is better than nothing. If you would like, we could turn around and go farther down the street to another place."

She stood there for a moment before replying. "No, this is fine for now. However, there are many cafés and restaurants here on this street. It is hard to know where to eat for each café provides appetizing breakfasts and delicious Italian lunches and dinners."

Francesco began speaking, "In the future, maybe you can take me on a tour of the cafés and restaurants, and we can decide between us, which we like best."

She stood gazing at him for the right words to say as they waited to be seated. "We would have to go on a tour together for I'm not sure that I know the best places to eat either." She wondered what she was thinking about when she agreed with him that she would take a tour of the cafés.

"We've been standing here talking for a little bit, but we don't know each other's names. What's your name?" asked Francesco as he extended one hand.

Her eyes widened as she looked through her dark eyelashes, "My name is Lucia."

"Lucia is a pretty name and is quite appropriate for you," replied Francesco. "If I can remember right, the name Lucia means light. I need some light to shine on my world. Maybe you can light up my way in this unfamiliar place. I will need all the help I can get."

"I don't know how much I can light up your way, but in the neighborhood where we are both staying, most of the immigrants have come over from Italy. It is pleasant to the ear for the majority speak Italian, and each one helps in any way possible. They understand how frightening it is coming to a strange country where you don't know anyone, and the English language is a barrier. And your name is?"

"Francesco is my name. I come from a little town in Italy called Bari. As you know, *Little Italy*, where my two brothers and I are staying, reminds me of our town with its architecture. Of course, we haven't been here long enough to assess the area for its true potential. Today, we are supposedly looking for jobs."

As she stood still looking back at him, she felt that she could have told him her life story. "I come from a town farther south toward Sicily. It is a very poor place, and jobs are scarce. The name of the town is Palermo. There are many back streets that anyone wishing to embark upon for a little adventure to discover things can do so successfully. Do you know where that town is located?"

"I think that I might have heard of the town where you are from in southern Sicily," said Francesco as the feeling within him kept returning that he had known Lucia for a long time. "Let's make our way to the round wrought iron table across the room since we aren't being seated by the café."

While crossing the room, he began the conversation by telling her of his life back in the village of Bari with his parents and siblings on the farm. Reaching the wrought iron table, he pulled the chair out for her to sit down. Time didn't seem to matter for the moment. She seemed to brighten his day after black despair had settled around him from the journey to America. She was a new acquaintance, but she appeared quite easy to talk with and seemed understanding and pleasant was his first observation.

They were still chattering about their lifestyles blocking out those around them. Now, the world was standing still. Suddenly, their conversation was interrupted by a short plump waiter attired in a black and white uniform with a little bell pinned to his lapel as he approached their table. "What are you two having for breakfast?"

Francesco replied, "I only want some black coffee since I have already eaten."

Lucia thought a little while before she answered, "I will have something more than coffee for it will be a long while until I eat again." Lucia hesitated, then began speaking, "How about some pastries and juice?" Pastries are filling. She didn't want a stranger paying for her meal. "Put my order on a separate check."

The waiter smiled as he turned to leave; he paused saying, "The pastry today is filled with a vanilla cream pudding with a few strawberries on top. Is that sufficient?"

Lucia answered, "That will be fine."

"I'll be back shortly with your order," responded the waiter.

Francesco asked Lucia, "Where are you working?"

"I work a few blocks down the street at one of the finest New York hotels," she remarked.

"What would you be doing at a hotel?" he asked.

"Well, when we came over from Italy, I had to get a job. I took whatever job I could to make some money to help my family. I am sort of....uh.... uh.... what you call a maid responsible for cleaning the guest rooms, arranging flowers, and changing the beds throughout the day. The pay isn't the best, but it helps my father with expenses. Consequently, one day while I was working as a maid, I overheard several of the workers talking about tryouts for a performance to be held during the holiday season."

She continued, "The hotel where I'm working is hosting it on their stage. I understand that topnotch performers are coming here from several parts of the country to stage this show. They said that they needed some extra locals, which I recently became. Well, I never have worked on stage, but I thought maybe I could be a line dancer attired in a beautiful costume for the audience to enjoy and maybe get a laugh or two. Because I cannot speak good English, I could not try for a speaking part."

Francesco shook his head, "Why would you want to be on stage?"

Lucia resumed talking. "You know it's every girl's dream to dress up in a beautiful costume for an audience to see. I thought maybe this is my opportunity if I get chosen. It will make me a little bit of extra money. Tryouts were a few weeks ago. I went to the theatre part of the hotel where I tried out. They had a person at the theatre to show you the routine. They were judging how well each dancer performed to make their choice. There were at least 100 girls auditioning. I was told only 40 would be chosen. Believe it or not, I got a part in the Christmas show dancing. Last night when you saw me swirling about as you call it, I was practicing for my part in the show. Several times a week, we've been rehearsing for the show.

Practice makes perfect is what they say. I'm trying to get conditioned for my part."

Francesco sat still with amusement in his eyes. "That's truly wonderful that you will get to perform on stage," Francesco chuckled. "It's not every day that a regular person gets such an opportunity." Francesco was reflecting in his mind on how beautiful this woman was and had no doubt of her gracefulness when moving in step to music.

"No, it's not every day that this advantage would come my way especially when we arrived here from Italy not long ago. Truly, I'm excited by all of it. The best part is that the hotel rents the costumes at no expense to the participants."

For the moment, Francesco was amazed by it all for he never talked to a woman on this level before; and he didn't have any difficulty or uneasiness when he spoke. It seemed quite natural to share with Lucia. As he sat there looking across the table at her, a thought crossed his mind. Wouldn't it be nice to have this fair maiden sitting across the table from him each day for the rest of his life? He had to stop these kinds of thoughts, but he was captivated with her. He never thought that he would want a woman in his life. What was the matter with him? All his life he only communicated with his parents and siblings, not some stranger that he didn't even know.

This moment of silence from his thoughts was broken by movement coming toward him breaking the spell as the waiter approached with their breakfast items.

"I apologize for taking a little too long delivering your food. There were more orders back there than a few waiters can handle at one time."

Looking over the appealing pastry made Francesco feel hungry all over again. It certainly took his mind off the morning's search of a job for a little while. He thought he was filled up, but maybe he was wrong.

Francesco didn't mind the little wait. Honestly, it didn't seem like a wait at all. Time was going too fast as it was. He could spend forever with this woman, and forever would never be enough time. Puzzled, he shifted in his seat while he wondered why these crazy thoughts are coming in his head.

"Francesco, I really must eat quickly. I need to be on my way very shortly; if not, I'll be late." she said. "Not only am I working today, but tonight is another rehearsal for the show." She didn't even know the man. Why was she telling him information about herself? She felt like she could fling herself into his arms, but he was a stranger that she had recently met.

"I'll wait while you eat quickly. Lucia, it's been nice for the short time that we've had together." He could not let her go and never see her again. He hesitated then said, "Maybe we can meet again sometime later. I should be on my way too for I need to try and find a job for myself since arriving here from Italy after several weeks journey across the ocean. Later, my brothers and I will meet at our room to go for supper. We are going to stay a short time here in New York until we make a little money. We will then be on our way to our destination."

"What is your destination?" Lucia inquired.

"It's a place called Pittsburgh located in the state of Pennsylvania. There are supposed to be a lot of coal mining and steel industry jobs there," Francesco said.

"Well, good luck to you! I hope you find a job here in New York; then, you can travel on. My family is planning on staying here in New York. There are some other family members around the New York area. My father feels this would be the best place to stay. This part of the city is good for it resembles the part of Italy that was our home, and we all feel safe here so many miles away from home. There is plenty of activity here in the city, but I haven't decided where I'll live permanently—time will tell where I live in the future."

"Yes," he proceeded speaking, "maybe a rich young prince with his white horse will sweep you off your feet to another foreign land where you will remain in his castle forever."

She shook her head laughing.

"What are you laughing about?" he grinned.

"I don't know any rich young princes with a white horse for one thing! I don't want to live in a castle! The only thing I care about is someday meeting the right man and falling deeply in love and having a lot of babies that were conceived out of love. I don't need a castle to live in. My theory of a home is any place where two individuals are in love, and they live happily ever after. It isn't material things or the size of a house. It can be very lonely in a castle if you don't have the right prince to share your life," she said. Why was she telling her feelings anyway? She barely knew him, but she felt he was a man of character.

"I agree with you. There can be a lot of emptiness in life regardless of how much money you have if you don't find the right person to share your life."

"Well, Francesco, I need to go to work. Otherwise, I will be late, and I don't want to lose my job. I must pay for my breakfast and be on my way."

"No, I promised I would pay for your breakfast if I could join you. I will stick to my bargain. This is a little attribute for you picking me up off the ground." He replied chuckling as he reached into his pocket and pulled out some money to pay the waiter. He thanked the waiter as he pulled her to her feet as they headed out to the street.

"When can we see each other again? Maybe tonight would be good, that way I can tell you about my job hunting experiences today," he replied as he stood gazing into her eyes.

"Well, better yet, why don't you walk down to the hotel with me because I believe they are hiring some bellboys?" Lucia questioned. "It is a nice, crisp day for a walk, and we can talk as we walk getting to know each other and enjoy the sights of the city. You will not feel so alone, and you won't get lost in the streets of New York. Maybe if you're lucky, you will land a job where I work, which would be quite convenient for you for it isn't too far from where you are staying. As far as seeing you again, I don't know when that will be possible for I am quite busy with everything I'm doing for the present time."

"Come on then, we can walk and talk on our way there," he urged.

As the two of them walked down the street, Francesco was floating through air on the pavement. The two were chatting in their native language continuously as they strolled along the street. He never felt as happy as he did at this moment. Walking with this beautiful porcelain doll with black hair flowing across her shoulders was unexpected today for he had planned on looking for a job by himself. He never for one moment thought he would have the pleasure of meeting this lady that he spied in the window last night. He knew that this wasn't wrong because it's not good for man to be alone, but he also recognized he had to keep his focus to achieve his goal. It's nice to have companionship. Where would this lead anyway for he was not staying long here in New York. All kinds of thoughts were coming into his mind, but he felt he better pay heed to his head instead of listening to his heart for the time being.

She was walking fast as he followed for she realized that she only had a minimal amount of time until she had to be at work. She had spent too much time for breakfast this morning. The streets, this morning, were quite busy with people passing by on their way to work. Aromas of coffee and all the breakfast commodities hung in the air this morning as they passed by several cafés along the way to the hotel.

"Hurry, Francesco, it's only another block," as she held out her hand. He took her small tiny hand in his as they walked past the five and six story buildings with their Italian architecture. As they crossed the street, it was as if the city structure changed. Now, the buildings stood higher gracing the sky. She headed partway down the street suddenly stopping as she crossed the street entering toward the doorway with a movable glass door entrance.

Lucia pointed toward the left, "Francesco, you can go to the desk through these doors where you can ask the manager if he is hiring anybody."

"Lucia, how will I find you after the work day has finished if I get hired? Will you wait for me at the entrance?" Not waiting for her response, he continued. "We can walk back to our places together, so I don't get lost. If not, we can meet later this evening."

"Francesco, I don't know if I can meet you here or not for I have no way of knowing if you will get a job. Besides, I won't know what time you are quitting. Tonight, I have practice for the line dancing. It will be quite late to tell you that I'll be able to see you later today. As I told you before, I am extremely busy, and it will be hard to commit to you for a meeting of any kind."

Francesco was disappointed. "If you can't meet me tonight, how about having breakfast with me tomorrow morning at 6:00 AM at the same café?" Francesco asked.

"I don't know—that's pretty early," she replied. "I usually grab something quick then head to work. Today was quite unusual for I awakened earlier than usual. For some unknown reason, I decided to eat at the café for a better breakfast."

"I know it is a little early for you, but I want to spend some time getting to know you better. Please say you will meet me?" he pleaded.

"Well, maybe tonight I will see you for a little while around nine o'clock before retiring for the night, and we can discuss break-fast tomorrow morning. I'm not promising anything, though, Francesco. I will have to see how the day goes from here. Be careful not to fall face first again for I might not be around to help pick you up." Lucia snickered.

Francesco wanted to blurt out that it was her that knocked him down causing him to fall face first, but instead kept his thought to himself. "Thanks Lucia, I will be looking forward to seeing you soon. Wish me luck with my job hunting," Francesco said as he reached out his arms to embrace her. She walked toward his embrace clinging to him as they captured the moment. A moment that seemed right, but he was a perfect stranger with a warm friendly personality that she felt she had known forever. He could be married or some type of criminal trying to escape from the law. Why was she feeling excited? Unexpectedly, he lifted her feet off the pavement swirling her in a circle as people passed by gleaming at them with happiness.

"Francesco, what was that all about?"

"I'm happy that you will see me again! Nine o'clock it is. Furthermore, you are the first person I got to know here in New York." As he spoke, he was thinking that the day would probably pass by slowly waiting for her return, but he must look for a job whether it's here or elsewhere. "Really, I may never want to leave New York either if I find the right job!" Why did he say such a statement? He must be losing his mind. He already suspected that opportunity was calling elsewhere.

As the door rotated with motion, she waved to him as she entered through saying, "I hope to see you soon, but for now, I must go to work." In her heart, she wanted to stay with him throughout the day, but she couldn't let him know her innermost feelings. She hoped he would get a job at the hotel. It would make things more convenient with him close at hand, but she felt it would be better to let him work a little at contacting her before jumping at the opportunity. He would appreciate her more if their relationship works out.

Francesco had to maintain his wits for he needed a job and had to present himself well to the manager. He knew that not only himself, but both his brothers, had to get a job to be able to stay on in New York for a short season. Francesco walked toward the left to a small office where a little stout, bald man was sitting behind a desk dressed in a white shirt with red tie and black pants. He had a pencil in hand as he sat looking down and writing every now and again in the black book that lay there on the desk. He was smoking a pipe that filled the entire room with a fragrance of some type of cherry scent. As Francesco stopped at the desk, the manager looked up through his black-rimmed glasses with beaded eyes and asked, "May I help you?"

Francesco had to think what he wanted to say for he felt very awkward asking about a job being that he only was acquainted with the world of farming back home. He stood there for a second scratching his head as he spoke softly, "Recently, I arrived here in New York. I am in search of a job. Do you know where I could find a job?"

The manager looked at him for a moment out of the corner of his eye saying, "You are asking where you could find a job. Well, maybe you could find a job right here at this hotel. What kind of job are you looking for, sir?"

Francesco shrugged his shoulders as he answered, "I don't know. With arriving from Italy yesterday, I haven't had time to think about the type of job I would like to work. I will take any type of job to pay expenses that I'll have while living here in New York."

"Well, if you don't know—I sure don't know what to tell you." The manager was speaking in Italian. "I have several jobs available if you are interested in working here for a small amount of pay. Being we are located a few blocks from the train station, a lot of the immigrants traveling from Europe and businessmen come to this hotel. You could use your native language when you speak to help those traveling into our city. Your English isn't too good, but you won't need to understand or speak too much of that language. For a little while, it would probably help you pay for room and board. The job that I feel would be perfect for you has the title, Bellboy. The job responsibilities include carrying luggage for travelers to their rooms and making sure they are comfortable during their stay. If a traveler needs you to run an errand, you will need to do it too. You would be at their beck and call. Do you think you would be interested in such a job?"

"Yes, of course I would be interested in the job. Choosing a top-notch job for now is limited with my inadequate language and trade skills. I would be happy for any job that would help with room and board for a few months until I make my way out of this city at some point. With my pay and possibly the help of my two-brother's pays, we will be able to survive for a brief time. Winter will soon be coming on and at least this hotel is only a few blocks from the Boarding House where I am staying, which is good because I can walk to work each day."

He didn't say this out loud, but he thought it while scratching his head. Maybe another benefit was that he could walk with Lucia, the girl of his dreams that knocked him off his feet, because she worked somewhere in the hotel. He couldn't be picky in his choosing for it is difficult to acquire a job in such a short time period. He could keep looking for a better job when he wasn't working at the hotel.

The bald manager put his pipe down on the desk looking intensely at Francesco. "I am offering you the job. Well, what is your answer, my friend?"

Fate was on his side apparently for he got this job right away. "When could I start the job?" Francesco asked.

"You could start today working only a few hours up until noon," replied the manager. "I will get you a uniform to wear and give you an extra one to take along home. This way you have a change of clothes. I'm expecting a few groups of travelers today. This will help you to get acquainted with your job responsibilities. Let's go over the layout of the hotel as well as the guidelines of the job and what I expect from you. I will give you a little orientation each day. If I give you some basic training, it will not be too overwhelming for you to comprehend. Later this week, though, you can begin working the full eight hours. Down the road, when we are exceptionally busy, you will be expected to work more than your eight hours, but for the next few days, plan on short days. Since you just arrived here, I know that you will need a little time to get adjusted to the city."

"Thanks for your consideration! That sounds like a plan to me," agreed Francesco.

"Before leaving for the day, I will give you a work schedule to follow that you can make your weekly plans."

Francesco didn't think the job sounded too bad. The manager informed him that there were several Bellboys, but right now, they were helping all the travelers that were arriving and leaving the hotel. This made Francesco feel a little less alarmed for he could acquire help from other employees. His mind instantly reflected to his work back home on the farm, which was hard-manual labor. There was nothing hard about this job only carrying luggage. He would be working mostly weekends and a few days through the week. He was told that the time when the hotel really gets busy is when the trains arrive, and passengers are looking for a place to stay. He wasn't necessarily accustomed to dealing with people—only the people he dealt with at the market selling vegetables, but he could learn new ways. Everyone said there were jobs in America. He knew now that it was true. He was excited about starting his new job. He couldn't wait until he told his brothers about the job, but more than anything he wanted to share it with Lucia. He was wondering if his brothers had found any jobs. The answer to that question was pending.

The hotel manager handed Francesco a small package. "You'll need to come behind my desk and change your clothes for there will soon be a ship coming into port, which more people will be looking for a place to stay. Besides, there is a popular show at the theater that will be bringing some more people into the city."

This statement was a reminder to Francesco that this was the show that Lucia was participating in.

Francesco went as instructed to a little room behind the manager's desk with a cloth curtain covering the doorway where he changed his clothes. The pants were a little baggy, but he would make due the best that he could in his predicament. Francesco was feeling a little nervous with the anticipation of beginning a new job. If he were home, Mama would adjust the pants for him, but he was too far from home to worry about that idea. As he exited the room, he handed the manager his clothes with the extra uniform and assured him that he would pick the clothes up at the end of his work day.

"The uniform is quite attractive with the navy color and a red stripe design on the sleeve and trousers and a matching cap on your head. You look pretty handsome in those clothes," chuckled the manager. "You will do fine. I will place your belongings here on the shelf by my desk. You can pick the clothes up when you finish today."

Francesco smiled as he turned around noticing a group of men entering the hotel with baggage in hand. He still felt a little nervous and awkward, but he had to get started with his job. "May I help you?"

One gentleman spoke up, "Yes, you may. We made reservations for a group of rooms because we are businessmen staying in New York for the week. Would you be able to help get us checked in and directed to our rooms?"

"Yes," replied Francesco as he ushered them over to the manager desk where they checked in and the manager pointed him toward the direction to find the rooms. After the group checked in, he loaded their luggage on a cart as he led them down the main corridor where the manager instructed him to go. This was all new to Francesco because he didn't know the layout of the hotel too well yet. Eventually, he would learn every nook and cranny, but as for now, he wasn't too confident of where he was going himself. He kept questioning himself whether this was the right area of the hotel.

One of the businessmen stepped up to the door by Francesco saying, "This looks like the right group of rooms that the manager said we were staying in. It looks like that the rooms are adjoined for easy access. Get your key out to try the door. This will be great for we welcome the idea that we are all staying in a central location in the hotel."

As Francesco examined the door for the specified number, he put his master key that the manager gave him into the keyhole. Suddenly, the door opened as a woman came through its entrance.

She looked familiar to him in every way. He stopped dead in his tracks as he stood there stunned without elaborating to the group of his recognition of this familiar face.

The head of the group asked, "Are you alright? You look as if you saw a ghost."

Francesco made up an excuse for the way his facial expression appeared. "I started the job today. The woman startled me. I was a little worried that I wasn't at the right room. It kind of surprised me when the door opened."

The businessman nodded.

The woman smiled at him as she stood there in a trance. She was very surprised to see him this soon. "I'm sorry, sir, if I startled you, but I was finishing cleaning this group of rooms for I was told that some travelers would be arriving soon. I was putting on the finishing touches by placing some fresh-cut flowers in the vases." The scent of the fragrance from the bouquets was permeating the room. The woman was dressed in a blue uniform with a little cap pinned to the top of her head. Her long black hair flowed around her shoulders.

He wondered how she changed her look from the time he left until now. He didn't think she had a uniform on when he left her. She must keep her uniforms at the hotel. She must go to a dressing room to pin on her cap and dress in the uniform that the hotel furnishes to prepare her for the day.

"No, you didn't startle me too much. When I inserted my key, I was quite surprised the door opened before I turned the lock," Francesco replied with amusement.

"Well, it's good that we don't have anyone falling through the door now," she snickered as she walked out of the room. "I will be a few doors down the hallway if you need anything for I have a few other rooms to clean. We are expecting some other travelers."

Francesco entered the room with amazement to see the beauty all around. He had not ever been in a classy hotel before now. There were two large soft cushioned sofas with end tables beside them. On the two end tables sat a brass lamp with a beige pleaded shade. Fresh cut flowers of various colors were placed in a large gold-coated porcelain vase beside the lamp sending a sweet fragrance throughout the room. Right at this moment, he felt close to Lucia for he sensed she was the one to arrange the beautiful bouquet in the vase. Even though she was absent from the room, he could feel her presence throughout the room. All the special touches were a reminder that she had been here. The sofas were of the French style design embossed with a medium blue fabric with light green pillows. Behind the one sofa was a wall clock with a gold pendulum hanging down to chime on the hour. A dark green with medium blue design Oriental rug lay between the sofas. In the corner of the room was a large oval oak table with six chairs sitting around it. Once inside, Francesco noticed there were several doors located off this sitting area to where the bedrooms were located. There was even an outside door to get to a balcony overlooking the city. This sitting room was like nothing that Francesco had ever seen or imagined. It was elegant and had to be designed strictly for the rich and famous. Francesco ushered the businessmen into the room. He returned to the hallway to wheel in their luggage. He was told by the one businessman which bags to take to which bedroom. The group had plans for staying at least one week maybe even two depending on how the meetings progressed. After dispersing the luggage to the separate areas, the head of the group handed Francesco money—thanking him for all his help. He alluded to the fact if there was anything else that needed done that he would call for him.

Francesco felt good about making a tip from the businessman. He would be going to the boarding room with more money than when he had left this morning. Upon exiting the room, Francesco saw a door cracked a little way down the hall. He stopped abruptly in his tracks; and sure enough, it was Lucia cleaning up the room to get it ready for the next arrival.

"I am shocked to bump into you again today." Lucia whispered as she looked up to see Francesco entering the room. "I had no idea that you were working here at this hotel today. You apparently got the job right after I showed you the way to the manager's desk earlier this morning."

Francesco responded as he glanced around the room. "Yes, I did start today, but the manager only wants me to work until lunchtime. I was glad to be able to get this job thanks to you. It will help me tremendously with my expenses while I stay here in New York. Thanks for telling me that the hotel was hiring, or I would have not been able to obtain a job so quickly. These rooms are elegant with all the expensive décor. You probably enjoy getting the rooms ready for guest. Well, I must be going for I know you are required to continue working and not waste time. I still may need to greet additional travelers coming to the hotel today before I leave." He hesitated for a moment then walked toward Lucia touching her cheek. "Lucia, I hope to see you tonight sometime."

Lucia drew her breath in as she whimpered from the touch of his hand on her face as she spoke softly saying, "I feel we will get to meet again sometime if not tonight. You will be working at this hotel, and I'm sure that we will periodically bump into each other now and again."

In her heart, she wanted to see him as much as he wanted to see her, but she could not let him know of her feelings for he may think of her as too aggressive. She would like to yell out to him that she would like to see him tonight and every spare moment she had. She would like to fill up her days with his presence.

"Well, Francesco, I must continue getting this room ready for the next arrival. I'll talk to you again. It's good to see you. Have a great day!"

Francesco turned around once again before leaving. "I will see you tonight no matter whatever the time!" he demanded. Thus, he stomped out of the room as the door slammed into the wall behind him. He was feeling a little hot under the collar the way she was putting him off with excuses, but this was not the time or place to take out his frustrations for they were both at work. After all, this was his first day of employment; and he didn't know Lucia very well even though he felt differently. He couldn't believe himself being persistent for this was not his character. What on earth has come over him? What was this feeling that he was feeling? Was he a man in love? He never had been in love before or maybe this is how one acts when you feel much love for another person. He wasn't going to think about this too much longer for he had work to do. He really must focus on his new job to keep it.

Lucia cracked the door open—watching him—her body motionless. She would like to run into his arms. No words passed between them. She then went over leaning against the door stepping away and immediately slammed the door shut. She stood in silence questioning the way she was feeling about Francesco.

As Francesco managed to make his way down to the main lobby, there were several guests waiting to be taken to their rooms. There were other Bellboys now helping with the flow of travelers.

The manager handed a schedule to Francesco saying, "After taking this group of travelers to their rooms, you can leave for the day and return tomorrow at 10:00 AM to help with the volume of guests expected."

Francesco was glad that the day was a little shorter today for all the feelings that were welling up in his spirit from leaving home coming to a foreign land. The feeling of separation kept sweeping over him because it was unlikely that he would ever return to his homeland again. He was homesick to see only a glimpse of his family. Another hurtle was not speaking good English. Also, he had to contend with his emotions that he was feeling toward meeting this lady of his dreams very unexpectedly.

After a few moments in his own thoughts, Francesco replied to the manager, "I know that the Christmas season is soon approaching. I am going to look around the city a little to see what I can find for my special lady friend to surprise her for the holiday. Gifts are magical, and I want to make her feel special."

He had only met her, but he felt compelled to surprise her with an extraordinary gift for this lady was already very special to him.

The manager stood assessing his face before speaking, "I hope you find that special gift for your friend. Besides, Christmas is the season of giving gifts to those that we love."

He stood by the manager's desk for a moment. "Is there anything else that I can do before leaving?"

The manager gave him a wave shaking his head saying, "No, I will see you tomorrow bright and early. Change your clothes and take your uniforms with you."

Francesco left the hotel and down the street he made his way browsing the various shops of the city as he passed. He came upon a unique boutique where red velvet material lined the window with several beautiful combs for a woman's hair sat on top. The choice that caught his eye were a set of combs adorned with precious colorful gemstones set within the gold decorative piece of the combs. He stopped by and asked the clerk, "How much do a set of these combs cost?"

The lady told him the price.

Francesco pulled some money out of his pocket. Unfamiliar with the value of the American coins, he asked, "Do I have enough cash to buy the combs?"

"You have more than enough money to buy the combs," she explained.

He replied without hesitation, "I will buy the special gift for Lucia. Please put them in a box and wrap them with special paper." He then handed the clerk the tip money he was paid that would make it possible for this purchase. Lucia would be able to wear these combs in her hair for the performance. It would add accent to her hair.

As he left the shop, he was excited to have purchased a gift for Lucia. The clerk had wrapped them in a small gift box with sparkling blue Christmas wrapping and placed a silver bow on top. He could give them to her when he decided the time was right. He may give them to her at the opening of the show, which would be perfect. She would look stunning with the combs in her thick black hair for they were of a gold metal with various color gemstones detailing the metal. These were the most beautiful combs he had ever seen. He felt that a gift is special when you give it in love no matter what the cost. This gift would be the first gift ever given to a woman by Francesco. He was sure that Lucia would treasure this gift.

He returned to the boarding room to find his brothers already there waiting for his return. He had the package in his pocket. When Vito and Alberto weren't looking, he would hide the little special box under his mattress until the day he would give it away. This was going to be his little secret.

"Where did you disappear too?" Vito asked as he and Alberto lay on the bed waiting for an answer.

"Actually, I found a job in a hotel where I will be a Bellboy believe it or not. I worked part of the day today, then went on a little mission exploring some of the shops here in the city," explained Francesco.

"What would you be looking for in the shops?" Alberto questioned.

"Nothing in particular," he proceeded to reply not telling them the whole truth. He wasn't telling his brothers about the beautiful lady that he met today or the gift he bought—not yet. Earlier, he had thought that would be the first words out of his mouth, but he decided against it for they would tease him to death. It was Vito that was always mentioning beautiful women. He had only met her. He didn't want to make a fool of himself for in a few days she may not even desire to see him again. "It soon will be the Christmas season. I thought I would get in the mood of the season by browsing the shops here in America to see what is available to purchase and to try to get familiar with the city. Christmas is a time of giving. It's nice to shop around even though you don't buy anything. It kind of gets you in the holiday spirit." Changing the subject, he asked, "Did either of you find jobs?"

Vito as well as Alberto shook their heads in answer to the question. "I found a job helping in a butcher shop while Alberto is across the street from me working in a café cleaning off tables. It will help us with expenses for a few months until we decide to move to acquire the jobs we were told about in the coal mines and steel factories."

Francesco would have a hard time leaving New York now with meeting this woman and having to leave her behind. He would have to think about this a while. He may never leave New York. If things worked out, however, he could send for her once he was settled into his permanent job. He could not bear the pain of losing his first acquaintance in New York. He would find some way to take her with him to wherever it is that he would be going. Hopefully, she would want to go with him. He was in a daze for a moment until Vito yelled out, "Let's go for a late lunch or early supper. We can look around to see some sights then retire for the night since all of us need to go to work tomorrow. We can say that this is a celebration supper to all of us finding jobs in the city today."

They went for an early supper, but Francesco's mind kept racing back to this beloved lady that he was falling in love with as the moments passed. The brothers were talking over dinner, but Francesco was in his own little world preparing his strategy. His mind kept focusing on the slender lines and angles of her body, the way her long black hair fell across her shoulders, and the delicate shape of her face with her dark brown eyes. How had this happened to him? How had he let this woman work her way to his heart?

Alberto asked Francesco as he chuckled, "Where have you been over our early supper? I was planning on sending out a search party for your brain! You seem to be preoccupied with thoughts of your own and haven't been paying much attention to what we are discussing."

Francesco stared at his brothers with a look of disbelief saying, "Uh…. uh…. you wouldn't understand. I've had something happen to me today. I'm not the same person you knew this morning!"

Vito spoke up as he crossed his arms gently across his chest, "Why do you say that Francesco? We leave you for a few hours; and now, you tell us you aren't the same person?"

Francesco met Vito's gaze, his eyes dead serious, "It would serve no purpose for me to tell you about my adventure today."

He didn't know whether he should tell his brothers about the lady or not. He pondered a moment then the words flew out of his mouth. He wasn't using good judgment apparently. He should keep it to himself, but when something good happens, most everyone wants the world to know.

"All I can tell you is that I met the most beautiful woman today! I'm planning on marrying her!" It would do no good to admit this woman meant life to him. Sharing his plans with his brothers would be colorless and dull and serve no purpose.

Vito stared at him in disbelief. "I'm not forcing the issue, but how could you plan on marrying a woman you don't even know? Did you pop the question?"

At first, Francesco didn't answer for he was trying to convince himself of his reasoning. He didn't even know why he blurted out marriage to his brothers. "No, I didn't pop the question. I know it's too soon, for I could change my mind, but right now I feel that it would be wonderful to see her face each day. I want to spend the rest of my life with this woman! If you must know, I believe it's called love at first sight!" The ache in his chest was worse than imaginable and unexplainable for him to describe to his brothers. "Leave it alone for now, Vito."

With that statement, they ate their meal and then left the café as they walked back to the boarding house enjoying the scenery of the city. Darkness had already closed in on the city. The days were getting shorter on daylight even though it wasn't late.

Upon opening the door, the room was silvered by the light of a full moon and the city's street lamps. Daylight seemed to fade away at such an early hour. Francesco told his brothers to go to bed regardless of the earliness of the hour if they were tired, but for now, he was going to sit up for a while looking out the window. He had an extreme burst of energy presently. The sky was overcast with barely a few stars shining through the clouds. Surprisingly, a dim light turned on above to the place where the porcelain doll stayed. Lucia stood in the dimmed light of the window that framed her body like a canvas with her long black hair flowing around her shoulders as the moon and city lights washed over her skin with a colorless light.

Did she know he was there, below, watching?

Francesco got his answer when Lucia lowered her gaze and looked straight at him waving her hand. Francesco didn't want to breathe. He didn't want to blink or move. He didn't want to miss one second of her glorious beauty.

His first deep breath brought a dizziness that was more than he could bear. They both started doing hand motions to communicate to meet out in the crisp night air.

Francesco strode across the room, pulled on a lightweight jacket, and ran out the door as fast as his legs would carry him onto the street. The night was cold from the breeze off the Atlantic.

Lucia hurried down the steps, taking two at a time. She was feeling that she was running away from something instead of to something. Suddenly, a distorted shadow came up behind her as Lucia gasp from fright, "Francesco, I'm sorry, but I thought you were someone else."

Francesco shook his head, "Lucia, I'm sorry to have frightened you. I appreciate your coming out on such a short notice. I had to see you tonight. Let's go to the café across the street to get something to eat or drink before retiring for the night. We can talk for a short time; though even a few minutes will make me happy."

Since the supper hour had passed, they noticed the café this time of night was a little isolated, which they were glad for they could be alone to talk privately. As they made their way to the table, Francesco shouted to the waiter. "Bring two cups of soup to our table to help warm us from the chill of the night air. We don't care what kind of soup. The only thing we care about is that it's hot."

A short, chubby littler waiter brought two bowls containing hot steaming minestrone sprinkled with cheese on top. "I hope everything is alright."

Francesco replied as he picked up his spoon, "I'm sure it is." He repeated, "We want a little something to warm us up." Francesco knew if he would get close to Lucia that their bodies would warm up very fast.

Lucia was placing her linen napkin on her lap as she sipped her soup slowly. Conversation never ceased throughout the evening. Lucia spoke of her first practice for the show and her day at work among several other topics including her family. Francesco sat there in awe taking it all in. The lite meal was more pleasant than he ever expected. He wasn't hungry for he had early supper with his brothers. He would do whatever he could to be close to Lucia.

Suddenly, Lucia glanced up at the clock as she stated, "The time has passed by rather quickly." Francesco watched as Lucia picked up her linen napkin to wipe her lips as she stood up throwing her napkin by the empty soup cup.

She stopped as she turned her gaze toward him saying, "I must apologize, Francesco, but the hour is getting late. I must return home since I rise early in the morning for work."

"Let me pay the bill." Francesco dropped the money on the table. He pushed back his chair and crossed to her in two strides placing his hands gently on her arms turning her toward him. "Come, we will walk together."

As they left the café, Francesco put his arm around her shoulder to keep her warm from the chill of the early night air.

"I guess we'd better be going." She whispered knowing deep inside—her feelings were that she didn't want to leave; she could have stayed with him throughout the night. The warmth of his body against hers caused her skin to tingle sending sensations to her inner nerves. She had never experienced this before. All evening she had a mixture of emotion. Even though the temperature outside was chilly, warmth was spread over her face; and the palms of her hands were damp.

Stepping into the cold night brought a flash of homesickness for some unknown reason. Maybe, the night sounds of traffic in the street with the rustling of the leaves underfoot in a city he did not know caused this feeling. It was such a big, unfamiliar place with many people that a person could become lost quite easily. What was he doing here alone with only his brothers? He understood that he was very far away from home. He was confused by the feelings he was having about this woman for he never was friends with any woman until now.

Crossing the street, he had to take a deep breath for he suddenly felt breathless. She seemed so incredibly petite and delicate. For a moment, the thought of being away from her seemed unbearable. Instantaneously, words beyond his control slipped out of his mouth. All at once, he stopped as he blurted out, "Lucia, may I kiss you?" He stared at her for he was spell-bounded by her slender, delicate features. He closed his eyes wondering if this was a mistake asking such a thing. He was making a complete fool out of himself. He then opened his eyes and looked at Lucia as she silently stared up at him. He moved his hand to her chin gently taking her jaw into his hand. He was under a magical spell that nothing could turn his thoughts around.

Lucia was in strange waters. She'd never felt like this before. She didn't know how to react. His mouth suddenly found hers and at the same time his hand was stroking her back sending shivers of delight throughout her body. "Oh, Lucia" he whispered against her lips, "I love you very much! Please say that you love me too!"

Suddenly, she wrapped her arms around his neck and tried to pull him close to her. Then, she opened her mouth to his in search of his lips. His lips took hers out of need that matched hers. She raised her hand to his face tracing her fingers around his cheeks and then touched his black curly hair at the back of his neck. "Yes, Francesco, I love you too; but it is too soon to be sure about our true feelings," her voice shaky as she snuggled even closer into his strong arms. He was crushing her into his chest that she could hardly breathe for a moment causing a sense of lightheadedness to strike her. It took several moments after the heat of the moment to focus her thoughts. Her heart was fluttering against his chest. "Francesco, I could stay here with you all night, but we really must be going. It's getting late. We both need to go to bed for we are working tomorrow."

He pushed her away, and he took her hand in his as they continued walking toward her place. Francesco said, "Yes, we do need to call it a night. As far as our true feelings, I am sure about mine." He was a little hurt by her statement. "I'll walk you to your door. Tomorrow, we can start where we left off tonight. Let's meet at the café at 8:00 AM for breakfast instead of 6:00 AM."

Lucia nodded, but didn't say anything for a second as they stepped in front of her door answering, "Alright, tomorrow it is. That will give us a little time to talk and then get to work for 10:00 AM."

This time he didn't have to ask. Francesco turned and slid his arms around her. She was beautiful. All he wanted to do was to hold her close and keep her safe. "I'm going to kiss you again!"

Laughing nervously, she threw her arms around him as she whispered in his ear, "Is that a promise? Then, I'm going to let you kiss me for I love you very much!"

As Francesco turned to leave, he stood there for a moment staring at her for it was like music to his ears hearing what she had said. His eyes met hers as he stepped toward her once again to give her one last embrace before striding away.

As Francesco made his way to his place of refuge, he was floating on air. He had such a wonderful feeling that nothing seemed to matter now. Upon entering, he swung the door open thinking what to tell his brothers. The place was quiet for the pair must be sleeping because of the lateness of the hour. For a second, he stood at the door stating softly in a whisper to his brothers that he had something to tell them. "Vito, Alberto, I know that I told you this before, but I have met the girl of my dreams! I'm positive that I'm in love!" These words fell on deaf ears.

Vito rolled over in bed opening his eyes looking straight at Francesco as he softly spoke trying not to awaken Alberto. "What are you muttering about at this hour of the night? Calm down Francesco and go to bed. I'll take whatever you are saying up with you in the morning when my head is clear." He rolled back over in bed and continued his pleasant sleep.

Francesco stepped over to the window hoping to view his lovely lady one last time before retiring for the night. Looking up, the figure that he was acquainted with was looking down right into his face. She gave him a little wave as she closed the curtains. "It truly is magic!" he said softly.

"You don't know what you are saying," a voice answered behind him for Vito was now a little more alert.

"Yes, I know what I'm saying. I met the most beautiful girl in the whole world that I want to spend the rest of my life with soon. She's the only thing I can think of all day long."

"How can you be so sure that this is true when you only met her today?" Vito whispered.

"You know when that right person comes along. It's like you've known them your entire life." said Francesco. "It feels perfect!"

"Go to bed, Francesco. You must be extremely tired to be talking out of your head as you are. Maybe in the morning you can see things more clearly." Vito chided.

Francesco didn't care what his brother thought because he knew how he felt. He would not let anyone take away the feeling he had for this woman out of his heart. As he laid his head down on his pillow, thoughts of her brought happiness beyond measure as he drifted off to sleep.

CHAPTER 9

NEW YORK, NEW YORK

A promise is an expectation of holding on to hope of the unforeseen happening.

Upon returning from work, Francesco sat on his bed thinking how they had settled in comfortably the short time that they were here in New York. Meanwhile, the days were passing by quickly from the daily routine. Signs of the Christmas season were in the air. The city was lit up with various colors of lights on the sparkling trees with music of carolers echoing the spirit of the season. He felt as each day passed, he and Lucia were falling in love deeper and deeper. This season was different than others for him. It was filled with great anticipation because he intended to spend the holiday with Lucia. She would be appearing in the Christmas Show at the hotel starting a week before Christmas, and he had every intention of watching as many performances as he could. She was practicing intensely several days a week to be ready for the dancing, which left little time for them to spend together. Every minute they had together was quality time. He was excited with the expectation of his quiet, shy maiden turning into a beautiful frolic dancer for the season.

The opening night for the show had arrived. Now, Francesco's surprise to Lucia became a reality. When Francesco arrived at Lucia's apartment, it appeared no one was at home. The door opened, and Francesco met Lucia at the door adored in her elegant holiday gown. Her floor length costume was of a deep, dark navy satin with gold trim. The skirt had three tiers with a large gold velvet bow adorned in the back. The long slender sleeves edged with lace at the cuffs and the bodice trimmed with gold emphasized her tiny features. Her hair was pulled up to the back of her head with little ringlets falling toward her face. The costume was gorgeous; the woman was beautiful. Francesco stepped back to catch his breath. After the greeting of kissing Lucia on the cheek, Francesco handed her the little box. "Lucia, this is for you. I've been counting the days down since I bought this gift for you. I bought it the first day I met you for I knew then that you had taken my heart. I give it to you as a token of my love for you. It's not real expensive, but it's something I hope you will always cherish to remember me in the days ahead. Always remember that it was the first thing I ever bought you. Please open the little package now."

Lucia shut her eyes trying to hold back the tears as she laughed and cried at the same time. No gentleman had ever bought a beautiful wrapped gift for Lucia. "Francesco, there are no words beautiful enough to express my appreciation for the gift."

Francesco shook his head as he reached up and touched her hair. "You need to open it first, my dear, before expressing your gratitude to me for you may not like what I'm giving you."

"Francesco, I would like anything that you give me. Anything would make me happy because it came from you." She smiled reaching out to pat his arm.

The little package was very beautifully wrapped. It was wrapped with a royal blue foil with a small silver bow. Upon opening the little box, she whispered with excitement, "Combs, you bought me combs for my hair. Oh, how lovely, Francesco! The combs are gorgeous!" The combs were made of a gold metal aligned with gemstones displaying various colors of the rainbow. Each stone sparkled as she tilted the combs in different directions.

"Let me put them in your hair now to wear for the performance tonight, if you don't care." Francesco reached up and slid the one comb in her hair followed by the other.

"This is a special moment that I will remember for the rest of my life," replied Lucia as she turned toward the mirror dazzled by the reflection.

He exhaled with gratification as he turned her to him lowering his lips to hers and kissed her. It was a demanding kiss of his love toward her that left her breathless. After a considerable time, he withdrew his lips murmuring, "I'm glad to place the combs in your hair tonight. You are very special to me! I bought them with the hope that you would wear them to the show's opening. They will serve to you as a reminder of me while I sit in the background watching. Christmas is the time of year for all kinds of surprises. Isn't it? The combs, I believe with their colorful stones are perfect." He suddenly grabbed her saying, "Come, Lucia, don't you hear the music. We must dance the first dance."

Laughing and crying, Lucia played his game and started swirling as she lifted her skirt quickening her step with her feet touching his following as he led the way. "Yes," she pretended, "I hear the music loud and clear." Really, the only music sounding in the room was the tune coming from the beating in their chest. These sentiments were felt between them as they swayed to the tune from their hearts.

"You're wonderful! Not only are you a wonderful person, but you are also a wonderful dancer." He told her as she stepped close to him. Francesco was elated finding a little opportunity of being alone with Lucia. Consequently, he knew that they must be on their way for time was of essence for the performance.

Making their way to the hotel early, Francesco dropped Lucia to the door where all the performers were to meet. Then, Francesco looked for his brothers to join him in the front row seats that were reserved for friends and family of the show participants. With front row seats, he could watch the performance and keep his eye on Lucia. He wanted to capture every second of this magnificent event.

It was 8:00 PM when the lights dimmed in the auditorium as the curtain began to rise with soft holiday music playing in the background. He turned around to notice that every seat in the house was filled, and the atmosphere of vibrant electricity was running throughout the audience for this special affair. Instantaneously, the cast was singing beautiful melodies that echoed throughout the place tickling the ears for all to hear. Everything was going fine for this performance. Francesco was captured in his spirit as he sat in awe watching every move that Lucia made while dancing across the stage. His eyes never left his lady for a moment for the color of the gown brought out the beauty of her skin. He was blinded to all else around him only the motion of his woman in front of him as he sat glaring. As the dancers danced, Lucia would shift a handful of fabric from side to side to avoid trampling the hemline. The satiny fabric of her dress fluttered and billowed around her with the gentle graceful movements. Francesco was inspired by the performance holding back the tears that would well up in his eyes as a million stars twinkled in the recesses of his mind. Was this a dream? If it was, he hoped it would never end; but if it wasn't, this was a new experience for him for he had never gone to a theater before this time. His heart was captured with much love that he could hardly contain himself. For a moment, he wanted to stand up in the audience and proclaim his feelings for all to hear. It was their night. He wanted to be alone in his own thoughts. He knew his brothers were being captivated by the excitement felt across the audience. He wondered if Lucia's family was touched by the magical feeling for he assumed they were somewhere in the audience. Tonight, it was all about his Lucia. He wanted to spend every second watching and being fascinated with Lucia for tonight.

As the performance ended, the curtain came down, and the lights dimmed as the audience rose clapping and yelling out in adoration for the performers. Then, the curtain rose again with the various brilliant colorful lights flashing on the actors while they bowed toward the audience. The audience remained cheering for a standing ovation. The glow shining from the lights brought tears to Francesco's eyes as he thought of the array of tiny colorful stones from the gift that brought Lucia much delight. The deep wine velvet curtains for the last time dropped to the floor and the overhead lights in the complex came on. People were now making their way to the exit. Francesco went in the opposite direction hurriedly making his way to the back of the stage, where the performers were gathered brushing passed each other, to find Lucia and walk her home. All at once, panic-stricken, he wondered in such a crowd if he would be able to find his lady. Out of the corner of his eye, he caught a glimpse of an image he believed was her standing with her back toward him. Racing toward her, Francesco's heart took flight for a moment when he turned her around slowing pulling her against him.

"Lucia, at last I found you. I was worried I wouldn't find you in this crowd, but I should have known that I would know you anywhere. Here, I brought you something. This is for you, my love," he quietly whispered in her ear as he handed her one beautiful embroidered, white-lace handkerchief as a keepsake. "Let's get out of here where we can talk. It's getting late, and it's time we go out into the street to make our way home. It will be heaven to be alone with you for a brief time. Let's get away from the crowd and noise. You can share all your joys of being on stage if you'd like on the way!"

Quickly, Lucia thought of this moment as a prince whisking away his princess. She turned nodding without speaking as he gathered her in his arms for a little embrace. Tears were in her eyes from the emotion of the show. The handkerchief was a perfect gift.

"This will be one of many nights to remember forever," Lucia whispered. Making their way through the room to the dimly lit street, they strolled hand in hand talking over the various scenes of the performance.

As they approached Lucia's residence, the place was deserted. It was a good thing for Francesco was overwhelmed with the many emotions that were running through his heart. He said, "You must be exhausted, but you are probably too excited to sleep now. Morning will arrive sooner than we think."

Lucia replied, "I am exhausted more from the anticipation of the show. Thank you for the evening. I am on a cloud right now, and I will have to come down. I will always keep this memory somewhere in one of the little compartments of my heart."

The stars shone bright over the city tonight while the twinkle from the light of Francesco's eyes was reflecting into the face of Lucia. Francesco smiled as he stood at the door watching Lucia, "I need to let you get to bed. I really must be going. With the holiday season in full swing, it will be busy at the hotel the next few weeks. We both need to get some sleep. Besides, your family will be returning soon." Francesco pulled Lucia close to his chest to embrace her in his arms one last time before turning toward the door to make his way home.

The journey was close to reach his room where his brothers were waiting for his return. Francesco thought how time was passing quickly.

In the days ahead, Francesco and Lucia continued their courtship. Each day, Francesco would start his day meeting Lucia for breakfast. The time was coming nearer for him to leave the city. The memory of these last few months with Lucia walking beside him, kissing her, dining with her, and sharing special moments were now ending. He wished that time could stand still, but his wish was beyond his control. His thoughts drifted to the day he gave her the small gift box with the combs for her hair as his fingers quickly grabbed one, and he plopped it into her hair. The look on her face from the gratification that she was feeling could never be erased with him for a lifetime. Lucia seemed to be appreciative of small things. He was remembering the night he gave her a sampling of chocolates. She loved chocolate and sampled several pieces as the chocolate ran out the sides of her mouth. They both stood laughing for all the happiness they were feeling together at that moment. Several memories were engulfing his mind while piercing his heart into pieces that he had to tell her that it was time for him to move on to the job he originally came to claim elsewhere. His brothers had been ready to leave town for quite some time now, but they were trying to stay a little longer because of Francesco. The plan was that they would leave together on their next venture. He had grown close to Lucia in these last few months, and he wanted nothing to change that fact. When he told her of his plans, he wanted to handle the situation with "kid gloves."

Today like many other days, he met Lucia at their special breakfast café before their workday began to have some small talk. Lucia was sitting at the far side of the café sipping on a cup of coffee. He noticed that she apparently was there for a few moments because she had a cup with coffee setting across the table waiting for someone to claim.

"As usual, I feel on top of the world being able to start my day by having breakfast with you. You light up my day before it begins," said Francesco as he sat across the table from where she was sitting.

Lucia put her head down. Her cheeks began flushing. "You're a little dramatic this morning," said Lucia laughing.

"I may be dramatic, but it's the truth the way I'm feeling right at this moment," replied Francesco. "We really have had some nice times together. I thought several times about how my life has changed since coming to New York. I'm glad I came this way."

"I'm glad both of us came this way. We would have never met if we remained in Italy. Now that the holiday is over, our work has slowed down a bit, but I think we better get moving to work to avoid being late," stated Lucia.

After eating breakfast, Francesco and Lucia arose from their chairs walking down the street, chatting while walking, to their workplace.

As Francesco dropped Lucia at the door of the hotel, he decided to ask Lucia to dinner tonight to discuss a few things that was on his mind.

The day dragged by as any other day when there was the anticipation of their night meeting. Spring was right around the corner causing the weather to be exceptionally warm for this time of year. Evening was now upon them. He had decided to take her to a little outside café with tables located on a balcony with a red-tiled roof for covering. Thus far, the evening was delightful with music playing softly in the background, and the only light was the soft glow of candles flickering as they were warming the place to capture the mood.

"I'm very hungry, Francesco." She could not take her eyes off his well-formed face for he seemed a little withdrawn tonight.

He had much to say, but for the moment no conversation came out of his mouth. The only sounds that could be heard was the music playing softly to inspire one's heart with wild imaginations.

After polishing off the roast beef, potatoes, and vegetables, Lucia sunk her teeth into her first bite of pecan pie alamode. The dinner was utterly delicious.

Francesco thoughts stirred for choosing the right words, "Lucia, I brought you here tonight to tell you something that I've been avoiding for a little while. There is no better place than dinner for a night to break the ice of a difficult situation. I want to talk my plans through with you deciding what we could do to remain together. I want to make this evening special. Uh..... uh.... through time I knew that I would have a farewell dinner in New York. Upon asking you to dinner tonight, I hadn't alluded to you that this would be farewell, but I suspected before the evening ended I would have to tell you."

She took a deep breath. She covered her face with her hands ignoring voices all around. In her heart, she already knew what he wanted to tell her. She tried to look away blinking back her tears. "You're leaving New York soon, aren't you?"

"Yes, that is what I am trying to tell you. How did you know?" questioned Francesco.

"Well, you mentioned the word farewell. Also, you told me that you would only be staying a short time here. I knew the day would be coming all too soon when you would have to leave. The question was when that would be." A sense of sadness swept over her. She already was missing him and felt alone thinking of his absence.

"My Lucia, you are beautiful!" he whispered. "You are the most beautiful woman I have ever seen! You are a gift that I will cherish forever! I love you very much and can hardly bear the thought of leaving this place without you, but I know I must leave with my brothers in search of our job and our destination."

"What is love anyhow?" She spoke up. Her voice was low that he could barely hear her over the sound of the music. "I know nothing lasts forever. How stupid of me to dream that we would be more than a brief encounter. Being loved has been wonderful, though, and having loved is to have lived even if it is only for a short time. It's worth everything!" She couldn't accept the thought of losing Francesco as she was sinking into self-pity.

As he gazed into her tear-stained face, his voice was low with anguish choking back his own tears, "It's not easy for me to leave you here in New York, but my plan is not to leave you forever but to return or send for you once I get settled. You will not be losing me." Francesco reached for her hand squeezing it tightly. "I love you, darling! If I had my way, I would take you with me in my pocket when I leave, but we know that isn't possible. While I'm gone, we will write until I can be with you once again. I can't live without you for I love you! I will miss you terribly! When the time is right, I will return or send for you. You must believe me! There are still many things my brothers and I must get organized to depart. Tonight, I will go to your father for his approval of taking your hand in marriage. You will marry me, won't you?"

Francesco pulled out of his pocket a beautiful pink rose embroidered handkerchief etched with white lace. He whispered as he handed it to her, "You can use it in the days ahead to wipe the tears from your eyes. I know that you will have tears flowing that stain your eyes from feeling the loss and emptiness here without me; also, there will be tears of happiness knowing that you will join me shortly as my wife." He explained, "This handkerchief is a little token of the love I feel for you. I could have bought you a rose to express my love, but it would wilt and fade away. At least, these roses are embroidered into the handkerchief to last until we can meet once again."

Francesco continued speaking, "I wanted to present you with a beautiful ring for such an occasion, but the lack of resources made it impossible to follow through with my desire. Anyhow, I was told that roses serve as a symbol of love. I hope that the handkerchief for now will be enough. Love really isn't measured by the size of a gift, but the thought from the one giving it from the heart." He loved this woman. In all his life, he never had such a deep physical attraction for another person as he did for his Lucia.

"If you keep giving me handkerchiefs, before long I will have a whole collection. I hope that I don't have to use them for drying my tears." She answered with amusement in her voice.

"No, I don't want you to be crying while I'm gone," Francesco replied.

As she held his attention, surprise and happiness flared up in her eyes, but it didn't take her long to answer his question. Breathlessly she replied, "I never thought you would ask. Francesco, I love you very much. I can't imagine my life without you either. I will wait for you no matter how long it takes. Yes, I'll marry you. My father knows how I feel about you. He would do nothing to upset me. I know he will give us his blessing."

Quickly, they headed out of the café onto the street for excitement was rising within them. Now, there was nothing in this entire world that could keep them apart. Passion, hot and wild swept over them. At his touch, she gasped for the heat that was penetrating her inner being. As he embraced her tightly, he placed a kiss on her lips saying softly, "Lucia, I want this to last forever. In the years ahead, I want to make you happy and spend my entire life loving you."

She smiled as her breath quickened, her breast falling toward his chest; she was deliriously in love. There could be no question about her love for him. She threw her arms around him saying, "I promise to love you forever. You will always have a special place in my heart."

He held her close trying to shield her from the cool night breeze. They both sensed that this was their last meeting until he would seize her. Heavy hearted, they walked slowly and quietly each in their own thoughts back through the streets of New York to Lucia's place.

Upon entering, Lucia's family met them at the door. Her father was a pleasant soft-spoken man. He was dressed in a red and navy plaid flannel shirt with dark pants. Lucia's mother had a gentle spirit with a smile on her lips. She was short and slender with her curly hair pulled up to the top of her head with a hair comb holding it in place. She had an apron wrapped around her for she was either cooking or baking in the kitchen.

A few greetings were exchanged. Francesco tried to speak to her father with barely a word coming out of his mouth. "May I speak to you privately?"

Her father replied, "Surely, let's go into the parlor where we can sit and talk about whatever is on your mind. Come this way, Francesco." They moved into the parlor sitting across from each other in soft blue cushion chairs.

Francesco was very nervous about what he had to say to Lucia's father. "I want to explain the arrangement I have made with Lucia. Tonight, something very special has happened."

"What special thing has happened tonight?" he quizzed.

"Uh…. uh…. I have asked Lucia for her hand in marriage," he clearly stated. "She has accepted, but before we make arrangements, I wanted to ask you if you will allow Lucia to marry me."

Before Lucia's father answered, he was out of the chair and calling for his wife. "Mama, come here quickly."

Mama scratched her forehead, questioning, "Yes, what is most important that you have called me to your conversation?"

"Francesco is asking me if I allow him to marry our daughter. I want to include you in this conversation for not only is she my daughter, but yours also." Both parents ran to Francesco and put their arms around him letting him know without any word exchange that things were fine for him to take her hand in marriage.

Lucia entered the room observing the three with their arms around each other joining into the circle. Lucia wasn't sure what was transpiring, but she thought it had to be something good.

Francesco continued speaking his plan for all to hear. "When I leave New York, I will have to stay in a boarding house until I find a job. Once I make enough money and see my way clear to be able to provide for Lucia, I will either return or send for her. I know it will take me a little time to get things in place, but I promise I will not change my mind on what I have decided." For a second, his heart was overcome with many doubts and fears. Becoming dizzy headed, he staggered backwards from all the emotion he was feeling. He wondered if he would be able to provide for Lucia, but he must because he could not live his life without her.

He hesitated for a moment then regained his composure to begin explaining once again his plan. "The train will be leaving New York around suppertime in a few days to take me to the place where I plan on getting a job. Not only will I be leaving New York, but both of my brothers will be going too. This has been our intention since our arrival here. Hopefully, this will be my permanent destination where I will begin my new life here in America."

After a moment, the pair strolled across the room leading Lucia with her mother to the window overlooking Francesco's place. The words her father spoke would be ones to always be remembered.

"Lucia, if you can find happiness with him my child, you have my permission to marry him. Love him with all the passion that your heart can give. I give you my blessing." As he spoke, once again they came near embracing each other in a family circle that would not be broken no matter how far they journeyed. Lucia's parents had tears of happiness and sadness in their eyes. They were happy that Lucia had found her soul mate in life, but the sadness was that Lucia would be leaving New York soon to meet Francesco to make a home together, which was quite a distance from New York. It wasn't the same distance they traveled from Italy, but still it would be inconvenient to make the journey often. Little money made it impossible to travel these days.

Realizing the time, Francesco glanced at Lucia as he walked slowly to the door. With reluctance, he opened the door speaking, "As God as my witness, I promise that I will either return or send for you. You must believe me! Now, I must leave for a little while. You will never be out of my mind for even a moment. It's tearing me apart having to say goodbye! I will not say it. I will only say that I shall see you soon. I know that the days will drag by waiting for me, but I will try my best not to have you far from me for too many days." With these statements, Francesco opened the door stepping into the night air with Lucia following him as they clung to each other giving their farewell kisses under the starry sky. Magic was in the air. Even though Francesco had to leave in a sudden departure, he still could not bear the pain of glancing into Lucia's eyes to see the hurt she felt from the affection that was held deep in her heart for him.

Lucia stood in silence blinking back the tears. "My heart is sinking, but I know that I must let you go. The sooner you go on this venture I know the sooner that you will return. I will hold on to hope until I can be with you once again. I pray that you will find a job quickly."

Many things happened over the next few days as Francesco and his brothers prepared for the trip that awaited them. They all had to pack up their belongings and leave their jobs to which they wouldn't be returning. Many emotions ran through each of their minds since they wouldn't be coming back here. It's difficult to live in a place that you call home for a while, and suddenly you're uprooted, and it's not your home anymore. The time spent here would always be remembered for it would always be their entrance into the new life to their "*streets of gold.*" They would be traveling several hundred miles away from New York. Tonight, they must get a good night's rest for the journey will begin late tomorrow. Where would this train take them? It would be a journey they weren't sure where it would lead. They made it this far to begin a new life, and they would continue not looking back, but only ahead, to what the future held. New life would begin for Francesco once he had Lucia with him permanently. He knew that leaving New York without his Lucia that time would go slowly until he could hold her in his arms once again. In his heart, he would hold on to the unseen vision of never letting go until he accomplished his desires. None of them had a place to live or a job to go to when they left Italy, but they all had faith in their hearts of obtaining the unforeseen. It was hard for Francesco to get a good night's rest tonight with many thoughts racing through his mind. At times, his mind would play tricks on him by telling him to stay in New York while his brothers moved without him. He hoped he was making the right decision to move on from New York for he did like his job here, but the pay was low and survival with a family would be tough.

CHAPTER 10

LEAVING NEW YORK

---

*Hope is holding on with a prayer of expecting
the impossible will be fulfilled.*

Morning came quickly. The brothers rose early to get their day started. Even though the day would be hectic, they all wanted to take one last look around the city before leaving, which was the one thing they all agreed upon. For Francesco, a charm had settled over the city that was unexplainable. The train would be arriving later this evening. There was only a little time to browse. Living in the city this short time familiarized them to the customs of America. They became more fluent in the English language with the passing of time. Instead of browsing, Francesco wanted to spend the last hour or two with Lucia, but he thought that it might be too painful. Therefore, they both decided not to have Lucia come to the station to bid him farewell. She couldn't bear the thought of watching him get on the train that would take him away from her. It was best to start the day as usual by going to work. Throughout the day, he was tempted many times to stop by one last time to see Lucia. If he saw her this one last time, though, he probably wouldn't leave but stay in New York. It was hard for them to face this departure. He had departed his homeland without looking back, but he held all the memories close at hand from Italy to make it through each day. Now, he must not look back once again for it was hard enough to think that he was leaving. This time was different for he knew that he would either return or send for his bride. He had to focus on the future.

Today, the temperature had dropped steadily as clouds were graying in the sky. The wind was blowing excitement in the air—excitement to find that special place called home. Meanwhile during the city bustle, the trio moved along patiently for one last tour before heading toward the railroad station to purchase their fare home. The railroad station wasn't a great distance in city blocks from *Little Italy*. *Little Italy* didn't seem far to reach the day they arrived not very long ago. Light of day was welcomed from the putrid smells that existed on the ship that any distance would not have mattered only the fact that their feet was on dry land. The day they arrived, there were mass lines of people purchasing tickets at Ellis Island. Today, it was different for there weren't as many lines here in the city. As they approached the ticket window, the ticket agent greeted them with a smile as the three stood by the booth waiting to purchase their ticket. They realized that they must purchase their tickets ahead to avoid any delay leaving New York this evening. Then, they headed back to the boarding house to finalize their housing payment and to pick up their baggage. A few more hours, and they would be heading to a place called home. Sadness flooded their very inner being for they became accustomed to this place that became their first home away from Italy.

Francesco stood as paleness washed over him looking out of the window in a trance. This was the very window that he first spied his porcelain doll. Vito spoke softly, "Francesco, I know it is tearing you apart to have to leave her behind, but you must go. There is no way that we can leave you behind. We are all in this venture together. If it makes you feel any better, Alberto and I will do whatever it takes to get her quickly in your life. There are no guarantees in life, but we will do our very best to make this dream of yours come true quickly."

Presently, the muscles in his entire body seemed to contract with pain. His throat tightened as he blurted out in a hoarse whisper, "Thanks for your understanding. I don't know what's wrong with me for feeling this way. I've never been with a woman before that captured my heart in such a way."

Vito replied, "I don't know exactly what you are feeling for I never experienced the way you feel about this woman. I have heard, though, that when the right lady comes along, it does unforeseen things to the very soul of man. If you decide that you want to talk, I'm here for you."

Francesco closed his eyes as he nodded saying, "I'll be alright." Francesco felt a feeling of reassurance sweep over him by the words spoken by his brother. "I wish I could see her one last time before I leave. We decided not to do that, but it is killing me emotionally knowing she's right across the street from me." Francesco glanced once again toward the window trying to catch one last glimpse.

Alberto yelled as he opened the door, "You'll never leave if you see her one last time. Come on, Francesco. Let's get out of here and look around one more time for a few hours before leaving."

"No, I am going to find Lucia. I must! I must see her one last time! I will be back within the hour to depart from here. Both of you can venture one final time up and down the several streets that are familiar during our stay here. There are many similarities of this city to our homeland."

Vito replied, "You do what you must do. Hopefully, we'll see you upon our return."

Out the door Francesco ran to meet one last time his lady. He would find her before leaving. Caught off guard in the distance was an image of a lady resembling Lucia running down the street toward Francesco falling into his arms. Francesco picked her up swirling her around the street murmuring love sounds in her ears.

"Tears again," Francesco asked.

Lucia nodded to catch her breath before speaking. "They're happy tears that I was able to see you one last time before your departure."

Francesco said, "I wish you could pack up now and come with me."

Lucia stammered, "Uh…. Uh…. it was a rough night last night knowing that you will be leaving without me, and I don't have much to pack. I am certain that I will come with you once we marry, but I must get some things organized to come with you to our new home. I will wait for you however long it takes for us to be together. I pray it's not too long."

Francesco pressed his hand to her cheek, "I love you so very much, and I will return for you." Lucia wrapped her arms around him as he then placed his lips to hers, kissing her for a long while, whispering love notes in her ears. "Okay, I will see you later. I will not ever say goodbye. The only thing I will say is that I will see you later." He then turned as he walked down the sidewalk to his place. He felt happy with the confirmation that Lucia gave him.

Vito and Alberto were waiting at their place ready to go for the adventure. Not a word was spoken about the lady. Silence was best today.

Now the time was at hand with the purchased tickets, the threesome scurried from the boarding house with luggage in hand down the street to the boarding section of Grand Central Terminal. Vito proclaimed, "Finally, several more hours and our journey will be complete! It's been fun seeing the sights of the city today, but now it's time to go."

Grand Central Terminal was newly built and opened February 1913. They were told that the building was as beautiful now with its marble staircase, 75-foot windows, and star-studded ceiling as it was a little over a year ago when it opened.

The brothers were becoming old pros with the English language. They had practiced some of the English language on their voyage over to America and while in New York spoke it quite frequently to make their way around the city and to become more acquainted with the words. Above the noise in the station, a voice yelled out, "All aboard!" They knew what those words meant. In the distance, the sound of the engines roared with the whistles blowing as black smoke permeated the air up into the sky. It was hard to see the train approaching because of the fog settling in off the Atlantic, but a light shining from within the car made it possible to see a man dressed in a black top coat with black trousers and a white shirt. He was yelling for different destinations. "All abroad" was heard once again as the train came to a squeaking stop. Under the dim lights, passengers lined up to the rails waiting to board for their ticket home. The railroad conductor continued his yelling as he directed passengers through the doors. The train only stopped long enough to be re-fueled and for passengers to board. While stopped, passengers were handed a box lunch as they boarded with their baggage. With the supper hour past, several passengers alluded to the fact that they would soon be eating the box lunch. Many of the passengers that were boarding were new arrivals to America from the ships. Most hadn't eaten for a day or two. Most of the crowd was thankful to have a little something for money was scare. They would probably eat the lunch and long for more. Baggage was light for the average passenger dressed in all the clothes they owned layering themselves with layers of petticoats, jackets, and coats. Some immigrants arriving from the ships carried grape vine cuttings to transplant.

With tickets in hand and clothes on their backs and only a few miscellaneous items of baggage, the three ran to board the train. It was early March 1914. The weather wasn't too severe now. It was cool, but there wasn't any snow on the ground. Francesco stopped, but for a moment, he looked toward the sky before boarding to sever the feel of freedom in his heart—along with the homesickness being far from his homeland. He couldn't believe that he had already been in

America for several months. Time passed by quickly. He was leaving behind his true love here that he met in New York, which saddened his countenance. He already was missing this beautiful princess that he met in New York. For now, he would try not to think about it, but many thoughts were invading his mind. Looking around quickly, he wanted to remember once again how it felt in this place called America. The place that he had captured his true love; but he questioned, where are the *streets paved with gold* that he was told about in Italy?

He was having feelings of fear rushing over him. He was worried whether he would leave this all behind him once again never to return? Tears of joy and sadness filled his eyes. In his heart, he wished very much that she was going with him. He promised that he would write letters faithfully until they could once again be bound together. What a difference a day makes. Could he keep this promise? He hoped that he could for he wanted her with him to start this new life together. Otherwise, if this venture didn't work out, he would find a way to return to New York to be with her and spend the rest of his life working in the city to make ends meet. The city wasn't such a bad place to live even though he came from the country. He would adjust to city life if he needed too. If he was with her, he imagined he would be happy anywhere, even though it meant living without any money. He was certain that he could not leave her forever.

Francesco stood for a moment remembering days gone by in silence as a voice rang out.

"Come on Francesco, we must hurry that we get a seat to take us home," said Alberto. Francesco wasn't in any hurry. He wanted to feel this feeling forever—not forgetting his lady and the memory of the lady greeting him upon his arrival. He remembered her standing for all to see as she reached toward the sky welcoming the foreigner to his new home.

Vito stated, "Let's try to get a seat where maybe some of the beautiful women are sitting."

Francesco replied, "You always have your mind on women. Hopefully, the time comes you meet a woman and fall madly in love with her." He hesitated from saying to Vito that he already found a woman that he was madly in love with for he knew his brother would laugh at that statement. He suspected that Vito deep in his heart understood for Vito had already responded to his need of the meeting before leaving the city.

Vito swung his head around saying, "It looks like up ahead there are some seats that we can sit down and enjoy our travel. We're in luck; it looks like there are some pretty ladies up there too."

Francesco wasn't interested in any beautiful women only the one he left here in New York that he planned on taking as his bride. As they reached their seats, many thoughts entered his mind. He would plan for his own best interest including having Lucia in his life. Life would be empty without her. He was determined to find employment fast.

Weary from arranging details in New York the last few days for today's travel, they were looking forward to gazing out the windows trying to see sights they could acquaint themselves once again in this new land. The light of day was dimming, but they would make the most to see what was in front of them veering out the windows as darkness would be settling in upon the earth. It wouldn't be long now until the engines roared, and movement began. When the train left the station, it was fascinating to wonder what the sights would be like compared to the sights of the city. Sleeping a little while to rest their weary bones at the present was the last thing on their minds. It was a little late in the day to start traveling. Any sane person would be thinking of being in bed in a few more hours, but they had to do what the train itinerary schedule allowed to reach their destination. They were hungry and tired from their travel by foot to the train station, but the thoughts that mostly plagued their minds were finding refuge to shelter themselves once again from the chilly nights. The train would be pulling into their destination on schedule. Beginning again is never an easy task. They were all a little apprehensive of going to a place unknown to them. They were aware that they had to find a job and a place to live quickly. They were told that jobs were plentiful in the coal mines, railroads, and steel industry. Many of the people who worked in the mines were immigrants who arrived from the Old Country. Maybe this place to where they were going would have *streets of gold* like they were told back home.

Silhouettes of buildings lined the darkening eastern sky. Francesco sat in his seat looking out the window with anticipation of the future. At this very moment, he felt like getting out of his seat and jumping through the door to stay in New York. He would run back as fast as he could to the city that he left to see that beautiful face once again. It would be like he never had left. A tear came to his eye with all the magical moments he had encountered while in New York. Reality hit him when a thought crossed his mind. To reclaim Lucia, he had to part from her for a little while. Francesco made a promise to Lucia before leaving the city. He would not break it intentionally.

What is a promise anyway? There are no guarantees in life. Francesco had nothing left to do but to hold on to hope and his promise. Otherwise, there always was the alternative of returning to New York to stay. Even though circumstances would come against him, he knew that hell or high water he would have her with him one way or another. It may take a little longer than he planned. Happiness is worth a lot more than money could ever buy. If he could be with Lucia, everything was alright. What is life worth without happiness? Happiness is different things to different people. To Francesco, happiness was enjoying the simple things of life with a special someone that you can share all your hopes and dreams.

Thoughts were running through his head once again of coming across the Atlantic on the ship with the tossing waters not able to see the light of day for weeks. It was refreshing to be able to smell through the cracks of the windows the fresh air blowing across the station. As the train doors closed to prepare its way to start slowly rolling down the New York tracks, Francesco was very content with knowing that he and his brothers made it safely to shore. It was more refreshing, though, to think of his beautiful woman waiting for him here in New York. Once again, tears of joy and sadness welled up in his eyes. These memorable thoughts would never fade from his mind no matter where he was.

Francesco's mind kept returning to their long voyage from Italy. At least the worst of their travels with coming to America was over. He remembered smelling the putrid air with vomit and body odors and nowhere for them to escape. It made one sick being confined to a small compartment with rattling pipes. Now, it was all behind them. Francesco wondered what his new home would be like away from New York. He found New York a comfortable place. Hopefully, he was making the right decision by leaving New York to go on this new adventure. Memory recalled how hard life was in the Old Country. As time passed by, he trusted life would get easier. At least, he wasn't alone. He had his brothers to console him for they were all able to talk Italian, but now they could speak the English language with some fluency. Maybe their new destination will be like *Little Italy.*

Sounds of different dialect chatter were heard faintly all over the car. Fear that gripped many hearts from their journey to America was now replaced with laughter for the moment. Many of the passengers' facial expressions now changed countenance. Passengers sat patiently waiting for the rails to take them to their new home. Many of the passengers shared the same feelings of beginning again. It's never easy to start over in anything, but a matter of speaking is that we can do it by pulling our self up by the shoelaces and begin again.

Once again, in the distance the conductor yells out, "All aboard!" The whistles sounded as the train slowly started to roll out from the station. Again, a black cloud of smoke was now peeling through the sky while the engines roared as the cars picked up speed to move down the tracks. Each person sat in awe in view of the city. Skyscraper buildings stood tall against the sky everywhere the eye glanced. There were a few things to compare in this modern city to the city of the Old Country with its medieval streets and monuments. Pigeons propped themselves on the tops of buildings watching pedestrians pass by through the streets. Where was everyone going? The hustle and bustle of the city at early evening was overwhelming to a newcomer seeing the streetcars, trucks, and cars with the traffic heading in different directions. Smoke stacks poured out a dirty sooty cloud of smoke across the city. The city appeared to be noisy to the ear. Now, the city was behind them; and the countryside was coming into view. There were mountains and hills where valleys of yellowish brown meadows sat in between. Now that spring was approaching, it wouldn't be long until the coloring of bright green would be seen on the rolling hills. Clumps of evergreens, pines, and a variation of hardwood and fruit trees stood as silhouettes across the sky with some bare branches bending low to the ground with weeds mixed in between. There were sparkling water brooks where rabbits, birds, and deer could nest along the banks making the quiet habitat their home. Then unexpectedly, a little town would come into view with dirt roads and houses with smoking chimneys clouding the sunny blue sky. In a little group of its own were a church, school, tavern, and several stores where townspeople apparently could make a purchase for their daily needs. In the distance, farmhouses sat with barns and silos, chicken coups, and fences. There was a brook with a covered bridge where a horse was pulling a carriage over the road with a couple of passengers. How Francesco longed that it would be he with his lady in the carriage with her black flowing hair while the wind rustled taking them to who knows where? The fences held cows, pigs, and horses with chickens scattered outside of the fence. The little towns with such array of scenery brought back the memories of the countryside where Francesco grew up. Francesco still hadn't seen the *streets of gold* that many had talked about back home.

"Well, I guess we should eat our boxed lunch food. Hopefully, this food will help to ease our hunger pains until we get off this train," said Vito breaking up the silence of Francesco's thoughts for the moment. Opening the lunch box with anticipation of what it contained was not a real priority presently; for being weary from the worry of starting over, wears down the body that any food item looked good. The trio talked about what they would do upon arriving at their destination. They practiced some English and talked Italian to several passengers on the train. Most of the passengers were of the same descent, and they were looking for a place to call home. The only difference was that many of the passengers came directly to the train from the ships, and they had a stopover for a few months before their departure. This made for a comfortable setting for everyone because each one had the same things in common. There were men, women, children, and elderly folks traveling on the train car. It was a relief traveling by train compared to the ship for passengers could get out of their seats and move from one car to another; where in the ship steerage, the only place one could go was to the open deck space reserved for steerage passengers. The train was a long train with the engine carrying a dining car for those with enough money to buy food, passenger cars, sleeping cars, and the caboose was at the end of the line.

After they finished eating food from their packed lunch, Alberto said, "Why don't we explore the train since we have a little time to spare? Night will be coming on soon, and we will have to remain seated. We may as well look over the cars now while it's still daylight. None of us has ever ridden a train. It will be interesting to see inside each car." Alberto was one for always exploring something new. Their legs were wobbly upon standing from their remembrance of all the days of traveling on the ship, and the train motion didn't help matters. At least on the train, you were above ground level to be able to enjoy all the sights and move around a little bit.

As they entered the next car, there were several men sitting around talking and playing cards. The one yelled out in Italian, "Do you want to play?"

Vito responded, "As soon as we look around, we'll be back to play." They noticed coins on the tables.

Francesco mumbled to Vito, "Why would you play with strangers especially when money is involved. You know Vito that our money is limited. Money is hard to come by right now until we get jobs. Besides, we need money for our boarding needs."

"Relax, Francesco. We will only use a few cents. When it is gone, the game is over for us. Who knows, we could get lucky and maybe win some money to make things easier as we journey on."

"Yes, Vito, or we could lose money to make the rest of the journey harder," replied Francesco.

Vito explained, "I have a little reserve for such things that I didn't tell anyone about. Don't worry and go along for the ride for once. You really are such a worrier!"

It was interesting to see the little nooks and crannies of the train. Everything was compacted to fit in its own little space. "Look here," yelled Alberto. "There is only enough room for one person, and you sure wouldn't want to spend much time in here. The bathroom contains a little bowl with a faucet used for a sink, and the commode was designed with a black toilet seat sitting on top of a can-like contraption with only enough space for a person to slide in and out without turning around. This little button must be pushed in to turn on some water to wash our hands."

"Vito, we'll throw you in there and lock the door. You won't be able to get out until we get to our stop; that way, you can't get into any trouble," said Francesco laughing beneath his breath. "I know how you have claustrophobia, and maybe that would cure you."

"Don't start anything you can't finish, Francesco," snarled Vito. "Even though we are all very tired, I still have enough strength to whip you if need be."

"Come on, let's keep exploring," answered Alberto.

As they traveled farther down the train, they came to the sleeper cars where people were in bunk beds sleeping with only enough aisle space to navigate from one end to the other of the car. A few of the sleepers had curtains pulled across to prevent observers from peeking into the bed for privacy, while other sleepers had locked doors. To walk from one car to the other, the brothers had to exit the door to the outside jumping the coupling and entered through the next train car's door.

"The rich and famous must be in the sleeping car that is a private room having a locked door," Francesco espoused. "It must be nice to be able to live this comfortably. Maybe, we'll be able to travel in comfort someday once we get a job and make some money. There is such a wonderful aroma filling the air up here."

Alberto replied, "We must be coming near the dining car where all the food is located. We did eat the food in those boxed lunches. I don't know about the both of you, but I'm still hungry. We do have a little money to buy some food. Let's look what food items are available, and we can decide once we see what's on the menu."

As they approached the dining car, the scent of cooked food lingering in the air grew stronger making the taste buds of one's mouth pour out extra saliva with the stomach rumbling from the emptiness of food. The line of food items included cooked chicken, baked beans, mashed potatoes, corn, potato soup, homemade bread, and a yellow cake iced with dark chocolate frosting.

"It looks that we can pick and choose what we want to eat and pay for only what item we take," said Francesco. "Young men have good appetites at this age." Francesco was still hungry. "I'm going to have a cup of soup to warm up from the cold and cure my hunger pains. It is a little cool in the passenger cars. Soup will sure hit the spot. Obviously, with the doors of the train opening and closing at every stop, it's making the cool evening air penetrate the cars. This is causing us to feel a little chilly from the brisk outside air since spring sunsets are rather cool."

Vito and Alberto spoke together, "We will have some soup to heat us up too."

The chef stood behind the food line watching as they approached. In his years of cooking for travelers, he knew the hardships traveling created. The chef was a tall black man dressed in black pants and a plaid shirt with a smile you wouldn't forget. Apparently, cooking was his specialty.

"I want all of you to know that my food is the best in all the trains that travel the tracks on the east coast." He had a big white hat propped on his head with a white apron tied on. He stood hovering, waiting to serve whoever desired to eat at his table. This was his territory, and he was in charge.

Standing with utensils in hands, the chef spoke up. "Do you men have enough money to buy something to eat? If you don't, I can give you a little bit of food to share to fill your stomachs to tide you over until your journey is complete. My intuition tells me that your money is scarce. I enjoy providing the needy with something to eat. I'll give you a plate of food to share to satisfy your appetites. You can pay for the cup of soup only."

Vito spoke up, "We accept the charity offered to us for our money supply is limited. We have come all the way from Italy in search of a job."

The chef said, "You can make your way down the food line with the tray in your hands to find seating in the next car where booths are located for passengers to eat."

Francesco murmured, "We are a little wobbly from travel. It will feel good to sit down and eat some home-cooked food. It will remind us of our days back home. Thanks very much for being considerate of us."

The chef continued speaking, "I know how exhausting it is traveling. I know how hard my life has been hopping the trains and not getting off until released when the order is given from headquarters. It sure isn't any kind of a family life when most of your life is spent traveling the tracks."

Steam rose hitting their faces sending scents through their noses and mouths with the anticipation of how heavenly the food would taste. They made their way to a booth in the next car down while the chef followed from behind.

Sitting down, Francesco began cutting his chicken in thirds to accommodate each of his brothers. He wanted each of them to have a little bite to eat.

The chef standing over their booth said, "The chicken is fixed with a few herb spices with one tasting like rosemary giving it a splendid smell while the mashed potatoes are flavored with parsley. The potatoes are quite creamy from the butter and milk added making each bite melt in your mouth. The potato soup is truly out of this world too with the special flavoring of melted cheese, parsley, and the little pieces of potatoes. It is thickened to the right texture for tasting. Here is a slice of warm homemade bread, which will fill a stomach up real fast when there isn't much food to eat."

The tasting began. Vito raved, "I have never had potato soup that tasted as good as this soup in all of my life. The soup sure has a way of warming us up for there is a chill in the air tonight. It is good traveling with a meal to eat while seeing daylight—not like the steerage when traveling was without daylight and a limited food supply."

"My name is Ben," commented the chef. He remained standing while they were sitting with a smile that lit up his pearly white teeth for all to see. He was a friendly black man and wanted to make them feel at home. "This train is pretty much my home away from home since I signed on with the railroad a few years back as chief cook. I get to set my feet on the ground a few days out of a month until I board again. I usually am on the north and south bound train making Philadelphia my home when I am permitted to get off. It is a good living that I know how to do being uneducated."

Ben seemed to want to talk even though they didn't know him. He continued. "I had to quit school to help raise the family when my mother passed away. Being the oldest and growing up on a farm without a mother is hard. My mother had died of childbirth to the ninth child. I was sixteen when I had to take responsibility of the family. We lived in the Richmond, Virginia area. My dad would work outside in the fields. I remained at home along with my younger siblings taking charge of the indoor work. Cooking became my specialty. Our large family had to eat to survive. I learned fast how to create menus that went far with our large family. I would create meals from almost nothing that would turn out to be quite a spread of food. One of my specialties is chicken and dumplings for my father raised the chickens. All you need is some flour with water and homegrown parsley for the dumplings that were filling to all the little mouths. I stayed at home until the youngest was 12-years-old and able to take care of himself."

Ben remarked, "At the age of 28, I decided it was time to make my own life. There are still a few siblings at home that can help with the chores for my dad isn't farming as much land. I decided to sign on with the railroad and never regretted doing it for I make a decent living. I have seen a lot of country in the few short years that I have worked. I anticipated that I could always return to my childhood home if need be, but now that a few years have passed, things have changed. Many of my brothers and sisters are now married raising their own families. There are only three children left at home. Since my father has remarried, the younger siblings at home will be forced to take a job to support themselves within the next three years for my father is talking about semi-retiring. It's time for the younger siblings to begin building their own future. Life has been hard, but it's been good. My father deserves everything good that comes his way in his later years. I want my father to be happy."

Ben informed the brothers, "I'm getting off the train this time in Philadelphia where I have a tiny sleeping room." He coaxed, "If you like, you could spend a day or two with me until you catch the next train taking you to Pittsburgh. I have a bathtub where you could clean up and get refreshed from travel. It would be nice to have some house guests!"

Ben alluded to the fact, "There is nothing like a good soaping up to make the body feel fresh and clean. The poorest should always be able to afford a cake of soap to keep their body clean. Soap is cheap."

Alberta was not the least bit apprehensive to accept the offer without any reservation. After Ben went back to his kitchen on the train, Francesco scolded him for accepting the offer without consulting with him and Vito. "We don't know Ben well, only from this brief encounter on this train. How do we know that he can be trusted?"

Alberto chided, "Francesco, you fear too much. Ben looks like an honest man and sure wouldn't be working on the trains if he wasn't. He could show us around the city, which would be nice for a day or two until the next train comes. I think that any help from anyone right now would be appreciated until we can make it to our destination. It would be good to set feet on land once again."

"Francesco," blurted out Alberto, "We may never pass this way again. We may as well see Philadelphia like we did New York while we are here. We can compare the cities to see which one we like the best. Anyway, we do have to transfer trains at Philadelphia to get to our destination. Since we must get off there, we'll take advantage of another little adventure."

"You're right, but he said he had a small sleeping room. How do you know that he'll have enough room for us to stay?" asked Francesco.

Vito urged, "Well, I guess if he didn't have enough room, he wouldn't have made the offer. Since you enjoy exploring, Alberto, we may as well explore this city as well while we're here. It will be another little venture for all of us, and we would be able to learn a little more about America. Anyhow, we made some money while in New York. What are a few more days to waste some time exploring? Maybe if we like it here, we won't go any farther."

Francesco shook his head, "Hopefully, Ben doesn't try and steal our money."

After finishing their food, the trio got up to leave finding Ben in the kitchen. Vito spoke, "Thank you, Ben, for your kindness to us." Vito speaks in broken English, "We assure you that when we get to Philadelphia that we will get off the train with you. We must make this stop to transfer trains anyway. Why not spend a few extra days with you seeing sights of the city? We can board the train heading toward Pittsburgh in a few days once we see Philadelphia."

"I am delighted that you are accepting my invitation. I'll be looking forward to having a few friends to spend some time with showing you my homeland. It gets a little lonely at times never staying in one place for long for I am always running the rails with little time to make lasting friendships. It's difficult to come into an empty place not having anyone waiting on you after being out for a time. The only friendships I make periodically are with the passengers that are traveling my way. Loneliness is one of the worst feelings in life that can affect man's inner being. When a man can share in a good conversation with friends, this gives a man hope in his heart and something to look forward to each day."

Francesco replied, "It does get lonely out here. Our family is all in Italy. We only know each other with a few of the acquaintances we made on the ship coming over and in New York. We speak a different language. We are slowly learning the English language. We aren't real familiar with places, customs, or the monetary system. Everything is an adjustment coming to this country from another. We're glad that we all came over together since we are far away from home."

The brothers headed down the car to find where they were sitting. There were all types of faint odors filling the air from one car to the other reminding them of the odors of the ship on their voyage to America.

They had to pass by the car where several gentlemen were playing cards. The old bearded man yelled out once again motioning to them. "Come and sit down and play a hand or two with us. It is only for pennies. Who can't afford a few cents? It will pass the time until your journey is complete."

"Alright! Alright! We'll take you up on the offer," Vito said as he reached in his pocket. In his one pocket was a little black bag tied up with a red ribbon-like string. It appeared to be a little heavy for it was filled with some coins. Vito continued talking to the old man motioning to his brothers to sit down. "We will play a hand or two, but not much more than that for we didn't bring much money with us and need some money upon arrival to our destination."

The old man replied, "Don't worry about money. Worry about what is happening today, live today and let tomorrow take care of its self."

Vito believed that there was some truth to his statement, but he also speculated that he had to have money for starting his new life in America. The old wheels of Vito's mind were turning. The old man might be the type to try and swindle money any way he could. Vito would guard that fact in his mind. Maybe, the old man was a card shark. Who knows?

They sat down. They introduced themselves by name the best that they could to the old bearded man whose name was Elijah. There were two other shady looking characters by the names of Jeremiah and Daniel. Small talk began of how they were all traveling by train from New York. Apparently, Elijah was affluent for he was a plant manager running a Steel Plant in Pittsburgh. The other two were workers that saw to it that the plant operation ran smoothly. They were returning from a meeting in New York to learn some modern techniques in the manufacturing of steel. By their general appearance, you wouldn't perceive that they would have such job titles. As the old saying goes, *you can never judge a book by its cover.*

Stories were shared of their life back in the Old Country. They also relayed stories of their journey from Italy to start a new life in America.

Elijah pulled out a cigar. "You don't mind if I light up, do you?"

"No," answered Vito. "There is something relaxing about the smell of a cigar."

Elijah shuffled the cards holding the cigar between his front teeth. He then dealt out the cards as each one sat at the table ready to start the game. It had been a long while since they had played cards for life was too busy in Italy to sit very long for any relaxation time. When you weren't working, you would go to bed to get ready to work for the next day. Of course, when they did play cards, it was a different game playing with younger siblings than playing with adults. Each one now had their hand and the game of poker began. Elijah asked if anybody else wanted a cigar.

Vito responded, "I accept your offer." As Vito lit his cigar, he coughed and spluttered.

Elijah laughing replied, "I believe this must be your first attempt to smoke a cigar."

Vito answered. "Yes! It is my first cigar I've ever attempted to smoke. I like the smell of cigars. This time being offered a smoke, I thought I would try it."

Elijah grinned. "You'll adjust once you continue to smoke not saying it's good for you."

The lighting was dim as the game was played. It was a fun-filled evening with none of them really losing any big money. They all shared stories of their life as the games were played. Laughter was good for one's soul. Some of the stories that Elijah and his pair shared were helpful to them for they understood a little better what life would be like in America.

Elijah told them, "If you find that you can't get a job in the coal mines as planned, be sure to look me up for I will try to give each of you a job in the steel factory. I will be hiring several workers soon if any of you are interested." Elijah handed them a piece of paper to refer to in case they decided to apply for a job in the steel industry.

Vito whispered softly, "I'm glad that I talked you two into playing cards with these men. It really was worth our while to stop and play cards even though little money was gained. Besides, we had a great time playing cards and sharing, and we gathered some information for another type of employment."

Elijah laughed, "You will always remember me by smoking your first cigar in America."

Vito snickered speaking, "Yes, I will remember my first cigar. I might take you up on the job offer for I'm not sure that I am seeking a permanent job underground. I have claustrophobia."

The old man answered, "The job is yours; yell when you're ready. Let's turn in for the night. Goodnight....until we meet again!

"Goodnight to all of you," answered Francesco. "It is close to midnight, and each of us agree that we better turn in for the night. We are all tired from the journey."

They left the lounging car and made their way to their reclining seat. As they approached their seats, Alberto spoke softly, "Have you noticed that the train is now dimly lit for the night hour has approached? Silence seems to be sweeping across the car by the passengers."

Francesco answered, "Sleeping on this train for us common passengers isn't going to be the most comfortable. We must sit up in a reclining type chair that is considered a bed for nighttime use."

Vito growled, "We'll only get to take a catnap since Philadelphia isn't much farther. With the dull chatter that can be heard throughout the car from the passengers, I doubt we get a sound sleep, though it might not be too hard to fall asleep sitting up for each one of us is weary from the journey and our preparation ahead to travel. When we wake up from our doze, we'll probably be in Philadelphia."

CHAPTER 11

PHILADELPHIA

*Old friendship is being able to look back over the past and to
reminisce the shared memories that are held dear in one's heart with
that special person and to be able to count them as an "old friend."*

Philadelphia, known as the city of Brotherly Love, is approximately 100 miles south of New York. It wouldn't be long that they would be arriving to explore once again another place. They were told by Ben that the way the city acquired its name was that a man named William Penn had envisioned the area as a place anyone of any color or background could live in peace and harmony. They felt at home knowing such a place existed.

The train now had slowed down to a complete stoppage. It was the middle of the night. Passengers were scurrying around lifting their luggage from overhead to pull down the pieces to get off the train. The doors were slowly screeching open as passengers moved to the steps to exit to the city. The night air was fresh with the wind blowing sand-like dust through the streets. There's nothing like a cool breeze hitting your face to wake you up.

As the brothers rose to exit with their baggage in hand, straightway Ben approached with a big grin on his face. "You three are really coming to Philadelphia." Car headlights beamed on the street corners shedding light for the pedestrian to see while lamp posts lit up the streets from the darkness. "We'll have fun. Come on guys; let's get moving to my place. I feel moisture on my cheeks from the drizzle of rain." The brothers had no idea of the direction to take, but they followed Ben down the winding streets in silence. "Hurry! We don't want to get soak and wet. My room is not more than fifteen minutes from the train station by foot."

Francesco alluded to Ben, "We don't mind following you for the little walk here is a lot less than our stay in New York when we walked more than fifteen minutes at a time to get to where we were going." This was nothing new to Ben for he was acclimated to tramping through the city at night to get to where he wanted to go.

Philadelphia was a large city lacking hills, which made pedestrian travel easy. Ben could have chosen the trolley cars for heavy wood and steel designed trolley cars with eight wheels ran through the city on tracks built right into the streets. However, this was a way to rapidly move through the city and get to a destination quickly, but Ben was usually never in a hurry. It was good to breathe some fresh air into his lungs after being in the stale air on the rails.

Suddenly, they were walking up to a red brick building with several small square windows with green shutters wide open with a solid green wood door. Several chimneys were embedded across the roof with a little smoke rising toward the sky. There was dim lighting glimmering through the window panes. Upon unlocking the door, Ben threw the door open as they entered the room. The room appeared to be quite spacious enough for Ben to call it his home. A big bed covered with an emerald and white colored quilt with four brass post reaching up to the ceiling and a few armed gold-upholstered soft chairs lined up against the wall decorated the room. On the other side in the corner sat a small wooden oak table with two chairs with a cherry wooden frame daybed. The daybed had an emerald green bedspread with big yellow roses. Ben threw his belongings on one of the chairs. Turning slowing he said, "Make yourselves at home. This will be your place to be comfortable in the next few days. I'm not here much, but the room is warm and pleasant to shelter you from the cold. There's a bathroom right through the door on the left side of the padded chair. A couple of you can sleep on the daybed. It pulls out into a full-size bed. I purchased it to have in case my family comes for a stay."

The brothers had always lived their life in the European culture. It was a little difficult to claim America and it cities to the imitation of Italy's class and culture.

"Last night we were in New York, and several hours later, we're in Philadelphia," said Francesco. In his heart, he was still in New York. A thought came to his mind that it doesn't matter where one lives if one is cared for and safe. He felt in New York he was cared for by Lucia.

Ben said, "It's quite early. I'm tired from all the days on the train. Let's take a hot bath and sleep until at least noon. Then, I'll take you on a tour of the city. We can see the Liberty Bell and Independence Hall, where the Constitution and Declaration of Independence were signed. We can grab a late lunch."

Wandering around the city would be welcomed after they acquired some rest. They would not be staying long. Each one took a quick bath and laid down to sleep.

Refreshed after their little snooze, it was now time to arise to embrace the day with new anticipations of sights and pleasures to enjoy. It was early enough in the day with the sun shining in the cloudless sky as they stepped out onto the street to catch a breath of the spring air. They would have plenty of time to explore the city before night fell. It was good to sight-see places they have never been before and to look for the *streets of gold* that was talked about in Italy. Maybe this time, they would stumble onto these streets. As they looked in the distance, they caught a glimpse of several beautiful Victorian homes lining the pathways in the center of the city, which resembled some of the architecture from the Old Country. Venturing down the cobblestone streets, they came upon the waterfront where numerous shops and restaurants stood. Various outdoor dry-stone terraces enhanced the mind to briefly travel back to the Old Country.

Such an aroma from coffee brewing was bursting through the air as Ben blurted out, "We'll eat at one of these places for a late lunch, but for now, we'll grab a cup of coffee and relax a bit unless you guys are hungry."

"I don't know about you guys, but I'm a little hungry right now," replied Alberto.

"Me too," shouted Vito.

"Then, let's pick one of these places out and have our lunch right now," said Ben.

Vito was pointing to the next place a little farther down the street. "That place over there with the red brick front and the green tile roof extended onto the street looks inviting for a nice hearty lunch. The black iron tables and chairs located under the roof remind me of some places back home."

As each one walked to the café, Alberto said, "Let's sit right down here toward the waterfront of this little outdoor café and enjoy the sights of the open doors on this nice spring day."

Ben began, "Look across the waterfront beyond the Navy Yard. This is where immigrants are making their way into America besides Ellis Island in New York."

Francesco was only listening with half an ear for he was immersed in his own thoughts. As he gazed across the waterfront, delusional reflections were creating images in his mind of seeing and hearing things that appeared lifelike for a split second. The imagination in his mind proved breathtaking as the view of a woman dressed in shades of blue, orange, and red was dancing across the water. She was smiling at him as she reached her hands to his coaxing him to come her way as she swayed to the music. Suddenly, he struggled to his feet reaching out his hands toward hers as he stared into her eyes. Patches of sunlight were muting the reflection coming his way. In that moment, he drew himself to attention, clicking his heels and bowing toward her stepping to the beat of the music. He was dancing in the street lost in his own thoughts. What could it hurt anyway? This was purely an exciting feeling as he caught the hint of a smile curving her lips. He truly enjoyed and savored the sensation of the moment that he allowed himself to feel from this gorgeous dancing ghost.

It was broad daylight as patrons were passing by observing this gentleman drawing attention to him dancing with his imaginary partner. Maybe the breeze off the water had him lost in the thought of a woman.

Suddenly, Vito jarred him back to the present as he blurted out, "Francesco, why are you dancing in the street? If you proceed much farther toward the waterfront, you could very well fall into the water and drown. People that are passing will think you have gone mad."

Instantaneously, Francesco jerked to his senses as the lady dissolved into midair replying, "Forgive me, I apologize, but didn't you see her there in the water dancing? I was going to reach out to touch her when you brought me back to reality, and she has disappeared."

"Francesco, there is nothing on the water—only the reflections from the sun beating down from the sky," replied Vito. "Maybe you better visit one of the gift shops where you'll be safe. I think that the light of the sunshine is affecting your brain." Everywhere Francesco went, he could not get the princess out of his mind.

It has been fun exploring this city, but now nightfall once again was upon them. Many things had happened today. They couldn't stay much longer for they had things to do to fulfill their dream. It was exciting taking the grand tour of another city, but more than that was the fact that they were in Ben's territory exploring his way of life. Friendship hopefully would remain forever even though distance would probably stay between all of them.

CHAPTER 12

ANOTHER PLACE

---

*Flowers bloom in the springtime, flowers bloom in the
summer, flowers bloom in the fall and flowers even
bloom in the winter. Everything has its season.*

Time was passing by very quickly. The next day arrived as a flicker of the eye. The brothers had to make their way once again to the train station to leave for another place. Ben walked with them to bid them farewell. Once farewells were exchanged, they boarded the train to depart for another city. Ben would not be going this time for his job allowed him only a few more days at home to refresh before starting work once again.

As they headed toward the rear of the car, they found suitable seating. Francesco yelled, "It won't be long now until we will reach the end of our rainbow where the promise of tomorrow hopefully will be fulfilled."

Settling into their seats, the train came slowly to a halt. Alberto explained, "This must be a popular stop since there are many passengers exiting through the doors with their belongings in hand."

The conductor came over and told them, "You will reach your destination in approximately another two hours." Once again after traveling for a short time, the train came to a halt. This was their stop. They glanced through the door onto the street where very little civilization seemed to exist. Thunder and lightning flashed as they stood waiting their departure from the train.

Vito shouted, "At this moment, maybe we should keep on railing it and not get off. We must find our way to the boarding house and find it fast to get out of this soaking rain that we are encountering. We were told that the boarding house is only one-half mile from the train stop that houses a lot of immigrants that work in the coal mines."

Francesco responded, "The way it's raining, we will be soaked 'til we get there."

The train conductor stood by the train's open door pointing, "Do you see that narrow winding path? That is the direction to follow." He shouted above the flashing from the lightning and roaring thunder saying, "You shouldn't have any problem what direction to take for there usually is a cloud of black dust hovering over the whole area where the mines are located. Stay straight on the path. Don't get off the path for it will lead you to where you can find shelter."

Francesco stood thinking; then, began speaking loudly. "It is a little unnerving to get off the train with no appearance of human habitation in sight or shelter being available from the storm. The only shelter seems to be tall trees that are swaying back and forth as the wind is blowing the branches in motion. We were told never to stand under a tree while a storm is going on for lightening can strike unexpectedly."

They all jumped down from the train taking the direction the conductor pointed them toward, running down the path with their belongings in hand, hoping that they will make it safely to the board-ing house.

Alberto ran ahead yelling, "Come on you two, let's hurry to get out of this storm. We sure don't want to be struck by lightning. It is a blessing to get off the train to know that it isn't far to our destina-tion. Many times, we had talked about coming to America, but now the reality of setting our feet on the pavement to what should be our destination is at times too much to handle emotionally."

Francesco confirmed, "Yes, it is overwhelming to me. Hopefully, it will be all that we dreamed and hoped for before com-ing to America."

Once again, lightning flashed as they proceeded farther down the pathway and saw hidden behind a small forest of trees what appeared to be a little town set back in a country setting. There were several buildings spread throughout this countryside, which hope-fully was the destination they were seeking. The little structures lined in rows with rough lumber boards, small windows, and sagging doors had the same similarities, which must be the company houses where the miners and their families lived. In the distance, they saw bigger structures with many windows resembling the wooden boarding houses, where they were told the immigrants lived. They had never seen a boarding house, but they had a visual image set in their minds of what to expect when one appeared. Back in Italy, they had the various descriptions in their mind's eye of what different ones had described to them. Several places were lined against the horizon resembling what they visualized. Several small houses and buildings ran in rows. Hurriedly running toward this little village to make their way from the storm was now the only thing that mattered. It was hard to observe the view around them with such an intense storm taking place.

As they made their way closer to the houses, they noticed a big sign in view in the distance along the hillside for which apparently was the entrance to the coal mine. There was a dark hole, which appeared to be approximately six feet high and about six feet wide. If this was the entrance, then it would probably be the place that would lead into the innermost part of the earth, which they planned on exploring soon. There were rails lined with coal cars. Coal was piled up in coal cars along the tracks near the mine yard.

The boarding houses sat adjacent to the coal mines entrance distinguishing the town to be a coal mining community. They were told that typically 30 to 40 young men lived together in these boarding houses. What they heard back in Italy was that the first floor contained a kitchen, dining area, and the quarters of the boarding house keeper, which was usually nothing fancy. The upstairs bedrooms accommodated the men sleeping in double bunks. It sure would be an interesting experience to live in one of these places. Because of the storm, they chose the structure the closes to the pathway. Hopefully, there would be room in the inn for the travelers.

As they approached the boarding house, Vito grabbed the door knocker. He steadily banged in hopes that someone would answer quickly. Unexpectedly, the heavy door was swung open by a much older man—probably in his late sixties of little stature. His unsmiling face embraced a mustache that curved down to the corners of his mouth. The mustache made him appear a little harsh. Francesco thought the man looked as though he was a little provoked from the steady banging of the door. Stepping back from the open door, the man seemed to place a stern look on his face that made them feel a little nervous.

Their heart thumped in their chest as the older man greeted them with a deep voice at the door speaking. "I take it that you boys are looking for a place to spend the night."

The thunder continued rumbling as the lightning flashed down and the earth shook. On each of their faces revealed a frightened look as they shook their heads up and down as a clap of thunder boomed loud and near.

Francesco tried speaking above the crash of the thunder in very broken English, "Yes sir. We uh…. need shelter from the cold. We have traveled many miles across the ocean to come to America to find jobs in the coal mines."

"Hurry, come in out of this storm. You're soaked to the skin," said the old man as he stepped farther backward to usher them through the door. "There is plenty of room here for a few more men." The brothers' hair was matted with their clothes clinging to their skin from the torrential downpour that was occurring outside. Several men stood around the room as they entered staring back at them solemnly. Most of the men seemed roughly the same age in their twenties and early thirties.

Upon entering the boarding house, long wooden tables lined the huge room with benches on each side to accommodate the boarders. Apparently, this was the dining area. Along with the tables and benches, a rustic fireplace stood at the far corner while the room was illuminated by the lit fire and a few candles shattered away the gloomy dark day. The fire was crackling to take the chill out of the air for the cold rain radiated a dampness that brought a shiver to the body. As the three stood there looking around in silence, it felt good to familiarized themselves with the atmosphere of the room and with the various personalities they would be making acquaintance with while staying at this place. This would be the place they would call home for now—until life's path would take them on their journey elsewhere. This was going to be a far cry from the lodging they left behind in New York where privacy was expected. Privacy is a good expectation whenever it can be found, but it's good to have the opportunity to share accounts in life with others, to walk them through their wilderness and valley, and to be able to offer encouragement to uplift and touch the innermost heart and soul of another human being.

Apparently, the man that greeted them at the door was the boarding housekeeper. He said, "There are 24 bedrooms upstairs with 6 bedrooms downstairs. I only have a few upstairs rooms that are vacant in this boarding house. I'll show you the available bunks where you can sleep tonight, and then you can get those wet clothes off and hang them up down here by the fireplace to dry."

As they started up the sweeping staircase, they heard the squishing of their shoes on the hardwood stairs. As they reached the top of the staircase, they noticed that the upstairs was divided into several private rooms behind a closed door. There was a plain big wood landing making for a long hallway with an oak banister wrapped around the outer side overlooking the downstairs dining area. Upon entering the closed door of the room, several bunks lined the inside of the room. There were two windows built into the outer wall with a few lights in the ceiling where a pull chain hung down for turning the lights off and on. As they stood at the far side of the room, they noticed that the room was illuminated by a fading light coming through the window from the street. The room was nothing fancy, but they found it acceptable and comfortable for the time they would be staying here. It was a room where little privacy could be found since sounds could be heard penetrating the thin partitions separating each room. The only privacy would be in each individual bed that could be called a solitary place.

At least for tonight, they would be sheltered from the raging storm that was going on outside. The boarding house with its lights beaming out into the night served memory of a lighthouse on the shores of the ocean that would lead one safely to shore. It was a reminder that there is light and a great refuge during the storm. It would be good taking the time to reflect on the simple things of life and all its blessings. The very thought of arriving safely to the shores of this great land called America was appreciated beyond each of their wildest dreams could even imagine. Dwelling on these positive good thoughts would bring peace and tranquility to the innermost spirit within the very soul of these men once again.

There was a heavy dark oak door with bronze colored handles lining the wall on the side of the room representing a closet that apparently was housing the little bit of apparel belonging to the guests. The quaint room was neat and clean. There were a few old wooden chairs sitting beside the bunks to accommodate one retiring for the night.

As the old man led the brothers across the room he said, "These two bunks are the open bunks that you can call your own sleeping space for the night. Change out of those wet clothes and come downstairs. A bath towel is hung on each bedpost for you to snatch up and dry off. I'll make you each a bowl of soup to warm you up from the cold before retiring for the night. We can talk a little later about your charge for staying here. Tomorrow, you can worry about looking for a job in the coal mines. I'm sure for the moment that you are quite tired from your journey and would appreciate some quiet time among yourselves to think of not much of anything and to get a little organized for your stay here."

"By the way, I forgot to tell you that my name is Dale. I'm the boarding housekeeper," he spoke softly in his deep voice as he walked through the door and down the stairway.

Alberto jumped down on the bunk as he laid his head across the pillow placing his legs and arms straight across the blanket imagining how it would feel to sleep in this bed tonight. "Well, I guess we can plan on sleeping here for a little while. Once we get acquainted with some of the guys, we'll feel a little less strange in these premises."

Vito yelled, "Stay off the bed for we are all soaked as wet rats. I sure don't want to sleep in a wet bed tonight for it'll sure be a long night. We need to change out of these soaked clothes for we are all drenched to the skin. Then, we can hang them up to dry down at the fireplace as Dale told us too. Tomorrow or the next day, we can go seek work in the coal mines, but for tonight, we'll be content to rest our weary bones and grab a bite to eat. Hurry! I'm hungry!"

Hurriedly, each undressed to put dry clothes on—pitching the wet clothes in a pile. Picking up the wet heap of clothes and damp towel from the floor, they returned downstairs placing the clothes by the fireplace to dry. Francesco glanced into the glowing fireplace visualizing her shining presence. A magical spell swept across the room as he envisioned her eyes beaming out at him with all the love she had deep within her heart. His chest tightened with the thought this evening that if he were in New York, he would be with her instead of being alone here with only the memory of one he held dear in his mind and heart. Hopefully, it wouldn't be long until he could send for the love of his life to come quickly to him.

There were times Francesco thought he would lose his mind wanting to reach out and touch her and not being able to do it. Suddenly, restlessness sank in on him for he didn't want to spend the rest of his days remembering what use to be. He wanted to remember each day spending quality time with her as she placed her hand in his to conquer all the trials of life that was thrown their way while walking by his side. There would be a lot of good times together, but realistically there might be some bad times too as in any marriage. If they loved each other, they could make it through anything as they held on together. Life wasn't easy these days, but happiness wasn't measured in material things. To have a perfect relationship, each one had to always think of the other person's needs. The very thought of her with him would help satisfy the emptiness from feeling alone, but it still would never be enough until she physically appeared. Otherwise, such emptiness would prevail in his heart without her by his side.

Until he could secure a permanent residence, he could not even correspond with her. In measuring distance, she really wasn't that far away from him, but even one mile was too much of a distance when one is separated from the one they love. Hopefully, she would be waiting for him as she had promised. All he could do for now was to place positive thoughts of hope in his mind to send him into a dreamland that would sustain him until he had her by his side.

The old man motioned for them to come this way. It was time to dine. He had set out bowls with spoons along with a cup on the long wooden table. As he dipped the chicken noodle soup from the pot to the bowls, the steam was rising through the air causing the taste buds in their mouths to yearn for satisfaction from the smell that was penetrating the room.

Francesco pulled out the bench as he plopped himself down along with the others to savor the soup to once again satisfy his appetite. At least for now the downpour outside had subsided, and the sunset was falling across the sky fading the colors into the darkness of the night.

The different men were gathering around to get acquainted with each other. Each one had their story of how they landed here at this boarding house searching for a job that would lead them to the better things of life.

The boarder with a partial left arm began, "I will take you to the coal mines tomorrow to sign up for work. If you like, you probably would be able to start immediately since the mines are hiring, and there is plenty of work to be done underground."

Francesco expressed, "Thanks! We'll take you up on the offer! We have all polished off the delicious soup. We all know it is soon time to retire for the night for the outside sky is darkening. Early to bed today is our goal for we all feel the day's exhaustion hitting us, and tomorrow will be another early rise."

The boarder stood and came toward them smiling brilliantly, "Gentlemen, allow me to introduce myself. My name is Marcus." Attired in a snowy white long-sleeved shirt with one sleeve rolled up with snug black trousers accented his small pudgy frame. He had a rounded face of character with black wavy hair.

Marcus continued speaking, "I have lived here at the Boarding House for a few years working in the coal mines until I lost part of my left arm due to an accident under the ground. Now, I have other responsibilities that I take care of here at the Boarding House to keep busy and to bring in money to survive. I don't know if Dale told you or not, but there is a bathhouse out back. When you come back from the coal mines, you will need to stop there first before entering the boarding house to clean up from the day's job."

Vito replied, "How nice to meet you, Marcus. In the days ahead, we will depend on your helping us to make our stay here pleasant." Without hesitation, they reached out extending a friendly welcome as they shook each other's hands.

Marcus extended his right hand of welcome saying, "I hope you were told that the mining industry is dangerous, but reality struck me with the truth when I lost part of my arm. Many dangers exist in mining coal underground. Methane gas, water, and falling rock are a few of the problems that prevail."

Sometime when they became more acquainted with Marcus, they would like to hear the details of his story on the loss of his arm instead of the brief details. Marcus still had a smile on his rounded face regardless of his work mishap. Conversation never ceased in the room as the boarders conversed in their private groups among each other. Each group was sharing the details thought important of their day's events.

Marcus raising his eyebrows, smiling, continued speaking, "I hope you gentlemen have brought along your appetites for Dale sure can outdo himself in the kitchen. Since I understand that you will be taking jobs in the mines, you can look forward to coming home to having a home-cooked meal prepared for you each day. One never knows from one day to the next what's on the menu, but everything Dale cooks is delicious. His specialty is throwing together a chicken pot pie with nice big pieces of chicken and potatoes smothered in a thickened style of gravy with the best flaky crust imaginable."

The new arrivals seemed to be embraced with wide open arms by the other boarders making them feel a part of an extended family now that their family remained back in the Old Country. It was interesting to see the different reactions among the men who were assembled under this roof tonight. The brothers never had experience living in such a large family type setting. Down the road would tell the tale, whether this type of environment would serve as a tranquil setting away from the workplace.

Tonight, the house seemed to be filled with activity with each boarder having a story to tell of their happenings today or in the past. Marcus stood up at the table tapping with a cup to get everyone's attention. Silence swept across the room for an instance. "Since we need to rise at the crack of dawn, I'm suggesting that we all retire for the night. Morning will come too quickly."

Inside the boarding house upstairs sleeping area, the brothers breathed easier relaxing from their day's journey. The room was still once the boarders retired for the night. It was as if all of life was sucked from the room. As Francesco lay on his bed unable to sleep, he noticed shadows were dangling through the windows from the trees that were swaying from the winds of the storm that once again sprang up. He tossed and turned in the moonlight as he caught a glimpse once again of the face he longed to see. He shut his eyes. It was all remarkably real. Once again, he opened his eyes and the same familiar face appeared. She turned her face to his; she was looking right at him with a smile on her lips. She was no strange visitor to

Francesco. The translucent figure of the woman made him catch his breath to the back of his throat whispering as he drifted into a deep sleep, "I can't take my eyes off you."

The sunrise was dawning as the rays of the sun sent a warm glow through the dingy room. Francesco arose and sat on the edge of his bed remembering the face he viewed last night. He longed for nights to look upon her lovely face. Some things were better off to keep in the secret compartments of the heart than to speak idly to those that would not understand. Morning was always a wonderful time to reflect upon yesterday's happenings.

The windows were cracked as the sound of the birds singing outside filled the room with a melodious song to anyone that was listening. There were voices echoing throughout their room from the various conversations heard from the neighboring rooms.

Francesco arising propped the door open as he walked out to the landing where he silently stood for a moment hunched over the banister to observe the morning routine in the dining area below. Through the door, he motioned to Vito and Alberto while they sat on their bunks to join him. They observed from the boarder's dress that they were all from similar backgrounds and preparing for a day's work. Everyone seemed to be a visitor from a faraway land.

They noticed that most of the men were attired casually in their long-sleeve plaid shirts, jacket with a handkerchief tied around their neck, overalls, and high-top shoes to begin their day down in the center of the earth.

Returning to their room, they sank down on their bunks. "I think we better get dressed to begin our day," stated Vito as he lay on the bed looking toward the ceiling. "Hopefully, we all get a job today." A sense of fear swept through him for he didn't know if he would be comfortable working underground where only darkness prevailed.

He was hoping he wouldn't acquire employment. He probably would contact Elijah, the witty old man from the train, who gave him information about the steel mills and was responsible for him smoking his first cigar.

"Alberto, did you sleep well last night?" asked Francesco as he turned his head to look at Alberto.

"As well as one could expect in this new environment. Once I get adjusted to this place, I'll feel more relaxed," stated Alberto as he shifted his position on the bed raising his head from his pillow. "I feel like I'm in a dream and need to wake up. It's like a dream that we have made it to America to our destination." For a long moment, they were silent assessing the statement that Alberto echoed. They sat in silence for a moment observing their surroundings when suddenly Francesco followed by his brothers arose to dress for the day.

As they made their way down the staircase, the smell of morning coffee infiltrated the air. Cups and bowls lined the long wooden table. A few of the boarders were already seated at the table smoking cigarettes and cigars with a cup of coffee in hand. Metal lunch boxes with a handle lined the far wall. It appeared that Dale and Marcus prepared the boxes for each worker to grab as they left the premises to begin their day's work.

Marcus once again appeared saying, "I hope you had a restful night last night sleeping. Today after breakfast, I will take you to the hiring manager to process your papers in order that you may get a job in the coal mines. One thing I must tell you is that coal mining is a back-breaking type of work. Bringing the coal from under the ground to the surface is very hard work. A world of blackness darkens the earth with dust and dirt filling your lungs where only the light of the miner's lantern brightens the hole. There are times you gasp for breath and your eyes burn. The only welcoming sound is when the whistle somewhere above the ground blows letting you know that the shift for the day is over returning you to the bright daylight once more."

Alberto replied, "The darkness will compare with our journey to America. We are not lazy. We are used to hard work back in Italy. At least here, we were told that you obtain a decent wage for your labor."

"Yes, that is true on a good day," Marcus replied as he stood looking intensely at each of the brothers, "but there are a lot of dangerous conditions that you work in. Believe me, the mine work is not all it promises to be. You will learn that every one of the miners becomes your underground family for they are continually watching out for you regardless of each man watching his own back side. The older miners took me under their wing, so to speak, and took care of me during my early years in the mines. Many memories will stay with me for as long as I live when I began coal mining. All I can say is that hopefully the mining jobs work for you and that none of you has claustrophobia."

Clearing his throat, Vito's voice was calm as he spoke, "We won't know that until we get under the ground. None of us have ever worked under the ground. This will be a new experience for each one of us." Pondering a moment, Vito speculated that he had claustrophobia, and he would seek a different job once he decided that he couldn't work underground.

Alberto laughing said, "This will probably be comparable to the cave on the side of the hill back in Italy where we played when we were small boys."

Marcus began his lesson, "It might be a little comparable, but the cave where you played wouldn't be as dark, large, or deep as the mine. You will notice that each miner has a hat with a tiny lamp clipped to it in order that the miner can navigate through the darkness. Truly, you could get lost in the sections. You will notice rails that lead into the dark mine. Each worker is taken by an elevator down into the depths of the earth; then, you walk along the rails to your section where you are working."

"The coal mine has sections of high and low coal usually as low as 4 feet and as high as 10 feet. Many days, there are some type of incidents that goes on. There have also been some fatalities. The other day a group of miners were bolting up the roof in the section on the northern portal when suddenly the earth shook, and rock started flying down. A couple of the miners were blocked behind the debris. It was a joint effort for everyone that was close around having to dig the loose rock in order that the way was not blocked, and the miners could get out. It was a miracle that none of the bolters hit anyone on the head or other places on their body. The purpose of bolting the roof is that the coal can be taken out to prevent an accident such as the roof collapsing, but that day it didn't work against the natural forces of nature. Also, there was no money made that day for the time was spent in taking care of the accident that occurred."

Vito spoke up, "It must have been a scary moment for all those involved."

"Yes, it was a very scary moment for if a lot more of the roof would have come down, many of the miners could have been trapped and could have been buried underground and not survived." Marcus replied. "All I can tell you is that a lot of the miners ate a lot of dust that day!"

"There are many things the miners have to watch out for survival underground. It's a very dangerous job. I will tell you a few of the details to enlighten you. To begin, the methane gas must be monitored non-stop for it will kill you from lack of oxygen. Gases in the mine can cause an explosion. You'll notice safety lamps under-ground. If the glow of the lamp glows brighter, then you'll know that gas is building up and can cause danger. Ventilation must be pro-vided. Furnaces located at the bottom of the mine shaft provide a draft of fresh air to our miners."

Marcus continued, "Some sections have water up to your knees and hips that you work in depending how tall you are being how far up the water goes on each man. Continuous pumping eliminates water from the mine to guard against flooding. A little water stream is continuously trickling from down the walls running across the floor. Dampness is a well-known trait of the down under. You always need to wear boots to avoid your feet becoming wet to keep the chill off your feet."

"Your pay is based on how much clean coal you bring to the top of the ground. You are paid for tonnage. If you have a good day, you make money; otherwise, you don't. You sure don't want to load slate, shale, or rocks for there is no money paid for those products. The coal you load in the car is the coal you get paid for each day. When you work in sections that are hazardous and poor conditions, it's hard to mine a lot of coal." The brothers were captivated by these stories coming straight from the mouth of one that was under the earth. "I could tell you story upon story of happenings under the ground; but for now, we don't have time if you want to sign up for a job today. There are many health issues related to mining. It can give you arthritis in your joints from the dampness. Some of the men have hard times breathing from all the dust over time. After break-fast, let's head to the lower level to pick up some of the things you will need in case the hiring foreman will let you begin work today."

After breakfast, the men made their way through the heavy wooden door to the lower level of the boarding house where there were tools awaiting them to gather up before making their way to their workplace. A few lanterns were hanging to provide light for this gloomy room. With the help of these lanterns, this room had a distinct appearance unlike any other room. It represented the possessions of the hard-working boarders to earn their wage for a day's work. Stacked neatly in various corners along the walls were the very necessities needed for a day's labor. There were black buckets, picks, shovels, boots, hats with a light on top, and gloves. Without these tools, it would be impossible to bring the coal to the surface. Armed with their picks and shovels that was given to them, the miners crawled into the dark and dusty mines and stayed there for 10 hours a day, every day, for about a little over $2.00 a day they were told.

As the boarders stepped out the door equipped to begin the job, they departed down the winding trail to the coal mine. Marcus led the way to the hiring foreman. Their steps slowed as they neared the entrance where they stood glancing around.

They were greeted by a friendly voice, "Good morning, Gentlemen! May I help you this fine morning?"

Marcus spoke up, "Yes, you may. These three gentlemen arrived here from Italy in hopes of acquiring a job in the coal mines. Would it be possible that they could complete a job application to be considered for employment?"

He shrugged his shoulders as he inched closer to where they were standing saying, "I am looking for workers immediately. If these gentlemen fill out the application, they can start immediately working underground. The pay amounts to approximately $2.00 a day."

Marcus eyes narrowed as he gestured toward them that they could begin today. The pay was exactly what Marcus had told them earlier. They were unable to decide what to do as their muscles became stiff with fear from the anticipation of working underground.

Vito was gasping from breathlessness from the panic he felt overtaking him. Alberto shifted his weight back and forth from one foot to the other trying to make the decision from the opportunity given to them. Francesco spoke in a squeaky voice from the nervousness he was feeling, "If you'd like, we…we can talk out here, but the way I see it, today is as good as any to begin work. Alberto, Vito, let's begin today." The sooner Francesco made some money to become established here; the sooner he would be able to have Lucia with him.

There was a lot of activity going on around here. Mostly young men were moving around the outside of the mine. They were all going about their business as they stood observing the busy scene.

Vito felt like his breath was being taken away as he sighed watching his brothers stand in silence, "I uh…. uh…. agree. We came today ready to work. Let's go for it."

Standing a few feet away, Marcus bid them good luck as he turned away and scurried up the trail to the boarding house.

"My name is Jonah. I am the hiring and underground foreman."

He stood idly watching the expressions on their faces, "I will teach you everything you need to know about underground mining. There sure is a lot of dirt and dust to swallow, but you will get use of eating a lot of dust as you work under the earth. Some miners chew tobacco feeling this helps with the dust consumption. I see that you are dressed for the underground with tools in your hands. All of you I'm sure has a lot of apprehension as we are making our way to the opening of the mine to be lowered into the dark, damp cold center of the earth."

Francesco confirmed his feelings out loud saying, "I guess this is where we begin our dream that started back in Italy."

Jonah said, "I know that each of you has fears about the job for once inside the earth the eye will not see the light of day until the end of the shift when a whistle blows. There is always the possibility that an accident can happen, and you will never come up out of this mine."

"Gentlemen, you have all come here to work. I expect you to have a good work ethic. Most of my crew works each day until point of exhaustion. The more coal you bring up the better the pay. I will train you the safety ins and outs of the job. I do not want any accidents because of the lack of training. We are a family underground that takes care of each other. Your first day will be getting use to the underground. Let's get underground to the mine."

As they were loaded in the elevator and dropped down into the coal mine, it was amazing to observe the work that was going on underground where the world could not view the hard labor taken from the earth to provide with the necessities for human life on the planet earth. Men were picking with a pick and shovel as they loaded coal on a wheelbarrow to put into a coal car to bring it to the top of the earth to use it for existence.

"The farther we walk, the dustier it becomes. It sure is dusty down here. Let's try to work together," said Francesco. "If we stay together, we can work as a team helping each other making money and being safe."

Jonah pointed to the men, "Over in the corner are some wheelbarrows. You will get to know the men while you work. This is not real high coal, you must always be careful that a coal bolter doesn't come rolling down from the ceiling hitting you on the head. That is why I expect you always to keep your hat on your head for a little protection."

They joined the other miners and followed the protocol with pick and shovel as they loaded coal to bring to the surface of the earth. Finally, the day ended with the whistle blowing for them to come to the top of the ground.

"Vito, Alberto, I guess we made it today to be called miners. This will be our life in the days ahead. I don't know about you two, but I can get accustomed to working below the earth."

Vito answered, "I don't know that I'm staying underground. I'm going to look for a job in the factory. We have the contact information from the man on the train, and I may pursue that avenue of work instead of the mine. I don't think I can survive for a long period of time under the ground. I am too claustrophobic to do this job the rest of my life."

Alberto shook his head as he began speaking. "I am probably going to stay underground with Francesco. The work is a little dangerous, but I am not worried for it will be a good living for me. Let's go into the bathhouse and get cleaned up. We are black as the coal."

The days were passing by quickly with one day going into another. Vito couldn't tolerate working in the mines much longer for he would lose his mind if he had to stay. Each day that Vito arrived for work, he felt panic-stricken until the end of the shift. Eventually, Vito would land a job at the Steel Factory by contacting his acquaintance on the train.

Francesco continued saving money while working underground for several months that he could now marry his bride. Not only had he money for his return to New York City, but he would be able to stay at the "coal patch" in a company house to shelter his love and raise a family. One night after a full day's work at the coal mine, Francesco sat down on the steps of the boarding house to write his letter that he longed to write for several months. The emptiness deep within him would now be filled to overflowing once his love returned to him. The fear of losing her haunted him daily. She worked at a hotel, and while he was gone, maybe another young man came and swept her off her feet in his absence. He didn't know what he would do if this would happen, but he was holding on to the promise that she gave to him before he left New York. There were many words that Francesco wanted to pen in his letter to Lucia, but with lack of experience in writing, it was hard to put the words down on paper. When he would see her in person, the words would be spoken regardless of the proper dialogue. He would pour out his heart to her even if he made a fool out of himself.

My Darling Lucia,

Finally, the day has approached that we can make our dreams come true. If you would still have me as your husband, I will return to New York within a month to marry you. Originally, I said that I may send for you, but I feel it would be better for me to come and marry you there, and bring you back with me to begin our life together. I would return today for I'm lonely without you, but I know I must be reasonable. I know you will need some time to prepare for our special day. If I give you a month, it will hopefully give you enough time to purchase a wedding dress and to make the necessary arrangements needed for a small wedding. We need to set an exact date that I may make the proper arrangements with the coal mines of my absence. I miss you very much, and I pray that the days pass by quickly when we can be united. A promise is forever, and I promise to love you for that long. Once we come back from New York, we will stay in a coal company house until we can look for a house together where we may live. I will anxiously be awaiting your reply to make my plans to return for you.

Love,

Francesco

Upon returning home from work each day, Francesco would anxiously check at his mailbox to see whether a letter was received from Lucia. The days seemed to drag waiting for her reply. Francesco worried that the letter may have been lost. A month almost two passed without a reply for Francesco to return to New York. One day ran into another as Francesco held on to hope to prepare for the happiness that awaited him. He hoped that his perfect day would come that had been promised him.

On a late day in August, it was unbearably hot and humid with the passing of a storm that the letter arrived. Francesco's hands were shaking as he opened the letter nervously reading the message of each line. What would the letter reveal? Would he find the strong proof of Lucia's love vowed to him in New York or would there be a change in feelings? His face revealed the applause he felt from all the negative speculation that clouded his mind over the last few months. The dark cloud at this very moment was being lifted. His mind had him imagining vain thoughts for he had no reassurance from the one he longed to hold dear to his heart. She was unavailable to touch and share in conversation because of the distance in miles standing between them. A tear of joy fell from his eye as he pressed the envelope close to his heart.

Then, he smiled as he kissed the envelope imagining vapors penetrating his nostrils from the sweet smell of her perfume as she penned out the words that silently played lovely music to his ear. The very scent of her stirred his passion and sent tingling sensations throughout his body igniting flames of desire. He could not wait to hold her once again in his arms and kiss her soft, sweet lips.

He would prefer to remain a bachelor than to marry out of convenience if Lucia did not wish to marry him for she would remain in his heart forever. He was head over heels in love with this woman.

Francesco and his brothers had to make the arrangements with their workplace to return to New York for a short period of time. There was much preparation for Francesco to make to travel once again to New York. It was good that Francesco anticipated this day for there was quite a bit of expenses that he had to pay to marry his bride. He and his brothers had to purchase a train ticket and suit for the wedding day. Most importantly, Francesco had to shop for the perfect ring that he could place on Lucia's finger to remain there forever. Francesco wanted to send a bouquet of white roses with purple orchids and a handmade embroidered handkerchief tucked into the arrangement for Lucia to carry down the aisle. Upon his arrival in New York, there would be no time for the traditional Italian wedding serenade.

There had to be some planning when a small wedding was in the design.

CHAPTER 13

RETURN TO NEW YORK

A true friend is one that you can share your deepest hurts.

Finally, the day approached that Francesco returned to New York with his two brothers to claim his bride. Once they departed the train, they made their way to the place where they had stayed upon arrival in America to revisit the place they called home before traveling on to the hotel where they would be staying to have shelter from the cold nights.

Strange how things change when you make a journey to the same place for a different reason than the first journey. There would be no meeting with Lucia before the ceremony upon their arrival. Lucia and Francesco felt this would make the ceremony more exciting. Besides, time did not allow for such a meeting. From his previous stay in New York, he knew exactly where the church was located for he and Lucia would stroll passed it on their lover's stroll.

All types of thoughts were clouding Francesco's mind now that he and his brothers had arrived here in New York. He was questioning himself whether he would recognize her once more as she walked down the aisle. He wondered if he would be able to pick out her face among a crowd. He reassured himself that he had to come to terms with these illusions for there would be no mistaking picking out that porcelain doll no matter how long he hadn't seen her face. Francesco's mind went as far as wondering whether Lucia would appear for their wedding ceremony. Maybe at the last minute, she might stand him up and run as fast as her legs could carry her away from this place. He had heard of such tales, but he hoped it wouldn't be his tale. He was apparently having a case of the prior wedding day jitters experienced by grooms.

Once again, they were walking down the streets that were all familiar to make their way to the hotel where Francesco had worked. The manager greeted the travelers. Francesco was not new to the hotel.

The manager began, "Francesco, it's good to see you again. I have missed your smiling face since you left New York. Your bride has not been the same since you left. She has been heavy-hearted. The days have dragged for her with the anticipation of seeing you once again. For a wedding gift, I am showering you and Lucia with a free few nights stay at the hotel while you remain in New York for I know that money isn't plentiful. I will provide a room for your brothers too."

"Thank you. I will never forget this awesome gift for as long as I live. Let's get checked in and go to our room in preparation of my great event," Francesco said motioning to his brothers. "I want to check on the bouquet of flowers with an embroidered handkerchief to see if it was delivered to the church as a surprise for Lucia to carry down the aisle. The handkerchief will serve as a reminder that Lucia can now dry all her tears for she will never be alone again. I want to take a walk to the church before retiring to be sure of its location."

Alberto agreed. "We better get going for we do have a lot to do before morning…. uh…. uh…. maybe we can grab a bite to eat."

Francesco was empowered with supernatural energy preparing for his special day before retiring for the night. He sat for a moment looking out the window reflecting on the past.

As dawn broke through the sky, the brothers and Francesco rose to prepare for the day's event. Vito teased, "Francesco, if you have a change of heart, we can turn around and head for the train station."

Francesco replied, "It seems that I've been waiting a long time for this day to arrive. There is absolutely no doubt in my mind that I don't want to follow through with my wedding day. I am excited the day has finally arrived that I may see my porcelain doll walking down the aisle to meet me. The sooner we get ready and arrive at the church; the happier I will be."

Upon entering the church, Father Smithton met them at the front door. Francesco gazed toward the front altar where there were two candle rings one on each side of the altar with a bouquet of purple orchids on each side as several musical selections echoed through the sanctuary. The church appeared to be ready for the wedding to begin.

The priest ushered him and his brothers to a side room. "Let's go over some of the ceremony before we begin," stated the priest. "We'll go over priorities only because of the time element." During Francesco's stay in New York, he had attended the church with Lucia several times before departing the city. The church was a beautiful stone building with a bell tower and decorated with stained-glass windows. The inside had marble floors with wood architecture making the appearance elegant.

He paused before speaking, "The wedding is small, but we want to make this a memorable day for both you and Lucia. Your bride is waiting patiently in the little room on the other side—up the staircase above the church, anticipating the day she has longed for these many months. We have a little time to prepare for the service to have things run smoothly. You will all enter the church and stand at the altar until the bride and wedding party meets you there. We will light the candles, then exchange the vows, take communion, and conclude with blessing the rings. Do you have your marriage certificate and rings with you?" He questioned. "We didn't get to have any marriage counseling classes, but with the circumstances, we will make due the best we can. Let's say, I'm doing an act of kindness for you."

"Yes, here in my pocket is everything I need for the day," said Francesco timidly as his brothers looked on.

"Good, then we are ready to proceed with the wedding. Come this way."

With his brothers at his side, Francesco walked toward the altar slowly. He noticed several guests seated in the church pews. Apparently, these were people that had become friends of Lucia's family while living here in New York. There was a beautiful young lady standing behind the pulpit singing *Ave Maria*.

Once *Ave Maria* concluded, another selection began as the bridal party attired in deep purple gowns made their way down the aisle meeting his brothers lined across the altar. Then, the musical selection of the Wedding March began; everyone rose from their seats looking toward the back of the church. Tenderness flooded Francesco's heart as he watched his nervous bride stroll down the aisle as his apprehensive thoughts at this moment disappeared. Francesco stepped back with surprise when he saw his bride attired in a beautiful white gown and veil coming down the aisle of the sanctuary with her father by her side. Francesco was amazed that Lucia would have enough time to shop for a bridal gown. She was carrying the white roses and purple orchids with a linen handkerchief neatly tucked and fastened into the bouquet.

It was a beautiful day! The sun was shining through the stained-glass windows. Various colors of light were filtering throughout the church inviting all the observers to feel the holy presence that was there in the sanctuary.

Francesco closed his eyes for a moment imagining that gentle touch he had longed to give to Lucia many times in the past months as he whispered, "You are so lovely."

His bride appeared in a full-length white gown with a high laced neckline and long sleeves covered with beaded lace appliqués. Her full-length veil was attached to a crown of white roses and pearls adorning her head as her sparkling black spiral curls fell across her forehead and temples reminding him of a princess in a storybook as she carried the beautiful bouquet he had sent.

Now that the vows and communion were completed, *The Lord's Prayer* was sung. Francesco floated through the ceremony when he heard the words from the priest concluding the ceremony, "I now pronounce you man and wife. You may kiss the bride." Francesco had missed most of the wedding by not hearing distinctly what was said because he was drifting on a cloud. Francesco smiled as he held Lucia's hands in his—squeezing her fingers gently—noticing the shiny gold band that he placed on her ring finger. He gently lowered his head cradling her face as he brushed his lips across hers whispering, "I love you," conveying his love and joy he felt of having her as his wife. She captured his heart and was very precious to him. Then, Francesco dug into his pocket pulling out a hand-made delicate white cultured pearl comb sliding it in under the veil to her beautiful locks of hair. He whispered, "I wanted to buy you a little something extra to let you know how special you are to me."

Lucia's eyes twinkling as she raised her hand to his mouth gently brushing her lips across his once more. Looking at this man in a different view now, it struck her that not only was this man the one she loved, but she had to remember that the man was now her husband. This was the man that she would be spending the rest of her life loving, honoring, and taking care of in the days ahead that she vowed today in the ceremony. This would always be a special moment for them to reflect on over the years lying ahead. It was their special day! This was a day to hold on to in the future. The ceremony was small—but elegant.

After the wedding ceremony, the wedding party stood at the altar posing for a few photographs before they made their way across the street to a little Italian café where soft music was playing to join their guests. White linen tablecloths draped the tables where in the center of the table sat one red rose in a small crystal vase. The décor appeared to be very classy.

The champagne was opened filling crystal goblets for a toast to the couple. The newlywed couple stood as they entwined their arms around each other holding their gaze looking intensely at one another as their lips sipped at the rim of the goblet. "Forever, I pledge my love to you Francesco," whispered Lucia.

"Forever is a long, long time," replied Francesco as he slid his hands to her shoulders, "but forever will never be long enough for me."

Vito stood to his feet while raising his glass to a toast to the couple, "My wish to the both of you is for happiness, love, and good health in the coming years." Francesco clicked his glass against Lucia's as she smiled taking a tiny sip.

"Listen to the beautiful music," Francesco said stepping to the beat of the music, "Come on Lucia, and dance with me." Lucia looked gorgeous as she swayed to the rhythm of the music. Momentarily, she was feeling that she was floating on air for her affection for Francesco ran deeper than she cared to admit. Both young and old were now swinging to the music.

The music stopped. Lucia's mother and father made their way toward the couple to congratulate and wish them well before dinner was served.

The bride and groom along with the bridal party were served followed by their guests. The food appeared to be quite tasty. Italian wedding soup, chicken, rigatoni and all the trimmings were served filling each one to overflowing. A separate table stood at the far corner of the room with a three-tier white wedding cake on it. The cake was decorated with pale purple orchids in the center surrounded by cookies and pastries. The small group of guests that attended was charismatic and was enjoying the reception. After dinner, the music set a tone for dancing endlessly.

After the cake cutting and bridal dance, Francesco swept his new bride into his arms and carried her out the door. They made their way to the hotel that was only a few blocks away. Familiarity gripped their hearts at the sight of the hotel with envisioned memories. He pushed the door opened and carried her across the threshold with the moon and stars shining dim light throughout the room. They noticed that their belongings were already in the room. His voice displayed such passion as he began, "I plan on making you my wife in every way possible tonight." The kiss was tender as his lips pressed upon hers. "I am very nervous, but I promise I will be very gentle. We'll take it slow. I have waited a long time to have you and now it's finally happening."

"Francesco, I am very nervous too." Lucia let out a whimper. She knew that she wanted him as much as he wanted her. Lucia had never been with a man, but she felt that when the time had come, she would know what to do to please him. As she finished pulling off her wedding attire placing it on top of his black trousers that laid across the floor, she laid down on the cherry wood poster bed with her silky black curls feathered across the pillow as her head sank down on the bed. She gazed at him as she slid her arms around his neck pulling him closely. Suddenly, he was on top of her as their thighs met responding to one another. Neither had known that much pleasure as their mouths met. His hairy chest felt exhilarating against her smooth breasts. Their spirits soared as an eagle throughout the night. Exhausted, the couple lay tangled with their arms and legs wrapped around each other until early dawn.

Sounds of activity from the street awakened them. Lucia smiled at Francesco as she draped the sheets around her shoulders. Last night would always be a night to remember. "Good morning, Francesco," whispered Lucia.

Francesco only smiled as he reached for her as his breath was hot against her face. Their bodies once more linked with passion moving as they whispered love words to one another. As they lay in each other's arms, Francesco crushed her to his chest as tears filled his eyes from the emotions he was feeling deep inside. "I am very happy that you are my wife. Don't ever leave me for I could never go on without you. You mean everything to me. Believe me, there are no words to explain the way I am feeling at this moment!"

"Francesco, I will never leave you." Without another word, she hugged herself to him. Lucia knew that the two of them belonged together for their entire life. Wasn't that the vows that they spoke to one another?

CHAPTER 14

A PLACE CALLED HOME

There are many hurting things as we pass through life. The hurts of life should be written in the sand where the waters can come in to wash them out to sea to remember no more, but the good things that are worth remembering should be written on a stone to keep forever in our hearts.

(Author Unknown)

After spending several days in New York, the newlyweds, along with Francesco's brothers, acknowledged it was time to return to the small coal mining town where they would call home. Goodbyes were exchanged to Lucia's family. There was more baggage to take home than what was brought to New York. There were Lucia's personals as well as the wedding gifts. It was pleasant to have Vito and Alberto help cart all the baggage for the newlyweds to lighten the load. There were a lot of stories being told to Lucia by the brothers about Francesco that kept Lucia laughing and lighthearted upon their return to their new home. The journey was quite enjoyable with the anticipation of starting a new life together. They were filled with unexplained energy as they were floating weightlessly through the air for neither of them had ever felt this way before in their life. Life was good, and they hoped that this feeling would last forever.

Lucia was pointing to the sky as they stepped down from the train. "Look, Francesco, there is a rainbow in the sky. I was taught that a rainbow is a symbol of a promise from above that the world will never be destroyed by a flood. To us, it will be a symbol of our promise that we made to each other in New York that can never be broken for as long as we live. Francesco, you know that you can never find the end of that rainbow no matter how hard you search. Well, that will be the same for our marriage—never ending."

Francesco nodded in agreement. Then, he bent down, turned around looking toward the sky, and reached down as he gathered up their belongings as he prepared for their departure saying, "Let's get moving to the company house that we can call home for now. Lucia, the last time I took this path, the rain was pelting down with only thoughts of how I wished you were here. Today, you are not only a thought in my mind, but you can walk the path beside me.

Eventually, we will set out on a search for a place to call home away from the coal patch."

Vito and Alberto grabbed some of the luggage as they made their way in the direction to where the newlyweds would be staying before they returned to the boarding house.

Lucia said, "The abundance of not having much doesn't matter to me. If we have each other, this is the most important thing."

Francesco replied, "Every day will be a new day that we can celebrate our love to each other. Hopefully, the magic of our love will remain alive and will leave us spellbound with the tenderness and love we can give to one another. It should help us fall deeper in love with the passing of time. It is rough for both of us leaving family behind, but now we are a family."

One day upon Francesco's return from work Lucia announced, "It is time now to find a place to call home where we can raise a family. Our arrangement was temporary; I don't want to live in this row of coal company houses for much longer. It wouldn't matter what type of a house that I live in, but I would like something with a little more open space. In my heart, for as long as you are in the place, I know I can live in a shack. I desire a home a little farther away from the coal and the dust."

Francesco replied, "Fortunately, it will never come to us living in a shack for I have saved up enough money to buy a comfortable place even though money isn't real plentiful."

Francesco tossed his lunch box on the table speaking, "In the days before your arrival, I found a few places that captured my heart in the western part of town not far from here. I decided to wait until your arrival when both of us could seek our dream place. I want you to be happy. I would call home any place where you reside under my roof. Hopefully, the places that I had found are still available."

Francesco and Lucia decided on one of the places that Francesco had searched for before her arrival. The house was a double story wooden structure consisting of seven rooms with a large yard.

Lucia smiled. "I love this house overlooking the green valley with a few trees and the cows grazing in the distance." It sat in a small rural community that had several houses that were designed basically the same. As they entered the door, Francesco and Lucia noticed that the rooms were covered with printed flowered wallpaper making for a cozy setting. Once the place was furnished with chairs, carpets, and lamps, it would be a comfortable home.

Lucia remarked, "The yard isn't a huge one, but it would be enough for children to enjoy the outdoors playing tag, hopscotch, and baseball. Over there, would be a nice place with the shade of the trees to set a picnic table to enjoy eating and for children to play when the weather would get unbearably hot. A little girl could enjoy making paper dolls from old Sears Roebuck catalogs.

Francesco noted, "At the far side of the trees, a creek runs through that would be a place for our children to catch frogs, crabs, or build a dam with the many rocks. We can plant a couple of perennial flower beds up next to the house, which would brighten up the place and require some outdoor care to keep them blooming each year. Besides, there is enough land that a garden could be cultivated to grow fresh vegetables in the summer."

Lucia confirmed, "This little picturesque place serves as a reminder of life in the Old Country, but now it can be a place that we can call our home here in America."

On the day that they moved, Vito and Alberto loaded up a few of the couple's belongings in an old red borrowed pickup truck. Their new home was only a few miles from the boarding and company coal houses, which made for a short journey.

It would be exciting to think of Lucia creating her own little special touches to this place. Francesco pondered how the unique beauty of his surroundings brought a feeling of serenity and satisfaction to him knowing the countless hours devoted by Lucia.

Francesco alluded, "I was told toward the east end of town is the nearest furniture store where upstairs, on the second floor, machine made furniture is sold. On the lower level, there's a drugstore, grocery department, general store, candy store, and a butcher shop too."

Several purchases were made and brought to their new home for arrangement. Lucia would get up each day looking forward to adding little touches to decorate their new dwelling place. Lucia polished the wood in various rooms making it gleam against the light, placing draperies that were hand-made at the windows. At the foyer, a mirror hung above a two-seated oak bench with a basket of dry-cut flowers sitting in the corner welcoming visitors upon arrival.

One of the first rooms Lucia decorated was the bedroom. Lucia brought a hand-made quilt that her mother had created with white lace sewed onto an eyelet cotton material around the bottom edges. In the center of the quilt, a design resembling a glimmering blue star with various colors of blue patches and hundreds of white stitches was sewn onto the heavy white fabric.

"We will surely always cherish this beautiful quilt. It will keep us warm when the cold nights come upon us," said Francesco. "The room looks lovely with the cherry wood poster bed adored with the hand-made quilt."

"Yes, I also placed these hurricane lamps with the big blue flowers to light up the room when darkness of the night arrives. I sat the white lace dollies under the lamps and underneath the white milk glass style dish with the blue ribbing to fancy things up on the large cherry chest of drawers," voiced Lucia.

"Let's go into the parlor where we can look at the furniture arrangement. I placed the oak style rocking chair and the two-seated green cushioned loveseat here. Between the rocking chair and loveseat is where this end table with the lamp that has a green flowered, glass shade with a brass base will stay," said Lucia.

Francesco looking at Lucia said, "For now, the parlor is cozy enough for the two of us to spend our evenings talking until we can afford to purchase some other pieces. The dining area with the big square oak table and six chairs will be quite sufficient for us to have our dinners."

"We will make things work with the bare necessities until we can have more money to buy a few more things. Uh……really Francesco, I have some other items to put out once the cedar chest arrives from New York. I have several hidden treasures that I have been saving up for over the years for my special day of matrimony. I always called it my hope chest. A hope chest is started from a very young age in hope of finding someone to share the contents with forever. I'm glad I found you."

Francesco walked over to Lucia wrapping his arms around her shoulders as he pulled her close and began kissing her on the lips saying, "It looks like one fine afternoon, darling. Let's get outside and enjoy the fresh air for a little while. We've done enough inside work for a day."

Francesco spoke with enthusiasm, "Lucia, let's hike the spacious, rolling grassy grounds where white lavender, and various red, yellow, and pink flowers seem to flourish among scattered bushes and trees. As you know, my brother, Alberto, always likes to explore. Let's take our pattern from him today. This is such a perfect day!"

Surprised, they approached an area where there was a type of moss lining the floor of the garden not made by human hands. It was the most beautiful garden capturing the heart with fragrances coming from the honeysuckle trees sending a sweet perfume throughout the air. Birds were singing a melodious harmony of songs. A huge stone serving as a bench sat under the little clump of pine trees. The trees were swaying slightly from the gentle breeze that was blowing toward the sky.

"What a beautiful day to be alive!" exclaimed Lucia.

Francesco walked over behind the bush and pulled out a net and large container with a lid tightened down. He did not let Lucia know his intentions until this very moment arrived.

Lucia laughed, "What in the world are you doing with a net and container?"

Francesco announced, "Lucia, I would come out to this field for relaxation when I wasn't working. I was in hope of buying a house in this neighborhood. I observed that there were a variety of butterflies that seemed to nest among these wild flowers calling it their home. I thought it appropriate that once we married that you and I could walk these hills to catch butterflies. It would be a great hobby when we have the time. Also, it isn't an expensive hobby. Once we catch the butterflies in our nets, we will put them in this netted box that I made to inspect the beauty of their wings. We can look for rare species."

Lucia spoke, "The flowers in this *garden of the wild* are plentiful. It seems to draw the butterflies."

Francesco replied, "I noticed the same. I have been doing a little research and talked to some locals to learn more about the butterflies."

Lucia interjected quickly before Francesco went on with his little tidbits of knowledge on the butterfly. "Butterflies seem to like the warmth of the sun and a little puddle of water to quench their thirst I'm noticing."

"That's right, Lucia. The Monarch butterflies seem to feed off milkweed I'm told, and the American Painted Lady thrives on daisies, hollyhocks, and thistles." Francesco pointing with his finger, "You'll notice over there that there are patches of white and yellow daisy flowers. The butterflies seem to dance amidst these flowers. Beyond these flowers are the Sunflowers and goldenrod where various butterflies like to make their landing for the nectar. The Queen Anne's lace and clover are attractive to the insects. I believe this is the perfect place to find butterflies. At the end of our hunt, we will look at each one for specific details, and then we will let them fly into the air where they are free once more. It will be great to watch all the colors flying up into the sky at once showing us the diversity of colors."

"What a wonderful idea, Francesco! We can examine the different butterflies with the various spectrum of color upon the wings to see which is the most beautiful. We will have to be very careful, though, not to break any wings for they are very fragile. We can then pick out the winner."

As they ran through the field, they caught the creatures that flew on the various blooming flowers. It was as if they were on a playground turning back the hands of time to their childhood once more when the pleasure of life was carefree. The birds were singing a song to be enjoyed by the listening ear in this lovely *Garden of Eden*.

Lucia bent down to gather various flowers to make up an elegant bouquet. "Francesco, isn't it amazing what beauty can be created by picking these flowering weeds? I can bunch them all together, and it will create a beautiful bouquet to place in a vase in our home."

Francesco watching her as she gazed up at him while he spoke, "Lucia, the flowering weeds are pretty, but the butterfly is beauty beyond description and will always serve as a reminder to us that no matter how complicated life can become that there is beauty in life with its many colors. If you look hard enough, you will find it. You can't repair a butterfly's wing once it has been broken—the same as in life and marriage, we must handle each other gently with our words in order not to hurt and break each other's spirit."

Lucia still on her knees smiling said, "Those words coming from your lips are truly beautiful." After a moment's hesitation, Lucia looking up at him began speaking softly, "Francesco, tell me again how you discovered this lovely place?"

He answered, "One day I was looking for something to do for I was lonely without you here with me. I decided to take a walk in the country pretending that you were walking by my side. I noticed a colorful butterfly perched on a bush and decided that I would follow it to see where it lives. It was a game that I was playing by myself to occupy my time because I was missing you. The butterfly was flying and landing—flying and landing. Finally, it took off, and I ran with it as it flew. It led me to this perfect quiet secret place. I knew when I saw it that you would enjoy coming here with me. I decided that this would be a little adventure that we could share together in the country air."

She raised her hands to his shirt as her arms wrapped around his neck. As he glanced into her face, bending his head forward with one yank, pulled her close taking her lips on his searching for her tongue as the warmth of his body met hers causing her knees to weaken. The prolonged kiss caused them to struggle for their breath.

With fresh flowers in her hand, she dropped to the ground. Her hair fell loose around her face. She composed herself. As she spoke, her voice was quivering. "Francesco, uh... uh... when we get back to the house, I will have to find a porcelain vase to place the flowers in."

"Lucia, when we get back to the house, we not only will look for a vase, but I believe we will first take care of some real important business between you and me." Lucia let out a whimper for she knew that Francesco's lovemaking drove her wild.

Passion was exploding between their bodies as Francesco's lips met hers saying, "Lucia, why wait until we get back to the house?" He questioned her in a whisper as he pulled her to the ground laying her down in the moss where the scent of flowers invaded their sensory organs. "Do you want me to stop?"

She shook her head for she knew they were beyond that choice. Sensations ran through their bodies. Both were quickly peeling off their clothes as their bare skin began touching each other lighting a passion in their bodies from head to toe.

This woman was amazing! Francesco stood grinning as he reached for her soft hand pulling her up not wanting the heat of the moment to end. Exhausted from pleasure, the two of them dressed and made their way back to their home. She placed the bouquet of wild flowers in a clear glass vase on the kitchen table. It would serve as a reminder of what had transpired between them in the rolling hills.

CHAPTER 15

PARENTHOOD

The spray of brilliant colors is there to represent that life is color and warmth and light as quoted by Julian Grenfell.

In February 1916, life took a different twist. Francesco and Lucia became the proud parents of their first-born child, Mary.

"Oh Francesco," said Lucia. "She is a beautiful little black curly headed five-pound baby girl. I think she resembles you a lot. I am very happy holding her. Here Francesco, you take your daughter and cuddle her for a little while."

"Alright, I don't know much about babies. The only thing was when Mama had my younger siblings, we all would help. It's wonderful the feeling I have holding our newborn. She resembles a little porcelain doll after her mother. Thanks Lucia for birthing our own child. We will love her, protect her, feed her, and shelter her from the cold."

Lucia smiling answered, "Yes, things are good, and as any parent taking on the new role of parenting their firstborn child, excitement will fill the air most days for us. Watching our little child grow brings on a new meaning to life for each day is a new experience for children are quite unpredictable."

Francesco cradling the baby said, "It will be even more pleasant once there will be the pitter patter sounding on the floor boards as the baby grows. I love our little baby."

There was a wooden cradle built by one of the neighbor gentleman that sat right next to the big poster bed. Lucia made a rag doll for the little girl to add comfort when the child was lying in the cradle. Some of the items that was being used for the newborn had arrived from New York. They were placed in her hope chest from her younger day. One such item was a hand-made knitted pink baby blanket with a little white bonnet with pink ribbons across the front side designed by Lucia's mother.

Winter turned into spring, and spring turned into summer followed by fall turning back to winter. One season went into another as the seasons passed making the years go by quickly. As the years were passing, the house was filling up with children and added responsibilities. Mary was the firstborn child followed by Leonard (Lenny), Joseph (Joe), Josephine, John, Maria, and Madelyn with a fifteen to 24 month increment between. Italian custom is naming children after other family members. The children were all born healthy; and as the years passed, the older children could help with the care of the younger children and chores that needed done for the day. Francesco and Lucia watched life bringing in various new experiences for every child was unique in his own sort of way.

Francesco remarked, "Most days, our house is in motion by early morning before I leave for work in the coal mines. You are usually in the kitchen starting breakfast with your back bent over the old coal stove cooking bacon and eggs, oatmeal, or pancakes for me. It sure causes the family's taste buds to come alive with the scent of food lingering in the air from your cooking."

Lucia responded, "With the hard-manual labor that you do, you must have food in your stomach to give you energy for the day. Even though the work is hard, you never complain. I'm sure memories return for you of your father and mother back in Italy. You're falling in the same footsteps of providing for a family."

Francesco smiled, "I enjoy working each day to provide for my family while you await my return. You make my life pleasant. I will do anything to provide for my family. Life has changed for us in the last several years compared to when we first arrived from Italy."

"I now can write Mama and Papa to inform them about our expanding family with enclosing some money to help them in Italy. It makes me feel good! Papa can't go down to the sea to fish much anymore because of his declining health. Mama can't take care of the farm work like she did when my brothers and I were at the farm.

Mama's energy level has weakened. The farm is downsized, but the few grown siblings do help with some of the farm work. They go to the marketplace to sell crops periodically to help provide some income. Mama and Papa are now aging, which saddens me. I can't imagine Mama without energy for she could outwork any man back when I was in Italy. I long to return to Italy, but I know it isn't feasible."

Lucia chimed in, "I know that it takes a lot of money to provide for a large family here in America. Our family always has food on the table, clothes on their backs, shoes on their feet, and a house that is furnished with the bare necessities needed for daily living. The luxuries of chocolates, snacks, and ice cream aren't often seen, but food that is brought home is food items that are necessary for daily survival."

Lucia reiterated, "Usually flour, yeast, and sugar are on the top of my list so that homemade items can be cooked and baked. In a week's time, it is nothing for me to bake at least ten loaves of bread for our family to eat. It sure taste good having homemade bread with the spaghetti that I make at least once a week. The big pots of soup or beef stew helps in providing enough food through the week for our family meals too."

"Regardless of all the hardships, life is better here than back in the Old Country," stated Francesco.

Lucia said, "We have lighting at night provided by kerosene lamps. When the weather is cold outside, everyone is nestled in their beds. Our children sleep with three to four in a bed with body heat radiating to one another. The comforter blankets thrown across the bed shields each one from the cold of the season."

Francesco commented. "There is a big old coal furnace in the basement that has pipes running into a few of the rooms. Heat in the winter comes from the old coal furnace radiating heat throughout the house. When the furnace is fired up, it provides heat to the whole house to take the chill out of the air. I get a load of coal from the coal mine and dump it inside the basement window to a coal bin within the basement. Some days when the nights are cold, but the days are warm, the furnace makes the house a little too warm. We then open the windows for the temperature is a little suffocating."

Lucia said, "What more could we ask?"

Francesco began, "We have been provided with all we need. The old coal furnace provides heat, which I am thankful for its miserable being cold. The older boys are responsible for cleaning out the grate of the furnace that fills with ashes. The shovel rests alongside of the furnace for the boys to use."

Lucia nodded, "The boys help you out while you are working. They load up the ashes once cool in buckets and place them in a wheelbarrow wheeling them to the outside of the house. Ash piles are made around the back of the house." Once spring came, some of the ashes were scattered into the garden before the earth was tilled up for planting. This was a good way to get rid of the ash piles and soften the ground for tilling. Francesco would sometimes scatter the ashes outside the doorways of the house in the dead of winter to provide traction for walking when ice settled onto the paths.

Francesco made his way off to the coal mine, while Lucia had specified days of the week set aside to do certain chores. There had to be organization in a family to make things run smoothly for Francesco was taken away most days with the coal mining process. Each child pitched in to accomplish the various tasks that needed done.

Lucia yelled to Mary. "It's Monday! It's the day that the washing needs done. We'll get out the washboards and the wringer washer to get started."

Mary complained. "It is sure a hard way to launder clothes, but we only have a few outfits besides the bed sheeting. I'll string the clotheslines across the yard to hang the wet clothes to dry. Besides the clothes, diapers for the babies need to be done today to keep the babies dry and covered."

Lucia whined, "Diapers are more time consuming than the regular clothes for they have to be soaked in Clorox before washing. Clothes will dry fast today since it is sunny and bright."

"Catch me if you can," shouted Lenny in his little playful voice coming from behind the bedsheets hanging out to dry. It was fun hiding behind the sheets for it was a maze running through from one path to another.

Mary urged, "Come to my little tent house. We can set up a blanket on the ground to shade us from the sunlight and play in this little house. We could go to the apple, cherry, and pear trees and pick some of the ripened fruit for a lunch break in the tent."

"Mary, I'll go and fetch a container to put the fruit in," answered Lenny. The afternoon was spent dragging some fruit into the tent satisfying the hunger of the stomach before picking and folding the clothes from the clotheslines.

Mary giggled. "Maybe one night we can let this tent house up and sleep outside. We could try and catch some lightning bugs."

"It sounds like fun to me for I love to watch the bugs light up when it's dark," replied Lenny and Joe together. The boys ran through the field with jar in hand lighting up the night with a flashing insect lantern.

Next day Lucia asserted, "This is our ironing day. Mary, you can begin today with the easy ironing. Start to iron the starched pillowcases since they are flat straight pieces without any buttons. The rest of the clothes are sprinkled with some water from a watering bottle and rolled in a basket ready to iron too. I have the old metal iron heated on the coal stove to make it plenty hot to take all the wrinkles out of the clothing."

"Alright mother, I will get started on this project," exclaimed Mary. She was thinking in her mind that this was a dreaded project that she had to master every Tuesday. She wished that she could find a way of escaping, but she never alluded her thoughts to her mother.

Lucia's day began with talking to Francesco and sharing her anticipated plan for the day. "This is the middle of the week already. This is our baking day. Breads, cookies, berry and apple pies, and cakes can be made. It sure is a great way to save on money and helps feed our big family. We always have plenty of food for the children to eat."

"I love your apple pie. If you like, you can make that for me. I will think about it all day with my mouth watering until I return from work for some of that delicious pie," said Francesco kissing Lucia.

Lucia wrapping her arms around Francesco's neck chuckled, "I will make you that apple pie that you are hungry for today. It doesn't take much to throw flour and lard together to whip up an apple pie for dessert. Flour is cheap, and the various berries and apples are picked from the bushes and trees on our family property. I can even make a large pot of chicken soup and serve it with my fresh home-made bread, which will make us a meal for today."

She reassured Francesco. "When money is scarce, I can make coffee bread. Bread is always a filling type of food. There are many things that can be created with bread. One of my favorite family's recipes is using bread to make bread pudding. Bread is placed in a big casserole dish with sugared hot milk and butter poured over the top. Then, a few raisins are sprinkled in before baking for a short time. I'm not making that today for I'm sticking to the chicken soup and homemade bread."

Francesco said, "You are clever with your recipe ideas. You truly amaze me with the different concoctions you come up with at times. I'm not picky so whatever you cook and bake, I will eat."

Thursday arrival brought out the duster and broom. Sweeping across the wooden stands and floor picked up the film of dust that accumulated for the week. Each of the children would help with this chore.

"Today is Friday. I'm going over to the company store to buy some food and supplies to stock up for the upcoming week," Lucia remarked.

"I'll see you later today when I return from work." Francesco kissed Lucia as he turned and headed through the door.

Lucia would pack up the children and walk down over the hill to a little country company store. Each child would carry eggs from their chickens or fresh vegetables from the garden for exchange of flour and sugar from the company store to save on money from Francesco's earnings. Various items were selected and charged until Francesco got paid.

Lucia smiled, "Children, here are a few items for you to carry back to the house in your little burlap sacks. Load them up so the weight is divided among you that they aren't heavy."

Leonard said, "I look forward to Friday's for I know that I can trot off to the store regardless of not being able to purchase many items. I like looking at the shelf that contains the big jars with lids on top located at the front of the store for us children to explore. Under the lids is where the excitement is for me."

Their eyes would light up imagining what they could bite into first. There were pretzel sticks, circus peanuts, gummy bears, various flavored candy sticks, licorice, hot fireballs jaw breakers, malt balls, and jelly beans to name a few items of interest. The items cost only a penny, which was the reward to the children from Lucia for helping with the daily chores and for carrying the groceries back to the house. Lucia always managed buying a few items for the children for in her heart she didn't want the company store manager to think of her family as poor. Lucia accompanied by her children on their way home reminded any onlooker of a mother hen with her chicks dawdling back to their nest.

Saturday was a family day to spend working and chilling out at the homestead. For Lucia, Saturday was the day to prepare some extra baking of breads for the week ahead and preparing desserts in case of company and washing the family clothes to have ready to wear for Sunday church. Francesco and the boys would work outside, weather permitting. In the summertime, the carnival came to town. Riding the Ferris wheel and buying ice cream was a special treat. Sometimes a professional boxer thrilled the onlooker for a few rounds in the ring.

On Saturday evening, the big washtubs came out and were placed in the kitchen. The children would grab a bucket and run to the outside pump to fill their buckets. Upon returning, the water was heated on the old coal stove and poured into the washtubs for the children to wash their hair and to take the once a week bath.

Francesco and Lucia tried to place aside time for family and friends on the weekend. Sunday morning, the family attended church. They would meet with Francesco's brothers and their families. Alberto and Vito had married and had families of their own. Each Sunday was spent in visiting and resting up for the new week to begin. The children looked forward in playing tag, hopscotch, and ball with their cousins. In the summer, it was easy forming a baseball team with all the cousins taking position on the field.

CHAPTER 16

CHANGING SEASON

As individuals, each one of us at times in our life has had our own storm going on in the recesses of our own minds.

The children were growing as one season changed into another as the years were passing. It was a cold winter day when Francesco had to run out to the shed to get kerosene for the lanterns. "Come Mary and Josephine out to the shed to get some kerosene for our lanterns. You can help me fill up the lanterns and carry them back into the house that we will have light tonight in our house."

Francesco hesitated for a moment looking at his daughters as he fumbled around the several cans in the shed to get the right can to fill the lanterns. "Josephine, bring your lit lantern that I may pour more kerosene in it to fill it up. It will continue burning if I put more kerosene in it."

Josephine took a few steps to reach where Francesco was standing. Josephine was a pleasant, pretty, little girl with big brown eyes with a head of black curly hair.

Francesco bent down pouring the liquid into Josephine's lit lantern when instantly a flame caused an explosion flying up toward Josephine catching her blue cotton dress on fire.

"Dash the fire out quickly!" Francesco screamed. "Roll on the floor Josephine." Sweat began pouring over Francesco's entire body from the panic he was feeling. "Roll.... Roll.... I tell you!"

Josephine wasn't paying attention to a word that was coming out of Francesco's mouth for she was frightened by the happening. She started running around the shed in terror screaming for help. "Papa.... Papa.... help me! Help me!" The fire took off from the air that was being fed by the child's running. Her dress was totally engulfed in flames.

Mary ran to her sister, but to no avail. She could do nothing to dash the fire out. She was panic-stricken. As Mary ran toward her sister, a flame hit her blouse.

"Mary, stay away from your sister." Francesco yelled hopelessly. Both girls were now on fire and out of nowhere came a bucket of water drenching the girls and causing the flames to subside. Then, Francesco found an old rag blanket lying in the far corner to wrap around the girls. Leonard stood there crying with the empty bucket in his hands.

Josephine fell to the ground crying and screaming in pain, "Papa…. I hurt so badly."

"Both of you lie still until I get back. I will bring wet towels to wrap around you. I must get you both to the hospital quickly."

Francesco ran into the house and cried to Lucia, "There has been an accident. There was an explosion. Both Mary and Josephine are burnt, but Josephine is burnt very badly. You stay here with the other children until my return for I am taking them to the hospital."

Lucia stood there with a blank stare on her face not comprehending what had happened. It seemed that she felt no emotion regarding Josephine's accident. Maybe, she was in shock and didn't know what to do at this point.

Then, Lucia screamed, "Francesco, I must come with you and help."

"No, you mustn't for someone needs to stay with the other children," roared Francesco.

Lucia stood still feeling helpless presently. Francesco was right regarding her remaining at home not only for the children's sake—but because she was very weak when trying to handle emergencies. Lucia stood sobbing as she watched Francesco run out the door.

Francesco hated to leave Lucia in such a state, but he had to sever ever moment for the welfare of his little daughters. He didn't want Lucia to see the girls' injury from the accident for it may send her into shock, which he would have something else to deal with at the hospital. Out the door he ran as fast as his legs would carry him.

"I'm here with cold, wet towels. I will load you both into the car to take you to the hospital. I'm picking the both of you up, and we will be on our way as fast as we can," hollered Francesco.

Upon arrival at the hospital, Josephine had fallen into a state of unconsciousness. The hospital staff whisks her away for treatment.

She was now in a hospital room with Francesco beside her bed. He was sobbing as he grabbed her little bandaged hand in his trying to assure her that she would be alright.

"Josephine…. Josephine…. It will be alright, baby. I am sorry for what has happened to you. It's my entire fault that this accident has happened. I must have filled your lantern with gasoline instead of kerosene causing the explosion. You must be in such pain all because of my mistake."

"Josephine…. Oh, my little Josephine…." Her name came out as a sob as he knelt by her bed. "I don't know where your sister Mary is presently, but I believe she will be alright."

A nurse brought Mary back into the hospital room, where her father and Josephine were resting, with several bandages wrapped around her arms covering the burns. She stood beside him with tears running out the corners of her eyes. On the other hand, Josephine was bandaged with only her eyes protruding through the white gauze. Suddenly, Josephine opened her eyes when she heard her name spoken. Pain radiated through her eyes.

"Papa, I love you! Don't leave me," whispered Josephine as she seemed to awake from her sleep.

A nurse dressed in white and a doctor wearing green scrubs walked into the room. The doctor had a stethoscope dangling around his neck. "Francesco and Mary, please wait out in the hallway."

"Papa…. is Josephine going to die?" Mary asked.

"No, sweetheart, she'll be alright. We must pray that she is alright. Right now, she is in pain because of the burns over her body. The doctor gave her a sedative, which will make her sleep, so she doesn't feel the pain. You are probably in pain with your burns too. You are being a brave little soldier."

"My burns on my arms hurt too, but they are only on a few places of my arms. I can't imagine how badly Josephine is feeling for she has burns all over her body."

"We must not think on that right now. We must think that Josephine will get well once again." Francesco contemplated that Josephine must get well for both Lucia and he would not know how to deal with losing a child.

After waiting for quite a while, the doctor called Francesco back into the room. "I'm sorry, but your daughter has passed away. There was nothing that I could do for her. Her body was burned extensively."

Francesco let out a yelp, "No! No! It can't be! I can't let her go! I can't! I can't! Oh, dear God, how can this be?" Francesco had to get his emotions under control. "I can't accept life without her!" Mary jolted back inside the room upon hearing cries of grief.

Francesco along with Mary remained by the bedside. Josephine was gone. How could he explain this to Lucia? A feeling of hopelessness raced through his entire body. Francesco knelt and cradled Josephine in his arms crying. It felt like everything in his body was draining out of him. He was in shock for he thought she would be alright after a week or two.

"How can this be, Lord? I am trying hard to make a good life for my family and now this tragedy. What will I tell my Lucia? How much more can I take?" Francesco dropped down on his knees by

Josephine's bed sobbing uncontrollably. "Lucia will be heartbroken losing her little girl."

The doctor reached over placing his hand on Francesco's shoulder while Mary reached down feeling pain from her burns to touch her sister's hand tearfully whispering as she sobbed, "I'll... see you in heaven someday my little sister. You'll be up there with the angels looking down at me until I get there with you. We must let you go to God now! Papa, we must be strong for Mama!"

Josephine's face was the picture of peace as she laid there. The doctor tried to usher Francesco from the room. Francesco glanced into the doctor's eyes and said, "What will I tell Lucia? This is such an unexpected tragedy. Let us have some private time with Josephine before we make our way home."

"Can we take you home?" asked the doctor.

"No, I will find my way home a little later. Let me sit down for a little while with my daughter Mary until I can get this in perspective. We will then make our way home." His very soul seemed to be taken from him.

Upon returning home late, Lucia met him and Mary at the door. Francesco scooped Lucia in his arms and buried his face in her shoulder weeping helplessly.

"I am sorry, Lucia! Why? Why?" cried Francesco.

"Francesco what has happened that you are crying?" asked Lucia. "Mary, are you in pain that you are crying too?"

"I'll be alright, Mama, but I have much pain from my wounds," replied Mary.

Francesco had to break the news gently to Lucia. His heart was broken with grief. He glanced at Lucia and Mary with tears streaming down his face. "Lucia, I don't know how to tell this to you. Mary, please leave your mother and myself alone for a little while. We need a few minutes of privacy to talk a minute."

"Alright Papa." Mary turned and made her way to her bedroom sobbing from the pain and brokenhearted emotion she was feeling, but watching her father cry really disturbed her.

His voice was gentle as he spoke softly. "Josephine has gone to live in another house. It's a place that there is no more suffering or heartache. It's a place where there is no more sickness. She's in God's arms now. She was in much pain from the burns that she had to leave us, so she won't be in pain anymore. The house where she will be living is a mansion far more beautiful than I could ever give to her. It's a place where there truly are *streets of gold*."

Lucia thought for a moment while trying to comprehend what Francesco was saying. She sobbed uncontrollably, "She won't be coming back to our home. Is that what you're trying to tell me? I want my daughter…uh…. uh…. you go get her wherever she is and bring her to me. I will make her well. Mother's always make their children feel better when they are sick. She doesn't need to live in a mansion or find *streets of gold*. Our home is comfortable to keep her safe."

Lucia stood crying while beating her fists into Francesco's chest. Pain was welling up within her as she stood crying like she never had cried before this time. The only time Lucia had cried hard was the night when Francesco was leaving New York unable to take her with him.

"Lucia… Lucia… you must get a hold of yourself for the sake of the children. We both must get ourselves together. This ordeal is not making it easy for us to keep our composure. It is difficult for me too. I feel like I was run over by a truck. Josephine is in a better place, and this situation is beyond my control. I want her back with us as much as you do, but there is nothing that I can do to bring her home anymore. It's all my fault!"

Francesco cradled her to his chest—crying on each other's shoulder. As he let loose of his hold on her, he watched Lucia fall to the floor. Seeing the hopelessness in Lucia's eyes was more than Francesco could bear. Lucia appeared to be falling immediately into a terrible downcast mood from the shock of the situation. Francesco felt that there might be no turning back for the love of his life. He hoped that time would help both Lucia and himself adjust to their loss, but things would never be the same again. Both parents were truly broken-hearted with no answer of mending their hearts.

Mary came back to where her parents were and stood watching with no words to speak. Francesco and Lucia were devastated from their loss that they failed to heed to Mary's needs. She kept all her sad thoughts wrapped up in a special compartment of her own heart. Not only was Mary in pain from her burns, but she was in emotional pain from the loss of her sister that she would play big sister too.

The morning arrived to celebrate Josephine's life. The day of the funeral, the sun was shining. Only a handful of people attended, being there were few acquaintances known to the family since coming over from Italy to establish their roots. Friends and family seem to stay at a distance when a child passes away for lack of words to say. Most weren't sure if this death was caused by a disease that was contagious.

Mary standing over the coffin whispered to her parents, "Josephine looks like an angel with her lockets of dark hair draped around her face and the flowing pink silk night gown covering her burns to disguise the pain she must have felt."

Vito and Alberto and their families came to the funeral trying to support the loss of their brother's child.

Vito replied hugging Mary to his chest, "Your sister is an angel. We must not think of what she must have felt. The pain is now over. She will never have any pain again. Think of all the good memories that you have with Josephine to get through this ordeal. Funerals sure seem to bring people out that you never see for years, but this funeral will be different for your family is new in the area. Uncle Alberto and I have been quite busy with our own families making it difficult to have as close of a connection since coming from Italy."

Mary stood staring without a reply.

The fond memory of hankies presented in New York now served for drying the tears staining the eyes for it was tough to lose a child. Sadness lingered in the air. Lucia's grief in the loss of her daughter caused much pain. It was hard for Francesco to see Lucia in such pain or to try to comfort and encourage her now. His heart was breaking into pieces from the sorrow he was feeling from the death of his child too. He felt responsible for this tragic accident. Lucia wasn't talking and had a blank stare on her face since this ordeal began.

At the funeral, Francesco continued blaming himself for the fire. "I can't believe instead of putting kerosene in the lantern, I had placed gasoline, which had caused the fire and explosion." Francesco cradled his face in his hands as he stood sobbing uncontrollably. "I apologize for making such a dumb mistake. I should have been holding the lantern; therefore, my little Josephine would still be alive. It would have been me instead of my little baby girl."

Vito began speaking, "You must stop torturing yourself. Mistakes happen for a reason. There are many things in life we don't understand, and sometime things happen that are beyond our control. You can ask a hundred questions, but you will never have an answer. It was one of those misfortunate accidents that occurred. The best answer may be that life bruises people."

Vito and Alberto with their families gathered around Francesco and Lucia and their family to try to comfort them in this time of sorrow hoping to help mend their broken hearts. Life had to continue regardless of the accident.

CHAPTER 17

HARD TIMES

—————◆—————

Grains of sand cause the oyster in his shell irritation.
The oyster lets loose, and this creates a beautiful pearl.
The same is found in irritating life's situations while
molding and shaping one into a beautiful pearl.

The good days were becoming a thing of the past. With losing a child, the good times remembered were now fading from view, and life was becoming very troublesome these days. Francesco remembered the rolling sea coming over from the Old Country. The ship had to keep sailing despite the storm. He now felt that he had been thrown on the sea of rocks where hope was dim.

The Great Depression of the 1930s was now in full swing. Gone now were the days of joyfulness. Money was growing scarce with the passing of days. Lucia was acting strange lately. Most days she felt abnormally anxious. Vain imaginations flooded her mind. In the past, Lucia was the one who would always bind the family together. Now the cord seemed to be slackening and things were not right anymore. The environment was growing tense with each passing day. Lucia was struggling with persistent sadness, and life's situations didn't help make matters any better.

Lucia took on a new personality and would become very irritated at the smallest of things. One morning Mary was happy and began singing softly like any teenager at fourteen would do. Lucia screamed at her at the top of her lungs, "Mary, I want you to go outside this very moment. I've had enough of your noise as I can stand this morning! Don't come in until I tell you that you are allowed."

"Mama, it is pouring down rain! I can't go outside in the rain. I need to get dressed for school or I'll be late," cried Mary.

"I told you to get out of this house and get out now! I don't care what it's doing out there! All I care about is that there is no noise coming from out of your mouth! When I instruct you to obey me, you must do it without question for I am your mother." As Lucia was speaking, she went over and grabbed Mary by the shoulder with her hair in her other hand and pursued to throw open the door pushing her through and locking the door as it slammed shut.

Mary hit the ground face first as she was crying loudly and speaking to herself, "What did I do to deserve such treatment. I was only singing a tune we were taught in school. I was taught that it is good to be happy."

Mary laid on the ground face down, crying her heart out for the way her mother was treating her these days. The rain had wet her night clothes. Every nerve in her body was screaming for help. Her head hurt from where her mother had pulled her hair and a bruise was forming on her shoulder of a deep purple color from the pressure of another's hand. She would be late for school if her mother wouldn't let her back into the house soon. Mary did not understand the mood swings that her mother was experiencing. She never knew what occurrence would set her mother off to become violent. Life was hard most days for Mary, and she hoped that the day would eventually come that she could put these bad memories behind her even though things seemed to be getting worse.

Suddenly, Jenny appeared on the scene. Jenny was quite a friend to Mary these days. Jenny lived adjacent to Mary's house. "Mary, are you alright? You must tell your father when he comes home from work today what is going on with your mother. This type of behavior cannot continue. You could get hurt very badly. I don't feel your mother is doing this intentionally. Your mother is very ill and needs some help from a doctor to make her well. I could ask my mother to take her to the doctors. People do get sick sometimes, and that is why there are doctors that can help."

Mary replied, "What you're saying is true, but how can you go to a doctor if you have no money to pay him? My father has little money with the Depression going on. He is trying to work it out on his own."

"Mary, come over to my house. We are about the same size, and I will lend you a dress to wear to school today. We can walk and talk about whatever you want to talk about as we go to school."

Mary lifted herself from off the ground and smiled as Jenny stretched out her hand to help her.

Mary began speaking, "Jenny, you are my very best friend that I can share my innermost feelings. We have run through the fields playing lightheartedly while I tell you of my deepest hurts and darkest nights. Without you as my best friend, I know that I would have no desire to continue living. My inner spirit is being pulled down with this family situation. It's hard to see a bright side when everything seems to be looking dim. Others don't understand until they walk through a similar valley. You are the only person that I can confide in with my secrets. Jenny, you are such a good listener and always accept me for the person I am."

Jenny replied, "Many times I have cried for you for I want to help you through these rough times, but I realize that there is nothing I can do except to lend an ear. I feel together that the void is filled to have someone to talk to and share hurts and heartaches."

Mary nodded, "You have a good heart, Jenny. Over the last few years, my father has worked in the coal mines acquiring all kinds of property and assets, but with the Great Depression settling in on America, the economy is changing. The renters he has in his rental properties are not paying their rent to him. It makes for a struggle to meet the bills each month. Not only is there the responsibility of paying the many properties overhead, but there is the problem of feeding the family when there is no money to do it. Happiness is being turned to hours of worry for money is scarce."

Jenny interrupted, "As in the days gone by, your mother would walk to the company store to acquire food to feed all of your family.

She would walk a mile or more with you children following behind her along the road as a duck with her ducklings to help carry back the groceries to the house."

Mary replied, "Yes…. uh…. uh…. things have changed. Now purchasing the bare necessities to feed us children is really all that matters. Items such as flour, bread, cheese, and powdered milk can get us through a week without going hungry. Some days picking up the pieces to go on seems impossible for my mother. Despair seems to spell defeat in her life now. Feelings of defeat are evident in my mother's life for she doesn't possess the determination to go on anymore. She has no will to finish the race that she is running. All hope seems to be gone. Upon rising each day, my mother feels that no day is a good day anymore since the loss of Josephine. There is no purpose in her life anymore. My father tries to assure Mama that things will be alright, regardless of the situation, because with loving each other they will make it through these dark nights someway."

Jenny began, "Your father has become stronger in coping with the loss of Josephine, but your mother refuses to see any brightness in any situation. She keeps looking through a dark glass not going forward; she keeps looking back at the past."

Mary nodded her head up and down saying, "Most day's Mama is experiencing fatigue with a tight band of pain around her head, sleeplessness, no interest, and feelings of fear. She says that inside all she feels is a feeling of wanting to die. She has not alluded this fact to the family, but she has told me of these feelings."

Mary stood thinking for a moment without speaking. If her mother had it her way, she would prefer being gone from existence. Mary felt that few people really cared about what her mother was going through anyhow.

"I must tell you that my father is taking on a different new personality too. Josephine's death has caused the family to be turned upside down. With the economy in such bad shape, it is hard to keep a positive attitude. The world seems to be crashing down on him. Coping not only with Mama's problems, but all the responsibilities of raising a family, is plaguing hard on him. On weekends, he comes home from work, but he then leaves and doesn't return until the wee hours of the morning from his card playing and drinking with his friends. When he is drinking, he doesn't have to face reality for a while. This has become the routine for my father to deal with this situation. My Mama seems to be second place in his heart now days from the grief he is feeling."

Mary continued espousing more of the story to Jenny. "Mama lays awake at night very tired from her daily chores, but she is unable to sleep in the empty bed worrying about father. She tells me that some nights she would fall asleep soaking her pillow with the many tears that fall from her eyes. Life seems to be at its lowest point with only despair at hand. Many nights she imagines father in the arms of another woman. She fantasizes him dancing the way they danced back in New York with another love."

"Each day Mama tries to believe my father that things will get better, but Mama cannot hold on to hope of brighter days. As the days pass by, the situation is getting worse with Mama. She is losing touch with reality. She wants no contact with the children like they don't exist. She dances through the house pretending of the past years spent in New York. The children, especially myself, has been taking over the role of being mother to the younger siblings. Many days, Mama stays in bed and locks the door without letting anyone in her room. She refuses to eat for days at a time. Some days, the family hears her dancing around the room singing at the top of her voice making a disturbance throughout the house. Sometimes, I try and talk to her through the keyhole; but Mama refuses to listen to any reasoning. Mama bangs very hard on the door creating a loud noise that anyone passing by outside would wonder where all the hammering is coming from inside the house."

"I am so very sorry for you and your family," said Jenny. "If there is anything I can do for you, please let me know. I will not let anyone know your secret."

"I do not want any of my friends at school to know my family situation. I am very embarrassed with the way my mother is acting. I will never invite any of my friends over to the house for milk or cookies to observe this problem. These kinds of problems are best hidden in a closet to remain in complete secrecy," alleged Mary upon arriving at the schoolhouse with Jenny.

Mary had arrived home from school to find her mother locked once again in her room.

"Mama, please let me come in to talk to you." Mary begged.

"No, I can't talk to anyone! No one understands how my head feels. It feels like there is a great pressure in it and that it is ready to explode," expounded Lucia. "Really, I'm happy being alone dancing in my room. I'm remembering New York. I'm practicing so that I can go back there to perform once again."

"Mama, if you would talk, it might help," said Mary trying to reason with Lucia. "Mama, you can't leave your home and children to perform. We want you to stay with us. We need you here."

"No, my life is over. There is nothing good anymore to live for on this earth," cried Lucia. "There is little money, and all the property we have will be lost in time. Your father doesn't want to admit it, but we are going to lose all our possessions after we worked hard all these years because of circumstances in the land. Your father stays out late at night. He doesn't care about me anymore! I will dance myself into my grave if I don't get back to New York."

"Mama, you are pushing him out the door by your actions and imaginations. You must stop talking this nonsense. You must admit that everyone is in the same predicament. We can go to the company store and get our food like the others—paying for it later. What is your worrying achieving? It's only making all of us miserable. Time will change things for us. It won't always be this way without an abundance of food and little money. If the situation doesn't change, look at the bright side of things by thinking—at least we have our health and each other."

"Each other is not good enough for me," yelled Lucia. "I want my Josephine back here with me. It's not fair that my little girl is gone from me forever. Why don't you take over being the mother to your brothers and sisters, and I can go away somewhere to forget all these struggles of life? I want to go back to New York where life is carefree."

Lucia was struggling daily with sadness from the loss of Josephine; but with the Great Depression coming on, it was making matters worse. Reasoning with Lucia when she was going through these spells was useless. Her reasoning power was clouded by whatever plagued her mind thoughts.

Mary was 16-years-old now. She had to quit school to care for her siblings. She was a very shy young lady. Many days, Mary kept many sad feelings deep inside. Sometimes, Mary would disappear with her siblings for a walk through the fields. She would pick up bouquets of flowers that were blooming. The beautiful colors of the various wild flowers were great for creating an arrangement to gather to place in a vase for brightening up the house. Even the wild dandelion with their bright yellow colors mixed with the Johnny Jump Up served a purpose. The array of the scents through the house seemed to cheer anyone's mood, but then upon return to reality the problem still was there. Feelings that seemed to overwhelm Mary at times brought tears to her eyes.

"Mary, you must not talk to anyone about your mother's strange ways," warned Francesco. "People will alienate us if you do. We do not air our laundry. I hope you understand what I am telling you."

Mary stood shaking her head as Francesco continued, "The only one you can talk to is me. Through time, your mother will get well if we treat her right. She is going through a hard time with losing Josephine and the Great Depression. Lucia can't seem to cope." Francesco explained to Mary that her mother appeared to have some type of illness. "I am taking her to the doctors, but with little money, I'm at my wit's end with no improvement in sight." He advised Mary once again, "I warn you, please do not talk to anyone about your mother! This is a family matter that should remain only in this house with you and the other children!"

Mary discerned in her heart that she had disobeyed her father's wishes for she had talked with Jenny venting some of her innermost feelings. She would never disclose her disobedience to her father.

Francesco would come home from laboring in the coal mines all day trying to make sense of it all. To make matters worse, Francesco still was going out at night with the guys drinking and playing cards. He told Mary that Lucia would get better, but he lost hope that things would ever be the same.

One night, he came home at 3:00 AM; and Lucia yelled at the top of her lungs throughout the house for all the children to hear. "Francesco, you are ridiculous! You're becoming a drunk! We have no money; and now, you go with the guys to play cards with the little bit of money we have playing poker. Maybe, you are not playing cards at all."

He would yell back, "You are not a wife to me or a mother to my children anymore! What do you expect me to do? At least with the guys, I can have a decent conversation and have a laugh or two. I detest your behavior! I am trying to help you, but you refuse any help from me. I love you very much, but you are hurting me by the way you behave! You expect Mary to do all the household chores and care for the children. It's not fair to Mary the way you are acting for sure, but more than that, it is certainly not fair to any of us in this house."

"I will not share my bed with you anymore for you don't deserve to sleep with me. You can sleep with the guys if they make you happy," said Lucia.

Mary was awakened and heard the entire fight. This type of situation was going on each week, and she would lay awakened many nights crying her eyes out wishing that things would get better in their home. She hated to hear her parents fighting. Her father would share bits and pieces of the puzzle with Mary. Apparently, he didn't want to worry her with grown-up problems.

One day her father returned from work and said, "Mary, we will have to sell our house here and move to a farm. I'm making one last attempt to help your mother. The doctor suggested that this might be better for your mother. It would be quiet. Your mother may do better in this type of environment breathing in the fresh country air. I hate the thought of leaving this place where your mother and myself first began for there are many memories to leave behind."

"You never leave memories behind. You take them with you wherever you may go," replied Mary.

"Actually, I found a small farm out in the country that I feel appropriate for us to try and start again. This country setting hopefully will help to encourage Lucia to get her mind working properly."

Francesco was crushed by the problems that he was facing each day. He was at "the end of his rope" not knowing which way to go. He loved his wife very much and hated to see the torment that she was going through frequently. He would try everything he could to try and make things alright once again, but nothing seemed to work. He felt Lucia was right about his playing cards and drinking. He didn't want to act this way, but this was his escape to have a little enjoyment during all the troubles he was experiencing. He was losing his patience and felt like a firecracker ready to blow up. Maybe the move to the farm would change the situation not only for Lucia but for his own well-being.

One day out of the blue Francesco shouted out to the children as they played in the back yard, "Let's gather around here to have a family talk."

Francesco talked earlier in passing to his children about making a move to the country, but he only dropped the idea for he was very apprehensive of picking up his family and settling once again to a new location. Times were hard these days with the Great Depression in full swing, and it would make it even harder to have to move his family to another location. Despite his reluctance, he must do what the physician advised by taking one last chance to see if his little porcelain doll would improve in a different environment. He wanted to bring back the days of happiness into his home as it was in the past. He would like to use a magic wand to turn back the hands of time. If only he could find the solution to the little mountain he was climbing, he would be able to slide down instead of climbing up. These days seemed to be colored in gloom and misery.

"I want to walk back in the woods as we talk. Your mother is watching out of the window, and I don't want her to get the wrong impression about what is going on out here. I love your mother very much, and I will do whatever it takes to make her well once again. She is not herself these days. I had told you previously that we may have to move to the country, and now the time has come that we will have to pick up and go."

The children stood in silence as each had their eyes fixed on Francesco as he spoke taking in every word that was being spoken from his mouth. They were of the age of innocence not realizing the full picture before their eyes.

"I like it here! I don't want to move," shouted Maria.

Francesco continued speaking, "I found a little farm that sits up on a hillside that seems to be affordable and the perfect place to raise you children. Lately, I can hardly remember the days when your mother was on top of the world with happiness. We came here to find our *streets of gold*. Some days, I feel we are looking in the wrong direction. Most days for her now seem to be spent in her losing the joy of living. She seems to be taking a downhill journey of dwelling on problems making everything tense in the house. The stress of these worries has your mother very disturbed most of the time. If I don't try to help her soon, I am afraid that her brain will snap. Truthfully, I don't know what to do to help, but I must try anything I can think of to see if it will help. Some days, she talks out of her head; and if this continues, I will eventually have to place her in a facility." Francesco had tears seeping out the corners of his sad eyes as he talked with the children. Mary had a handkerchief in her pocket handing it to him to wipe his eyes. The children stood motionless as if in a trance. Francesco hated his children watching him lose control, but the tears were a language that his family understood.

"I want to be able to help your mother to regain a few moments of happiness as I am remembering the days not too long ago. We didn't feel all our hearts sinking like a man drowning under the water.

This is a terrible thing that has happened. She is suffering within, but we must have the strength and courage to get through this problem. Even though we are going through this difficult time, let's try to show kindness and understanding toward your mother. I want her to snap out of this state."

Mary spoke up, "I heard the neighbors talking through the window one night that maybe an evil spirit has caused Mama to be the way she is."

"That's a lot of nonsense, Mary," snapped Francesco. "I believe that your mother is worrying herself to death, and she doesn't know for some unknown reason how to stop worrying. She seems to be overwhelmed with the littlest of problems. She is obsessed with fearing what will be in the future. I am very bewildered by our situation, but I know I must find a cure for your mother. The neighbors like to gossip for they haven't walked in our shoes. I told you Mary not to mention anything about your mother's illness, and now you can understand why I suggested that you not talk about such things. No one understands these problems for I don't understand it myself. We will try to keep this hidden. Only the doctor knows what advice to give us for your mother's improvement. We will hope that this storm soon passes."

CHAPTER 18

MOVING PLACES

———◇———

The promise of a Rainbow from the storm you're passing through,
When your way is clouded, and you don't know what to do,
There's a promise of a Rainbow that's soon to come shining into view.

Mary had a lot of hesitation about moving to a farm since her father made the announcement. She had friends where they lived; and if they left, she wouldn't see the neighbors and friends very much. It would be a real adjustment to live in a remote neighborhood with a few scattered houses.

One day as Mary and Jenny was walking home from school, they stood observing the playfulness of the children that was going on at the playground.

Mary began speaking, "Isn't it great to stand and watch the different groups of children playing under the sunny skies? Over there are youngsters swinging and giggling as they are swinging high to the sky. Swinging as high as the swing can take them. It makes one feel like a bird flying."

Jenny replied, "The sun is spraying fun and laughter for all to enjoy."

"I long in my heart to be carefree from life's burdens for a little while," said Mary. "I can't remember a time in my life when I was able not to have so many responsibilities hanging over my head."

Jenny answered, "I understand. Look over there. There is another group of boys that are tossing around a football as they tackle each other throwing one another to the ground."

"It looks like fun," Mary answered as she stood gazing toward the playground. "I wish that I could turn back the hands of time to the happy days because I long for their return. I don't want to move to a place where I don't know anybody in the neighborhood. It's lonely enough in this world. Soon, it will be lonelier not having anyone to talk to about what is taking place in my family life. The only one I share my secrets with is you. You're my best friend, Jenny."

"I can imagine how you're feeling. Mary, we aren't that far away. If things get bad, you still can walk to my house. It would be a little bit of a longer walk but not an impossibility," said Jenny.

Mary whimpered. "You always have understood and helped me at my low points in life. I don't know what I would do without you. Of course, I will see you at school."

"Keep your chin up! I'm here for you. I've been told that if we keep the right attitude, we can make it through anything," said Jenny.

The day arrived to start packing for the move. Packing things up was never an easy process, but the children were now old enough to help. Francesco had taken the children to the future home earlier to get them adjusted to the new surroundings.

Francesco explained, "Children, we must begin packing. The boys and I will lift the heavier pieces onto the small truck. I have a lot of newspapers that I have been saving to wrap the dishes, lamps, and breakable pieces. We don't have many items, but it will be a chore to pack the few breakable items. I have borrowed an old pickup truck from one of the men from the coal mines to move. With all your help, we will load up the truck with our few family possessions to move to the country."

Francesco announced, "Mary will go with me on a few trips back and forth to help unload the truck with the family personal things that have to be placed in closets at the old farmhouse. Each of you have your one church outfit and a couple of play outfits and a few school clothes. I want to make the move as stress-free as possible for your mother. Mary will be responsible of setting the furniture and belongings in place to make the house cozy and comfortable for all of us. Lucia is not in any shape for decision-making. She must depend on Mary to keep stress at a minimal these days. Your mother seems a little better with the anticipation of the change."

Mary spoke, "Loading and unloading boxes will take a lot of energy. At my young age, I still have the energy to accomplish the task. We'll place pots and pans in the cupboards. The towels, wash-cloths, and clothes should be folded and placed in drawers. There is an unending list of things needing attention before the family can live in the place comfortably, but for the time being, it will be a place called home."

Francesco shook his head in agreement with what Mary was saying. He went over and patted Mary on the shoulder to show his understanding.

The anticipation of all the things needing done made Mary a little nervous. Once she lived in the house, she could put the pri-orities needing attention at the top of the list; but for now, at least the family would have a roof over their heads and shelter from the cold nights.

The trip traveling up a hill on a long winding dusty, dirt road seemed to take a little while to get to the main structure. It would be a shorter distance walking through the field than taking the dirt road. The white wooden, two-story farmhouse sat on a little over five acres of land. There was a creek situated on one side and a building resembling a barn surrounded by some trees to the other side. The farmhouse and barn were out of view until reaching the top of the hill where the land leveled off to a flat parcel.

Francesco stated, "The house doesn't look like much, but it is well built and will be a warm dwelling place until I can make some improvements. Mary, I know the inside of this house isn't the great-est either. Most of the rooms are covered with wallpaper that appear to need replaced. When we have time and money, we will paint the outside and inside. We can change some of the wallpaper or paint over the old paper to at least make the house more attractive. It will give us the feeling of the house being fresher and cleaner with some of these improvements."

"Papa, I know that time is of essence, and the remodeling can be done while our family lives here. The exterior of this wooden house is dirty white with the paint peeling. A coat of paint is needed badly," remarked Mary.

Francesco replied, "I'm aware of the various repairs. The repairs will take a little time, but maybe keeping busy at the house will be good for all of us including Lucia. There will not be any time to think on the negative aspects the family is going through presently. It won't cost that much for what needs done here."

"I know that money isn't plentiful. It seems that these days that no one has money. We can depend on friends for some help," voiced Mary.

Francesco confirmed, "I expect to take care of most of the repairs myself with the help of my family to save on costs. At least, the family can move in regardless of the appearance of the place. It is a roof over our heads keeping out the rain and winds. We will be self-sufficient by farming. I'm experienced in farming to produce an abundance of crops if the weather cooperates. The house I lived at in Italy wasn't anything modern. I must say that I am a little disappointed that I will have to work very hard once again to acquire the necessities of life. I was promised a better life here in America, but with the Great Depression happening, it seems that life is hard here as well as back in the Old Country. I want to keep my assets and will do whatever it takes to keep them. I have no other choice."

Mary encouraged her father by saying, "You can farm the land to provide for our family all the vegetables, meat, and the dairy products needed. The fruit trees and berry bushes located around the barn will satisfy the stomachs of the family as well. It will be fun for the children to get their small bowls and buckets to pick berries. Of course, many times the children might eat more berries than what they put in the buckets."

"Now that we have worked very hard making our few trips with our material possessions, I believe it is now time to bring your mother to her new place," stated Francesco. "It would have been impossible without your help to have moved. I appreciate all you have done to help make the move go smoothly."

Francesco and Mary returned home to find Lucia and the family waiting to go to their new home. Loading everyone in the borrowed pickup truck, Francesco instructed the children to keep seated in the open-air bed while he drove the short distance to their destination. He took one last look at the house where he and Lucia began their married life together before departing as despair gripped him.

Arriving at the front door of the old white wooden farmhouse, Francesco led Lucia up the steps through the door. Lucia stood looking around at her unfamiliar surroundings.

Standing quietly for a few moments, Lucia said, "Francesco, I'm looking forward to living here. It is quiet with no close neighbors around. The calm atmosphere will be refreshing,"

The days were passing as the family was adjusting to the change with wide open spaces. One morning Mary, Leonard, Joe, and John went out to the side of the barn to where the raspberry and blueberry bushes were located with Mary carrying the deep-dish bowls. The berry bushes were drooping down to the ground with the heaviness from the ripened berries.

"Look over there, Leonard," yelled Mary. "There is a pile of berries that we can pick. The red raspberries and blueberries are both ripe."

"Let's see who can pick the most," cried Leonard.

"Here are your bowls to put them in," Mary said as she reached out handing the containers to her siblings.

John ran over to Mary with his little hand shut. "Look Mary, I have a few big berries. I bet these are the biggest berries of all."

Mary replied, "Wow, John, those are huge berries! What bush did you pick those from? They could win a prize."

John was proud of his little discovery of the big berry bush. The children were laughing and having a good time. Suddenly, berries were flying in the air. A berry fight had erupted. Each child was running around trying to hit the other in the face with a handful of berries.

"Stop, the berry juice will stain," shouted Mary. The children were tuning out what Mary had espoused. The children were amidst a berry battle, laughing and yelling in playfulness. What could one expect from boys nearing their teenage years?

With containers emptied, Leonard, Joseph, and John lay in the grass laughing with their faces and clothes of purplish blue and reddish color.

"Those stains will not come out of your clothing. It's good we all have old clothes on. I will wash these clothes, but it won't do much good. It's time to go in the house. Well, I thought picking berries would be productive, but it turned out to be a playful berry picking day. We didn't achieve bringing any berries back to bake pies."

The fields with the green grass were adventurous for the younger children to run through at times in playfulness hunting insects or picking wild flowers and berries for enjoyment. Lucia could take long walks through the fields smelling the fresh country air, which Francesco felt was a better way of life. Hopefully, this journey to a new way of life would help fulfill and inspire her to change into a happier, more content existence.

As the days passed, many hours of labor were going into the little farm. Besides laboring on the farm, Francesco worked the coal mines each day. The land was shaping into an abundant harvest from planting seeds, which is the theory of sowing and reaping. The boys were now of age to help with some of the farm work. It was delightful to watch the plants grow. Lucia seemed to be involved doing the house chores and in canning the vegetables and making jellies from berries to help lessen the cost of grocery bills.

Lucia was back in the routine of the days feeling safe and content once again. Staying busy seemed to keep her mind off the problems that the family was experiencing from the Great Depression and losing Josephine. Francesco held on desperately for each moment that things appeared to be normal regardless of the lack of conveniences found in this old farmhouse.

Without a furnace, the old black coal stove heated the house from the outside chilly air while kerosene lanterns provided lighting at night throughout the house. Kerosene would always hold a reminder of the tragedy that occurred. To wash one's body, there were washtubs to bathe in and washboards and a wringer washer to wash the family laundry. There were few comforts in life lately, but Francesco kept reassuring the family that a little work never hurt anyone. He alluded that as time passed, life would get easier if everyone would be patient until he could accumulate money to have a few more conveniences in the house.

Regardless of the hard ways of life, Lucia seemed to be steadily improving. She seemed to be finding her way back to becoming the person she once was. Francesco would return from work at the end of the day looking forward to spending time with Lucia. Her personality from New York was coming through the gray clouds causing sun rays to brighten the days again. No longer was Lucia lost in a maze all alone. Maybe, the suggestions that the doctor gave were working. The family was happier with Lucia being well again. The stress was being lifted as the days went by into weeks.

One morning, Francesco picked grapes from the grape harbor for Lucia to make some jelly for the family.

Lucia said, "Thanks, Francesco, for picking the grapes. I will now be able to begin making jelly. Children, come and nestle around the table. Take the stems from the grapes. Then, throw them into a pot to be washed. Upon washing the grapes, I will place them in a kettle adding sugar, pectin extract, and acid powder to be placed onto the stove to thicken. We will make this a family project to teach you little young ones what goes into the preparation for jelly to be made."

Mary spoke, "Mama, can I place the jelly once it thickens into jars? I can also melt wax to pour over the top of the jar to harden to preserve the jelly. With all of us helping, it will make the completion of the process go faster."

Lucia replied, "I'll let you take care of placing the jelly into the jars and melting the wax. I will be the designated one to take care of the cooking process since the fire of the stove could become dangerous for the younger children."

Lucia was cooking jelly on top of the stove at a high degree when unexpectedly the jelly began to roll into an uncontrollable boil. Lucia screaming, "Help me someone, the boiling is out of control with the jelly shooting up to the ceiling and boiling over!"

"Mama, I am here! Let me help you," cried Mary. "Turn the heat down to slow up the boiling."

"Mary, I have turned the heat down. The lid is off the pot, but it seems to be getting worse," yelled Lucia.

"Maybe we need to lift the pan off the stove to stop the boiling," screamed Mary.

A panic sounding voice echoed throughout the house calling, "It's too late! It's beyond our control. Oh.... Mary, please help me! The sugar in the jelly is causing a fire now. If we don't get this out fast, the whole house will go up in flames. Help me, please!" Lucia continued pleading with whoever would listen.

"Oh, my goodness," squealed Mary. "We need to do something fast! Help! Help us!" This episode was bringing back the hidden thoughts of the fire that took her little sister away. Uncontrollable tears were running down Mary's cheeks. A thought flashed across her mind of who would be able to help without a neighbor in sight. Papa was at work now. The only ones in the house were the younger children.

"This jelly is causing a fire on my stove, which is scaring me to death," cried Lucia!

The children were running around needlessly trying to determine what help they could provide to assist her with dashing out the fire.

"Mama, we will fill water pitchers and throw it over the flames," called Leonard.

"No, water will only make matters worse," Lucia yelled. Lucia stood frozen by the stove screaming helplessly. "Stop the fire! Stop the fire! Someone, please help us!" Her color was as the color of cotton.

One of the children called out, "What shall we do, Mama?"

Suddenly, Mary came to her mother's rescue by throwing a big bowl of flour over the pan, which immediately stopped the fire and ruined the jelly. The fire appeared to be smothered by the flour penetrating over the hot volcano type of mixture spewing its hot sugar over the sides of the pan.

Lucia looked straight at Mary with terror in her eyes as she spoke, "Mary, you take care of things here in the kitchen. I must go and lie down. Tomorrow, I will not get out of bed once again. This fire has startled me out of my mind. I must go to my room immediately and lie down."

"Mama, it is alright. The fire is put out now. Please know that there was no harm done. Go lie down and after you rest a little while you will feel better."

"Think what you will, Mary, but I will never feel better. Now, I must rest before I collapse," exclaimed Lucia.

Mary had a lot of unspoken fears held deep inside from this incident. She would tell her father upon his return from work. He could maybe help in making things alright. She hoped that her mother wouldn't experience more mountain climbing with starting once again at the bottom of the mountain scaling to the top. Fear overtook her at this moment that her mother may never reach the top again. Mary turned to walk away to hide her tears from the children. It was bad enough with the jelly causing a stove fire. She didn't want to make the situation any worse by shedding tears in front of her siblings. Mary's pain would stay buried with all the other pain. Hopefully, there would be no more valley experiences to walk. She sure didn't want to begin again walking on pins and needles all the time not knowing what situation would set her mother's mind in a tail spin.

"Let me clean up this jelly mess. You can all help me. Then, let's all gather together to go outside. It will keep the house quiet that Mama will be able to rest peacefully. Mama will be alright with a little rest and quiet time," said Mary reassuring the children.

If a little incident like this would set her mother back, Mary perceived that any hope for a full recovery was looking very bleak these days.

"Are you all okay?" asked Mary as she looked directly at the children. The children stood by her shaking their heads in silence that they were alright. "I know you are all a little frightened. We do have a little problem for each of us is worried about Mama in various ways."

Maria held out her hand to Mary as a tear trickled down her cheek trying to smile while clenching her little hand in her big sister's hand. "Let's go over and sit on the big tree stump, and I will tell you a story. Some fresh air will clear our heads and get our minds off Mama's little episode."

The younger siblings sat on Mary's lap attuned to every word that was being spoken. Mary started the story, "Once upon a time, there was a princess living in a castle located in the middle of the ocean surrounded by water. There was no way for her to leave for the water would drown anyone attempting the escape unless they could take a boat to shore for the waters were rough. The princess would dream every day how she would one day plan her escape from this castle because she was made to work very hard. She was losing her childhood of being the little girl that she should be at her age."

Madelyn, the youngest girl spoke up, "Why was she made to work very hard?"

"I have found that sometimes things in life are not fair and for no explainable reason other than the princess was the oldest child living in the castle surrounded by water. She was a very beautiful little lady. I guess you could say that the others were younger and were not given the same responsibilities because of their age," answered Mary.

"Why did age matter that they were not given work to do, Mary?" John asked.

"Apparently, they were not as mature as the princess. The better you do, the more work you acquire. Sometimes grown-ups don't realize what they do. They think that because the princess was the oldest she could handle all the storms that life threw in the pathway. Adults don't realize how they treat others badly. They don't do it intentionally. I am telling you this story to remind you that when you grow up, you should treat people fairly no matter what the situation. Don't expect one person to do all the work. It's very unfair to expect one person to pick up the pieces when darts are being hurled in one direction and are out of control. Everyone must pitch in to get the jobs done."

"Well, one day her Prince Charming came to her rescue in a boat. She finally made her entrance off the island and lived happily ever after."

It was soon time to return to the house when Mary noticed her father returning from work. Mary ran to meet him at the lane. "Papa, while we were making jelly today, we had an accident. The jelly boiled over and caused a fire on the stove. Luckily, I threw flour over the flames, which quenched the fire from being uncontrollable."

Francesco replied, "Why are you so fussed up? Accidents happen sometimes, but I don't see this being any major dilemma."

Mary squalled, "Not only could our house have gone up in flames, but I believe that Mama is having a backset from this little ordeal. I am concerned that Mama will be sick again, and it's all my fault."

"Mary, don't worry. We'll try and think positive that your mother will be alright. This incident probably brought back thoughts of what happened to Josephine." Tired and weary from the coal mines, Francesco was very troubled by the anticipation of the unforeseen, but he did not speak of his feelings to the children.

The night had passed like any other night, but the morning brought on a new day. Mary's suspicions were accurate. Once again,

Lucia was not herself. She had taken on a new personality all because of the event.

As the days passed, Mary was overwhelmed with taking care of five small children at such a young age while her father had to work the mines. She would rise early to do the laundry, baking, and cooking for the day too. Moreover, there were the animals and the barn that required attention. Her younger brothers would lend a hand in this task, but Mary felt responsible for overseeing the work that needed finished each day. She would pray daily that her mother would get better. The future sure looked bleak. Little conversation was exchanged most days between mother and Mary and family. Her mother was talking nonsense and had become very violent. Mary was always trying to assure her siblings that things were fine; although, their mother had sunken into a deep, dark mood.

CHAPTER 19

STRANGERS IN THE HOUSE

---

*It's funny when you think life is going well; then
suddenly, the carpet is pulled from under you.*

One day while doing chores on the farm, Mary looked out the window to see a caravan of wagons pulled by horses coming up the road. In the distance was an echo of music and laughter with the clacking of tin banging as the wheels of the wagons came slowly up the narrow lane. Mary ran out of the house to where her small siblings were playing and yelled for them to get into the house immediately for she did not know who these people were. She remembered her father telling her about traveling gypsy caravans coming to the farms and kidnapping the young children. Mary used precaution; she could not take any chances these days. Life was hard enough these days without dealing with another tragedy.

As the wagons came to a halt on this dusty road, the middle-aged man seated in the front wagon holding the leather reins in his hand yelled out, "Hello there, my pretty maiden." He had a bald head with a hoop earring in his one ear with a handkerchief tied around his neck with copper tone skin. His long flowing beard touched down to his chest area.

"Hello sir!" Mary replied. She noticed that pots and pans were tied along the side of the wagon to which the clacking could be attributed. There were four covered wagons with several men, women, and children seated on the front seat of each wagon. They were all dark-haired with dark-complexion dressed in bright colored clothing. The men wore knee breeches and short sleeved shirts with hobnail boots.

The women were adorned with expensive gold hoop earrings through their ears, large gaudy necklaces, and a bright colorful bandanna over their heads. They were attired with flowing apparel of long hoop skirts with a middy blouse and knee-high boots while the children were outfitted with various colored pantaloons and shirts in their dusty bare feet.

The man that had spoken previously to Mary had a big smile on his face. "My name is Louis. You must realize that we are quite weary from our days of travel. We would like to water our horses and rest them for the night. We will not bother you for we could go to the north end of the property and set up a little camp site if it is alright with you. All we would need is a few watering buckets that we could use to help us with this task."

Mary stood there for a moment in awe not knowing how to reply. Her mother was at the door of the house dancing around for she was quite not herself these days.

"Hello everybody," hollered Lucia out of the door twirling like a ballerina. "It's great to have some company out here in this lonely place."

Mary was hoping that these travelers wouldn't have an inkling that her mother was quite ill. She hoped that the travelers would think that Lucia was hitting the bottle this afternoon to be feeling quite energetic. Mary felt that there was no use in asking her mother for this type of request because she couldn't comprehend what was being said most days. Frightened, Mary would try to distract these strangers so that she wasn't overpowered by them until her father's return.

Mary realized she needed to make some type of decision quickly to suffice these people's request. One more thing to think about was not something she needed at this moment. She wasn't sure whether to tell the leader of the caravan to be on his way or to respond in a positive manner to his request. It could possibly be a ploy to get inside the house to rob them of all that they had in possessions from the house, which wasn't much. The caravan could be a tribe of petty thieves and pick pockets. It seems that they led a life-style of wandering. Money was skimpy these days. It was best to be on guard always for trust was a thing of the past.

Francesco was hard at work in the coal mines most days. Upon returning, he was drained at the end of most days; and he looked forward to a meal on the table that was followed by a few farm chores, sleeping, and beginning the next day the same way. He had very little quality time to spend with his family. He depended on Mary to take care of the family, meals, and the house. His younger boys would help with milking the few cows, feeding the chickens, and tidying up the barn. Francesco trusted that Mary was quite capable of handling the home front; even though, it was a lot to expect, but in the situation, someone had to take the responsibility.

Francesco had to work in the mines to bring money in to support his family. He understood that to keep Lucia hid in a closet away from the pressures of life that Mary had to pick up the slack regardless of her young age. Francesco was in denial that Lucia needed help. He assured family and close friends that this dilemma would pass as in the past, but he didn't share much information with anyone what chaos was taking place in the family circle.

Once again, the lean-faced, bald-headed man with the startling brown eyes and sharply cut features yelled, "If you would help us with our horses, my pretty one, we would be glad to help you with some of the farm chores if you would like us too."

Mary stammered for the words failed to protrude from her mouth from the nervousness she was feeling. Shaking her head was all she could do. She could use a little help these days with the farm chores. God knew that at the end of each day her strength was drained. The only words that came out of her mouth stammering were, "Uh…. uh…. my father will be here very shortly. He's doing some work." She didn't want these people to know how long it would be until her father's return home for she had no idea what these people wanted.

"Alright then," he yelled, "unload the wagons down at the corner of the little barn for the young lady allows us to stay here for a little while. You won't be sorry for giving us this privilege. We are very good workers. Besides, we will play some music to soothe your very soul tonight."

Mary once again shook her head and sighed, "Yes, I know—I know! The one thing I must say, though, is that upon my father's complete approval—the conditions and guidelines will be set for you to follow during your stay here. If he allows you to stay, he will expect you to abide by his rules. He may decide not to let you stay here at all. The decision will be totally up to him; but for the time being, you can stay here to feed and water your horses and rest the weary until he can talk to you in a little while."

Consequently, this was one of those days when her father must be working more hours than his shift required for he was not home at his usual hour. In the mine, there were many days when Francesco didn't return home for twelve to sixteen hours upon the start of his morning shift's beginning.

"Fair enough, my child, at least that will give us a little time to rest the horses along with us travelers," exclaimed the spokesman.

"Leonard, Joe, and John, please come outside and help unhitch the horses," yelled Mary.

There were several little eyes looking through the windows observing what was going on outside the walls of the house. Lucia made her way through the door asking Mary, "Are these the performers from New York City that are coming to visit me and are taking me back to the city?"

"No, Mama," replied Mary, "Stay in the house for now. I'll be in to explain a little later. Have the boys come outside for I don't think that they heard me when I yelled."

It was late in the day, and Mary didn't realize the boys were finishing up in the barn when she asked for their help. Leonard came quickly around the barn door pushing a wheelbarrow of manure out the side door on the south side of the barn with Joe and John by his side. "I need you to lend a hand to our unexpected guests to give their horses a drink. The horses are thirsty from traveling."

"We will be glad to give a hand with the horses. You will not need water pails for we will take the horses down to the creek where there is plenty of water for the horses to drink," confirmed Leonard.

Suddenly, a few barn swallows burst high into the air upon opening the door while a little yapping black dog stood by their side. Leonard tipped the wheelbarrow over on its front wheels to dump the load into the pile that was along the side of the barn.

Louis whistled as he waited to be sure the dog was not interested in approaching him where he stood. Louis yelled out, "James, Tommy, and Zac, let's get the horses watered and fed once we unhitch them. The boys over there offered to help."

No instructions were needed for Leonard, Joe, and John were familiar with the routine of unhitching. Once the horses were unhitched, the watering could begin. As they approached the horses, they grabbed the reins leading them down to the creek with several of the travelers straggling behind following the path to reach the creek that was located a little way past the barn.

"Come on," Leonard gestured as he spoke. "The spring water pouring into the creek from the hills above is cool and fresh that will quench the thirst of the horses from their long journey. The clean water supply running down from the mountain springs comes bursting forth daily with a new supply that will never run dry. After we water the horses, we will lead the livestock across the pasture to graze. If any of you are thirsty, go over and stick your head into the stream for a cool drink."

James, Tommy, and Zac ran over for a drink. "Boy, this water sure tastes good. It sure quenches our thirst after the dust we've picked up in our throats from our journey," said Tommy, who was the oldest of the three boys. He had black curly hair with bronze skin and was quite slender in stature and had a pleasant personality. The horses stood in the creek with their heads bowed low with their tongues lapping up the water shaking their heads in playfulness as the water sprayed around the boys' heads. After the horses finished their drinking, the boys followed the horses across the field. Nature in the fields would satisfy the hunger the horses had from their journey. There was old wooden fencing and plenty of grass at the back end of the property to make the horses comfortable. The old fencing needed repair, but it would serve for safety of the horses not leaving the pasture for now.

Tommy yelled out, "If the horses are still hungry after being in the field, we have a few bags of oats on our wagons that will satisfy their appetites if needed, but for tonight the pastures will provide enough food for the horses' stomachs. Papa says that we don't have a lot of money to buy food for our horses. We should save the oats for another time."

Mary felt a need to explain her mother's behavior to the travelers, but she kept it to herself. She wondered whether the travelers would understand after the explanation. She wanted to explain to Mama her decision of letting the travelers stay on the property and watering their horses. Mama would probably not even comprehend what Mary was trying to explain for she was in a world all her own most days. It was very sad to see Mama in such a downhearted state not able to comprehend what was happening in her surroundings. Most days concentrating for her was difficult. She had lost interest in everything that was once important to her. Mary had to watch her mother continually as a precautionary measure for Mama could inflict injury to herself if one wasn't careful. Many times, she would fantasize that she was on stage in New York dancing and singing throughout the house. If only someone could do something to restore Mama's mind once again, the family was going to pieces and losing its happiness along with Mama. Friends were not welcome here at Francesco's house for it was quite embarrassing for anyone to see Lucia in such a mind's state. This situation made for a very lonely life. It seemed that a black cloud was hanging low in this dark valley of despair that Lucia was passing through with no way to escape.

Mary was being affected emotionally by her mother's behavior. It seemed to be taking a downhill journey on her mind. Many days, she would vanish to a secret place to have a good cry. She didn't want to upset the rest of the family and thought it best to go off alone to let the floodgates open.

Amid Mary's thoughts, a small white dog wagging its tail jumped down from the wagon running and barking toward the chickens that were propped outside of the chicken coop. As the dog was circling around the chickens, he spotted the black farm dog and ran directly to greet it with its tongue licking the dog's mouth. It appeared that the dogs became friends immediately as they stood on their back-hind legs leaping playfully trying to embrace each other with their front paws in the air leaving out soft whimpering sounds together.

Laughter and talking was coming from all around the wagons as the various passengers were jumping down to the ground from the wagons. It appeared that relief had come to each traveler once their feet hit the ground. It was truly amazing how many passengers were in the wagons.

Louis asked, "What is your Mama talking about us being performers?"

"Before we children were born, my Mama lived in New York City and did some stage work there," replied Mary reconsidering sharing her mother's problems. "However, presently she is ill and not quite herself. Numerous times, her mind goes back to those days and times in New York. My father has taken her to several doctors, but we were told it will take time for her to get well. Maybe, someday my father will take her back to New York to where they began their life together. The trip could serve as a little boost in her treatment to help get her on the pathway to quicker recovery."

The man could see the hurt and worry in the young girl's eyes as she spoke. He tried to keep the conversation lighthearted saying, "My child, you will be delighted that we will perform for you and your family this evening and cast a magical spell on your mother that she may once again return to New York. It is fun to sing and dance! Music soothes the soul."

He turned around placing his hands at his hips as he spoke out, "Hurry everyone! We must prepare for our evening here. Let's gather some wood for our campfire tonight that we may have a feast with a lot of music and dancing!"

"Maybe, you should wait to prepare for the campfire. My father may not permit you to stay here," stated Mary.

Meanwhile, Mary captured a man's silhouette in the distance. It was later than the normal time that her father would usually return home. She was trembling inside not knowing what reaction her father would have to this situation. Many thoughts were running through her mind with anticipation of how to handle her father's interrogation.

"Look over there, my father is walking up the road," squealed Mary pointing toward the road. As Francesco ventured up the road from a hard day's work under the ground, he found a caravan of wagons in a circle to the side of the barn. As he looked past the barn, he saw the horses lying down in the pasture. The horses appeared to be beautiful stallions of various colors. He wanted to hurry into the field over to the big brown shiny coat horse and pat its head. In the back of his mind he thought—what on earth was his family thinking to have total strangers staying here at the farm? Hopefully, these people were stopping to rest for a short time. These days, it was hard enough to earn money for food let alone having more mouths to feed. Maybe, they were some relatives visiting from New York that Francesco didn't know existed. Many thoughts were racing through his mind. Francesco groaned as he placed his palms of his hands to his head from the sudden pain he was experiencing in his head from the anxiety he felt.

As Francesco turned around, a small boy with black curly hair dressed in red shorts and a white button-down shirt ran from the side barn door. The boy ran in his bare dirty feet as fast as his legs could carry him running directly into the path where Francesco was standing and was knocked down from the force to the ground. Suddenly, he left out a yelp from the sudden jar felt by the blow. Following him was a little black-headed girl with dark skin yelling loudly in some type of gibberish with the words coming out, "Can't I be the queen?"

The boy composed himself from his fall yelling back, "I don't know, Natalie, for I am the king of the castle, and I will have to make the decision later in my kingdom."

Francesco stopped dead in his tracks to where the children were standing, "Who are you children?" As he pulled the young boy up to a sitting position, Francesco raised his face toward the sky breathing in the clean smell of the summer air and wished he was a child once again. He stood there for a while remembering similar playfulness as a lad in days gone by. This incident brought his mind back to the days in Italy with him and his siblings playing in the hills of his homeland.

"My name is James," replied the boy with a big grin on his face, "and this is my sister Natalie. We arrived here today with my parents and will be staying to help out in this castle." The boy continued speaking, "My father is a magic man that helps sick people get well. The young lady told my father that her mother is sick and needs to get well to make her father happy."

Francesco was taken back with the child referring to this place as a castle, but children are innocent and see things through the eyes of a child. Maybe this was a castle to them for all they had known were wagons. Pondering, Francesco didn't perceive the impact that Lucia's sickness was having on Mary until he heard the child spout those words out. The children were only five to seven-years-old judged Francesco. The children seemed pleasant, but with little money and food, it was a concern to provide for Francesco's own family without having the worry of having more people to feed. To keep harmony in the family Francesco learnt early in life's game that silence is golden. Francesco thought maybe he could kill a few chickens that would provide something to eat. He could have a big kettle of chicken noodle soup made that would feed everyone.

He may as well resign himself to accepting the decision that was made earlier today for there was no sense to make a disturbance with Lucia being ill. Everything had to be handled with "kid gloves" to have a peaceful environment. Besides if this child's father can help restore Lucia's mind, it would be worth every inconvenience to have these travelers stay for a little while.

Francesco approached the man standing by the wagon. "What is your business here at my place?"

"My name is Louis. If you don't mind, we would like to stay a few days before continuing on our journey."

Francesco replied, "I am returning from work. Let me think about it a little while. Maybe, you could be a help here on the farm. Even though the farm is small, there is always something to do. There are certain jobs that must be done such as hoeing and weeding the garden, cleaning the barn, feeding the chickens, and taking care of the few livestock to make the farm workable. It would be my payment from you for letting you stay here."

Louis chuckled, "It sounds like a fair deal to me."

Francesco nodded, returning worried eyes to Mary, "It would eliminate the younger boys from some of their daily duties. My wife and children live on the farm that I purchased a few months back. We are trying to get a breath of the country air while raising our own crops with the Great Depression that is now going on. Food is not plenteous, and there are few jobs to be found. To survive, we thought it best to make our own provision without depending on others for our livelihood."

"This is very good of you to be able to provide for your family from the land," replied Louis. "I was told by your daughter that you would make the decision if we could stay here on your land. I understand that your wife is ill and needs some help. Your daughter said that you have taken her to several doctors and nothing seems to be making her well. She talks tales and imagines things."

Francesco speaking with tears in his eyes softly spoke, "That is another reason why I moved out here in the middle of nowhere. I felt that the clean country air and quiet environment may help her get well. When you look across the hillside, it's amazing how much beauty spans as far as the eye can see. I love my wife very much and want the best for her. I promised her when we were in New York before marrying that I would give her a good living. The way that the economy of the country is going has turned my hopes and dreams that were planned into a big pile of ashes."

Louis lowering his eyes said, "I believe that I was led here for a purpose. Hopefully, I will be able to help you if you permit me to stay with my family and friends a short time on your farm. Tonight, we will light up a campfire, and we will eat, drink, and be merry as we dance and sing around the fire having fun."

Francesco loved Lucia and worshipped the ground that she walked upon. Standing thinking quietly for a moment, Francesco understood that he was at this point willing to try anything offered to have Lucia well again. He started speaking, "To have Lucia happy and fancy free once again is my only desire in life that I contemplate time and again. I long for her gentle touch to warm my inner being where now the world seems hard and cruel in these depressed times. I remember the many times that I was told back in the Old Country that in America there were *streets of gold*. I've looked time and again for these streets, but I still have never found them. For a short time, I found happiness and prosperity, but the circumstances of life seemed to bring unexpected hardships to me at this point. Maybe uh...uh... if I would have remained in New York with Lucia, things would have not been as difficult. While in New York, we were content and joyfully jubilant. Lucia would be closer to having family ties. She could have continued working and taken part in the stage shows at the hotel. Here, the place we call home, has little activity except for the familiar bird songs in the early spring dawn making melody to the listening ear. It is a small community that is a good place to raise children, but there isn't any social life other than family and a few friends."

"I understand," agreed Louis, shaking his head.

Francesco looking at Louis spouted off recklessly, "You see these days, friends are in short supply with us leaving one place to settle into another area. It's always an adjustment to leave a community to move to another where becoming acquainted with the people takes some time. The area is a rural area with houses spread out all over the community with a considerable distance in between each house. Once my family is in the neighborhood for a little while, I'm sure we will become acquainted with several individuals. Though, right now I must always be on guard to protect Lucia against the hard, cruel world for this type of illness she has must not be spoken of and has to stay hidden for my family's well-being."

Francesco continued to glare at Louis while saying, "Right now I don't have much choice in the matter of where my family will live. The bargain between my brothers and me before leaving Italy was to remain together; and since money these days is scarce, I have no alternative. I can communicate with my brothers in Italian easily. Of course, in the New York neighborhood that we settled for a little while was a place where a vast amount of Italians had settled. It was very easy to communicate there too."

Louis sighed, "It would be too expensive to move your family back to New York with housing costing a lot more there than a rural area. I know how difficult it is for us moving from place to place."

Francesco nodded his head to show his understanding said, "Family is of importance to Lucia, but she always had assured me that home would be wherever I was living. Life is a little hectic being far from home and no family member to confide in only my two brothers. Lucia is very young with having few conveniences of life to sever. I guess in marriage there are quite a few adjustments that have to be made—especially with me being away from home working most of the day."

Louis answering Francesco, "Uh…. uh…. these days there are many pressures with the Great Depression in full swing. The pressures of raising children with little money to buy food and provide shelter are at the top of the list."

Francesco began, "Yes, many weeks pass without me even receiving a paycheck regardless of a full day's work in the mines. Another problem is I must rely on my daughter to stand in the bread lines to obtain food for the family for these lines are not an uncommon sight during these hard times. You're lucky to get flour, cornmeal, coffee, and sugar that are amongst some of the food items distributed to provide relief for our needy family."

Louis remarked, "These food items help, but you have to think of ideas of how to ration amounts so that meals go farther to avoid hunger."

Francesco said, "My daughter, Mary, bakes at least twelve loaves of bread each week for the family to exist. It's great to have warm bread right out of the oven with lots of butter for a meal."

Louis elaborated, "It sounds to me that if you have bread and water at the table, it is called a meal some days at your house."

Francesco answering, "That's right. Some days though, Mary makes bread pudding, which the family fills up on as a meal for the day too. Butter and cottage cheese are churned by hand from our cow's milk. For her bread pudding, she has milk and butter from the cows and eggs from the chickens with adding a little sugar. It doesn't take much to put together such a cheap meal. At times, our family goes into the woods to pick berries or gathers them by the barn, which are placed in the bread pudding that makes for a zesty taste. See over there are a few apple trees lining the property edge. We pick apples when in season and make up applesauce, dumplings, and pies. Living off the land is required for a family to survive in these depressed times. There is plenty of free food on the land to give a variety of choices if one takes the time and work to gather it. We can in jars the different berries and vegetables in order that the family has enough to eat throughout winter."

Francesco continued speaking, "A neighbor down the street where we lived prior to moving to the farm had taught Mary how to make low-cost simple meals to have nutrias food for the family to exist in these troubled times. Other meals that she prepares are huge pots of chicken soup from the chickens raised on the farm with fluffy dumplings sometimes dropped into the soup with a few pieces of home-grown potatoes and carrots. She also makes salads with endive and raw mushrooms picked from the fields or she will cook the endive and flavor it with cooked bacon. Cornmeal is eaten for breakfast. It's fried and buttered—comparable to bread for the dinner meal. One cannot be particular with food in such short supply."

Louis replied, "The average family is glad to have any type of food to eat to avoid starving. We eat coffee bread or fried bread dough. This is another commodity for these breads are quite inexpensive to prepare."

Francesco didn't want to communicate to Louis his personal business. Additionally, Francesco and Lucia had several rental properties purchased with tenants living in each place. Many times, the tenants were unable to pay the money owed to Francesco and Lucia. Francesco had taken a large loan at the bank to buy the properties depending on the renters to pay the mortgage. Most people had little money to buy food without the responsibility of shelling out money to pay the rental cost. Francesco had to take money from his savings to pay the mortgages. Money was dwindling; and if things didn't change, he would be running out of money that would make it impossible to pay these mortgages. Francesco and Lucia had a heavy burden placed on their shoulders. It was useless to think that they could sale the rentals for who would be able to buy them with most people losing their jobs for lack of work. When Francesco and his brothers left Italy the economy was poor, likewise poverty was running rampant right now on the home front of America.

Francesco being weary spoke, "My children seem to be suffering from their mother's illness and poor economy. It is placing the weight of the world on Mary's shoulders. Mary works from sunrise to sunset to have the children fed and the necessary things of living taken care of each day. I'm sure that Mary questions in her own mind many times the unfairness of the situation."

Francesco didn't know it, but Mary would long for her Prince Charming to come and take her away to a fairyland where there was only happiness. She would tell her younger siblings the story of the princess being rescued by her Prince Charming, but she failed to tell them that she was the princess to whom she was referring. Most girls her age was having fun with their girlfriends. Lucia was becoming a handful to care for each day. Mary had to be on guard constantly for she never knew what would trigger Lucia to react violently. Some days the sun kept shining, but most days seemed to have a big black cloud hanging over the house.

As Francesco walked toward the field, he noticed the group from the caravan having a gay time. They were sitting in the grassy area on the north side of the house laughing and talking. He couldn't quite hear the conversation—only heard the laughter faintly echoing in his ears. Immediately, another leader of the group jumped to his feet to greet Francesco.

"Good afternoon, sir," said the young man. "You must be the father of the children that live on this farm."

"Yes, I am Francesco. As I explained to Louis, my wife and children live on the farm that I purchased several months back." Francesco continued making his way from the field into the house with his children following behind. "I will see you later for Louis promised a delightful evening tonight."

Upon entering the house, Francesco spoke softly to his family. "Let's get ready for the evening. Louis assured me that we will have a fun-filled evening."

CHAPTER 20

THE DANCING BEGINS

Retracing one's pathway is not always easy,
But it brings one to face reality that the element of time
changes things.
Also, the mirrors of our mind bring back
pictures differently then and now.

It was early evening when Louis, the leader of the caravan, decided to light the fire to begin the festivities of the evening. The sky was dark with only the glittering of the stars above shedding light for the world to see. The wagons circled the blazing campfire as the dancing began providing for a perfect atmosphere this evening. Violins and guitars echoed throughout the neighborhood. The music transported peace and tranquility to one's heart. As the dance began, the women formed a circle lifting their skirts quickening their steps to the beat of the music. The circle was made up of beautiful individuals each having different needs. It appeared that the life of these people was music, dancing, and adventure. The music seemed to be absorbed into their mind and soul causing each one to feel lighthearted and joyous.

The camp was set up as the fire was blazing and tunes were being played for the onset of dancing; Francesco brought his family out of the house to participate with the activities that were taking place. The children ran over and took their places in the circle holding hands and joining in the rhythm of the music. Mary felt an inner peace as she watched her parents' playfulness tonight. She kept reassuring herself that maybe tonight was the night for a miracle to happen. She has been living her life in such a distressful situation at the edge of a nightmare watching her mother dwindling away into a person that she didn't know anymore. It appeared that a stranger moved into their home from another place in time. This sad state of affairs was sure taking a toll on all the family members. Mary was playing the part of the mother to the children and her mother. She was the mother they knew more than the natural mother that bore them. When Louis spoke to her earlier in the day, he did assure Mary that he could cast a magical spell upon her mother for her to regain her health.

Francesco took Lucia by the hand as she stayed close to his side to join in the fanfare of adventure in the night happenings. "Lucia, you look very radiant tonight." Lucia had her hair pulled up and tacked with a fancy comb to the back of her head with little ringlets cascading toward her face. The comb was a memento brought back from their days in New York. Mary had fixed Lucia's hair to help improve her frail appearance.

Francesco whispered, "Let's dance this one dance to remember for a lifetime. We'll be celebrating a new beginning of our life here instead of New York. I don't believe we've ever danced here since coming from New York. This will bring back to us some fond memories." The guests were all on their feet turning and swaying to the music.

Lucia sighed, and leaned her head against Francesco's shoulder, "Oh Francesco, Francesco…. if only we could go back to New York." She still was holding on to his hand.

"Lucia, this is our home. You're safe here with me and the children. God knows that we are greatly blessed for God has given us seven beautiful children. We did lose one of the seven, but we must go on. I don't know what has happened to you or where you've been, but you must believe me that I love you more now than ever. We can make it through these hard times for it won't always be this way." Francesco cuddled her in his arms touching his finger lightly to her lips. He pulled her close placing her head to his chest burying his face in her hair. In that instant, passion was flowing out of his heart intensely that he gasped for his breath was being taken away for the moment. He then placed his hands around her face and kissed her squarely on the mouth and drew back to see the expression on her face. It was as if a magical spell had been cast tonight on Lucia. For tonight, it appeared that Lucia was once more a normal human being. She was no longer excessively pale and sad hearted, and her dark hair made her porcelain face glow tonight in rare beauty.

The faces in the circle had expressions of interest and amusement to what was happening between these two lovers. One of the young men yelled out in laughter, "Kiss her again, my friend. Women need a little kissing now and again."

Francesco was a little embarrassed as he felt color rising on his cheeks not realizing that he was being watched by the crowd. Slowly, they walked over to join in with the singing and swaying to the music. Francesco and Lucia never missed one beat of the music. Lucia's mind seemed to be back on the stage of New York when life wasn't this complicated. Violins and guitars were being played creating beautiful music that satisfied every listening ear.

Francesco lifted her off the ground, and the sound that came from his throat was unlike his voice. "Lucia, I want to treasure this moment for the rest of my life." He was ecstatic to have the flames of their fire burning brighter liken to a sensation of a rushing wildfire.

Louis stepped out of line as he walked closer to where Francesco and Lucia were standing. He hesitated for a moment as he gazed toward the open blazing fire unable to speak. He stood with his hands in his pockets listening to the sounds of the voices dancing around the campfire. He stood for a moment still saying nothing trying to compose the right words, "I would like to help you. I have a magical crystal ball in my wagon that will help predict your future. He gestured toward the wagon saying, "I'll be glad to take you both there."

Francesco had a smile on his face, "Yes…. of course, I'll be glad to pay you for this service." Francesco couldn't tell Louis the fear he felt inside for a man is taught that as an adult he should rarely know fear. The saying that came to Francesco's mind that brought a calming over him was that *there was nothing to fear but fear itself.* (Roosevelt)

"It's free of charge to you for letting us stay here. I can't expect payment when money is hard to come by these days," said Louis.

Obviously, it appeared that Louis was very concerned about them. "Usually, the crystal ball will see solutions to life problems that we are not capable of seeing. It can tell us of the present, past, and future."

He led them up into the wagon where there were benches around an old wooden table on each side to sit down upon. He went into a wooden shelf cabinet fumbling through it with his hands.

"Here is the object, my children, that has the power to forecast the present and future of our life." The crystal ball was covered with a red velvety cloth. Reaching toward the object, he sat it down on the table requesting that Francesco and Lucia sit down on the wooded benches to wait what the magical ball had to reveal to them for tonight.

Louis placed the red velvety cloth that covered the ball over his head saying, "Let's see what the crystal ball has in store for you, eh?" Louis reminded them of a king adorned in the red velvet cloth lying over his dark head of hair with his sparkling gold adornment.

Francesco was going back in time remembering bedtime stories of his youthful days. Louis appeared to be a wizard that had the power with one magical touch that could change the journey of life to where Lucia and Francesco were heading. The crystal ball brought a reflection of different mirrors from life's events that seemed to be liberating their hearts from sadness in these perplexing times no longer having a hold on them for the moment.

"Francesco, please gaze into this crystal ball with a wish for the future, and tonight I assure you that you will be granted whatever your wish shall be."

"Louis, how do you know that I have a wish in my heart?" Francesco asked.

"Francesco, I can see it in your eyes. People's eyes tell it all, I believe. Most people have at least one little wish. Please look into the crystal ball with that wish, and I know that tonight is the night that your very wish will happen to you."

Francesco closed his eyes with the very wish he desired as the shine of tears began to gloss over his eyes. His mind went back to the days of wrapping his arms around Lucia and robbing her of the very breath she breathed because of his lips touching hers. He remembered how he would comb through her hair with his fingers touching her porcelain face with his lips. She always looked beautiful. Even now, she hadn't lost that trait. His heart groaned for the very need to be wanted by her once more. He sat there trembling for a little while because of the love he was feeling. He would do anything to have his porcelain doll well and the emotions she felt for him from the past return once again.

Lucia reached out to touch Francesco's wrinkled shirt as he sat trembling. She said, "I love you very much! Can't we stay under this spell for the rest of our life?"

Francesco stood up and bent over to kiss her long and hard. When they finally pulled apart, Louis stood up staring at Francesco saying, "My crystal ball is telling me that I will need one of your chickens sacrificed tonight. It declares that if a chicken is sacrificed, then your very wish will be granted to have brighter tomorrows with Lucia."

Francesco dropped another kiss on her lips. "If the crystal ball tells you this revelation, then, we must act at once in order that my very wish shall come true."

Francesco's anxieties seemed to be fading away with having a glimpse of the future. His heartaches were gone at the present. He gathered up Lucia as they stepped out of the wagon to find their prime chicken to sacrifice. Turning around he yelled to Louis, "You find the prime chicken you want to use as a sacrifice. I have more important matters to attend to presently."

Lucia softy spoke, "Thank you Francesco for rescuing me once more. I don't deserve your love, but you have always been kind and gentle toward me regardless of my frailties."

Francesco was tired of the storm that he was passing through. There had to be light on the other side of the storm if he could get to the other side where the thunder would sound no more.

Tonight, there was much dancing and adventure around the campfire. Francesco's family was spinning around the blazing camp-fire dancing and clapping to the beat of the music with all the cares of life drifting away.

It was well after midnight when Francesco gathered up his family to retire for the night.

The music, dancing, and campfire tonight were like something out of a dream. It was a new world of exploration. Regardless of Francesco's family's departure, the music played on well into the wee hours of early morning. This event was not planned, but it proved to be a lighthearted happy time.

CHAPTER 21

STRANGERS DISAPPEAR

---

*Can you mend a butterfly's wing when once it has been broken? Can
you recall an unkind word when once it has been spoken? Can you?*

(Author Unknown)

It was a Saturday morning with the sun breaking through the gray light of dawn that Francesco arose from a deep sleep. He reached for his trousers pulling them up as Lucia lay beside him sleeping. In the dim light, he noticed her silky head of hair fanned across the pillow. He sat their remembering last night, but also the days gone by when her arms would slide around his neck as he would tangle his fingers through her hair. He never took his gaze off her face. He hovered over her for a moment bending down to kiss her lips. "What more could I ask for but to kiss your lips?" he whispered. "Oh, yes…I made you a promise that I will forever keep come what may."

Awakening suddenly, she rolled away as he bent down to reach for her. There was no body response as there was last night. Francesco was saddened as he squeezed his eyes shut to hold back the tears shaking his head in disbelief. He muttered softly, "I wanted you naked in my arms once more. If only, I knew what to do to make it happen. Go back to sleep my dearest. Maybe, you're still in dream-land. At least, I'm glad we had last night."

Standing up, he pushed the bedroom door open as he restrained himself from running out the door never to return. The happy days for Francesco seemed like a distant memory, but he would hold on to the memory of the moment from last night.

He had his family to think of their welfare. With the strain of the situation, it would be easy to leave this house without looking back, but the love and passion he felt for Lucia contained him to stay through this ordeal. He had to keep reminding himself that Lucia was suffering and not herself lately.

Francesco was struck with the notion that Lucia would be healthy upon arising because of last night's prediction. Silently, he was reflecting on the happy times with Lucia when they would sit on the back porch sipping lemonade from their glasses enjoying each sip on those hot summer nights. Now, the person with whom he sipped the lemonade seemed to take on a total new personality, which appeared at times to be a stranger that was unrecognizable to Francesco. There was no more laughter, sharing, or talking. Dreams were turning into ashes falling slowly like dust to the ground. Happiness was being replaced with sadness. Was he a fool to think he could find happiness here in America? All he wanted was a normal life like others had in this land. Was that too much to ask? He kept replaying his hope again and again in his mind that maybe Lucia would be more herself upon arising today.

He ran out the door of the house to speak with Louis, but he noticed there were no wagons to be found. Complete silence now filled the air. Sunlight was dancing across the lawn as he strolled out toward the barn. Apparently, the caravan left through the night to his disappointment. Francesco circled around the barn in hopes of finding the caravan, but there were no wagons in sight. For a moment, Francesco felt that the caravan was only a fragment of his imagination until reality struck him. As he opened the barn door, he was astonished to find that one of his prime cows and a work horse was gone. He then trotted down to the chicken coop swinging the door open to find several laying hens were gone with the fresh eggs. He depended on these hens to provide eggs each day for the children to eat a hearty breakfast. Panic-stricken, he dashed through the front door up the stairs into each bedroom to check that all his children were in their beds. He settled down a little when he comprehended that these travelers didn't take any family members. In the back of his mind, he remembered that material things in life can be replaced, but life itself once it has been lost can never be restored. Several memoirs were flashing across his mind while he stood reminiscing in hope that the events of last night could come alive once again and not die to the wind.

To his utter astonishment, he realized that he donated to the gypsies without his consent. What a fool he was to place trust in these wanderers. This incident was an endangerment for his entire family. In the future, he would be more cautious whom he welcomed into his home. This incident was a reminder to him what people do in desperation.

Again, his blood was starting to boil at the thought of the injustice of this situation. His family must have been cast under some type of a magical spell from the playing of the music not to hear the caravan leaving in the middle of the night without as much as a goodbye. It was as though they vanished into thin air. What in the world could he have been thinking to let these people stay on his property? He was told that petty thieves were roaming the land with the economic situation. Now, he learned first-hand the result of the thieves. Francesco was at a complete and total loss of this situation. He was angry, but he had a heart of gold. He clung to the idea that if they didn't help themselves to what didn't belong to them, they probably would have to hunt in garbage cans for food like several people were doing in these perilous times.

Maybe, it was worth the loss if Lucia was well upon awakening.

With the Depression in full swing, Francesco had lost a lot of his financial stability. He couldn't afford to lose much more. He had heard the horror stories of many people having their dwellings padlocked and their families turned into the street. There were house foreclosures all around the area. Regardless, he was going each day to work to provide for his family, but with work hours at the coal mines being cut and the added financial responsibilities on the rentals, the future appeared bleak. The American dream that Francesco had dreamed seemed to be turning into a nightmare. Francesco tried to keep a positive perspective about the country's economic collapse.

Anger was draining from Francesco as he went back inside the house to inform Lucia what had happened right before their eyes. Francesco had to handle this little problem with delicacy. Lucia was in a very fragile state. He didn't want to break the spell that she was under from last night, but nothing hurts more than losing one's belongings to those thought to be trustworthy.

"Lucia, wake up. I have something to tell you," Francesco began.

Lucia raised her head off the pillow opening her eyes into slits staring at Francesco. "What could possibly be that important to wake me up this early in the morning that couldn't wait until I woke up?" Lucia snapped.

"The gypsies are gone! Apparently, they fled through the night."

"What do you mean that the gypsies are gone? Why didn't we hear them leaving?" Lucia stared at Francesco as she rose from the bed pacing a few steps.

"Lucia that is not the worst of things that I need to tell you. Not only are they gone, but they took some of our belongings with them. Please, try not to be upset."

"Don't be upset! I'm not upset because of their departure, but I'm upset because they are thieves. We trusted them to stay on our property, and now you come and tell me that they left without as much as a goodbye. They played beautiful music for us. How could we be so vain? Don't you think I have a right to be upset? I like people whose character is made up of integrity. It hurts me to have been deceived by such people. Do they not have hearts? What belongings did they take? Did they take some of our children?" Lucia questioned with fright arising in her voice.

"They took a cow, a horse, and some of our laying hens with eggs to the best of my knowledge. Hopefully, they took nothing else. I'm not sure."

She took a deep breath as her eyes widen. "Oh, this is truly awful! As it is, we are short on money, and to make matters worse, we will probably have to let some more of our rentals go. We had people that we trusted come in and steal from us right under our noses. We should report this to the authorities. There are many people these days eating out of garbage cans. Probably before you know it, we'll be the ones eating out of the garbage cans."

"Hopefully, Lucia, that never happens. You are a constant worrier. I will always try and provide food for our family. We could tell the authorities if we want, but then I thought about it and realized maybe they would starve to death if they didn't steal from us. I could go on a search for them. Uh…. uh…. let them have what they've taken. They must live with their conscience. I don't want to get anyone in trouble. The few things they took with them will be a payment for the advice they gave us."

Lucia stood pacing as she was wringing her hands. After a few seconds, she started speaking loudly breaking her silence, "Maybe, they have no conscience. Let your family eat out of garbage cans instead of them! Why should we let them take the easy way out? If we let them go, they will steal from someone else. It isn't right Francesco. If you don't want to tell the authorities, I can report them. Would you answer me one question, how is it that we did not hear these people leave in their noisy wagons?"

"Possibly they gave us something in our drinks to put us to sleep that we would not hear them as they left or maybe they continuously played high-sounding music while the wagons were moving to block out the noise of the wagons as the wheels moved. I don't have a clue, but whatever they did; it put us in a sound sleep. Perchance, we were cast under a magical spell. Really.... I can't figure it out either. Perhaps, we were exhausted from what we've been going through and that is why we had such a sound sleep."

"Try to go back to sleep for I have several things I want to attend to right now. Our animals for one thing need taken care of despite this difficulty."

"I can't think of sleep now. All I can think of is how angry I am with these people doing such a thing to us. These travelers seemed like nice people. This is too unbelievable for me to comprehend." She dropped down on the bed crying to think for a moment about what had happened.

One thing that was positive was that for this moment Lucia seemed to be able to focus on what was happening. Hopefully, this incident would not set her back. Presently, Lucia seemed more like her personality before the sickness occurred.

"It looks like today will be a gorgeous day!" said Francesco. Huge white clouds are rolling over a bright blue sky bringing a promise for a perfect day!"

Sometimes when the days were bright with sunshine, it would lift the dark clouds that surrounded Lucia. Francesco went downstairs to find some buckets for what better day would there be than today to take the family to gather berries and mushrooms to help feed the family in these days with the economic crisis going on. Maybe with this new day dawning, Lucia would join the rest of the family for the little adventure into the woods through the paths tramped down from the traffic looking for berries.

"Wake up everybody. Let's get dressed to go berry picking!" Francesco yelled throughout the house. "I know that it's early, but get on some old clothes. Be sure you all wear long pants and long sleeve shirts for where we are going there will be thorny bushes and poison ivy, and I don't want you getting your arms and legs scratched more than necessary or picking up any mosquitoes or ticks or poison."

"The weeds can make your skin very itchy," replied Mary's voice echoing from her bedroom.

"We will walk with our buckets and bowls down by the creek into the woods. I saw a lot of big berries hanging off the bushes the other day. The bigger the berries the less time it will take us to fill up our buckets. Besides, with all of us picking, we will be able to take less time getting the number of berries that we need for a couple of pies. If we get enough, we will prepare some in jars to have for winter when the berries disappear. Also, we can make jelly for our bread."

Francesco yelled up the stairway, "Lucia, come along with us to enjoy the day in the company of our children picking berries. If you get tired, we will return home, but I beg of you to come. It will do all of us well to go for a little outing since it is such a beautiful day."

Mary stood listening to her father trying to encourage her mother to join in the day's activity. Mary and Francesco had much compassion for her mother in her illness. Many times, she would try to come up with a plan that might work to lead her mother through this unfortunate problem, but all plans seemed to fail regardless whatever she tried to devise. With all the dancing and music last night, Lucia did seem to improve.

All the children came down for breakfast while Mary made them some hot oatmeal with Francesco pitching in to help the process go faster. When breakfast was almost over, Francesco met Lucia at the top of the stairway dressed appropriately for the day. Apparently, she was going to join in the day's fun.

Francesco cradled his arm around Lucia's shoulder saying, "Lucia, it's very good to see you dressed and ready to go. I am going to make you some toast, scrambled eggs, and coffee. We still have a little time; and then, we will be on our way to the weed world," chuckled Francesco kissing Lucia on the cheek. "Hopefully, it won't be too much exertion for you."

Lucia kissed Francesco on his cheek and brushed her lips over his lips. Then, she made her way down the staircase joining the family laughing from the comment that Francesco made. Each child gave her hugs welcoming her into the group of berry pickers. The younger siblings jumped up and down clapping their hands in their excitement saying, "Mama, we are glad that you are coming with us."

"I'm glad for the invitation," said Lucia as she was making her way to the kitchen.

"Come my dear and eat your breakfast." This was the first since last night that Lucia had spoken attractively and continued to show him affection. Lucia did appear to be a little despondent; but maybe while in the woods, the bright summer sunshine would elevate her mood. Most days, Lucia would not speak a word. She would only nod her head to respond to a question. It was as if her voice was taken from her. It was good to hear her voice again. It was a mystery what the thoughts in her mind were for her life had become one of silence most days.

Mary thought back to the time when the children were having their berry battle. All the colors of blue and purple were embedded on their clothes that day. It's amazing how children can have fun making up their own little games for the sake of being busy.

Mary shook her head a few times trying to come out of her daze saying, "It is summertime, and it's going to be hot with long sleeve shirts and pants on this time of year especially in the afternoon. It will be a little warm this morning, but not as much as later. It's better to be protected from the briers and poison than to have all of us scratched up and itchy. Maybe by lunchtime, we will have all the berries that we need to avoid the heat. Be sure to put on socks to protect your feet. I sure don't want to get the vinegar out to use on each of you to take the itch out on your arms, back, and legs."

Mary thought it would be nice as a family to do this activity. Everyone seemed to be of a happy countenance. It would be nice for a short period of time to be fancy free and enjoy the nice change of her mother's mood. Mary stood reassessing last night, and she believed that some type of a miracle did take place from what she observed with her mother today. She would take what she could get whatever the time allowed. Wishful thinking was that Lucia would never return to her dark bleak ways again.

Francesco lined up the children with their individual bucket as they walked through the door for their morning venture. Francesco was smiling, and his appearance was more relaxed than it had been for days.

"Mary, we must pick as many berries as we can so that we will have food in our house for a while," remarked Francesco. "Money is in short supply; and with the gypsies stealing from us, it will help replenish our food. You can make us some desserts. Our family can even have a dish of blackberries with milk upon our return, or we can eat them for breakfast."

"Papa, we will all pick berries to help out in this situation. I know money and food are not plentiful," Mary replied in a worried tone of voice. "With the big garden you plant and picking berries in the woods, we always seem to have enough food for our family." Mary would try to encourage her father in this situation that was playing hiatic on his mind.

Francesco came toward Lucia engaging his mouth on every part of hers with a deep kiss. He tried to take the stress of finances and the hardships of everyday living out of her mind for the moment and take her back in time of the good old days. Only a small fragment was left of the girl he remembered marrying. Now, her face had a blank stare placed upon it without a smile on her lips. He wished many times that the personality of the one he married would return, but for now it had vanished. Many times, he would close his eyes to try and imagine his lover returning once again to him. Francesco felt that upon looking in the depths of Lucia's eyes, there was a smile on her face, but one had to look very hard to see it for it was not visual.

"Come Lucia and children, let's get started. You are all lined up waiting for me. Come, follow the leader from out of the house into the woods we will go."

Francesco held out his hand for Lucia to grasp. Lucia placed her hand in his for the first time since last night when her personality took on this new person. Together with buckets in hand they walked into the path along the woods to find the berries that Francesco discovered a few days ago.

The woods were adjacent to the house. Wild flowers were blooming and birds high above were chirping songs only that they understood. An eagle was soaring in the sky with its wings spreading a span of seven to nine feet. Mary thought of how the wings served as a covering of safety for all those that remained under those wings. If possible, the family should remain forever under the eagle's wings.

"Look at all the beautiful berries. There are even mushrooms along the shaded areas, which we can pick. I love to eat mushrooms," Francesco proclaimed.

Francesco was stooping, picking a basket of mushrooms, contemplating how tasty they would be fried in a skillet with butter. There was nothing like a fresh crop of mushrooms.

"We've been picking long enough, let's go home now. I believe we've picked and eaten enough berries and raw mushrooms for today. It's approaching noon, and the sun will make it too hot to be out here in the weeds."

"Papa, Mama, please look at my bucket! The berries are huge," cheered John.

"You win the prize for being the best berry picker on this side of the hills," laughed Lucia. "Tomorrow, I will use the berries to make some pies for all of us."

"I'll help," yelled Mary. Mary didn't want to suggest making jelly for the incident of the past cured her of ever wanting to make jelly again. Today, it appeared that Lucia had once again taken on a normal personality.

"Let's make our way back to the house and have some lunch out under the trees. We will have a bowl of berries with milk," said Francesco. The children were happy to return to the house. There were several trees for shading where they could sit down and have a picnic lunch.

Night had fallen across the land. Francesco was awakened by feeling very sick in his stomach. "Lucia, please call the doctor. I have been vomiting profusely for several hours, and I am very weak. I feel like I could pass out. I have chills and a fever too."

Lucia replied, "It's the middle of the night. Can't you wait until dawn?"

Francesco answered, "No, I may be dead by then! There is something seriously wrong."

Now, the whole household was awake. Each one was trying to help Francesco until the doctor arrived.

"It's quite good you called," said the doctor. "I believe Francesco must have eaten a poisonous mushroom today making him very sick.

In a few days, he should be alright. I gave him medicine to counter-act the poison. In the meantime, he'll be quite ill until it passes."

"Thanks for coming in the middle of the night," sniffled Lucia. "I'm glad I listened to Francesco and called and didn't wait."

CHAPTER 22

THE ASYLUM

"The way it is now, the asylums can hold the sane people, but if we tried to shut up the insane we should run out of building materials."
Mark Twain, Following the Equator

The severe worldwide economic depression had ended. The poor economic situation had turned around, and everyday living was becoming easier.

One brisk fall afternoon, Francesco was sitting at the kitchen table when out of the corner of his eye he spotted a figure running out through the field in the distance. Suddenly, he let out a holler, "John, Joe, Leonard, and Mary, please hurry through the field after your mother! I believe that she is running toward the high creek. We must catch her and catch her quickly!"

Shooting quickly out of the house and yelling at the top of their voices, "Mama, come back to the house! You will get cold without a coat on. The water is cold and high, and you will drown!" The boys ran as fast as their legs could carry them. They finally caught up to her grabbing her in a tackling position to throw her to the ground. They sat in amazement wondering what caused the sudden change of personality.

Lucia was sobbing uncontrollably for sadness seemed to prevail in her spirit. "Mama, take my hand in yours, and I will lead you back to the house where you will be safe once more," affirmed Leonard. "Today is cool, and the wind is tossing your hair all around your head. We love you! We need you too!"

Lucia stood motionless with sad emotions falling across her face as she made her way back to the house in the crisp chilly air mumbling in an unknown language. "Why couldn't you have left me go to the water and drown?"

This up and down roller coaster ride was beginning again for some unknown reason. With all the emotional chaos today, it was now time for Lucia to leave home to obtain medical help for this strange illness. This incident proved that she was capable of physically harming herself. Francesco thought the storm had passed, but now he felt overwhelmed once again. He didn't know whether there was much help for those suffering from this type of illness, but he had to take the necessary steps to find help if possible instead of living in denial. It was only by chance that Francesco had gazed out of the window to see Lucia running toward the creek. The creek was deep with the current of the water strong. Anyone wading into the creek would be swept downstream. There could be a time he would not have been at a window to see her wandering off to harm herself. Francesco had no alternative but to commit her to an institution where she would be at least safe. He had hesitations on taking such actions, but he had to pursue taking care of this dangerous situation soon.

Troubles seemed to mount once again. Many nights Lucia would lie in bed panic-stricken with terrifying thoughts running through her mind. She shared none of her thoughts with her family, but she kept them concealed deep within her heart. Lucia was not getting enough sleep at night, which made it difficult taking care of her children. Lucia would now and again come out of her silent world to speak, but there were days at a time that passed that she wouldn't speak one word.

"Francesco, I hear a noise in my head like a gun going off and voices talking to me."

"Lucia, relax your head against your pillow and try to think on good things that you will be able to relax and fall asleep."

"I can't, Francesco! You don't understand what I am going through!" Lucia cried out. "These strange feelings I have are sweeping over my mind. I can't relax! Will I ever be healthy again?"

"You must get well Lucia for me and the children. We need you! Presently, you are exhausted and need to get away to get some rest. Tomorrow, I will take you on a little vacation."

Francesco was at his lowest point of life with having lost a child to death and now having to follow the doctor's advice to help Lucia recover. He always looked for the *streets of gold*, but wondered where they were because his life seemed to be filled with a lot of heartache and pain. His deepest longing was to have Lucia the way she was. The situation at home was getting out of control.

One morning before the children arose out of their sleep Francesco said, "Lucia, I have packed the necessary things for your survival in a large bag to take to the facility. Now, it's time for you to dress for the trip ahead."

He didn't know how Lucia would react in front of the children, but he realized that he must take this last chance to have Lucia well once more. Now, he was wondering about his own sanity as he prepared to let the dream of his life make her departure. Francesco kept this dream in the corner of his mind refusing to accept the reality of what was happening. He was holding a steady grip knowing that his fingers needed to be pried loose to let go. Unfortunately, he had his family to consider, but it wouldn't be easy to let her go. Common sense told him he had to let go.

Francesco went to the children's room to awaken them from their sleep. "Wake up sleepy heads before we leave this morning. Give your mother a goodbye kiss." Each child ran to their mother for the kiss that they didn't understand.

"Lucia, we must go for a little ride now. You look lovely today. Let's think that this is a little getaway for you that you can get some rest for a short time away from us. I know that we will all miss you while you are gone, but the important thing is that you get some rest." Lucia stared at Francesco without talking with a blank look on her face as Francesco was speaking.

Lucia espoused, "Mary, you are going to marry that fellow from town someday! I believe his name is Mike. When I get back, you'll probably be married."

Mary smiled as her mother made such an "out of the blue" statement. Mary was devastated by such a remark although she knew that her mother was ill. She squeezed her eyes shut to stop the tears flowing down her cheeks from the frustration that she was feeling. Mary didn't know any fellows from town; and at this stage of life, she had no desire to marry anyone. Mary couldn't think of another thing to do to try and cheer up her mother before she left home. All that she wanted to remember was the face of the one she loved very much.

Francesco had instructed Mary a few days earlier about having the children lined up in front of the house to bid their mother farewell. Leonard, Joe, and John tried to be brave and not shed any tears watching their mother climb into the car while being carted off for a vacation away from home leaving them behind.

"No! No!" cried two-year-old Madelyn. "I want to go too, Mama."

Mary reached down to grab Madelyn in her arms to try and comfort her. "It's okay. Mama will return to us soon. I'll take care of you while she's gone."

"I don't want you taking care of me. I want my Mama." Madelyn replied in gibberish language.

Maria stood pouting with tears running down her face. "I don't want Mama to go without us."

Each family member hated the thought of Mama leaving; but despite their feelings, it was good reasoning to let her go. Francesco had reassured them that upon her return she would be well, although it failed to bring peace to their little hearts that explanation brings when you're a child.

"Your father is going to take me for a joy ride out into the country where I can dance all night. Aren't you, Francesco?" Lucia yelled out the open car window.

Francesco nodded in agreement. "Dancing…dancing will bring back the good memories that have passed us by quickly." Francesco wondered whether he would ever hear the music to dance once again. Francesco looked at her with sadness in his eyes, "Lucia…. you will be able to dance and enjoy whatever it is that will make you happy."

Francesco was worried that sending Lucia away may not be the right thing to do for she may never return to her home again. He was at his wits end, and he didn't know what other decision to make.

Lucia climbed back out of the car staring into his eyes as she started twirling around and clapping her hands in the air. "Do you hear the music, Francesco? We need to dance for the children."

This seemed not to be having a positive effect on the family. It made the children all have a worried countenance watching their mother in such a confused state. The pain was welling up within their deepest inner being.

"Listen…. I hear the music in the distance. Let me have this dance to remember the rest of my life," said Francesco pretending to hear the musical sounds.

Francesco tried to justify the unfortunate scene by falling in step with Lucia for possibly the last dance with his lady. Their audience appeared to be captivated by the motion of the dance, but the curtain seemed to be coming down on their stage when there would be no more dancing. He wasn't prepared for the ache deep inside that he was feeling. Happiness in life was his only desire.

The children seemed to cheer up once they saw their father participating in the dancing. After a few dances, Francesco threw the luggage bag into the car. Then, he yanked Lucia by the wrists while she was in a joyful mood kissing her one last kiss and loading her in the car waving to the children as they began their unknown journey.

The children stood cheering while clapping their hands.

As Francesco drove down the road, he felt exhausted from lack of sleep from the worry he was experiencing from the problem with Lucia. He wished that there was a way that he might pull her out of her sadness, but all hope of a brighter tomorrow seemed to be fleeting. There seemed to be no help in sight for Lucia's mood swings and severe sadness. There seemed to be no alternate course but to take her to this institution where he was assured she could be cured.

Lucia rested her head on Francesco's shoulder while driving to the institution. Her illness had taken a toll on everyone. Few words were exchanged, but Francesco wrapped his arm around her to try comforting her. If he allowed himself to think about what was happening, he might change his mind.

In the distance sat a huge red brick building in a field. Upon approaching the building, Francesco and Lucia were met at the front door by a lady dressed in white resembling a nurse. There was a distinct odor that was noticeable to Francesco as he and Lucia entered the foyer.

"Welcome." The lady reached out her hand to greet Lucia and Francesco. "I take it that you are Lucia and Francesco." Francesco stood nodding his head in agreement looking uneasy.

She continued speaking, "We have been expecting you. The doctor called to tell me that you were scheduled to arrive at the institution today. I have been waiting for your arrival. My name is Rose. I am one of several nurses working here at the facility. This will be your home Lucia for a little while. You can get a little rest, and hopefully it won't be long until Francesco can take you back home with him." The nurse avoided mentioning Lucia's children for she may make a scene and not want to stay here without a fight. She continued, "I will show you the way to your room where I have a bed prepared for you to lie down. It will be quiet. Quiet is what we all need when we are not feeling well. I will see you to your bed."

Francesco was paying little attention to the nurse for there were several patients along the hallways that Francesco viewed as a little out of control. There was a lot of commotion not quiet in this place. Some of the patients were rambling loudly in sentences that made no sense to the human ear. Others seemed to be withdrawn from their surroundings. Strange feelings were sweeping over Francesco in a negative way. He questioned himself at this moment that he made the right decision for Lucia's well-being.

As they moved down the hallway, there was a wall clock chiming and floor lamps in the far corner throwing a dim lighting over the area. Several rocking chairs lined the dark corners of the place. An old man was sitting in one of the rocking chairs that apparently was moved from the far corner to the entrance way. He wore glasses without lenses. He had some type of a wrist band on his wrist, with a t-shirt, pants and no shoes on his feet. A dress brimmed hat was perched on top of his head. He was gazing out the window in his own little imaginary world.

Lucia pointed toward the old man questioning, "Francesco, is that my father?"

"No Lucia. He is a patient here. We do not know him."

She began saying, "Francesco, I believe that I know him. It is my father. You are not telling me the truth."

*

Francesco stepped back with a hurtful look on his face saying, "Lucia, why would I lie to you. I have no reason to lie."

Lucia paid no attention to what Francesco was saying as she began speaking softly, "Hello, Papa. I hope you are alright. I haven't seen you for such a long time. Have you been waiting for me to return home?"

The old man let out a yell toward her saying, "Shut up! Don't bother me!"

"I'm not bothering him, Francesco," Lucia said with sadness echoing her voice. "It's been such a long time since I saw him last that I thought he might like me to talk to him." Francesco wondered if that may be some of Lucia's problem of homesickness. He thought he someday would return to New York with his family, but it was difficult financially to make this wish happen.

"It's alright Lucia. You did nothing wrong. He doesn't know what he is saying," stated Francesco. Francesco answered her in a quiet voice realizing the confusion that Lucia was experiencing. The nurse gazed with compassion in her eyes toward the couple wondering if there were any right words to be said that might not upset Francesco.

Once through the foyer, halfway down the hall, there was a little room situated in the middle of the hallway with window shades pulled shut with no lights in view. The nurse spoke as she pointed, "This is the beauty shop for keeping the haircut and clean in these situations. The things we sometimes take for granted in the outside world are a vital function here in the life of the residents. We have everything needed for the patient to remain comfortable while staying here."

On the other corner across from the beauty shop, a miniature glass-enclosed cage stood that measured approximately 8 feet that served as an aviary. It contained several exotic birds. The birds included the American Singer Canary, Finches, and Orange Cheeked Waxbills. Next to the cage sat a bearded gentleman with wire-rim glasses strapped in a wheelchair. He was tapping on the glass and mumbling words only understandable to his vocabulary.

There were several patients parading the entrance and hallways. Psychiatric aides stood observing the patients and giving assistance when needed. The sound of out of tune music radiated through the hallway from the room to the right on their journey to the unknown. A voice roared, "Don, sing out the words to the song. We want to hear you." They stood for a moment to observe the activity that was going on. Tears filled Francesco's eyes as memories came streaming from his mind—for these same old songs and tunes were now one more thing of the past but of a different tune. He had to catch his feeling to avoid sobbing in front of Lucia. He wanted Lucia to feel that this was a good place for the rest that she needed, which he had second thoughts himself. He noticed the patients were all in a similar situation with being out of touch with reality. He finally got control of himself. He wasn't crying inside for what is at the present, but what was and could be if Lucia would be well.

Francesco noticed that most of the patients had tousled hair and a sober countenance as they were blurting out the music and mimicking tunes of the past. He wondered whether in a few weeks when he returned for a visit if Lucia would be in the same category as these patients. Maybe she would be farther out of touch with the world than she is already.

Passing several rooms, Francesco noticed that some of the patients were restrained in a white cloth-type garment tied to their bedpost preventing movement of their arms while lying in their beds, while others were sitting in a chair that had leather gloves on the armrest with their hands through the glove restrained to avoid hurting themselves. This appeared to be inhuman treatment. The restraints appeared to be confining for the naked eye could not view any limbs of the patients. Suddenly, fear gripped Francesco sending him in a panic thinking if restraints were placed on Lucia how upset she would become. As far as he was concerned, this would create the patient to become more mentally distraught and wild. Francesco immediately took a slow deep breath to release the fright he was feeling. Francesco was following the doctor's orders for Lucia's well-being. He felt as if he was viewing a group of wild animals.

Francesco felt like he could run out of this crazy place with Lucia's hand in his never more to return. He probably should have checked the place out before making such a final decision, but he was under such strain with the weight of the world resting upon his shoulders. He never had dealt with this type of sickness in the past. An old saying, he recalled was, *wouldn't it be nice if everyone could throw their troubles in a field, then go and pick out the one they wanted.* He had written Lucia's father for advice, but the only answer he received was silence. It was easier to sweep this problem into a closet and let it rest.

Finally, they reached their destination, noticing the door was shut. For a moment, Francesco stopped. His mind was imagining familiar voices ringing out with the sound of laughter permeating the air. Maybe upon opening the door, he would encounter scenes of the past of New York and the life that was. Walking hand in hand through the brisk night air not caring about what was happening in the city was a good memory he held in his heart. They were on top of the world feeling only love for one another. He remembered all so well the laughter between him and Lucia in those days. Now there was no laughter—only silence and pain filled the air. Francesco had a broken heart seeing Lucia in such a state that was beyond his control. Many times, he had retraced in his mind their paths to try and figure out if there was something that he could have done differently to change life's circumstances, but there was no answer to the problem. He wondered whether the pleasures of life that created good memories would ever return. All he knew that the formula to mend his heart was to have a miracle performed that would return Lucia's sanity to make life easier. He seemed to be on a downhill pathway leading to nowhere.

As Francesco opened the door, a distant voice rang out, "You have a nice body."

Francesco turned around to notice that a little white-haired lady at the end of the hallway was yelling out the message creating an illusion once again to his mind of things from the past from his special lady.

Francesco took a deep breath as he gazed at Lucia. His lingering stare reminded him of his promise to her back in New York to make her happy. Now, his world seemed to be crumbling, and all his dreams seemed to be falling to pieces at his feet. He stepped toward her pulling her to himself one last time before leaving for the day as he softly said, "Lucia, you must get well for me. I will miss you, but I will be back to visit you and one day take you home with me to pick up our life where we left off. You must come back to me. There are times that I feel that I can't face another day without you."

Lucia turned her head away from now the familiar voice.

"Lucia, look at me." Francesco guided her eyes to look at him, but she only had a blank stare evident in her eyes. The nurse assured him that they would take good care of Lucia; but regardless, hopelessness washed across him as he turned about taking long strides toward the door. He felt lonely and afraid as he left the institution to make his way home to his family.

The psychiatrist recommended that Francesco and family stay away from the institution for a little while until Lucia regained some of her mental focus. Francesco was told that he could check in at the institution to inquire about Lucia's progress.

The weeks were passing by without her gaining much progress was the information he was given. Francesco was very discouraged with the whole situation, but he refused to give up regardless of the circumstances. He would confide in Mary with the details of her mother's condition.

One day after several weeks of not having Lucia in the house, Francesco asked the family to get dress. "We are all going for a visit to see your mother. I'm finished paying attention to the directives of the institution. I am very aggravated with the institution."

Waves of hopelessness were taking over him. "I am packing you children into the car with the anticipation of seeing your mother in hopes that she has made a little progress is all that I desire."

Upon arrival to the facility, Francesco began speaking, "Mary, you and the children must remain down here in the lobby until I check if we are permitted to see your mother. If you can't see her, I will bring her to the window where she can wave to you. The nearest window where her room is located is directly above the lobby area. I will show you where to stand to see her."

"Okay, Papa, that will be fine," replied Mary as a whimper caught in her throat. Mary spoke softly saying, "I will take care of the children until you can return." Francesco spun around heading down the hallway disappearing from view. Mary was trying to keep her composure for the children's sake even though her heart was breaking in two. Her wounded spirit spiraling through her made it hard to have strength to move. It was as if she was a block of ice frozen in place.

Francesco met a nurse a little way down the hall. "I am here to visit my wife."

The nurse looked at Francesco for a moment then she began speaking, "You're Francesco."

Francesco shook his head up and down as the nurse continued speaking, "Francesco, why are you here? You were told that we would let you know when the time is right for you to visit Lucia."

Francesco was insistent as he proceeded to speak, "Listen, she is my wife; and I have every right to see her. It's been several weeks without her at home. I can hardly bear to go on without her. Don't you understand that I love my wife? I miss her! You must stop putting me off! You can bring me to her bedside! I must see her and see her now!"

The nurse flung her arms in the air. "Francesco, I will take you to see her. It's sad how our environment causes some people not to be able to cope. Your wife is suffering from a depression problem. Sometimes, life circumstances cause people's minds and personalities to change. I believe with losing a child and the Great Depression that had hit our country has taken a toll on Lucia. She talks about fire and is very worried about financial problems and the children. It has thrown her into such a state that the psychiatrist had to give her shock therapy to try and snap her out of her present state."

"Has the therapy helped her?" asked Francesco as he viewed the overcrowded conditions of the facility. Everywhere he looked, there were patients sitting and standing wall to wall in every area of the room. At least, he felt better that Lucia was not one of the patients sitting in the hallway.

"Lucia seems very confused in her thinking. She is very withdrawn from reality. Most of her days are spent in her dark room alone. She refuses to socialize with other patients. Sometimes, she dances around the room as if she is performing for an audience mumbling out loud for anyone listening to hear. Hopefully, this passes with time, when and if she has healing of her mind."

"What is your name?" asked Francesco.

"I'm Diana the head psychiatric nurse in this section of the institution. I've worked here for several years trying to help the patients focus on reality. Some patients leave the facility never to return, but others leave and come back in a short time period. There are others that never leave. I pray that Lucia recovers never to return here again. She is a nice lady, and you two deserve the best." Diana understood that Francesco wasn't making a pest of himself pursuing Lucia's good health.

Panic-stricken, Francesco began speaking, "I beg of you not to put me off for another minute. I demand that I must see Lucia. I don't want any excuses why I shouldn't see her. Besides, I have my family with me to help cheer her up. They are waiting outside her window."

Diana led Francesco to Lucia's room. The door was closed; and upon opening it, he views a woman with her arm in a sling with her hair standing straight up into the air with a sad appearance on her face. There were multiple bruises over each arm. She had lost a tremendous amount of weight. This couldn't be his Lucia. Her eyes were sunken into her face. She looked worse today than the day he brought her to the institution.

Francesco spoke softly, "My dear Lucia. I've come to see you. Are you alright?"

Lucia answering, "I will dance for you like I did in New York. You can determine for yourself if I know the dance well enough to come home."

Francesco thought that Diana didn't realize why Lucia danced around the room. He knew that Lucia was capturing her life from the past.

Diana was small in stature with caramel-colored shoulder length hair flowing around her face with an electric smile shining across her face. "After Lucia is finished dancing, we will bring her to the window to wave at the children."

Lucia yelled as she laughed hysterically, "Here I am! Watch me dance for you! I love dancing! I want my children to see me dancing with the happiness I am feeling. They are a great audience." The children couldn't hear her words through the closed window, but waved to her as she danced for them. She danced for a little while until Diana took her by the arm and sat her down on the bed.

Diana spoke softly, "If your oldest daughter would like to come up and visit her mother, she is permitted."

Francesco kissed Lucia whispering under his breath of his deepest feelings to Lucia. He then turned and left to have Mary come and visit her mother.

Upon entering the room, Mary was taken back by her mother's appearance. Her hair was standing straight up as if she had placed her finger in an electric socket.

"Mary, did you get married to the man down the street? You would make a beautiful bride like I was when I married your father." Lucia was talking out of her head to Mary and made no sense whatsoever with the words she was speaking. Mary didn't even date a man let alone marrying one.

"Mama, I know no men," replied Mary hesitantly to Lucia.

"Well, it's about time that you get to know a few men. You sure don't want to become an old maid," laughed Lucia.

Mary was very upset with seeing her mother in this state. She appeared to be worse now than when she left home. She felt like running out of the room, but there was no place to run. Embarrassed, she concocted an excuse to leave.

"I will have to be going soon for Papa is waiting outside with the children for my return. I will come again and visit you. You must get well. We need you at home," cried Mary.

"I will never get well, Mary! You will visit me at the graveyard your next visit," exclaimed Lucia.

"Mama, don't say those kinds of things. You must get well." Mary bolted from the room joining her father and siblings. Leaving the institution on such a negative note was very heartbreaking for Mary.

Many weekends were set aside for visitation of Lucia. Francesco and Mary would try and cheer Lucia up with each visit. Weeks were running into months with no improvement. Then, one day the family was told that they were not permitted to see Lucia for she had contracted tuberculosis.

CHAPTER 23

SAD HEARTS

———◆———

The beauty of the blooms in early spring from the special variety Dogwood tree will serve as a reminder that life begins once again.

After several months of agonizing over Lucia's hopeless state, Francesco received the call that Lucia was gone. Gone! There were many unanswered questions. He stood silently in shock. Crying was all he could do for his heart was breaking in a million pieces. Finally, he got himself composed to be able to speak.

He didn't know how to tell the children, but he felt that he must. As he went to the upstairs, Mary was lying across her bed. Francesco stood contemplating for a moment. "Mary, I have something I must say to you," Francesco said as his voice quivered.

"Okay, Papa. I did hear the telephone ring. It's Mama, isn't it?"

Francesco shook his head up and down to reply.

"Something bad has happened to her, hasn't it?" Mary questioned as her voice trembled as she began crying.

Again, Francesco shook his head as tears welled up in his eyes. Francesco could not bring himself to talk about his Lucia. He took his handkerchief from his pocket as he reached out to Mary wiping his eyes, but his tears would not stop. "Life has lost its music! There will be no more dancing!"

"Mama is gone, isn't she?" Mary asked.

Once again, Francesco shook his head as he held on to Mary weeping uncontrollably. "I have lost my happiness and all I cared about in life. I don't know how I can make it without her, but I know I must go on for you children. She lit my world with love and happiness."

He couldn't say the words. Francesco's heart was being pulled out of his chest. He felt like he was gasping for breath. "We must go to the institution one last time before she's taken away. Then, we must make arrangements."

"Papa, I will try and help you with all the sadness you are feeling, but I'm so sad and upset too," sobbed Mary. "It will be hard breaking this news to the children."

"We'll tell them in the morning." Francesco made his way to where the children were standing in the hallway. Francesco spoke to the children, "Mary and I must go to the institution tonight. We will be back as soon as we can. Go to bed. Leonard and Joe will be here with you until we return."

Out the door Mary and Francesco ran quickly to begin their journey to reach the institution in a timely manner. As they arrived at the facility, Diana met them at the entrance.

"I will take you to your Lucia. I am very sorry that we could not make your wife and mother well. We tried everything. She refused to eat and became very weak. Then, she contracted the tuberculosis. Put this mask on before we make our way to the room. Remember, do not touch her!"

"I know you tried to make her well," said Francesco sobbing. "It is all that one can hope for is that you tried. It was out of all our hands for Lucia seemed to be out of reality these days. Hopefully, one day a cure is found for this illness."

Walking into the room, Francesco went over to the bed where Lucia was still lying. Speaking softly while Mary and Diana stood silently, "I truly loved you Lucia. I wish that I could have made you well. I will always hold the good memories of you in my heart. No one can erase the memories from my heart." Francesco broke down weeping uncontrollably with Mary and Diana trying hard to comfort him.

At the dawning of the morning, Francesco made the announcement to the children. They all stood weeping for quite a while. Each one handled their grief differently.

Francesco contacted Vito and Alberto to talk about the situation and to help in his hour of need. "Vito, I am very brokenhearted that I cannot bear to talk to anyone right now about the passing of Lucia. I feel numb this instant as I feel a deep pain penetrating throughout my entire body. Lucia and I had shut ourselves in away from the world for a short time taking care of our young family. Very few people became more than an acquaintance. The few good friends we did have seemed to disappear from our territory because of Lucia's emotional condition. It didn't bother me for as long as I had my Lucia, I felt I had everything for she was what made my heart beat. Even in her sickness, I still loved her dearly."

Vito answered, "Francesco, you really never accepted Lucia's emotional weakness. You avoided the topic, but I understand since little is known about this sickness."

"Vito, I feel very helpless! If you could, I would like you and Alberto to make all the arrangements for the funeral. I need to come to terms with this unfortunate event that is happening in my life. The one thing I ask is that she has a handkerchief in her hand as a reminder of me in New York."

Vito replied, "We will take care of all of this for you. You get some rest now before the viewing and funeral."

At the viewing, few friends and family filed passed Lucia expressing condolences while Francesco and Mary stood next to Lucia. "Mary, your mother was a beautiful lady," a little voice softly spoke. The voice belonged to Jenny, Mary's best school friend, who lived across the street from where they had once lived.

Francesco interrupted replying, "She was my special lady. She had such beautiful porcelain skin. How can one tell someone they love goodbye?" Without spoken words, he stood observing that her skin was pale from her sickness and her arms had deep purple bruises in a few places. The mystery of the bruises would always haunt his mind for nobody seemed to give an explanation when questions arose—only a result of shock therapy. He spoke softly looking at his dear wife. He was weeping as the words came forth, "I am saddened from the sorrow that I am feeling at this moment. I wish things could have been different for us, Lucia. At least, I knew love for the short time we had."

Mary heard the words that her father had spoken to her mother replying, "I wish things would have turned out differently for the both of you. My heart feels as if it could explode." Mary replied as she broke down into an emotional outburst. Francesco came to her and threw his arms around her trying to comfort her in her distress, but he needed comfort himself. His brothers, Vito and Alberto, and their families were there supporting Francesco's family during this hour of need. The younger siblings sat in the chairs dazed trying to understand all that was happening as their mother lying there held onto the embroidered handkerchief.

At the final viewing, Francesco's family struggled knowing this would be the last chance to view the lovely face never again for their eyes to see.

Upon arrival the day of the funeral at the little red brick framed church, the outside church bell was ringing for all to hear that the service was about to begin.

Francesco and his family made their way toward a front pew sitting down with Vito and Alberto's family. Music was playing softly. The scent of incense penetrated the air. As the clock approached the hour, a man attired in a purple robe started up the aisle to the altar carrying a large brass cross. Another man dressed in a red garb followed holding a gold cup lined with white porcelain and some type of porcelain stir. Then, Father Murdock followed the two men making his way to the wooden box covered with a white linen cloth that was adored with a beautiful embroidered gold cross overlay centered in the piece of linen material. The music ceased as the priest turned facing the congregation saying a prayer.

Then, a few of the congregation with the church choir began singing an opening hymn. The priest shared many thoughts of the good times unfolding memories of Lucia when life was at its best. Many of the parishioners were wiping their eyes with their hankies from the emotion they were feeling of losing such a young woman to death at 43-years-old with young children left behind.

The family was seated at the front of the church each one in their own thoughts helpless in their sorrow. Francesco was trying to remain strong for his family, but it was good to shed tears for tears can help heal the wound in one's hour of brokenness. Mary sat close to her father, weeping as memories kept flooding her mind. Some of the younger children sat in their seats expressionless not knowing what their reaction should be at such a time as this. They were not grasping the full meaning of the sorrow.

Every now and again incense would fill the air as a soft tingling sound of bells rang out in the distance as the bread and wine was administered. A clear voice echoed *Ave Maria* throughout the sanctuary from the back balcony inspiring every ear that heard the tune, but serving as a reminder to Francesco the happiest day of his life of their wedding day in New York of the same tune.

As the service ended, a ray of sunshine sprayed through the stained-glass window showering a sign for all to see bringing hope that a brighter tomorrow would prevail.

As friends departed, Francesco stopped to speak with Vito and Alberto. "I don't know how I'm going to make it through this adversity." Francesco broke down crying holding his hands to his eyes.

Viewing Francesco's sadness Vito spoke up, "There are no words to say that can make you feel better. All I can say is that you will never get over your loss; but with time, you will adjust. You must pick yourself up and go on regardless of this tragedy for the children's sake."

Francesco replied, "Hopefully, you are right. I wish someone could tell me that I am in a dream; and when I wake up, it will all go away."

Alberto spoke softly, "We both wish we could make this nightmare disappear from you, but we can't. If it's any consolation, you will always have a part of Lucia with you even though she's not physically present with you. She's in the children. If you look hard enough, you'll see her in different places and feel her gentle touch and feel her presence. No one can wipe away your memories that you had with her. She'll be forever in your heart."

At that remark, Francesco burst into tears saying, "Most of us think that we always have tomorrow when we only have today. It's hard to imagine life without her for she left this world at such a young age. Today, part of my heart was buried there with Lucia."

Vito grabbed Francesco hugging him, "You must be strong for the children. I never went through this type of experience myself, but I imagine how hard it must be for loss is never easy. Lucia would want you to live happily and take good care of the children for they need you now more than ever."

Francesco began explaining, "Her body was weakened from lack of nutrition. If only she had eaten, she would have recovered and avoided tuberculosis. The facility couldn't do anything to help her for she was very frail. I know that death is a part of life. None of us know how long we have to live, but it still doesn't make it easier."

After the burial, everyone went their separate ways. Francesco sat alone at the gravesite to quietly pause and reflect on his loss. He had to hold on to all the pleasant memories of the days with Lucia to get through this trial. He could travel the world to try and find his true love, but Lucia would never return to him. He had to let her go. At that moment gazing across the site, Lucia seemed to appear.

Francesco was astonished and got up from where he was sitting speaking softly, "You came back to bid me one last farewell. Oh, Lucia, I love you very much! Lucia, do you hear the music? Let's have this one last dance before I let you go."

Lucia smiled at him as her hair flowed across her face. Francesco placed his hands across her back to hold on to her tightly dancing in tune with the music he was hearing of the days that had longed passed. Tears were flowing down his cheeks with the remembrance of the dancing and happy times. He was stepping with Lucia to the beat of the music and did one last swirl, and she was gone.

Stepping back into reality Francesco stood pondering for a moment capturing his thoughts. He realized that he had enjoyed the pleasures of life with Lucia. Why had he been so blind not to see? He had found the *streets of gold* that he came seeking here in America. Francesco could read the invisible sign that proclaimed, "Welcome to America" where he had found the promise of a better life. He was blessed by walking on the *streets paved with gold* to find the precious treasures given to him. Francesco appreciated having Lucia and his lovely family and finding true love for the brief period that most people have never known.

As he turned to leave, he noticed an embroidered handkerchief beneath his feet. He whispered through a smile, "Thanks for our beautiful last dance!"

EPILOGUE

---

*A life when it is gone leaves a sweet-smelling
fragrance as a blossom to those left behind.*

Francesco's heart seemed to be mending slowly as the mountains he once scaled seemed to be parting for him to make his way to the other side. He was rebuilding his life once again from the loss of Lucia. Traveling back to Ellis Island after all these years held a special memoir in his heart viewing the place then and now. As they disembarked years earlier in New York, he didn't know anyone here in America. He believed he was blessed to have Lucia cross his pathway.

As Francesco reflected this day on his life since coming to America, he looked across the sky. There was a silhouette of trees lying against the various colors of red as the sun was setting in the distance. This picturesque scene served as a reminder to him that as the sun sets in the eastern sky, our life is filled for a little while with the beautiful colors of the sky for us to enjoy for a short season until the sun goes down and our life folds away into the setting.

Francesco had reminded himself many times when he looked over his life, life had been good. Life's circumstances molded him into who he had become on his journey through life.

Suddenly, a sweet-smelling fragrance filled his nostrils making his heart feel alive once more for what he had enjoyed. It served as a reminder that things that bring happiness in life can appear only for a season, but things can pass by in a fleeting moment. Once again, he would hold onto hope for a new beginning in finding a place of solitude, peace, contentment, and happiness. He reflected for a moment on the good times—running through the fields, picking bouquets of wild flowers with echoes of laughter from the children as they presented their bouquet to Lucia. Small things in life bring happiness. Time with his family was one of the most precious moments to remember. Suddenly, his eye caught a glimpse of the gates he passed through at Ellis Island, he recognized he had to begin looking beyond the gates once again for future dreams.

REFLECTION

As the sun sets in the evening, it's a reminder how things of life come to an end, but the memories remain. When I look at a sunset, I think of you and hold close the memories of the things I hold dear to my heart. Not only in a sunset, but every place around that I look remains memories that no one can take away from the recesses of my mind. Tomorrow, the sun will rise in the sky once again reminding me how the rays shine across the earth bringing brightness to my life once again. I am reminded that the sun will shine in my life once again with the happiness that I once knew if I hold on to the memories and start building more memories to view.

ABOUT THE AUTHOR

Lucy Byers lives in Western Pennsylvania along with her husband and a chocolate-colored cocker spaniel dog with a lifetime collection of books in their library.

Before beginning her debut historical romantic novel, her entire career has been devoted in education, working as an administrative secretary in Elementary and Special Education for a local school district. She obtained her Associate Degree from Westmoreland County Community College with acquiring several honors and awards. She has attended numerous Writer's Workshops and Conferences to enhance her writing skills. Reflections of the Journey to Streets of Gold was birthed because her grandfather and grandmother were Italian immigrants.

She enjoys stories from the past enlightening her to be able to pass on to readers—a historical adventure with some inspirational thoughts or a love story to melt their heart. When she isn't reading or writing, she's probably playing the piano, singing, cooking, baking, or traveling.

LucyByers@Facebook or LucyByersBooks.com on the Website.